**PRAISE FOR *SMOKE SCR[EEN]***

'Alongside Jo Nesbø's *Knife*, [...]
anticipated read, and it doesn[t dis]appoint'
*Tvedestrandsposten*, Norway

'A pr[...] [...] Kurt Wa[...] d[...]r – a
middle-aged man suffused with loneliness and regret, and trying to
connect with his younger daughter. The dramatic, violent twists
bring to mind Jo Nesbø' Crime Fiction Lover

'An addictive and thrilling read that keeps the reader guessing
while enjoying an intricate puzzle that requires excellent police
procedural work to unravel it. Highly recommended'
Live & Deadly

'Beautifully atmospheric in its icy Norwegian setting, *Smoke Screen*
is a mesmerising tale, an intricate and intelligent, yet high-octane
story, and highly recommended to fans of Nordic Noir and lovers
of thrillers alike' From Belgium with Booklove

'Horst and Enger have written a compelling follow-up to *Death
Deserved*, with a host of characters that are all vividly portrayed, as
are the locations and settings. The chapters are short, adding a great
sense of urgency to this very clever story that completely captured
my attention from the tantalising prologue. I'm intrigued to see
where these two gentlemen take Blix and Ramm next'
Swirl & Thread

'An expertly written crime thriller, fuelled by the experience of two
best-selling authors who fuse their creativity seamlessly, with an
emotional connection not only to the series leads but even the
deeply troubled souls at the heart of their investigation'
Live Many Lives

'Tense, thrilling and with a beautifully emotive narrative, this series
just seems to be getting better. Thankfully we are getting at least a
book three and I, for one, cannot wait' Jen Med's Book Reviews

'A thrill a minute, *Smoke Screen* is full of suspense and intrigue. With a clever and intricate plot, plenty of twists and turns and a cast of engaging characters, there is a lot to keep you glued to the pages' Novel Deelights

'A fast-moving, punchy, serial-killer investigative novel with a whammy of an ending. If this is the first in the Blix and Ramm series, then here's to many more!' LoveReading

'A clever, gripping crime novel with personality, flair, and heart' Crime by the Book

'A stunningly excellent collaboration from Thomas Enger and Jørn Lier Horst ... It's a brutal tale of fame, murder, and reality TV that gets the pulse racing' Russel McLean

'Now – what happens when you put two of the most distinguished writers of Nordic Noir in tandem? *Death Deserved* by Thomas Enger and Jørn Lier Horst suggests it was a propitious publishing move; a ruthless killer is pursued by a tenacious celebrity blogger and a damaged detective' *Financial Times*

'After the case mushrooms into a succession of eerily planned and executed homicides of amoral celebrities, Blix and Emma concoct a brilliant but dangerous scheme to catch the culprit. A devilishly complex plot, convincing red herrings, and well-rounded characters help make this a winner. Scandinavian Noir fans will eagerly await the sequel' *Publishers Weekly*

**The Blix and Ramm Series**
*Death Deserved*
*Smoke Screen*

## ABOUT THE AUTHORS

Jørn Lier Horst and Thomas Enger are both internationally bestselling Norwegian authors. Jørn Lier Horst first rose to literary fame with his No. 1 bestselling William Wisting series. A former investigator in the Norwegian police, Horst imbues all his works with an unparalleled realism and suspense.

Thomas Enger is the journalist-turned-author behind the internationally acclaimed Henning Juul series. Enger's trademark is his dark, gritty voice paired with key social messages and tight plotting. Besides writing fiction for both adults and young adults, Enger also works as a music composer.

*Death Deserved*, the first book in the Blix and Ramm series, was Jørn Lier Horst and Thomas Enger's first co-written thriller.

Follow them on Twitter @LierHorst and @EngerThomas and their websites: jlhorst.com and thomasenger.com.

## ABOUT THE TRANSLATOR

Megan Turney is originally from the West Midlands. Having spent several years working between the UK and the Hardanger region of Norway, she is now based in Edinburgh, working as a commercial and literary translator and editor. She was the recipient of the National Centre for Writing's 2019 Emerging Translator Mentorship in Norwegian and is a published science-fiction critic. She holds an MA(Hons) in Scandinavian Studies and English Literature from the University of Edinburgh, as well as an MA in Translation and Interpreting Studies from the University of Manchester. Follow Megan on Twitter @meganeturney and her website: www.megane-turney.com.

# SMOKE SCREEN

JØRN LIER HORST & THOMAS ENGER

TRANSLATED BY MEGAN TURNEY

**ORENDA BOOKS**

Orenda Books
16 Carson Road
West Dulwich
London SE21 8HU
www.orendabooks.co.uk

First published in the United Kingdom by Orenda Books, 2021
First published in Norwegian as *Røykteppe* by Capitana Forlag, 2019
Copyright © Jørn Lier Horst & Thomas Enger, 2019
English translation copyright © Megan Turney 2021

A catalogue record for this book is available from the British Library.

ISBN 978-1-913193-56-0
eISBN 978-1-913193-57-7

This book has been translated with financial support from NORLA

Printed and bound by CPI Group (UK) Ltd, Croydon CR0 4YY

For sales and distribution, please contact *info@orendabooks.co.uk* or visit
*www.orendabooks.co.uk.*

# PROLOGUE

*1st January 2019*

The heavy iron door at the end of the corridor slammed shut. The sound reverberated along the brick walls.

Christer Storm Isaksen lifted his head from the book he was reading and listened. Short, slight steps on the linoleum floor.

It was Frankmann. He was the only one who would ever bother doing the extra round, if there were a reason to do so.

The steps came to a halt outside Isaksen's cell. There was a rattling of keys before the sound of a knuckle knocking lightly on the door.

Isaksen put the book down.

'Yes?'

The upper hinge creaked as Frankmann appeared in the open doorway. It looked as if he had lost even more weight over the last week. His uniform hung loosely from his thin torso.

'Happy New Year,' he said, accompanying the greeting with a nod. He had a white envelope in his hand.

'Happy New Year,' Isaksen nodded back.

He wanted to ask him how his Christmas had been, but held back. He was curious about the envelope.

'A letter came for you,' Frankmann said. 'I thought you would want it sooner rather than later.'

Isaksen took it from him.

No stamp or address. Just his name, written in small, round letters. The writing was a little slanted and somewhat unclear, as if the writer had been in a hurry.

'It was in the post box at the visitor entrance,' Frankmann explained.

Isaksen felt the envelope. It contained something stiffer than a letter. Maybe a postcard.

He rubbed his thumb over the place where the stamp should have been, turned it over. No return address.

He couldn't remember the last time he had received a handwritten letter. The Christmas cards had stopped coming too, after his mother had died.

Frankmann was still standing at the cell door, an inquisitive expression on his face.

'We would normally check it over first, with the rest of the post,' he said; an explanation as to why he was waiting to watch Isaksen open it. 'But the mutt won't be here until Friday,' he added, referring to the sniffer dog.

Isaksen peeled away the flap on the envelope and gently unsealed it. With two fingers, he opened it just wide enough to peek inside.

It was a photo.

He took it out and felt an instant tightening in his chest.

The girl in the photo was eight, maybe nine years old. She was wearing a blue hoodie and had her long, brown hair pulled back into a high ponytail. She was sat behind a school desk, resting her hands on a book. She had braces too, which she hadn't managed to hide – the photo capturing the exact moment she had grinned at the camera. There was a sprinkling of freckles across the bridge of her nose. Her eyes were ice blue, identical to his own.

'It's her.' The words escaped from between his lips.

Frankmann took a step closer.

'Who?' he asked.

Isaksen didn't answer.

*It's her*, he repeated to himself. Her: the girl everyone had told him was dead.

# 1

*Twenty hours earlier*

The New Year's Eve fireworks illuminated the city. Shrieking arrows shot into the sky and exploded in an array of multi-coloured patterns. Each eruption varied in strength and intensity. Over the last few minutes, the explosions had become more and more frequent.

A heavy mist had drifted across the fjord and lay like a lid over the harbour in front of Oslo City Hall. The drop in temperature had forced the spectators to button up their coats and tighten their scarves. They huddled together in the snow, laughing and shouting.

Emma Ramm was well wrapped up in a thick winter coat. She was wearing wellies, with two pairs of woollen socks. But she was not part of the crowd milling around in the square – the New Year's revellers staring up at the sky, holding their phones out in front of them. Neither was she among those frantically trying to get in touch with their friends and family, moments before midnight. Instead, she was making her way through the crowd, studying those she passed, looking for a sign, for anything that would indicate whether they were actually there to celebrate, or if they were there for another reason. She was unsure, however, what the signs for *that* would even look like.

It had been a little over half an hour since Emma had left Irene's flat, halfway through a quarrel she had been having with Kasper, who had suddenly decided that he didn't want to go to the annual New Year's party in Amager after all, as *he'd rather start the New Year in bed next to her*. He could not understand why she absolutely had to be down by City Hall when the clock struck twelve. She didn't even like fireworks.

'I just have to,' she had replied.

Kasper had laughed at her vague and childish answer. He was grumpy by that point as well, so had replied: 'Fine, but you can go by yourself. I'm not going out just to get cold and wet.'

'I'll go,' Martine had chimed in. 'I want to see the fireworks. Can't I go with you, Aunty? Please?'

Emma had smiled but shook her head. She didn't want to have to explain to her niece that it might be too dangerous for a small child. And for adults too, for that matter. Lots of people end up ringing in the New Year in A&E with a firework-related injury.

But there was another reason.

Over the last few months, Emma had played a major part in exposing what the media had called 'the countdown murders'. In fact, she had almost been one of the victims. The killer had intended to make her murder the grand finale to his countdown. So as New Year's Eve approached, and with that the public countdown to midnight, she had grown anxious that someone else might be inspired to attempt something similar.

Emma had confided in her therapist about this irrational fear. He had nodded and said that he understood her logic, but that there was no reason to believe something like that was going to happen again. Emma had tried to convince herself that her thoughts were just ridiculous speculations, but the idea had already taken hold and had only gained momentum. Her mind kept returning to the huge firework display that was always held on the square between the harbour and Oslo City Hall, where thousands of people gathered every New Year's Eve. Her therapist had eventually suggested that she should go down to the harbour that night, that she should tackle her fear head on, see for herself that nothing bad was going to happen, and then learn from that experience.

In fact, in the end, she had decided to leave the whole thing be, but earlier that evening an almost claustrophobic panic had washed over her, a sudden fear of what Kasper might do once the clock turned twelve. Not that she thought he would get down on one knee and propose or anything – they had only known each other for eight months – but it wasn't out of the realms of possibility that he might confess his love for her. Emma was still not quite sure how she felt about him, other than thinking that he was a nice guy who she enjoyed spending time with, so long as they lived in separate cities and didn't see each other all that often. She just wanted to carry on enjoying her relatively uncomplicated existence as the new crime reporter for news.no, without having to think too much about the future.

She took her phone out. Kasper had tried to call about a minute ago, but she couldn't be bothered to call him back. It was 23:59. Emma took a deep breath. People had started throwing their arms around each other. They shouted and sloshed around in the melting snow. The sounds of fireworks crackling and booming, people yelling and screaming filled the air around her. Emma didn't miss a single thing about the nights she used to spend out partying in Oslo, except perhaps the momentary bliss she would feel after a glass or two, before it inevitably tipped the other way.

Someone had started the countdown. Emma felt as if something sharp and uncomfortable were bearing down on her stomach and chest. She tried to hold on to her therapist's assurances that nothing bad was about to happen. Soon she could go home to Irene, Kasper and Martine, free from worry, ready to begin the New Year.

*Five!*

*Four!*

*Three!*

*Two!*

*One!*

Everything was suddenly bathed in a blinding light. A violent explosion shook the ground beneath her. The wave of pressure and heat knocked her off her feet. Debris tore through the air. She curled up on the ground, her arms wrapped around her head, trying to make sense of what was happening.

At the edge of the harbour, about thirty metres away, an immense column of orange, yellow and red flames that had just erupted into the sky was now starting to collapse, the flames cascading back down to the ground. Her ears were ringing, but she could still hear the cries, she could see the people in the crowd, who had only a moment ago been celebrating together. Now they were clinging on to each other, pushing past each other, panicking, searching for their friends, partners, children, something to explain what had just happened.

Emma got up. Black rags and scraps were descending from the sky. A man came staggering towards her, one of his arms on fire. He yelled and feverishly slapped at the flames before managing to tear his jacket off.

While the rational part of her had tried to hold on to the belief that her countdown hypothesis was absurd, an irrational prediction, the sensation she had felt growing over the last few weeks had still twisted itself into a painful knot in the pit of her stomach.

But there was no ominous feeling anymore. There was no fear.

It was now reality.

And around her, the fireworks continued to erupt.

# 2

Alexander Blix battled his way through the flood of terrified people. He leapt over a flowerbed that was hiding under the snow and slipped on a patch of ice, somehow managing to stay on his feet. Sofia Kovic was close behind him. He listened through his earpiece as she radioed into the operations centre, alerting them to the explosion that had just occurred in front of Oslo City Hall.

A man was stumbling towards them, a charred open wound on his face and a bottle of champagne still in his hand. A woman with something sticking out of her leg limped nearby.

Blix ran past her. People were sprawled across the ground, blood-soaked, groaning with pain. Others were sat half upright, dazed, their clothes in tatters. A dark, grey smoke screen had engulfed them.

He stopped, unsure where to begin.

Four bodies lay motionless near the end of the harbour. He ran towards them and knelt by the first body. A young woman with blonde hair. Shrapnel from the explosion had punctured her left eye. He searched her neck for a pulse but couldn't find one. He moved over to another woman who had injuries to her chest and stomach. Her mouth was agape, her eyes wide open. He couldn't find her pulse either.

Kovic had bent over a man wearing a grey coat. She looked up at Blix, met his gaze and shook her head.

Down at the water's edge, slumped across one of the mooring posts, was another body, scorched from the waist up. A man, by the looks of it. His injuries were more severe than the others'. Half of his face and most of his chest had been torn to shreds. There was no point checking for a pulse.

Four dead.

The explosion had left a huge crater in the asphalt. The remnants of whatever had exploded were scattered around them, still on fire. Orders had started to come in over the police radio, something about a bomb, and that they should treat it as a terrorist attack.

*Terrorism*, Blix thought. *Christ.*

A shout close behind him made him spin round. Two well-dressed men were pointing into the dark water. There was a body floating face down, arms outstretched.

Blix tore his earpiece out, pulled his jacket off and detached his duty belt. He took a step to the edge of the quay and dived in. He hadn't stopped to think about how cold it would be, but when he broke the surface he felt like he'd leapt into a pool of ice. The muscles of his face froze. It felt like a hard, cold clamp was tightening around his head. The water penetrated through his shirt, seeped into his trousers, filled his boots. His chest clenched. He had never tried this hard to move his limbs before, but they refused to obey him.

His buoyancy sent him back up to the surface. He struggled to catch his breath, and had to stop and wait for his muscles to relax.

He could hear someone shouting at him from up on the square.

'Ten metres, to your left.' It was Kovic's voice. 'Be careful!' she added.

Blix drew in a breath and tried to command his body to swim, but his clothes were weighing him down, sticking to his skin. The intensity of the cold water was making his movements slow and ineffective. It felt as if he were barely moving, and his heavy boots were dragging him down.

'Just five more metres! Further left.'

Blix propelled himself forwards with a few wide strokes, stretching out his hand on the final one. He made a grasping motion, as much of a grab as he could command his fingers to make. Clothes, a frozen, lifeless hand. Blix clutched the body just as it began to dip below the surface. He tried to roll the person over but only managed to turn them halfway before they slipped out of his grip. The effort sent him below the water again. He swallowed a mouthful, spluttered, coughed and spat. He had no choice but to wait until his body had stopped protesting, so that he could concentrate on turning the lifeless person onto their back.

It was a woman.

Her face was partially concealed by her long, dark hair, which was pasted across her severely burned skin. Blix took hold of her under her armpit and swam backwards towards the square.

'Over here!' he heard Kovic yell.

He turned his head and saw his colleague standing with one foot down on the jetty, ready to pull them up. His body stiffened with each kick. He spat and gasped as he struggled to keep the woman's head above water. Behind him, Kovic took another step down into the water.

His body was about to give out. He managed to grab one of the steps and draw himself and the woman up onto the ladder. His right foot found one of the steps. With one last push he hoisted the limp body out of the water so that Kovic could grab her jacket collar. More people were rushing over to help. Blix was finally able to let go of the woman, and he clung to the jetty, gasping for air.

'Do you need a hand?' he heard Kovic shout down to him.

Blix coughed a few more times before shaking his head and attempting to heave himself up and out of the water. But his legs would not obey him. His arms were frozen stiff. Kovic reached down anyway and grabbed his forearm with both hands. Someone else came over to help. Together, they managed to haul him up.

The paramedics up on the square were already seeing to the lifeless woman. Blix leaned forwards and rested his hands on his knees, letting the water drain off him. He was not trained for this. Not in the slightest. He usually sat behind a desk. He investigated crime scenes, questioned witnesses. It had been nearly twenty years since he had last been on active duty. He had only volunteered to work on New Year's Eve so that his younger colleagues with children could celebrate with their families at home.

He expelled the water from his nose, straightened up slightly and noticed that he was bleeding from a cut on one of his hands.

The explosions of the New Year fireworks merged with the sound of sirens. Kovic appeared with a woollen blanket and wrapped it around him. A woman was standing beside her. Blix hadn't noticed her at first, but, recognising who it was, he attempted to smile.

'Hi, Emma,' he said.

# 3

The harbour looked like a battlefield. There was blood everywhere. The injured were leaning against one another, crying. It was unclear what had exploded, but what was left was spread across the ground and continued to burn. Emma tried to avoid looking directly at the bodies of those who were clearly dead.

The New Year was only a few minutes old. A cacophony of noise surrounded her. The sound of sirens, a firework exploding somewhere above them, the blaring of a car horn, the thumping bass of a song being played far, far away. Oslo was under attack again, Emma thought, seven and a half years after the last time, when a car bomb had been detonated in the Regjeringskvartalet area of central Oslo, killing eight people. It was well known that Norwegians enjoyed a good party, so she had often thought that the capital would be an easy target for terrorists. The streets were always packed, and never more so than on huge national celebrations like the seventeenth of May, or New Year's Eve.

The woman Blix had rescued from the water was now laid out on a stretcher. Paramedics were attempting to fit her with an oxygen mask, but were struggling to remove the hair that had melted into the wound on her cheek. A man was kneeling beside her, performing chest compressions. If she survived, she would be forever marked by the events of that night. Emma thought of her own physical defect. A rare illness had caused her to lose all her hair. At least her condition, and the emotional scars that came with it, were easy to hide from the outside world, with the help of various wigs and a resolute attitude. A facial burn was much more difficult to conceal.

The police had started carrying out their routine operations. They had already rolled out the barrier tape and had secured the area around the site of the explosion. They were now in the process of expanding the perimeters.

Emma's phone rang. *Anita Grønvold, news.no* flashed up on the screen.

'Where are you?'

Emma could tell that her boss had been drinking, and that she was somewhere where the party had not yet ceased.

'The square, in front of City Hall,' Emma replied. 'I came down to watch the fireworks.'

She recounted what she had seen, the bodies of the dead, the injuries of those who had survived, the woman who had been rescued from the water.

'Have you taken any photos?'

'Not yet.'

'We need photos,' Anita said. 'You don't need to write much, but we need those pictures. Go with the terrorism angle first. Make sure to mention the casualties and the other victims, the extent of their injuries. I'll get Henrik Wollan to help, and some others, regardless of how drunk they are.'

'I had thought about linking it to the countdown murders,' Emma said.

'Huh?' Anita said. She didn't understand.

'The fact that whoever did this chose a particular time,' Emma explained. 'Twelve o'clock. The countdown to midnight, and the New Year.'

There was a moment's silence.

'You don't think it's just a coincidence?'

'No.'

'Well, copycat killer or not, you won't be able to get the police to confirm or disprove that theory, certainly not tonight, anyway. Just focus on getting those photos and figuring out the scope of the situation.'

Emma sighed inwardly. 'Will do.'

'Tomorrow, you can get started on a piece about Blix and the woman he rescued. Find out who she is and how she's doing.'

Emma hung up, swiped up to open the camera on her phone and began walking around, holding it out in front of her. She took a few shots of the first responders, the police officers rolling out more barrier tape, the flashing blue lights, the blood-soaked victims, the armed officers. She thought about calling Kasper or Irene – she should let them know she was still in one piece – but settled on sending her sister a quick text to say she was okay. She could pass on the message.

Emma caught sight of Blix again. He was sat in the open door of a police car, wrapped up tight in a blanket. Steam was rising from the top of his head.

Blix had saved her life once too, nineteen years ago, in an incident the media had subsequently named 'the Teisen tragedy'. Blix had shot Emma's father – he hadn't had any other choice; he had to do it before her father had a chance to shoot Emma too. He had already shot and killed his wife, Emma's mother, only minutes before, leaving her in a pool of blood on the kitchen floor.

Emma hadn't fully understood Blix's role in the events of that day, not until circumstances had brought them together again years later, with both of them working towards solving the countdown murders. He had kept an eye out for her then, giving her information he hadn't shared with the other journalists. But that wasn't the reason that Emma had grown to appreciate his presence in her life – even more so as time went on. It was because she felt that he actually cared. In conversations with her therapist, she had come to realise that she saw Blix as a kind of father figure.

Emma took a step closer to him. Blix's lips were blue, contrasting with the stark white of his face. One of his hands was bundled up in a bloody bandage. She snapped a photo of him without him noticing, and moved on. A reply from Irene had popped up on her screen, but Emma swiped it away, resolving to read it later. Kasper hadn't called or sent a single message to check if she were safe.

Now that there were fewer people inside the perimeter, the extent of the damage was much clearer. Her gaze was drawn to the black hole in the ground, about a metre wide. Emma held her phone in front of her, continuing to take photos of the scene. She zoomed in closer to one of the casualties – a man on his back. He was wearing a grey coat with a high collar. It was singed from the explosion, and was drenched in blood. He had black trousers and black gloves. Matching black shoes too. They were made of leather, and they looked like, as if they could be...

Emma drifted towards him, stepping over to the other side of the body. She heard a voice shouting her name, but didn't look to see who it was. She only had eyes for the man on the ground in front of her, refusing to acknowledge who she was looking at. It was not Kasper. It was impossible, it couldn't be him.

'You can't be here,' the voice said behind her, closer this time. 'You have to stay behind the cordon, Emma, like everyone else.'

But Emma wasn't listening, she just edged closer and closer to the man lying there on his back, staring straight up at the sky. At the fireworks and the stars. The ground and snow around him were stained with the blood that had drained from the open wound in his stomach.

*No*, Emma whispered softly. *It can't...*

She shook her head, gasping for air. She felt a hand on her side, but didn't turn to see who was talking to her, pulling at her. All she could do was stare at his black curls against the white snow. His stubble. His eyelids. She desperately hoped they would start blinking, but they remained as they were, just as motionless. Just as dead.

# 4

Blix thought he knew what it felt like to be cold, to be frozen to the core. In his younger years, he had gone through a period of taking a swim in the sea every morning. Autumn or spring, summer or winter. It made no difference. He had been living on the peninsula at Bygdøy at that time, so it was only a short drive to the beaches at Huk or Paradisbukta. Gard Fosse, who was now his boss, would join him from time to time. Hollering and panting, they would race out into the water, only to sprint back to shore again a few seconds later, to a dry towel and warm clothes. Maybe even a flask of coffee.

With all the roadblocks and chaos in downtown Oslo, it had taken much longer than usual to get back to the Oslo Police Headquarters. The locker rooms were packed. The extra officers who had been called in were preparing themselves for action. The room was buzzing with activity. It was difficult to hear anything else over the sounds of weapons being loaded and the crackling of the radio transmitters.

Blix had torn off his wet clothes, closed the shower door behind him and stood under the warm jets of water until he was absolutely sure that he had fully thawed.

The cut on his hand probably needed seeing to – he had managed to bandage it up himself at least – but he decided to stay at the office regardless.

Kovic had remained at the harbour. He called her to see how things were going.

'We're trying to track down witnesses,' she replied. 'But none of the people I've spoken to so far were sober, and no one's provided any new information. Hopefully, the CCTV cameras can help us out.'

Blix nodded. Cameras didn't lie. Unlike people, they couldn't be persuaded to change their story. And the city was full of them.

'A lot of people were using their phones to film at the time as well,' he commented, dropping into the chair behind his workstation. 'We can encourage people to send us whatever footage they've got.'

'We've already secured some,' Kovic replied. 'But it'll be a massive job to trawl through all of it, especially when we don't even know what we're looking for.'

'Do we know anything more about the explosion?' asked Blix.

The line crackled.

'The bomb was placed in a waste container,' she answered.

'A waste container?'

'Yes, one of those litter ones. Green, about a metre high. God, I can't think straight – what's the word I'm after?'

'A rubbish bin?'

'Yes, that, a rubbish bin.'

Blix had turned his computer on and headed straight to the news website *VG Nett*. Photos from the scene at City Hall dominated the front page, already supplemented with witness statements: 'blood everywhere' ... 'mindless terrorism'.

'The bomb squad believe that the force of the explosion measured in at around seventy millibars,' Kovic continued.

'Is that a lot?'

'Not enough to break windows or damage the nearby buildings,' Kovic explained, 'but enough to inflict fatal injuries on those closest to the explosion.'

'I see,' Blix replied.

'There's something else you should know...' Kovic began.

'Go on?'

Kovic hesitated before continuing.

'None of the casualties have been formally identified, but Emma's boyfriend is one of them.'

Blix moved his phone to his other ear.

'She was inside the cordon,' Kovic said. 'I was next to her when she saw him. Kasper Bjerringbo. A Danish journalist.'

'I know who he is,' Blix replied, swallowing hard. 'He was a good guy.'

'From what I managed to get out of Emma, he wasn't meant to be there.'

Blix had seen Emma that night, but she'd been alone.

'How is she?' he asked.

'What can I say? I think she's in shock. She just stood there. Didn't cry or anything. And I didn't have the heart to pull her away when the paramedics came for him.'

Blix felt a strong urge to see Emma. Talk to her. Not that he could say much to help, he just wanted to be there for her.

'Is there someone looking after her?' he asked.

'Yes, I think so.'

'Can you make sure?' Blix requested.

'Will do.'

The line fell silent.

An officer walked by behind his desk. Blix straightened up a little and cleared his throat.

'Any news on how the woman from the harbour is doing?'

'I've just spoken to someone at the hospital, about ten minutes ago,' Kovic said, sighing. 'They said it's too early to tell.'

'Have we managed to identify her?'

'We have. Bear with me.'

Blix listened as Kovic fumbled with a notepad.

'She had a bank card in her jacket pocket.'

A few more seconds went by, before Kovic found the name.

'Ruth-Kristine Smeplass,' she said.

Blix's mouth opened involuntarily. 'What did you just say?' he asked.

Kovic repeated the name. Blix ran a hand through his hair.

'What's wrong?' Kovic asked. 'Do you know her?'

'Don't you?'

'No?'

Blix thought of the long, curly hair. That perpetually irritated expression. The hours he had spent staring at her face, searching for the truth.

'Ruth-Kristine Smeplass is Patricia's mother,' he said. 'The Patricia who's been missing and presumed dead since 2009.'

'Shit,' Kovic said.

In all his years as an investigator, Patricia's disappearance had been the case Blix had spent the most time working on. It was a case that he returned to time after time, reviewing all the information they had, going over everything again and again, looking for a sliver of information that he might have overlooked the first time.

First, Kasper. Now Ruth-Kristine.

Two people he knew, both victims of that night's attack.

Bloody hell.

He heard a siren start to wail on the other end of the phone.

'Are you coming back to HQ soon?' he asked.

'Not entirely sure yet,' Kovic replied. 'There are still a lot of people here.'

'I understand,' Blix said. 'Take care of Emma for me. See you soon.'

# 5

It was only three hours and six minutes into the New Year when Gard Fosse emerged from his office, decked out in a black suit and white dress shirt, now unbuttoned at the collar.

'The large meeting room,' he said, pointing to the floor above them.

Kovic had just arrived.

'I should've grabbed some food first,' she grumbled, chucking her notepad and pen onto the desk.

Blix pushed his chair back and stood up. He had called and messaged Emma several times over the last few hours. He was still waiting for a reply.

They followed Fosse upstairs. The seats around the long conference table filled up promptly. The leader of the Emergency Response Team, and the heads of the Intelligence and Investigation Departments were sat together at the end of the table, next to a number of leaders from various other specialist units. A handful of investigators were scattered around the table, as well as a few men and women Blix knew from Kripos, Norway's National Crime Investigation Service, someone from the Norwegian Police Security Service, or PST as they called it, and a couple of other people he didn't recognise. A lot of the attendees were still dressed in the clothes they had been wearing to parties they must have been attending only a few hours earlier. Some of them were struggling to keep their eyes focussed.

Blix and Kovic found a vacant chair each. A door at the far end of the room opened, and the chief of police strode in, followed by the communications advisor and another man who had the sleeves of his tuxedo rolled up.

'Welcome,' the chief of police announced as he sat down. 'Let's get started.'

He nodded at the man in the tuxedo, indicating that he should take the lead.

'My name is Raymond Rafto,' the man began. 'I am one of the chief inspectors at PST, and will be the lead investigator on this case.'

He looked around, with a somewhat arrogant air, before continuing:

'At midnight, an explosive device was detonated in a rubbish bin at the square located between Oslo City Hall and the harbour. As the situation stands, four people have been killed: two men and two women. Another woman has suffered life-threatening injuries. Twelve people have been seriously injured and, thus far, seventeen others are at the hospital being treated for minor injuries. We currently have no ID on the casualties. There is nothing to indicate that the victims are anything more than innocent bystanders.'

Blix felt the urge to interrupt him and inform them all about Kasper and Ruth-Kristine, but decided to leave it be.

Rafto continued: 'No one has claimed responsibility for the bomb yet. And we have no substantial intelligence that would have led us to suspect such an incident might take place. There was some minor activity regarding restricted materials over the Christmas weekend, and further tracing has been initiated. We are also working closely with the usual security services in other countries, but no other threats have been detected. We do consider it likely that another attack may occur, however, simply because one terror attack is often followed by another. With that in mind, the national threat level has been raised to substantial.'

He pushed the sheet of paper aside and turned to Fred Malmberg, head of the Emergency Response Team.

'What's the current status on the ground?' he asked.

'The area around the harbour and Oslo City Hall has been secured,' Malmberg explained. 'The injured have been taken to hospital. Paramedics are currently working on the casualties, who'll then be taken for post-mortems. Crime Scene Investigation are now on site, working with the bomb-disposal technicians. We have personnel stationed at key points around the city centre, to maintain calm and for surveillance, and we're receiving assistance from the armed forces to search for any other explosives.'

The PST investigator nodded his approval and looked to the far end of the table.

'Investigation?'

The head of the Criminal Investigation Department sat up.

'We've interviewed the witnesses with minor injuries,' he began, 'but nothing much has come of that. There were a lot of people who were close to the harbour and weren't directly affected by the explosion, not physically anyway, but of those who were near the site, none have provided any useful information.' He cleared his throat and carried on. 'Several people have called in already with tip-offs, claiming to have seen men who they've assumed are of a Muslim background, but so far it seems that these tip-offs are mainly based on prejudice, not on any particularly suspicious behaviour. Large parts of the area are monitored by our own cameras. We've already begun a review of all the footage, and have started collecting recordings from other sources. And I expect to be informed of the type of explosives that were used sometime later this morning.'

'What about the design and trigger mechanism?' Rafto asked.

'We should find out about that sometime in the next few hours as well. Some of the components have been secured and brought in, and we have divers in the harbour as we speak, searching for more remains from the bomb, seeing as the bin was located so close to the water.'

Rafto glanced at his watch. 'I'll be meeting the justice minister for a briefing in half an hour,' he said, looking around the table. 'Does anyone have anything else?'

The head of the Undercover Police Unit spoke up.

'We've been tracking an escalating gang conflict,' he said. 'We know that the Balkan Brothers were at a bar just up the road, about three hundred metres from the site of the explosion—'

'Details,' Rafto cut him off. 'Chase that up with the relevant departments.'

He began collecting his papers. 'The investigation will be conducted from our premises in Nydalen, but everyone will be assigned important tasks. I ask that the unit heads remain. Everyone else can go.'

Chairs scraped against the floor as people stood up. Blix caught up with Fosse.

'One of the injured, one of the most seriously injured, has been identified,' he said.

'File a report,' Fosse replied.

'It's Ruth-Kristine Smeplass,' Blix continued. Fosse slowed his pace momentarily. 'Patricia's mother,' Blix clarified.

'Some people just can't catch a break,' Fosse sighed. 'Will she survive?'

'It's too early to say,' Blix answered. 'But it might be worth looking into a bit more.'

They had reached the top of the stairs.

'How so?' Fosse asked. 'You think the bomb could have something to do with Patricia?'

Blix struggled to justify the suggestion, but that was how he worked – always starting with whatever stood out most, following any random angles and irregularities in a case.

'The bomb was not positioned to inflict maximum damage,' he said.

Kovic had appeared at his side.

'It wasn't intended to harm anyone other than those in the immediate vicinity,' she added. 'Most of the pressure wave was sent out into the fjord. The bomb would have caused far more damage if it had been located anywhere else on the square, or along one of the streets closer to the centre, like on Karl Johans gate, for example.'

Fosse scoffed. 'It did more than enough damage,' he retorted. 'We should be thrilled that more people weren't killed.'

'It may have been a targeted attack,' Blix pointed out.

'And who would be the target?' Fosse asked. 'Ruth-Kristine Smeplass? The last I heard, she was nothing more than a haggard drug addict. Neither she nor any of the casualties were people of importance.'

Blix felt a wave of anger wash over him.

'They were important to someone,' he said.

'You know what I mean,' Fosse replied. 'They were innocent by-standers. That's what terrorism thrives on. Inciting fear.'

'One of the casualties was a Danish journalist,' Blix said. 'Kasper Bjerringbo.'

They had made their way into the corridor on the sixth floor. Fosse glanced up at the meeting room directly above them, where there had been no mention of a dead journalist.

'How do you know that?' he asked.

'He was Emma Ramm's boyfriend,' Blix explained. 'They were both there.'

Gard Fosse's lips tightened. He disapproved of the close relation-ship Blix had with the young journalist. Fosse had been working with Blix that day, on the patrol nineteen years ago that had ended with Emma's father, armed with a gun, barricading himself and his family in their home. While Blix had decided to go in, Fosse had stayed outside, waiting for back-up.

'I understand,' he said. 'But that doesn't change anything. He was an innocent bystander.'

Blix wasn't ready to let it go. 'I think we should look into it,' he re-peated.

'Look into what?'

'The possibility that this could be something other than a terrorist attack.'

Fosse stopped again and looked directly at Blix, shifting his gaze to Kovic and then back.

'Our department will be handling the incoming tip-offs,' Fosse said. 'You're a part of something bigger this time, Blix. You can't just do what you want, following your own initiative. You will have to play as part of a team and do as you're told, for once.'

Blix waited until Fosse had disappeared into his office, then turned to Kovic: 'I'm going down to the archives.'

He pressed the button next to the lift doors.

'What are you going down there for?'
'To get the files for the Patricia case.'

# 6

As the lift made its way down to the basement, Blix leant back and thought about the first few weeks and months that had followed Patricia's disappearance. The intense search, the close connection he had formed with the girl's father. His despair, which had quickly become Blix's own. It had been so easy to imagine that something similar could have happened to Iselin, his own daughter.

The lift juddered as it came to a stop on the bottom floor. He rarely visited the archives, but it was a well-organised system that stored every single one of their cases chronologically, regardless of whether it had been solved or shelved. The case files for the investigation into Patricia's disappearance consisted of nine separate ring binders, all stacked inside a cardboard box. A cloud of dust swept into the air as he lowered it from the shelf.

He found Kovic waiting for him when he arrived back upstairs, eating a cold tortilla wrap.

'It's going to be a long night if you're expecting us to get through all that,' she commented, swallowing.

Blix put the box down on the desk between them.

'It's mainly dead ends,' he said. 'A lot of documentation from an investigation that led nowhere.'

Kovic wiped her mouth with a napkin. 'Can you give me a quick run through of the main details?'

The open-plan office was packed with police officers and other investigators. It was much louder than they were used to. With a lot more people than usual, too.

Blix lifted the main folder out of the box, sat down and took a deep breath, unsure where to begin.

'Patricia was kidnapped on the eleventh of August, 2009,' he started, removing the band from around the folder. 'Her au pair was assaulted on her way home, after picking Patricia up at the nursery in Tangenten. She was beaten and pushed into one of the bushes in

Bjølsen Park, and the perpetrator disappeared with the pushchair. The au pair couldn't remember anything about the attack. No description, other than the fact the perpetrator was wearing dark clothes.'

Blix put the folder down and took out the first few pages.

'Patricia's father, Christer Storm Isaksen, had full custody of the child at the time. Ruth-Kristine was one of our first suspects, seeing as she and Christer had fought so vehemently over who would get custody of Patricia. A lot of people thought she had been involved.'

'So what was the reason Ruth-Kristine didn't have custody of her own daughter?' Kovic asked. 'It must have been serious, if the father was granted full custody.'

'Mental-health issues,' Blix explained. 'A long history of psychoses, personality disorders, hospital admissions, rebellious behaviour and self-harming. She was also an addict and was deemed a potential danger to the child, so she was only allowed limited visitor rights.'

'But she wasn't involved in the kidnapping?'

Blix rubbed his hands over his face. His cheeks were warm. He would probably end up catching a cold after his dip in the harbour.

'She had an alibi,' he said eventually. 'There was nothing to suggest that she had anything to do with it. That was until Patricia's father met with a man named Knut Ivar Skage about two years later, in the car park that leads into the forest at Solemskogen.'

'I remember that,' Kovic said, eagerly. 'Skage was murdered, wasn't he? Patricia's father killed him?'

'Correct,' Blix nodded. 'He was after the reward that Isaksen had promised for any information that might help him find Patricia. According to Isaksen, Skage admitted that he had seen his daughter after the kidnapping, and that the person behind it was a woman who Christer knew well.'

'Ruth-Kristine,' Kovic concluded.

Blix nodded. 'That's how Isaksen interpreted it anyway. As did we.'

'But why would he kill the man who could give him all the answers?'

'When they met, Isaksen asked for some sort of reassurance, to make sure Skage actually had reliable information. Skage told him that Patricia had a birthmark on the top of her thigh, just inside the groin. Isaksen presumed the worst. He thought his daughter had been abused.'

Kovic bit her lip thoughtfully.

'But that was unlikely,' Blix continued. 'The last thing Skage said before he died was that all he had done was change Patricia's nappies. He hadn't been involved in the kidnapping itself. He had just been contacted afterwards because the kidnapper didn't know how to look after a baby.'

'Oh God,' Kovic moaned.

'Tragic. And even more so as Knut Ivar Skage was already a dying man.'

'What do you mean?'

'He ran a garage in Kalbakken, his own car repair workshop, so he'd been inhaling all sorts of solvents for years. He was riddled with cancer. The doctors had given him a few months to live.'

Kovic looked at what was left of her tortilla wrap and, with a grimace, chucked it in the bin.

'So, he really did just want to tell Isaksen what he knew before he died?' she asked, wiping her hands clean with the napkin.

'And probably to cash in on the reward, to leave some money for his wife and children,' Blix nodded. 'He couldn't carry on working, being that ill, and they were struggling, financially. It was discovered that he hadn't been paying his taxes from the business either, so was basically left with no income.'

'Did he have a criminal record?'

'Nothing much. One or two cases about his lack of bookkeeping, and one report of fraud relating to a car sale,' Blix explained. 'When we went through the garage after he died, we found spare parts from various stolen cars. It was probably how he managed to stay afloat. Bought cars that had been written off and then repaired them with parts from stolen cars, before reselling them.'

'Did he have any connection to Ruth-Kristine?'

Blix shook his head.

'Where was she when her daughter was kidnapped then? You said she had an alibi.'

'She was with a friend – her neighbour. They were out shopping that day. And there were CCTV recordings and card receipts to prove it.'

'Wasn't it a man who had kidnapped Patricia, anyway?'

'All the evidence we had seemed to point to that,' Blix confirmed. 'And after Christer told us about what Knut Ivar Skage had said, we began the search for a man in Ruth-Kristine's social circle who had no children of his own.'

'Because of the thing with the nappies?'

Blix nodded again. 'We found a few who fit the criteria, but they checked out.'

'Could the au pair have had something to do with it?' Kovic queried.

'Carmen Velacruz,' Blix said, trying to pronounce the Spanish name correctly. 'We didn't find anything to indicate that was the case either. No motive. Besides, the attack was quite brutal. The hit she took to the head that day could easily have been fatal.'

'Have you kept surveillance on her since?' Kovic asked.

'We've checked up on her now and then,' Blix said. 'She's back in Spain now. I've looked into her movements occasionally, just to see if she's had any contact with a child who might match Patricia's age – if she's still alive that is.'

'And she hasn't?'

Blix shook his head. 'There is also a limit on the amount of resources I can request from our colleagues in Madrid.'

'What sentence did Isaksen get?'

'Twelve years. He's still in prison.'

Blix could tell that she was thinking about something, and sent her an inquisitive look.

'It's nothing. I was just thinking that, if Ruth-Kristine did actually have something to do with the kidnapping, there couldn't be anyone else who has a greater motive to kill her than Isaksen. But, if he spent New Year's Eve in a cell, then...'

She turned to her computer and opened up the criminal-records database, the directory where all prison violations and requests for furlough were registered.

'I don't think he's ever applied for furlough,' Blix said as he watched her type in his personal details.

Kovic nodded and squinted at the screen.

'He hasn't left Oslo Prison since the trial,' she said. 'Except for when his mother died.'

Blix could hear the lingering suspicion in her voice.

'He could have asked someone else to do it for him,' she suggested. 'He could've met someone in prison, someone with explosives expertise – or who has a connection to someone who has. Foreign criminals, maybe. What do I know? People who are willing to do that kind of thing for money.'

'Christer has practically isolated himself while he's been in prison,' Blix said. 'He barely interacts with the other inmates.'

'Still,' Kovic pressed. 'We should check it out.'

Blix stood up and started to gather together the papers that were now spread across the desk. He put them back in the box with the rest of the files for the Patricia case, suddenly feeling lethargic and drowsy.

'We'll approach this one thing at a time,' he said. 'First of all, I suggest we get a few hours' sleep.'

# 7

With trembling hands, Emma unlocked the door to her flat on Falbes gate and stepped inside. She found herself immediately looking down at a pair of Kasper's trainers, one shoe left haphazardly on top of the other, next to her neatly positioned winter boots.

The door closed behind her. She shut her eyes and stood there for a few seconds. Her ears were still ringing from the explosion.

Emma drew in a short gasp and blinked a few times. It would have been at this very moment that he'd have walked down the hall to greet her, open arms and a wide smile. She would have taken in his unruly curls, his glasses, the white shirt that he had probably untucked, maybe even undone a few of the buttons, now that he was home, now that the evening, the party, was over. She would have noticed his chest hairs, just peeking out. His stomach, the slight hint of his defined muscles beneath his shirt. Emma had always been most attracted to men when they weren't completely undressed, when she could still imagine what the rest of their body looked like underneath. For some reason, she also liked Kasper most when he was a little bit tired and surly, as he might have been now, at half past four in the morning.

She would have welcomed his embrace, kissed him. His lips might have been dry. They might have tasted a little like stale alcohol. A cigar, maybe, too. He would have pulled her in close, and they would have stood there in the hallway, silently holding each other. She would have whispered an apology into his ear, having left Irene's New Year's dinner without him. She would have explained why she had felt it necessary to have been down at the square, at that exact time. And he, as she knew he would, would have said that it was fine, that it didn't matter, that the most important thing was that she had come home to him in one piece.

Emma pulled her wellies off, threw both pairs of woollen socks aside. Her feet were clammy. She made her way slowly into the flat. His suitcase was pushed up against the wall outside her bedroom, wide open. She stopped in front of it and stared at his clothes. She squatted down and lay a hand on one of the white T-shirts he had been wearing a few days ago. She took it out, held it up to her face. It wouldn't have mattered whether she had been there or not. She couldn't have prevented the explosion. People would have died anyway. But Kasper would not have been one of them.

Emma got up and walked into the kitchen. A bread knife had been left out. Three glasses on the table. A plate. She loaded everything into the dishwasher and closed it. She pulled her phone out of her pocket. Anita had called three times, Blix five. Irene had sent her a text. It dawned on Emma that she had not yet read her sister's reply after she had sent her a message earlier, assuring her that she was fine.

She opened it.

*I'm so glad to hear that. God, how awful! Have you found Kasper? Is he okay? He changed his mind and went after you. Said he wanted to surprise you.* ♥

Emma closed the message. She tilted her head back and took a deep breath, and felt her lips begin to tremble.

# 8

Blix woke with a start. The feeling that he was late for something made him sit bolt upright, before he realised what day it was and what had happened the previous night.

He had only managed to get a few hours' sleep, but he rubbed his eyes anyway and picked up his phone from the bedside table. There had been no new internal police bulletins since he had gone to bed, sometime around five o'clock that morning. He hadn't received any breaking news notifications from the newspapers either, no new developments. A swift sweep of the largest online publications showed Norway's media waking up to a rare, disoriented frenzy. The fear of another terror attack reigned.

Blix loaded the news.no website. They had posted full coverage of the incident too. None of the articles had been written by Emma.

Blix's thoughts had frequently drifted back to Emma the previous night. He knew she was strong and resilient, and was always determined to not let anything or anyone control her life. He had occasionally wondered whether it was all just a façade, if she was still that scared young girl he first met. He had a feeling that if her defences did start to crumble, then the entire fortress would collapse.

In any case, he would try to help her as best he could. How he would actually go about that, he did not know. There was a limit to how much he could do. He hoped she would call back sometime this morning at least.

Blix poured himself a cup of coffee and sat at his kitchen table with one of the folders from the Patricia case. He had taken the box home and leafed through the old documents until he succumbed to the fatigue. It hadn't taken him long to reacquaint himself with the key suspects. Blix and the other investigators had mapped out Knut Ivar Skage's social circle extensively, in search of a man who had no young children among his immediate contacts, but they'd found no obvious contenders. Two years after Patricia's kidnapping, all of the recorded telecoms data from Skage's phone had been erased too, so they couldn't even trace who had called him.

As he ate breakfast, his thoughts alternated between Ruth-Kristine Smeplass and Christer Storm Isaksen. He had always wondered how two people as tremendously different as they were had managed to find each other, and have a child together. Their relationship had gone awry well before Patricia came into the world. At one time Blix had become fixated on why and how they hadn't been able to work out their differences, and whether one of them had previously dated someone who might have been seeking revenge. The list of potential candidates had been substantial, but they had all checked out.

Blix headed over to Kovic's to pick her up for work just before eleven o'clock. It was a grey day. A light drizzle was slowly washing the snow away from the roads and pavements. There was hardly anyone out that morning, aside from one or two who had begun the New Year with a morning walk or jog. The remains of a few burned-out fireworks and other rubbish from the celebrations littered the pavements.

He decided to call Nikolaj Smeplass as he sat waiting for Kovic outside her flat. Ruth-Kristine's parents had been living in Spain for the past three years. They would have received a formal briefing about what had happened to their daughter at some point that morning, but Blix wanted to talk to them himself. He had been in regular contact with Ruth-Kristine's father after Patricia's disappearance, and he still had his number saved.

He didn't need to introduce himself when Smeplass picked up. He expressed his sympathy.

'Thank you,' Nikolaj Smeplass replied, his voice wavering slightly. 'Do you know who did this?'

'No,' Blix replied. 'Everything seems to suggest that she was an innocent bystander.'

Kovic appeared at the car door and climbed in. Blix transferred the call to speakerphone so she could listen.

'We're trying to book tickets home,' Smeplass said. 'But there are a lot of people flying back to Norway at the moment. Looks like it'll be Thursday at the earliest.'

'I hope we have some better news for you by then,' Blix replied.

Smeplass sounded frustrated. Or maybe worn out.

'Ruth-Kristine has an extraordinary ability to get mixed up in things she shouldn't be involved in,' he sighed.

'How do you mean?'

'It was always one thing or another. Always with the wrong men. Bad people. We tried to tell her that she was ruining her life, but then she would say that it was *her* life to ruin and we had to stop treating her like a child. She was right, of course, but ... you never stop caring, no matter how old they are.'

'Was Ruth-Kristine in a relationship that you know of?'

Smeplass took a deep breath.

'She's had this *friend* for a few years. They've been on and off. A lorry driver who lives on Kolbotn.'

'Do you know his name?'

'Haugseth. Svein-Erik Haugseth. We've never met him.'

'What about her sister? Do you know if they were in touch?'

'I don't think so,' Smeplass answered. 'Britt and Ruth-Kristine are very different people.'

Blix thanked him for the information and promised to keep him updated if there were any developments in the case.

'Please send my regards to Sonja,' he added, and hung up.

He turned to greet Kovic: 'Good morning.'

'Hi.'

She smiled weakly. She had deep bags under her eyes.

'Did you get any sleep?' he asked.

'Not really,' Kovic answered. 'But I'm fine. I'm used to it. Thanks for picking me up though.'

'No problem. Fancy a trip to Kolbotn?'

She looked at him. 'Shouldn't we go to HQ first?'

'You know what it's going to be like there,' Blix objected. 'How investigations into bombings go. PST will sort through everything, and then all the irrelevant tip-offs, which are usually backed up by little more than unfounded suspicions, will be sifted down through the system and end up on our desks. So we'll be left with the routine work that almost always leads nowhere – the only reason we have to carry it out is so the lead investigators can say that every single lead has been followed up.'

Kovic stared at him.

'Now, I usually don't mind chasing down every potential lead, no matter how small,' he continued. 'Someone's got to do it. Before we do end up doing that though, I want to have a look into something that might be a little more interesting.'

'You don't think we should talk to Christer Storm Isaksen first? Wouldn't that be more interesting?'

'Christer isn't going anywhere,' Blix said. 'Anyway, Kolbotn is closer.'

Kovic had no further objections and spent a few seconds searching for Haugseth's address. She typed it into the sat nav – it would only take them fifteen minutes to get there.

'I'll see if he's home,' she said.

She dialled his number. She didn't introduce herself when he answered, simply asked if he was at home.

'Yes. Why?' he asked cagily. 'Who is this?'

'Excuse me,' Kovic said. 'I think I've got the wrong number. Sorry for bothering you.'

She hung up. Blix sent her a quick look.

'He might search for my number online and find out that I work for the police,' she said. 'If he does, and then runs off before we get there, we'll know that he doesn't want to talk. He might have plenty of reasons for doing that, of course. If he stays though...'

'Then we won't have gone over there for nothing,' Blix concluded.

Kovic shrugged.

'Smart plan,' Blix said.

Kovic smiled.

Blix put the car into gear and set off.

'Fosse is going to wonder where we've gotten to,' she said.

'Fosse has more important things to worry about than the two of us,' Blix replied.

They drove in silence for the next few minutes. Blix glanced over at her occasionally. Kovic seemed to be staring off into space.

'Everything alright?' he asked.

Kovic gave a start. 'Oh. Sure, yes. I'm just a bit...'

Blix looked down at her hands. They were shaking. Kovic had noticed too and placed one hand on top of the other. She paused for a moment, before explaining:

'What happened last autumn ... the explosion at the TV studios, where your daughter...' Kovic stared out of the window again for a few seconds. 'It had a bigger impact on me than I've been willing to admit. And then last night, everything just...' She took a deep breath.

'Everything came back,' Blix said, finishing the sentence for her.

'It did. And I wasn't even in the damn building when it happened.'

Blix nodded. 'Have you spoken to anyone about this? A therapist?'

'A few times. And everything's fine during the day. But then the night comes. I wake up with this intense pounding in my ears, as if my whole head is shaking. And then I have to get up and go for a walk. Get some fresh air.'

Blix pulled out into the left lane, overtaking a car that had a bed wrapped in plastic tied to the roof.

'Do you get that?' Kovic asked. 'Do you ever wake up and...?'

She stopped herself.

'Forget it,' she said after a while. 'I know how you reacted afterwards, of course...' She made a dismissive gesture with her free hand.

'It takes time,' Blix said. 'I don't think it helps if you try and speed up the process. It'll work itself out in its own good time.'

Kovic nodded slowly.

'But it does help to talk through it though, from what I've heard,' Blix continued, thinking back to the time he had shot and killed Emma's father.

'That was probably one of the many mistakes I made after the Teisen tragedy. I couldn't let go, and I thought I had to fix the problem by myself.'

'Men,' Kovic said. 'Hopeless.'

Blix smiled. 'But I'm fine now,' he said. 'Finally. I've just started to get the feeling back in my lips. Christ, that water was cold.'

He let his tongue glide over them. It made Kovic laugh, before she sank back into her seat.

❄

Svein-Erik Haugseth's house looked as if it had been built in the seventies and hadn't been decorated again since. The grey coating on the walls was flaking away, and parts of the tiled roof looked like it had been ripped off and then chucked carelessly back into place. The garden was completely buried in snow.

Kovic and Blix parked next to a lorry that had *HAUGSETH TRANSPORT* plastered onto the side.

There were three bin bags full of empty Swedish beer cans piled up outside the front door. The charred base of a firework was sticking out of the snow beside them, along with a bunch of burned out sparklers.

Blix rang the doorbell, and accompanied it with a knock. A man appeared at the door about a minute later, dressing gown wide open and wearing a pair of grey woollen socks. His thin hair was sticking out in every direction. He looked as if he had only just woken up, or was still in the middle of hosting a sleepover.

Blix introduced himself and Kovic, holding his police ID up as he did so.

'Svein-Erik Haugseth?' he asked.

'Yes. What's this about?'

'It's about Ruth-Kristine,' Blix said. 'Your ... girlfriend?'

Haugseth rested a hand on his hip. 'Not anymore. Or, well, I don't think we are anyway. Why?'

Blix and Kovic looked at each other.

'Can we come in?' Blix asked. 'It'll be easier to explain inside.'

Haugseth looked at them as if he thought they were having a laugh.

'By all means,' he said, opening the door fully to invite them in.

They manoeuvred their way through the piles of newspapers, bottles and old pizza boxes and sat down opposite Haugseth on a leather sofa that had so many cracks in it, it was only just possible to tell that it had once been black. The TV was on – a programme about restoring old cars. The residue of old cigarettes and dregs of spilled beer plastered the table between them. Haugseth didn't bother cleaning any of it up. Instead, he rubbed his face slowly, which didn't seem to revive him as much as he might have hoped it had. There was an open beer can in front of him.

Blix informed him that Ruth-Kristine had been one of the injured in the explosion the night before, and explained her condition.

'What kind of relationship did you have with Ruth-Kristine?'

Haugseth took a moment to work out what was going on. He blinked a few times.

'We've been together for a few years now,' he said slowly, swallowing. 'She lived here with me, for the most part,' he added.

Blix glanced around the room quickly, but couldn't see any clothes or other items that would indicate that a woman had lived there.

'But I haven't seen her since...' he thought about it; '...the day before New Year's Eve,' he concluded. 'No wait. The day before that.'

'The twenty-ninth of December,' Kovic clarified.

'Yeah. I think so.'

'Can you think of any reason why she would have been down at the harbour last night?'

Haugseth shook his head. 'In all the time we've been together, she's never spent New Year's Eve *there*. She wouldn't. She doesn't like crowds. Doesn't like fireworks either. She'd always stay inside when we've...' He made a gesture as if he needn't explain.

'Did she have any close acquaintances that you know of?' Blix asked. 'Anybody she could have been there with, or someone she trusted?'

Haugseth took a moment to think it through.

'That would be Nina.'

'Nina who?'

'Nina Ballangrud,' Haugseth answered. 'They're always together.'

Blix jotted the name down on his notepad.

'Do you have a phone number or address we could contact her at?' he asked.

'Sure, I've got it written down here somewhere,' Haugseth said.

'You said you didn't think you were together anymore,' Blix pressed. 'What makes you say that?'

Haugseth sighed. 'She changed, out of nowhere. Decided she didn't want to party, drink, things like that. She borrowed some money and left with my car just after Christmas. Didn't come back until a few days later. And then she was quiet, closed off. Wouldn't spend time with us, wouldn't drink or do anything. She wasn't herself.'

'Do you know where she went when she left?'

'Didn't say. I thought she'd gone back to her own place.'

Kovic looked through her notes.

'In Holmlia?'

'She's got a two-bedroom flat there,' Haugseth nodded. 'I've only been a few times. Not a fan of tiny flats with low ceilings myself.'

Haugseth picked up the beer can and raised it to his mouth, thought about it for a second and lowered it.

'I sent her a text yesterday morning,' he continued. 'Asked if she wanted to come to the party I was having here, since it was New Year's Eve and all, but she said she couldn't.'

'So she had something else planned?'

'I mean, most people have something planned on New Year's Eve don't they? So yeah, that's what I figured.'

'But she didn't say what she was doing?'

'I asked; she didn't reply. I thought that was it then, it was over.

When she didn't even want to spend New Year's Eve with me...' He let the sentence trail off. Took a swig.

'Do you know if she had any enemies?' Blix asked.

Again, Haugseth considered the question.

'There was this one guy.' He scratched at the thick stubble on his chin. 'Or at least I think it was a guy,' he added. 'She was arguing with someone over the phone anyway.'

'When was that?' Blix straightened up.

'The last time I saw her,' Haugseth said.

'The twenty-ninth,' Kovic added.

'Yes.'

'What were they arguing about?' Blix asked eagerly.

'I've no idea. I just walked in here, and she was stood over there, talking on the phone. Stormed out of the room and slammed the door behind her. All I could hear was that she was angry. Or she was being aggressive anyway.'

'But you couldn't hear what she was saying?'

He shook his head.

'And you didn't ask who she was talking to?'

'I did, but I was told that I could go fuck myself. Then she went out again. And that ... that was probably the last time I saw her.'

Blix and Kovic took turns asking a few more questions, but the fact that she had been arguing with someone over the phone remained the most interesting piece of information.

'We need to get a copy of her phone records,' Blix said as soon as they were back in the car. 'Find out who she was arguing with.'

'And we should have a look at her flat too,' Kovic suggested.

Blix put the car in reverse. His phone pinged twice. The same notification appeared on Kovic's phone. She opened it.

'They've found a photo of someone who they think might be the bomber,' she said quickly, holding up her phone to show him an image of a man in dark clothing. The picture was grainy and blurred, but it looked as if he was carrying a green-and-white shopping bag, one you would get from the supermarket *Kiwi*. Kovic swiped to the next photo, this time showing the man standing next to the rubbish bin. In the next picture he was walking away, without the bag.

'At 11:32 last night,' Kovic read aloud.

'Do they not have any photos of his face?' Blix asked.

'I'm sure we'll get one soon,' Kovic said. 'They're probably trawling through the whole city to find more footage of him.'

Blix pulled out onto the main road.

'Ruth-Kristine's flat can wait,' he said. 'I want to see the photo for myself. On a better screen.'

# 9

Emma was curled up under a blanket on the sofa. The TV was on – a programme about a lioness and her fight to protect her new-born cubs. There was a cup of ginger tea on the table in front of her. She hadn't touched it yet, even though it had been well over half an hour since she had put the bag in to brew.

The screen on her phone lit up from time to time, but she didn't check to see who was messaging her. She had sent Anita a brief text that morning to explain why she hadn't posted any articles last night. And to say she wasn't sure when she would be coming in to work. Anita had sent three texts in return. Emma hadn't read any of them.

She thought about what she would say to Jakob and Asta, Kasper's parents. She had only met them the one time, in Copenhagen last November. They had met for a far-too-expensive dinner at Kiin-Kiin, an Asian-fusion restaurant in Nørrebro – an evening that Jakob had insisted on paying for. Two lovely people who were about to be so utterly, irreversibly crushed, all because she had been so stupid. So unbelievably, bloody stupid.

She wondered what Jakob and Asta were doing at that moment. They must have been informed by the Danish Ministry of Foreign Affairs by now. Perhaps the whole family had come together, to comfort one another – a family Emma barely knew anything about. It was something she now regretted, not having asked about them more often. She knew that Kasper had a younger brother. Emma couldn't even remember his name.

Ritzau, the news agency he had worked for, had probably held a memorial ceremony too. Perhaps the editor-in-chief had delivered a thoughtful, touching speech about how great Kasper was, how much they were going to miss their warm, kind, caring colleague. They had likely honoured him with a minute's silence. There were certain to be hundreds of people at the funeral.

Emma closed her eyes again.

The funeral.

She had to be there, of course. Kasper would have to be taken back to Denmark first. His clothes, suitcase, toothbrush, toiletry bag. Emma would send them everything. She didn't want anything of his left behind; there should be nothing to remind her of what had happened, how incredibly foolish she had been.

She stared at the Advent candles on the coffee table. Four of them, all purple and almost completely burned down to the wick. A little glass Santa was sat next to them, as if he had chosen to plop himself down there to watch the flames. She had asked Kasper to help her take down the Christmas decorations the day before.

'You want to do that now?' he had asked.

'Christmas is over.'

'Is it?'

'And the tree is shedding everywhere. I wouldn't have bothered getting one if Martine hadn't insisted.'

He had asked politely if they could keep the decorations up for a few more days, and she had agreed to wait until today before she would take them down.

The lioness had picked up one of her cubs, barely two weeks old. Holding it by the scruff of its neck, she carried it up a small mound, into a den. She laid it down carefully and gently licked it clean. Emma closed her eyes. A tear trickled down her cheek. Wiped it away with her thumb.

There was a knock at the door. Emma couldn't be bothered getting up. It didn't matter who it was. She curled up tighter under the blanket and continued to watch the lions.

A few moments of silence followed, then another knock. 'Emma?'

It was Anita. She knocked a few more times, accompanied by an: 'Are you there?'

Emma sat up. Resting her elbows on her knees, she buried her face in her hands. She was dizzy. She didn't know how she was even going to stand up. Didn't know how she was going to manage to walk. Talk. Think.

She could hear keys rattling on the other side of the door. Emma turned and watched as Anita pulled the key out of the lock and stepped into the flat in one swift motion. The door slammed shut behind her.

'Shit,' Anita uttered, casting a look at the door as if to tell it off. 'Made me jump.'

She smiled meekly at Emma, held up the key between two fingers.

'I spoke to your sister,' she explained. 'Told her what had happened. She'd been called in to work, so I went to Ullevål and borrowed her extra key. Something told me you weren't going to let me in.'

Emma couldn't bring herself to answer.

'She told me to say hi,' Anita carried on, filling the silence as she took her boots off. 'And to ask that you call her.'

Anita glanced briefly at Kasper's suitcase before she sat down on the other end of the sofa. She left her phone on the table.

'How are you doing?' she asked, after a pause. Emma raised her head to look at her.

'Forget it,' Anita said with a gesture. 'Dumb question.'

She looked around, nodding to herself, as if she recognised the flat. She turned to watch the family of lions drinking from a watering hole. The lioness looked up, surveyed her surroundings.

'Where's Martine?' Emma asked.

Anita smiled reassuringly.

'With a neighbour. Karina, I think.'

'Karin.'

'That's right, Karin.'

They were silent again.

Anita peered over at Emma's now-cold teacup. 'Shall I make you a new one?'

'It's fine, it's not a big deal.'

'No, but it's important. You need to remember to eat and drink.'

Emma couldn't argue with that.

'You know, I knew this photographer from AFP once,' Anita

began. 'From France. Really sweet guy.' She shook her head and smiled, as if reminiscing about something he had said or done. 'We got to know each other pretty well, while I was on an assignment in Afghanistan. We had dinner together once or twice, shared a few bottles of wine.'

Emma watched Anita.

'The day after I left to come home, there was an incident in Kabul. Double suicide attack. Twenty-six people died.' She paused. 'Pierre was one of them.'

Anita picked up the remote and muted the TV.

She remained silent for a while before continuing.

'I found out the second I landed. My bosses asked if I could go back and cover the attack. But I...'

She looked away.

'At first I was in shock, naturally. And I was scared. If I had delayed my trip home by just two days, it could have been me.'

They sat in silence again.

'But I thought about it for all of three minutes, and I called back and asked them to book me onto the next flight. Do you know why?'

Emma shook her head.

'Because, first and foremost, I wanted to report on what had happened. Cover it like a regular journalist. I felt there was an extra significance in reporting it, since Pierre had been a close friend. But I also did it *because* I was scared. I couldn't let the fear or my grief for Pierre overwhelm me. I had to be there. For myself, so I could see it, where it happened, and process the event. The best way for me to do that was to work. Work like hell. Prove that it wasn't going to break me.'

A text popped up on Anita's phone. She checked to see who it was, but didn't open it.

'I've always been like that,' she continued. 'And I think you're the same, Emma. You're tough. This won't break you.'

Emma stared down at the floor.

'But I'm not going to push you to come back to work. You need to figure that out for yourself, when you're ready. And I won't lie: we need you. Now more than ever. So, from your cynical boss: come back as soon as you can. From Anita, who only wishes you well...' Anita lay a hand on her arm. 'Come back whenever you feel like it. We're always here for you.'

Emma felt the walls start to close in again.

'Right,' Anita said, squeezing her arm. 'I'll leave you be.'

She took Irene's spare key out of her jacket pocket and left it on the coffee table. 'Your sister wants that back tonight,' she added. 'She said something about a New Year's Day tradition?'

Anita stood there, looking down at Emma for a few seconds, before she headed back into the hallway and put her boots on.

'Call me,' she said, taking hold of the door handle. 'Keep me updated.'

With that, she stepped outside and gently closed the door behind her.

Emma lifted her shoulders and released them slowly. She rubbed her fingers over her forehead and watched the lioness unsuccessfully hunt for her prey, watched as she slunk back into the tall grass, ready to pounce again.

Emma got up and took the teacup with her. Standing in front of the sink, she scooped the bag out and poured the contents away. She put it aside, grasped the edge of the counter with both hands.

*You are tough.*

*You will not let this break you.*

Emma pushed herself away, put the kettle on and fetched a fresh tea bag from the cupboard. It only took a few seconds for the water to start boiling. As she waited, she picked up her phone and turned it back on. She had received a torrent of calls and texts. The last one was from her therapist. Gorm Fogner. A long message that filled the entire screen. He was sorry that the very thing she had feared had become a reality. He offered to bring forward the appointment she had booked for ten o'clock on Friday.

With everything that had happened last autumn, she had started going to therapy sessions once a fortnight. She felt that the conversations they shared had helped her to process everything she had gone through with the countdown murders, and that the sessions had finally given her the opportunity to talk through the experiences she had been carrying with her since her childhood. The fact that her father had killed her mother, and that he had then been shot and killed by Blix. She knew that she needed to talk to Fogner soon, but she couldn't bear the thought of verbalising what she felt just yet. She swiped the message away with her thumb and began to type out a text to her sister instead.

*Hi, Irene. I'm fine, surviving. Not everyone did.*

She stopped herself, unsure whether to delete that and start again. She erased the last part and replaced it with:

*There's something I wanted to ask you. I helped to rescue a woman from the harbour last night after the explosion. She was probably taken to one of your wards. I want to know who she is and whether she survived. Can you help me? Would be nice to know if I helped at least one person last night.*

# 10

An extensive collection of recordings from various cameras in the area had been gathered, stretching back over the forty-eight hours before the explosion, and for the hours that had followed. A dedicated unit had been set up to analyse the footage, to first find an image of the man who had placed the bomb, and to then track his subsequent movements. Blix, however, was most interested in seeing whether they could find Ruth-Kristine in any of the recordings.

'You're better on that than I am,' he told Kovic, nodding at her computer.

She turned it on and logged into the shared server, where all the files for the investigation were stored. She spent some time clicking around the folders before she found the one with the images from the cameras closest to the square.

'God, there's so many,' she exclaimed, opening the first file.

The image that popped up had been taken by a CCTV camera located just below the Akershus Fortress, higher up and quite a distance from the edge of the harbour where the bomb had gone off. Although it did provide a useful bird's eye view of the area, there were so many people walking between the harbour and the fortress that night, it was quite hard to even see the rubbish bin.

Kovic clicked through the shots until she reached the image that had captured the moment the man had placed the bomb in the bin. The footage they were looking at was from a slightly different angle and a greater distance than the image that had been sent through the internal police bulletin.

The man with the Kiwi shopping bag appeared from the right of the frame. It looked as if he had been waiting for a crowd of teenagers to pass by before he walked over to the bin and placed the bag gently on top. He stood with his back to the camera for a few seconds before hurrying away. There was nothing particularly memorable about his clothes or his movements. Nothing identifiable.

Kovic adjusted the settings and played it back at double speed. Blix squinted at the screen. Once or twice, someone would stop at the bin and throw something in before quickly moving on. The quality of the recording was only good enough to decipher the shape of people's bodies, and to just about determine the clothes they were wearing, but certainly not enough to distinguish their facial features.

'We need to keep an eye out for a woman in a dark-green jacket too,' Blix reminded her.

He leaned forwards, closer to the screen. Every now and then, fireworks illuminated the area surrounding the harbour, making it easier to see what was going on.

The time on the recording passed 23:45. Another five minutes went by as more and more people gathered in the square to watch the fireworks display. People were lingering in front of the camera, blocking the view of the rubbish bin.

A person in a dark-green jacket appeared at 23:55, strolling towards the harbour, the hood on their jacket pulled low over their face. Blix pointed to her without saying anything. Kovic paused the clip and let the recording play at the normal speed.

'That's a woman, right?' Blix asked.

'Think so,' she answered.

It looked as if the person were slowing down. She came to a stop about a metre away from one of the other bins dotted along the edge of the harbour, but not the one with the bomb in it.

'What the hell is she doing?' Kovic asked.

Blix wasn't sure either. The woman paced around the bin before moving closer and peering into it. Without throwing anything in, she moved on.

'Strange,' Blix commented quietly. They lost the woman in the crowd.

'Load the next video,' Blix said, noting the time. 'I want to see it from a different angle.'

On the next recording, the camera was aimed almost directly at the rubbish bin. Kovic fast forwarded to the 23:58 mark. Again, they watched the woman take a lap around the bin, at about a metre away, as if trying to inspect it from the outside.

'Can we zoom in a bit?' Blix requested. 'On the woman and then on the bin?'

'I can try,' Kovic said. 'But it'll probably be quite pixelated.'

They followed the woman as she made her way further down the edge of the harbour, over to the next bin. She walked around it, exactly as she had done with the previous one, before moving on to the last bin, where the bomb was.

Blix blinked hard, trying to focus. The camera was placed so far from the bin that her face was completely blurred. Not to mention the fact that it was, naturally, dark out at that time, and that most of her face was hidden beneath the hood. But Blix was certain that it was Ruth-Kristine.

She stopped at the next bin. Fireworks were filling the night sky now, shooting upwards one after the other. The time on the screen read 23:59:50. A man in a dark coat walked by. He had curly hair. Blix thought of Kasper, Emma's boyfriend. She still hadn't returned any of his calls. Blix would visit her as soon as he had the chance.

They watched the screen as the entire area was blanketed in a blaze of light. Even though Blix knew it would come, it still made him jump. A pillar of flames burst into the sky, closely followed by a thick, grey cloud of smoke.

People fled in panic. Bedlam. As the blanket of smoke dissipated, they could see the bodies of the dead and the injured who had been left behind. A man pushed himself up into a sitting position. They watched as Blix ran towards them from the right of the frame, Kovic just a few metres behind. Watching it back, it was almost as if Blix were reliving the chaos, as if he could hear the screams and the sounds of the fireworks still soaring above them. He could almost smell the smoke.

'That's enough,' he said with a nod to the screen.

Kovic stopped the recording just as Blix was getting ready to dive into the water.

Neither of them said anything. Blix sat and fiddled with a pen, thinking about Ruth-Kristine, about how she had gone from one bin to the next.

'It was like she was looking for something,' he said eventually.

Gard Fosse entered the room. The police superintendent clocked Blix and Kovic and walked over to them.

'I was expecting you both here earlier today,' he said. 'You missed the briefing.'

'We were following up on a lead from last night,' Blix replied.

Fosse didn't seem too interested in hearing the details.

'Did we miss anything?' Kovic asked.

'Well you've received the footage of course,' Fosse said, pointing at the computer. 'The bomb was probably home-made, most likely triggered by a remote control. Other than that, it wasn't particularly advanced. The images have been printed out and pinned up in the common room.'

Kovic opened another folder. All of the items that had been recovered from the site of the explosion had been photographed and given a number, with no explanation yet as to what the objects were. A distorted piece of metal could easily be part of the bomb, or part of the bin. Still, Kovic immediately started clicking through the full-screen images. Most of the items were obviously contents from the bin. She paused when she arrived at the image of a larger, blackened piece of metal.

'That's part of the bin,' Blix commented.

'Look at those marks though,' Kovic said.

Blix and Fosse bent down, leaning towards the screen. Kovic zoomed in on a particularly charred section of the bin that had a white streak across it.

'Is that chalk?' she asked.

Fosse unfolded a pair of glasses from his chest pocket.

'Some kind of symbol,' he concluded. 'Maybe an Arabic or Muslim character?' He straightened up. 'I'll call PST and see if anyone else has noticed it. Maybe they've found more.'

Blix ran his finger across the part of the screen where it was just about possible to discern some of the blurry white lines.

'I think it's a cross,' he said after Fosse left. 'Someone had labelled the bin. That's what Ruth-Kristine was looking for.'

'But why?'

Blix shrugged. 'Maybe there was something she was meant to pick up. Or it could've been a meeting place. Remember what her boyfriend, Haugseth, said? That he thought she had something planned with someone?'

Kovic carried on clicking through the images. A photo of a shoe that had obviously come off amid the havoc, a phone that looked as if it had been retrieved from the water. It took them three minutes to look through the entire collection.

'No house keys,' Blix noted. 'Do you remember seeing if she had any keys on her?'

Kovic shook her head. 'Just a bank card, a pack of cigarettes and a lighter.'

Blix stood up.

'Let's go have a look at her flat anyway.'

# 11

Ruth-Kristine Smeplass.

Emma stared at the name Irene had sent her, wondering where she had heard it before. She sluggishly made her way back into the living room, to the coffee table where she had left her laptop, opened it and logged in. It felt good to be doing something. Her fingers sailed over the keyboard. She typed the name in and hit enter.

'Shit,' she exhaled, scrolling through the first articles that had come up. It didn't take long to realise that the face of the woman who had been launched into the water the previous night had dominated the news once before. But it had been a while since anyone had written anything about her daughter, or the father of her child, who had become a murderer not long after.

Emma opened one of the articles, all about the scene Christer Storm Isaksen had caused during the trial. He had thrown repeated accusations at Ruth-Kristine, who he firmly believed to have been behind the kidnapping. Emma guessed that the police must have made that assumption too.

She read with increasing interest. Blix was mentioned several times. It looked as if he had had a central role in the investigation, making his actions last night even more meaningful.

Ruth-Kristine's sister, Britt, was cited in a number of articles as a sort of spokesperson for the family. Most of the articles included a photo of Patricia. The same photo, the one everyone recognised – taken over ten years ago, when she was only one year old – with two small teeth peeking out as she smiled at the camera. It had been taken just a few weeks before she was kidnapped.

Emma looked up. She hadn't eaten for about eighteen hours, and it felt as if something heavy had been boring into her chest. Every time she tried to take a deep breath, it was like something had a tight grip around her lungs. But it was slowly getting easier. Emma thought about what Anita had said, and told herself that she was tough and strong, and that no one, nothing, would break her.

But she had to do something.

She couldn't just sit quietly in the flat, with Kasper's stuff.

She spotted a brown banana on the kitchen counter, promptly picked it up and ate it. Opening one of the cupboards, she grabbed a handful of peanuts and stood there, thinking of Ruth-Kristine, about how Blix's rescue operation would make a good article, and that combining the two stories could make a particularly good feature. If she could bring herself to write it.

She stood there for a long time. She would need to find someone who could tell her about Ruth-Kristine, what her life had been like in the decade since Patricia's disappearance.

Sat behind her laptop screen again, she looked up at Ruth-Kristine's sister. It turned out that Britt Smeplass owned a detached house in Grefsen, on Aschehougs vei.

If she were to get through the next few days, she would have to keep herself busy, physically and mentally. Use her head and her body.

She poured a glass of water and drank it in one go. She could feel her body objecting, along with a growing desire to curl up under the duvet again and let the world carry on without her. But she had made her mind up. She found her cycling shoes and put them on.

As she stepped outside, the icy arctic wind blew right through her. Her legs felt numb as she climbed onto the bike and rode off. Her arms were weak. Just holding on to the bike's handlebars required more effort than usual. She was breathing faster and heavier than normal, as if her whole body were resisting her efforts to be active.

A little over fifteen minutes later, she found herself standing outside a house with a garden, a garage, and a solar panel on the roof. The leaves on the apple trees were brown and were drenched from the rain, drooping down over the dull lawn, most of which was buried under the remaining snow and ice.

There was a light on in the living room. Emma let herself in through the gate and locked her bike to the fence on the other side.

The path leading up to the front door was paved. The giant trees and shrubs planted between the houses shielded them from one another.

Emma rang the doorbell and took a step back.

She rang the bell again and waited.

She could hear a dog barking from inside the house, and then a voice immediately after, telling it to stop. After half a minute had gone by and no one had answered the door, she rang the bell again, knocking this time too. The growling from within was followed by another loud bark. Emma tried to look in through a window, but it was too high up.

The sound of approaching steps. Someone opened the door slowly, and only a fraction. A woman peeked out. Emma couldn't see her whole face.

'Britt Smeplass?' Emma enquired.

No answer.

'My name is Emma Ramm, I'm a reporter for news.no. I was wondering if I could have two minutes of your time?'

'I'm not interested,' Smeplass replied.

She was about to close the door when Emma added quickly: 'I just have a few questions about your sister.'

Britt Smeplass stopped. It was the first time Emma could properly see her face, see how drained the woman looked. The only photos Emma had seen of her were from a good ten years ago. Time had taken its toll.

'News.no is a newspaper,' Emma continued. 'Online. I assume that you're already aware that your sister is among the injured from the incident that occurred outside City Hall last night?'

The door opened a touch wider. Emma felt a few icy drops of rain land on her face.

'May I come in?' she asked, as gently as she could. But Britt Smeplass made no sign that she wanted to open the door any further.

Emma looked down to see the snout of a dog pushing its way through the gap between the frame of the door and Britt Smeplass's leg. It was black, with a large, white spot around one eye. She wondered if she should bend down to say hello – dogs were often good icebreakers. But the growling and the sight of its bared teeth convinced her to stay where she was.

'I was there,' she said instead. 'By the harbour. A close friend of mine died. I helped rescue your sister from the water.'

Emma had hoped that it would affect the woman in front of her in some way, but it didn't seem to have worked.

'What do you want?' Britt Smeplass asked.

There was venom in her voice. The dog forced its head further into the doorway, growling more ferociously.

'Shut up, Eddy!' the woman said sharply, yanking it back into the house.

'I'm planning on writing an article about your sister,' Emma tried. 'A lot of people know who she is, but they might not know anything about her life over the last few years. I...'

'Can't you write about your friend instead?'

Emma tried to explain that she was too close, too involved, that she needed a way to process what had happened. A project, in a way, but she could tell immediately that she had said the wrong thing.

'I don't want to talk to you about Ruth Kristine,' Britt Smeplass answered. 'I don't want to talk to you at all.'

With that, she slammed the door in Emma's face. From outside, she could hear that the dog had started to bark again.

# 12

The housing association estate where Ruth-Kristine Smeplass lived consisted of four low-rise blocks of flats and ten terraced houses. It was located on the edge of the dense forest in Åsbråten, out in the Søndre Nordstrand district, a little less than fifteen kilometres south of Oslo city centre.

Blix spoke to Emma over the phone while Kovic contacted the chairman of the association, Mustafa Jamal Hayd, who agreed to come down and show them to the right flat. It was on the ground floor of one of the low-rise buildings.

'Over there,' Mustafa said, pointing.

Neither he nor anyone else on the estate had a key to Ruth-Kristine's flat. Blix was prepared to call a locksmith, but wanted to check first to see if she had left any windows open, or if there was any other way to get inside.

'Wait!' Kovic said as they approached. She held out an arm to keep the chairman back and indicated to Blix. The door was ajar.

Blix and Kovic exchanged glances.

'Stand back,' Blix ordered Mustafa, who promptly did as he was told. Blix edged closer. Where the lock had once been, there was now a large, strangely shaped hole.

He nudged the door open and peered around the frame, into the small porch and the hallway beyond. There was a man just inside, bent over a chest of drawers and rifling through its contents. Seeming to realise that someone had entered the hall, he turned sharply and bolted deeper into the flat.

'Police!' Blix shouted as he chased after him. Running through the flat, he just about registered the fact that there were clothes and various other items strewn everywhere, and that several pieces of furniture had been overturned. He hurtled after the intruder, and found him trying to open one of the windows.

'Police!' Blix yelled again. 'Stop!'

The man wasn't listening. He heaved the window open and was just about to jump out when Blix grabbed hold of his leather jacket and dragged him back in and onto the kitchen floor. He rolled the man onto his stomach and held his arms behind his back.

'What are you doing here?' Blix asked, trying to catch his breath.

'Please,' the man underneath him gasped. 'I was just...' His breathing was fast and ragged.

'You were just what?'

'I was passing by,' he mumbled into the floor. 'The door was open, and no one was home, so I thought I could ... I could see if...'

Blix fastened the handcuffs and let go. He got up and took in the rest of the flat. There were dishes piled up on the kitchen counter. A couple of glasses with a few dregs of something or other stood next to them. Two of them looked as if they had been used as ashtrays.

Kovic came into the kitchen. 'I've called it in,' she said.

'Good. Who are you?' he asked, turning to the man lying below him.

No answer.

'Do you know the woman who lives here?' Kovic asked.

He shook his head. 'Not really.'

The chairman appeared behind them. 'Adel,' he exclaimed. 'What have you done?'

Kovic looked down at the man on the floor. 'Do you live here?' she asked. 'In this building?'

Mustafa answered for him: 'He lives in 8C.'

Kovic hoisted the man up onto a chair.

'Do you usually come this way then?' she asked. 'Down this corridor?' she added, pointing out into the hallway.

'Sometimes.'

'When was the last time? When did you last walk by here?'

'Earlier today,' he answered.

'When?'

'I don't remember. Ten o'clock, maybe.'

'Was the door open then?'

He shook his head.

Kovic led Blix out into the corridor, away from the others.

'The lock looks like it's been melted away by something acidic, or a similar kind of substance,' she said. 'Something that can dissolve metal, anyway.'

'Bloody hell,' Blix said. 'Who has access to something like that?'

Kovic didn't have an answer.

'The whole flat looks like it's been turned inside out,' she said instead. 'And if the door has been like that for a while, then Adel might not be the only person who's been in here, looking for something to steal.'

'But to break into a flat in that way,' Blix said. 'That's advanced.'

'Silent too,' Kovic added.

'And whoever's responsible must have done it after New Year's Eve. After Ruth-Kristine was injured in the explosion.'

A silence settled between them.

'Someone was looking for something,' Blix concluded.

Kovic nodded, making a sweeping gesture across the mess inside the flat.

'The question is what,' she said. 'And why.'

'And if whoever it was found what they were looking for.'

# 13

The trip to Grefsen had been unsuccessful. Everything had gone wrong – everything. She hadn't been ready or prepared. At least the ride over to Britt Smeplass's house had done her some good. She had moved her body, got some fresh air, had managed to push Kasper out of her mind briefly too, if only for a few moments. But he had returned. She also felt guilty about having not written a single article about the explosion. News.no was only a small news agency, so Anita was dependent on everyone contributing. Emma thought about how Kasper would have reacted if the situation had been the other way round.

The photos she had taken last night were no longer relevant. The only thing she could use that no other journalists had, and that she felt she could bring herself to write about half a day later, was Blix, and how he had rescued Ruth-Kristine from the harbour.

As soon as she got back home, she sent him a text:

*I'm planning on writing an article about you and the woman you rescued from the harbour. Would be nice to get a quote or two, and an update on how Patricia's mother is doing, if you have one.*

It only took a few seconds before Blix had called her back.

'How are you?' he asked immediately.

Emma could tell he was worried; she could hear the concern in his voice. That, and the fact that he had called her at least ten times over the last twelve hours, without her answering any of them.

'Alright,' she said with a sigh. 'I'm fine. I'm trying to get some work done. Think of something else. Right now though, I'm thinking of Ruth-Kristine Smeplass.'

'Are you sure that's a good idea?'

'I'm not sure about anything at the moment,' Emma replied. 'I'm just taking everything an hour, or actually a minute, at a time.'

There was a brief silence on the other end of the phone.

'How ... did you find out about Ruth-Kristine?'

Emma didn't want to mention Irene, let slip about her assistance from the hospital. She had breached her duty of confidentiality by helping her, and that could land her in hot water.

'Is it important?' she asked instead.

He thought about it.

'No, maybe not. But we're not releasing the names of the casualties or the injured for the time being.'

'How's she doing?' Emma asked again, seeing where the conversation was heading and redirecting it.

'Not good. The odds of her surviving are pretty low.'

Emma took a seat on the bar stool closest to the kitchen counter and grabbed a pen and notepad.

'Could the explosion have anything to do with Patricia's disappearance?' she asked.

'I can't comment on that,' Blix replied.

Emma moved the phone over to her other ear. 'You would have said no if there wasn't,' she said.

Blix sighed.

'I won't quote you,' she assured him.

'No, but this is a huge investigation. And I'm not leading it either, so it's not my responsibility to comment on the details.'

Emma could hear that he wasn't happy with the direction the conversation had taken. She hesitated for a moment, before changing the subject again:

'You know what my first thought was? Last night?'

'No?'

'That someone had been inspired by the countdown murders and everything that happened last autumn, and they'd orchestrated everything so the bomb would go off at midnight. That's why I was there in the first place,' she explained. 'I was convinced that something was going to happen, something similar. I mean ... I hadn't anticipated what actually happened would happen, but...' Emma wasn't sure how to finish the sentence.

'I'm quite certain that this isn't a copycat killer,' Blix said.

'Terrorism seems most likely. We can see if someone else crops up eventually.'

'Someone other than Patricia, you mean?'

Blix didn't answer. Emma jotted down a few notes: *1. Terrorism. 2. Patricia.*

'What has she been up to?'

'Hm?'

'Ruth-Kristine, what's her life like now, ten years after Patricia was kidnapped?'

Emma knew that there had to be a story there.

'Has she had any more children, for example?'

'I think she's led quite a quiet life,' Blix answered. 'But I don't know enough to answer that properly.'

Emma felt a pang of hunger.

'So, how does it feel to be a hero?' she carried on.

'I was just doing my job,' he answered. 'And anyway, you're only a hero if it all goes well, and we don't know that yet. Do you *have* to write about it?'

'We need a positive story, with everything going on right now,' Emma replied.

'I'm not sure it will be all that positive. Ruth-Kristine is only just hanging in there.'

'Then I'll write that,' Emma commented.

'What?'

'I'll write that you were just doing your job and that you're worried about her. I don't really need that much anyway. I got some good photos.'

Blix sighed and eventually agreed.

'But don't write about Patricia. Not yet. You'll be the first to know if it turns out that there is a clear connection between the bomb and Patricia's disappearance.'

'I can live with that.'

'Good. Take care of yourself. Remember that you're allowed to feel what you're feeling – you're allowed to be sad.'

'I *am* sad,' she replied. 'And then I get angry. At the person, or the people, responsible. If the police can't figure out who's behind it, *I'll* figure it out.'

Emma wasn't sure where that thought had come from. She was surprised at its sudden appearance, the sudden anger, how determined she sounded. How motivated she was, out of nowhere.

'Whatever you do,' Blix said. 'Be careful.'

'Always am,' Emma said. 'You know me, right?'

'That's why I said it.'

# 14

The phone rang the moment Blix sat down at his workstation. He didn't recognise the number, but answered anyway.

'Incoming call from Oslo Prison,' a gravelly voice informed him on the other end of the phone. 'We have an inmate here requesting to speak to you. Christer Storm Isaksen. Would you like to accept the call?'

'Isaksen?' Blix repeated in surprise.

Christer couldn't possibly have known that Ruth-Kristine had been injured in the explosion. The names of the casualties hadn't even been released yet, let alone the injured. It must be a coincidence, because he was next on the list of people Blix wanted to talk to.

'He says it's urgent,' the caller added.

'Put him through,' Blix replied.

An automated voice alerted him to the fact that the conversation was being recorded, before the call was redirected.

'It's her!'

He could hear Christer Storm Isaksen practically hyperventilating on the other end of the phone.

'Who?' Blix asked. 'What are you talking about?'

'Patricia!' Isaksen cried. 'I'm looking at her right now! She's grown up. She looks about eight, I think, in the photo.'

'What photo?'

'It came in the post,' Isaksen replied, agitated. 'I just opened it.'

'And you're sure it's Patricia?'

'Yes. No doubt in my mind! Who else would it be?'

Blix bit his lower lip. 'Who sent it?'

'Doesn't say. Someone left the envelope in the prison's post box. There's nothing else, just the photo.'

'How do you know it's Patricia?' Blix repeated.

'She's my daughter!' Isaksen shouted. 'I recognise her. I knew it. I knew she was alive, all this time. I told you...'

Blix was struggling to gather his thoughts.

'I'm coming over,' he said eventually.

'You can see for yourself,' Isaksen continued. 'She's alive. And she's somewhere out there. You have to find her.'

Blix ended the conversation and contacted one of the prison officers to inform them that he was on his way. He hung up and sat for a while, trying to come to terms with the growing feeling that everything was somehow connected, and trying to grasp the fact that the investigation into Patricia's disappearance was starting to open up again.

He was about to grab his jacket from the back of his chair when Kovic came in. He filled her in about Isaksen's phone call.

'How can he possibly recognise her?' she asked. 'Patricia was only a year old when she was kidnapped.'

'I don't know,' Blix said. 'Probably wishful thinking, but with everything that happened last night, and now this, it does seem interesting. Are you coming? You said we should talk to him as soon as possible.'

Kovic nodded eagerly.

Although there was a tunnel stretching the short distance between Police Headquarters and Oslo Prison, Blix and Kovic decided to use the main entrance on Åkebergveien instead.

The high walls of the prison towered over the pavement. A glass-domed security camera was positioned next to the visitor entrance. There was a grey, steel post box fixed to the wall below it. Blix rang the bell and looked directly into the camera as he introduced himself.

It was getting dark and starting to drizzle. They stood outside and waited for a prison officer to come and let them in.

Kovic buried her hands deep into her coat pockets and peered up at the prison wall.

'Tell me more about him,' she said.

Blix took a deep breath and told her about the evening Patricia's father had become a murderer. The cold rain. How they had found Isaksen, sat on a rock, staring blankly ahead of him. His bloody hands. The blue lights flashing brightly through the trees. Knut Ivar Skage sprawled on the ground below him. The dog-walkers and joggers who had started to gather around the crime scene.

'Poor guy,' Kovic commented. 'Can you imagine? You wait that long for an answer, for anything, and when you think you're close, that happens. You're suddenly a killer. Twelve years ahead of you, under lock and key.' She shook her head. 'It's almost a miracle he hasn't killed himself in there.'

Blix had visited Christer in prison regularly during the first few years after his sentencing, mainly to update him on the investigation, but to check up on him too. He arrived each time with a guilty conscience, having failed to find Patricia. The visits had become shorter and shorter. There hadn't been much to tell him. The investigation had come to a standstill. After each visit, Blix would leave the prison with a feeling that he was gradually contributing to another man's destruction.

'What was his life like, before his daughter was kidnapped?' Kovic asked.

'He worked for Nordea Finance, something to do with shares,' Blix replied. 'Made good money.'

The door buzzed as it was unlocked. A guard appeared. He let them in and took them into one of the visiting rooms.

Christer Storm Isaksen was in there already, standing in the middle of the room, waiting for them. He was unshaven. The white hairs that peppered his dark beard were sticking out at odd angles. The hair on his head was shaved short but looked as if it had been hacked at. The receding hairline and a large, shiny circle on the crown of his head made him look much older than he was. As did the deep, dark-blue bags under his eyes.

'See!' he exclaimed.

He handed the photo to Blix and glanced at Kovic.

Blix took it from him and held it gingerly between two fingers. It was a photo of a young girl. She had braces and chestnut hair, which had been tied up into a ponytail. Blix spent time studying it, looking back and forth between Isaksen and the photo, comparing the two faces.

He had kept a photo of Patricia tucked inside a plastic wallet beneath the mouse pad on his desk for years. He had looked at it almost every day, but couldn't find any similarities between the photos. Other than the blue eyes.

'I don't know...' he started. 'We need to get the experts to look at it. Get them to do a forensic image analysis.'

'You're not her father,' Isaksen interjected. 'I'm telling you, it's Patricia.'

'Who could have sent it?' Kovic asked.

Isaksen threw his arms up, as if to say he had no idea.

'Someone who knows something,' he surmised.

Blix nodded. 'We'll have to take this with us,' he said. 'Examine it for fingerprints and the like.'

An agonised expression appeared on Isaksen's face, as if it hadn't occurred to him that he would have to give up the photo.

'I'll make you a copy,' Blix added. 'Tonight. We just got a new photocopier in the office. You can barely tell the difference.'

Isaksen nodded. Kovic found a plastic wallet.

'Do you still have the envelope?' she asked.

He took it out of his back pocket and handed it to her.

'Shall we take a seat?' Blix suggested. 'There's something else we need to talk to you about.'

They each pulled up a chair in the small seating area.

'It's about Ruth-Kristine,' Blix said.

Christer's eyes flashed momentarily. 'What's she done?'

'She's in hospital.'

Christer didn't seem to fully grasp the fact that something had happened to Patricia's mother.

'She's in pretty bad shape,' Kovic added. 'She may not make it.'

'We're looking into the possibility that someone was trying to take her life,' Blix said.

Isaksen raised his eyebrows. 'What do you mean?' he asked. 'What happened?'

'She was seriously wounded in the explosion by the harbour yesterday,' Blix explained.

'But that was a terrorist attack,' Isaksen objected.

'It may well be,' Blix said. 'But we're trying to look at it from as many angles as possible.'

'Okay, but what was Ruth-Kristine doing there?' Isaksen pondered. 'Outside City Hall?'

'That's what we're trying to find out,' Blix said.

'Could it have something to do with the photo?' Isaksen suggested.

'As of right now, all we know is that she was there when the bomb went off.'

'Alone?'

'Looks like it,' Blix nodded.

Isaksen shook his head. 'That can't be,' he said.

'What can't be?'

'Ruth-Kristine has never been anything but drunk out of her mind on New Year's Eve. Watching the fireworks at City Hall is the last thing she'd do. That may have changed, of course. But I doubt it.'

Blix and Kovic exchanged a look before Blix asked:

'So what do you think she was doing there?'

'All I'm saying, is that if she happened to be there right at that particular moment, there was probably a good reason.'

'Have you had any contact with her while you've been here?' Kovic asked.

'Absolutely not.'

'Spoken to anyone about her?'

'Not since the trial.'

Blix looked at Kovic. 'We should get going,' he said.

They stood up, and Blix rang the button on the intercom to let the officers know they were done.

Christer Storm Isaksen was escorted back to his cell. Blix and Kovic were accompanied to the security room to talk to the prison officer who had emptied the post box.

'I only found it about half an hour before he called you,' he explained.

Blix hadn't been paying attention when he had introduced himself, so he glanced down at the officer's ID. The name *Frankmann* was stitched into his shirt pocket.

'When was the post last collected?' Kovic asked.

Frankmann shrugged. 'Friday, maybe?'

'So four days ago?'

'We don't really have a set procedure for dealing with the post that gets delivered directly to the door, at least not over the weekend. And then it was New Year's Eve yesterday, of course. But there was nothing else in there. Just the letter, so it probably hadn't been there that long.'

Blix looked at the two screens behind him, both displaying live footage from the CCTV cameras. Each monitor was divided into eight smaller squares.

'Do any of the cameras face the post box?' he asked.

The officer clicked on the screen labelled *ENTR: Family – Visits*. The image was grey and grainy in the gloominess of the evening. A drop of rain was distorting the lens. It was the same camera that Blix had stared into when he and Kovic had arrived earlier. It was angled so that the visitors waiting at the entrance were captured, and very little of the people passing by on the pavement behind them was seen.

'The post box itself isn't actually in the frame,' Frankmann said. 'But whoever puts something in there should be caught by the camera.'

'Was the camera running?'

Frankmann nodded. 'I'm not an expert,' he admitted. 'But I can have a look.'

He navigated through the recording and found the footage of himself emptying the post box. From there, he began rewinding. A few pedestrians hurried by in both directions. Those who carried on walking to the end of the road were only seen from the waist down.

'Has Isaksen had many visitors lately?' Kovic asked without taking her eyes off the screen.

'No,' Frankmann answered. 'I don't think he has anyone on his visitor list. No one's been here since his mother died.'

A cyclist appeared, peddling backwards into the frame. He stopped, bent down and checked the hub on the rear wheel, then rode on.

'Has he made any contacts in here?' Kovic carried on.

'Isaksen pretty much just keeps to himself,' Frankmann replied. 'Why?'

Blix understood that she hadn't given up on the theory that Christer Storm Isaksen may have had someone try and murder Ruth-Kristine for him.

'Has anyone been released recently who he was particularly friendly with?' she asked.

'I've been his contact officer for six years,' Frankmann replied. 'I think I might be the only one he talks to in here.'

'Has he ever said anything about Patricia's mother?'

Frankmann didn't answer.

'There!' he exclaimed instead, pointing at the screen.

Blix couldn't see anything other than a shadow. Frankmann pressed a few keys and played the recording at normal speed.

The time indicated the photo had been delivered just thirty-seven minutes before Frankmann had found it. Someone's back appeared at the very edge of the frame. Then a shoulder and an arm. The person stood almost exactly where they had seen Frankmann standing when he had opened the post box.

The person was wearing a dark waterproof coat. They could see just enough of the back of their head to tell that they had a hood pulled up. Then they disappeared.

'Well, that must be the person we're looking for; they were right next to the post box,' Kovic commented.

Frankmann clicked back through the recording and stopped on the image that had most of the person's body in the shot. It was impossible to say anything about their height or gender.

Blix took a photo of the screen. 'We'll need all of the recordings from that evening,' he said.

'That'll have to be done by the day shift tomorrow,' Frankmann said.

Kovic got up. 'We'll also need a list of all the inmates Isaksen has served with over the last six months,' she said. 'And a log of his phone calls.'

'We'll need a warrant in that case,' Frankmann replied.

'It's on its way,' Kovic assured him.

They thanked him for his help, and he escorted them out. It had stopped raining and the temperature had plummeted. The pavement was covered with a thin sheet of ice. Blix walked cautiously and cast a glance behind him, up at the grey walls of the prison. He tugged his jacket collar up to his chin and bowed his head against the bitter wind.

# 15

It had been a New Year's Day tradition for as long as Emma could remember, eating the rest of the *pinnekjøtt* from the night before with her sister. They would always take turns hosting the festivities, and this time it had fallen on Irene.

The plan had originally been for Emma and Kasper to arrive together at six o'clock that evening, but with all that had happened, Emma had no intention of going. Irene had called once she had finished her shift at work, and while Emma had been in the middle of telling her that she wouldn't be joining them, Martine had snatched the phone out of Irene's hand and insisted that Emma *had* to come. Regardless of how she felt, it had been impossible to say no.

It was her niece who opened the door when she arrived a short while later. As always, she threw her arms around Emma's neck.

'Hi, Sweetie,' Emma said, hugging her tight. 'It's so good to see you,' she murmured into her hair.

It was one of the best hugs Emma had ever had.

She stepped into the hallway and let go of Martine. Irene emerged from the kitchen and made her way down the hallway to them. The sisters stood there for a moment, staring at each other. It was all Emma could do to keep from crying. Irene took a step closer and pulled her in tight. They stayed like that for quite a while. Emma held back the tears.

'Martine doesn't know,' Irene whispered. 'I thought you might want to tell her yourself, or ... not say anything at all.'

Emma sniffed as they parted.

'Are you hungry?' Irene asked.

The smell of traditional *pinnekjøtt* always made Emma hungry.

'There's loads of leftovers,' her sister assured her.

Martine came back into the hallway with the TV remote in her hand. 'Can we watch a film?' she asked.

'Maybe after we've eaten,' Irene said, looking at Emma.

'As long as it's not a sad film,' she said. 'I can't deal with that today.'

'*Ice Age*?' Martine suggested. 'I know that makes you laugh.'

'True,' Emma replied with a smile. 'All of that series make me laugh, even though the last two were pretty rubbish.'

Martine cheered, and disappeared back into the living room. Emma followed her sister into the kitchen. Irene lifted the lid from the pan of *pinnekjøtt* and had a quick peek inside.

'Nearly there,' she announced and sat down at the table, opposite Emma. They stared at each other for a few seconds before Irene finally spoke:

'He was a great guy.'

Emma nodded. 'He was.'

She had visited Kasper twice in Copenhagen, but this was his third trip to Oslo. She had been sure that he had felt something for her, but she had been a lot less sure about how she felt about him. In the days leading up to New Year's Eve, she had really just wanted to be alone. It wasn't that she wanted to be single, she just preferred her own company, preferred to make her own plans, to see to her own needs. Whether that was because the relationship had started to progress a little, that it had become more serious, or because she had simply started to tire of him, she wasn't sure. They hadn't talked about the future.

'Have you spoken to his parents?' Irene asked.

'Briefly,' Emma nodded. 'Earlier today.'

'How did that go...?'

'It was ... awful. Completely awful. They were fine, of course. With me, I mean. Said that it was all just an unbelievable coincidence. A terrible accident.'

'They're not wrong,' Irene said. 'You can't blame yourself for his death, Emma. Nothing good will come of that.'

That's what Kasper's father had said, too.

'They invited me to Denmark,' Emma said, shaking her head. 'If I wanted to go and ... just stay with them for a while.'

'How do you feel about that?'

'That there's not a chance in hell of me going.'

'Why not?'

'Because...'

She thought about it.

'I'm not good at being in other people's homes. Overnight. I get uncomfortable, especially when I don't know them very well.'

'Because of the wig?'

'Because of everything,' Emma replied. 'I don't know them, and I don't really have a connection to them anymore.'

'I just think that it might be good for you, to go. Have a break from work for a while and get out of here. Process everything that's happened, from a distance.'

'But I wouldn't exactly be distancing myself if I'm staying with his family,' Emma argued.

'I meant geographically,' Irene said. 'Distance yourself from your life *here*.'

Emma shook her head again. 'I have too much to do.'

Irene was about to say something, but chose to return to the stove instead. She stirred the pot of mashed swede and took the potatoes off the heat, tipped them into a colander. The steam rising out of the sink engulfed her face.

She walked over to the fridge and pulled out a bottle of aquavit and two cans of beer. Carlsberg. They had been drinking another brand the night before.

'I thought we should have some Danish beer tonight,' she said.

Emma felt the lump in her throat return.

'How did you get hold of that?' she asked.

'My neighbour,' she said. 'He's always in Denmark. And I think he might fancy me a bit.'

Irene winked. Emma stared at her sister.

'That's not hard to believe,' she said tenderly.

'Ha,' Irene exclaimed, rolling her eyes and calling her daughter through for dinner.

'God, I'm bloody starving,' Irene said.

Martine came into the kitchen. As if she were an adult, she placed her hands precociously on her tiny hips, and said:

'You shouldn't swear, Mummy.'

# 16

The windshield was frozen solid. Blix started the car, turned the heating on full blast and let the engine run, while he got out and started to scrape the layer of ice away.

He had just finished the passenger side, when a noise coming from his jacket pocket made him pause. Kovic had set up a new alert on his phone for when the operations centre sent out internal bulletins. He dropped the ice scraper and fumbled with his jacket pocket until he managed to pull his phone out.

*Explosion in a rubbish bin in Frogner Park. Stand-by plan Golf Bravo initiated. All operational units subject to U-05.*

Blix hastily scraped away the patch of ice obscuring the view from the driver's seat before he threw himself behind the wheel and reversed out onto the street. He had no need to be there – he didn't have an official operational role in the emergency response to such events, but he headed to Frogner Park regardless. A second explosion would directly interfere with the ongoing investigation he was pursuing. Kovic was now on board with the theory that Ruth-Kristine was not just a random victim. Another bomb would suggest otherwise. Either way, there would be a need for investigative assistance at the scene.

Blue lights appeared in his rear-view mirror. He pulled over, let the ambulance pass and then followed it.

The mobilisation of the emergency services was already under way.

Fire engines, police cars and ambulances had gathered at the main gate. Blix pulled up behind them and rushed into the park. Smoke was still billowing into the heavy, grey sky.

He manoeuvred through the crowd that had gathered by the gate, flashed his police ID when he arrived at the barriers and ducked under the tape. He made his way quickly to the site of the explosion, and stood close to the inner cordon. The rubbish bin looked as if it had been blown into four pieces, and the explosion had blasted a crater into the ground. Chunks of grass, soil and gravel from the foot-path had been scattered across the snow and the surrounding area, but no one appeared to have been injured. The paramedics were standing around, waiting. The police officers who were already at the scene didn't seem to be particularly busy either.

Blix walked over to the incident commander, who was stood next to one of the specialists from the fire department, and requested a progress report.

'One minor injury,' the commander explained. 'A broken leg which, strictly speaking, was not directly caused by the explosion.' He slid his right boot back and forth across the icy path to demonstrate how slippery it was. 'We're currently waiting for the bomb-disposal technicians to secure and clear the area,' he continued. 'The bomb was significantly less powerful than the one from New Year's Eve, but its placement may indicate a connection.'

'Do we have any witnesses?' Blix asked, looking around.

'None as far as I know,' the incident commander answered.

Police had started to usher people away from the perimeter they'd set up, back towards the gates. An older police officer with an automatic pistol strapped to his chest waved Blix over. He was standing with a young woman around Iselin's age.

'I think I saw him,' she said as Blix arrived.

'Saw who?' he asked.

'The man with the shopping bag, the *Kiwi* bag.' Her breath sent plumes into the chilly morning air.

Blix stared at her for a moment before guiding her to the side of the path. She introduced herself as Gøril Kittelsen. She explained that she had seen a man while she was out jogging about an hour earlier. She lived nearby, and had run back when she heard the explosion.

'A lot of people carry those shopping bags though,' she said. 'So that wasn't weird. But last night you released that statement saying you were looking for a man who had put a bomb in a shopping bag, so I thought maybe it could be the same guy.'

She seemed pleased with her own reasoning. It could have been a random passer-by, Blix thought. There were probably hundreds of *Kiwi* shops in Oslo.

He looked at her sceptically. 'What did he look like?'

'A little shorter than you, I think. Wearing a dark beanie. Black gloves. Black coat as well. Or it could have been a jacket, I'm not entirely sure.'

'How old was he?'

She thought about it for a moment.

'Forty, maybe fifty? Hard to say.'

'Did you see his face?'

'No, he had a scarf pulled up over his mouth and nose.'

He could have done that because he was cold, Blix thought, yet the description did seem to match that of the man with the shopping bag they had seen by the harbour. But she would have seen pictures of him too. Her description could be influenced by them.

'Did you notice anything else?' Blix continued. 'Any other details you remember?'

She thought about it.

'He was wearing brown walking boots,' she said. 'The shoelaces on one of his boots was undone. And the laces were blue.'

'Blue?'

The girl nodded. 'They were hard to miss.'

Blue shoelaces, Blix thought, taking out his notebook. That was something.

# 17

It had just gone half past nine when Emma walked into the offices of news.no. Anita Grønvold was stood beside the coffee machine, talking on the phone. The TV on the wall behind her showed a live broadcast from Frogner Park.

Henrik Wollan's eyes widened when he noticed Emma. She walked past, taking off her bike helmet.

'Hey,' she said, removing her jacket. 'How's it going?'

Wollan span around in his chair to face her. 'What are you doing here?'

'Working,' she said, pressing her hands to her cheeks to get some warmth back into them. It had been a cold bike ride. 'Have you been to Frogner Park?'

Wollan stared at her for a few seconds before answering:

'I just got back. There wasn't much to do there, seeing as everything was blocked off. But I took a few photos of people who certainly won't be throwing their rubbish into any old public bin anytime soon.'

He rolled his eyes, as if he thought they'd been overreacting.

'But I'm sure that's exactly what he wants,' he added. 'Make people scared to go about their daily lives.'

'That's terrorism for you,' Emma commented, chucking her jacket onto the back of her chair.

Out of the corner of her eye, she could see that Anita was still busy on the phone, but that she was gesturing for her to go over. Emma grabbed a cup that had *DON'T MESS WITH EMMA* printed across it – a gift from Wollan after the countdown murders last autumn – and walked over.

'As soon as possible,' she heard her boss say to whoever was on the other end of the phone. 'And by that I mean half an hour ago,' she finished, pressing her finger firmly on the screen to hang up.

'Don't ask,' she said, exhaling heavily.

A whiff of stale coffee and smoke hit Emma's nostrils. Anita was staring at her inquisitively. She turned away, busying herself with the coffee machine. She found a purple capsule, put it into the machine and pressed the button for the largest cup.

'I wasn't sure if you were going to show up today,' Anita said.

'Me neither. But I had to do something. Keep myself busy.'

An image of the man who the police were searching for flashed onto the screen behind Anita. It was the same blurry image every media outlet had been showing over the last twenty-four hours.

'The police will be keeping their cards close to their chests,' Anita shouted over the noise from the machine. 'And there's not much we can do other than run after them with a microphone. Have you got anything else? Preferably something we can set today's agenda with?'

Emma's coffee was ready. She waited for the machine to release the last few drops before lifting the cup to her mouth and blowing lightly on the surface.

'Maybe,' she said.

Anita looked at her, waiting for her to elaborate. Emma took a careful sip.

'The first bomb,' she said, 'wasn't particularly effective, not as a terrorist attack anyway. It was effective *enough*, but if the goal was to cause the greatest possible damage, then they pretty much chose the worst rubbish bin in the entire area. Most of the explosion blew out over the fjord. So, if the first attack was carried out by terrorists, then I would say they were pretty amateur.'

Emma raised her gaze towards the TV screen. A grave-looking reporter was interviewing Raymond Rafto of PST, who was emphasising that they were still in the early stages of the investigation.

'The bomb this morning was even less powerful,' she continued. 'And it was detonated at a time when there weren't many people in the park. And yet everyone is still talking about terrorism and ISIS, when no one's even taken responsibility for either the first *or* the second attack.'

Anita frowned.

'It may very well just be a teenager who's been on the internet and wanted to test out their own DIY bombs. I don't think it would be particularly difficult.'

Anita looked at her doubtfully. 'Can you find an expert or someone who can prove that?'

'That's not what I'm getting at,' Emma said.

'So what's your point?'

'That this might be about something else.'

Emma hesitated a moment, before asking: 'Do you know who Ruth-Kristine Smeplass is?'

Anita snorted. 'Every journalist knows who Ruth-Kristine is. It...'

She stopped herself and suddenly looked up at the TV. The names of the casualties were being released, with their ages and places of residence.

Kasper's name was third on the list. Black letters on a grey background.

'She was the woman Blix rescued from the harbour,' Emma explained, blinking rapidly and looking away.

Anita seemed to disappear into her thoughts for a while.

'Wow,' she breathed finally. 'Why didn't you mention that in the article you wrote about Blix yesterday?'

'Because they weren't sure if she was even going to survive yesterday,' Emma explained. 'And because they haven't officially identified her yet.'

Anita raised her cup to her mouth and took a small sip.

'Get someone to confirm that it's her, and that her relatives have been informed, then we've got ourselves a story.'

# 18

The box containing the Patricia case had been relocated to one of the filing cabinets in the office. Blix searched through it and found the photo of Patricia. She was smiling at the camera, only a year and four months old. He held it next to a copy of the photo Christer Storm Isaksen had received in prison. The original had been sent off for a fingerprint examination, and another copy had been forwarded to a specialist investigator who tracked images of abuse posted online. They could work out *when* the photo had been taken and could interpret the surroundings and background of the picture to work out *where* it had been taken.

He looked from one face to the other. There were a few similarities. The corner of the mouth, around the eyes, maybe, but nothing conclusive. Yet he still couldn't rule out that both pictures were of Patricia.

On the TV at the other end of the room, the faces of the four casualties were just in the process of being released. Blix moved closer. The sound was muted, but the name, age and place of residence had been provided below the photos. He stared at the third image. Kasper Bjerringbo.

The only other face he recognised was that of a blond man with ice-blue eyes and a slightly crooked nose. The body they had found on the mooring post. His details appeared on the screen: Adam Hanssen from Fredrikstad.

Blix looked around the room. The spacious office had been set up for that day's investigative tasks. Each investigator had their own workstation, but none of those sitting there now seemed to be watching the TV.

The broadcast switched to a report from Frogner Park. Blix picked up the remote, turned it off and walked back to his desk. Kovic looked up from her computer screen. Her eyes were bloodshot, and her face was pale.

'He came from the northern district,' she said before Blix had the chance to ask her if she had slept at all.

'Who?' he said instead.

'The bomber.'

Blix sat down. Kovic angled the screen towards him, showing him a map of central Oslo – it had been marked with three red spots and two blue ones. She covered her mouth with her hand as she stifled a yawn.

'The analysts at PST found him on CCTV camera footage from some of the side streets,' she explained, clicking on the red marker positioned closest to Oslo City Hall. 'He took the same route, there and back.'

She opened an image from a recording that had come, by the look of it, from a camera inside the lobby of a business with premises on one of the streets. The analysts had labelled the marker: *Haakon VII's gate 2 at 00:01:17*. Through the glass doors, they could see a man wearing a dark beanie, black gloves and a black duffle coat, head bowed, walking away from City Hall.

'That could be him,' Blix said. 'Which would mean he left as soon as he detonated the bomb.'

Kovic clicked on the next marker, this time a blue one. The picture was of the same man, in the same place. This time he was on his way towards the harbour, a green shopping bag from *Kiwi* in his hand. The time on the image read 23:27:18.

'There we go,' Blix said. 'It *is* him.'

Kovic explained that the blue markers plotted the man on his way to the scene, the red markers showed the route he took after the explosion.

'None of the images are particularly good,' she added.

The next photo came from the CCTV camera at a bank on Munkedamsveien, about three hundred metres further north. After that, all they had were the images from the GP practice at the Stortingsgata crossroads. The blue lights of a police car could be seen in the background.

'Could he have taken the tram?' Blix suggested, pointing to the tram stop over the road, by the National Theatre. 'If it was even running on New Year's Eve that is, and after midnight.'

Kovic shook her head doubtfully. 'He'd have been spotted in that case,' she said. 'They have a good CCTV system.'

A notification popped up in the right-hand corner of the screen, informing her that she had just received the records from Ruth-Kristine Smeplass's phone.

'If the same man is responsible for both bombs, then there would be little evidence to suggest that Ruth-Kristine has anything to do with this,' Kovic noted. 'Which would mean that we're probably on the wrong track.'

Blix couldn't argue with that.

'I still want to know what she was doing outside City Hall that night,' he said. 'Why she happened to be right there, at that exact moment.'

Kovic opened the attachment. The list detailing Ruth-Kristine's phone usage was difficult to decipher, as it contained every single type of data that had passed through the telecommunication networks. She spent some time filtering through it so that they were left with just dates and times, who Ruth-Kristine had called or messaged, who had contacted her, and where she had been when her phone was active. The last time the phone had been used was in the Holmlia area. An outgoing call to Oslo Taxi at 22:58.

'She took a taxi into town,' Kovic said. 'We have to talk to the driver.'

Blix nodded.

'Her boyfriend mentioned she was arguing with someone on the phone two days before New Year's Eve,' he remembered. 'See if you can find that.'

Kovic scrolled down to the 29th of December. A total of eighteen numbers were listed. Some came up a few times. One of them belonged to Svein-Erik Haugseth. They had exchanged some text messages and had spoken three times. Another frequently used number belonged to Nina Ballangrud, her closest friend.

'I've tried to call her, but she's not answering,' Kovic said.

'Well they certainly had a lot to talk about,' Blix observed, pointing to a call at 16:43 that had lasted nineteen minutes.

'Have you looked her up on the database?'

Kovic nodded. 'A couple of minor drug violations,' she said.

Blix looked at the next number in the phone log. One call at 17:02, lasting four minutes and thirty-four seconds. Over the next half hour, Ruth-Kristine had tried to call the same number six more times. Each time, she had let the phone ring until it went through to voicemail, as if the person she was calling wasn't picking up. The name of the recipient was listed in a column on the right of the page: Sophus Ahlander.

The same pattern occurred the next day. Ruth-Kristine had called Ahlander five times, until he had finally picked up. The conversation had lasted twelve seconds. She had then tried several more times throughout the day, each time letting the phone ring out.

'Who is Sophus Ahlander?' Blix asked.

Kovic was already in the process of typing his name into the criminal-records database. Several results appeared on the screen. Mainly violations for drugs and betting. A few car thefts and burglaries, a couple of charges for fraud. No domestic violence cases, as far as Blix could tell.

'Petty crime,' Kovic noted. 'Most of these are old cases.'

'Had they been in contact before then?'

Kovic copied Ahlander's phone number and pasted it into the search box, checking the entire call log. Nothing at all from the last three months, which was the extent of what they had requested. On both the 30th and 31st of December, however, Ruth-Kristine had tried to call him several more times, all of which had gone straight to voicemail.

'Hm,' Kovic mumbled, scrolling up and down twice more.

'What are you thinking?' Blix asked.

'There's a gap here.' Kovic pointed at the screen. 'She uses her phone a lot, but on the twenty-seventh of December, there's nothing. No calls, no texts.'

Blix studied the screen. The last time the phone had been in use was in the early afternoon of the 26th of December. A text from Nina

Ballangrud. It wasn't until later the next day that the phone was active again. Then there was a flood of incoming messages, as if the phone had been turned off and the texts had piled up, waiting for it to be turned back on again.

'Her boyfriend said she took his car and disappeared for a couple of days,' Kovic recalled. 'But where do you go without your phone?'

'Can you get an overview of which toll booths the car went through?' Blix asked.

'Shouldn't be a problem,' Kovic answered.

She opened up an application form for the road toll department of the Norwegian Public Roads Administration.

Blix felt his phone vibrate inside his pocket. He pulled it out and saw that Emma had messaged him:

*I'm outside. Do you have time for an informal chat about the Patricia case?*

He sat with his phone in his hand, but didn't reply. Kovic had just found the licence-plate number for Svein-Erik Haugseth's car and submitted the form. She returned to Ahlander's criminal records, the page displaying a mug shot taken about eight years ago. A man with a round face, wispy hair and an unruly beard.

Sophus Ahlander.

'I'd like to know what Ahlander and Ruth-Kristine were talking about,' Kovic said, returning to the list of phone calls. 'And what was so important that she had to get hold of him.'

'Where does he live?'

Kovic found the address. 'In Haslum, on Vallerveien,' she replied, suddenly realising why he had asked. 'Gard Fosse won't be happy. PST are sending us more tasks today, and we've not even finished the last ones.'

Blix stood up.

'Let's go,' he said.

# 19

The rancid stench of stale cigarette smoke lingered inside the small work car. It was technically Anita's own car, but anyone in the office was allowed to use it, as long as it was for work.

Emma had parked on the opposite side of the road to the Police Headquarters. She leant over the steering wheel and peered up at the sixth floor. She had hoped, and believed, that Blix would take the time to discuss the new lead in the Patricia case, but he hadn't even responded to the text.

She still had her phone in her hand, waiting. She swiped up and searched for an old article she had read – an interview with Ruth-Kristine that included a photo of her and a friend. The two women had gone shopping together the day Patricia had disappeared. The photo had them both looking solemnly into the camera. Emma noted the name of Ruth-Kristine's alibi, Jette Djurholm, as a potential interviewee.

The Danish-sounding name made her think of Kasper. She felt the sensation course through her again, as it had many times since New Year's Eve. An overwhelming feeling rising in her chest, settling in her stomach. And then a clenched fist that punched and punched. She thought of Kasper's parents, what she would say to them. In many ways, it felt wrong to still be in Norway, at work, while her boyfriend's family wanted her to be with them, in Denmark. Emma had said that she just needed some time to work out when she could get over there. It hadn't been a question of whether she wanted to or not.

Emma craned her head up at the building again. Still no answer from Blix. She typed out a new message and was slightly more specific about what she was after:

*I spoke to Gard Fosse. He confirmed that Ruth-Kristine Smeplass was one of the injured in the explosion. I'm writing an article about what she's been through, what happened to her after her daughter disappeared. You know that investigation best. I'd welcome any input, anything that might be interesting to look into.*

She pressed send and sat back to wait for a reply. It was getting cold, and the windows had begun to steam up. Emma turned on the ignition.

She had just put the heating on when her phone vibrated. A reply from Blix:

*Not now.*

Emma sighed and considered just heading back to the office, when an unmarked police car drove out from the car park beneath the building. A grey Passat, the same kind Emma had seen Blix drive.

An old woman with a walking frame was taking her time crossing the road. The car came to a complete stop. Blix was behind the wheel. She recognised the woman in the passenger seat: Blix's colleague.

Emma slid down in her seat, ducking slightly as she watched the car turn left and drive off. She made up her mind on the spot. Starting up the small car, she followed them.

The unmarked police car headed south, through the city centre and onto the interchange that would take them into the Opera Tunnel and out of the city. They sped up when they emerged on the other side. Emma made sure to keep at least one car between her and Blix. They passed the exit to Bygdøy and Skøyen. Emma looked at the fuel gauge. A little under half a tank.

She had been following Blix for about fifteen minutes when they crossed the Akershus county border. Emma wondered whether she should just turn back. She hadn't really thought this through; she just knew that Blix must be heading somewhere important, seeing as he hadn't had time to stop and talk to her.

Then the car turned off the main road, away from the motorway and into the residential area of Høvik, carrying on further north towards Haslum. The tramline ran parallel to the road for a while. The buildings began to change character, from grand, suburban houses to clusters of cramped neighbourhoods.

Blix's car began to slow down and eventually swerved into a car park. It was an open area surrounded by terraced houses, with a playground and several paths, only just visible beneath the snow.

Emma pulled into one of the other vacant spaces, hidden between a substation and a van covered in a thick layer of snow, about thirty metres away. She turned the ignition off and stayed seated as she watched Blix get out.

# 20

A cold gust of wind forced Blix to dig his hands deep inside his jacket pockets. He stood in the car park and looked around. Each terraced house was split into three separate flats – one per floor – and had a small, walled garden out front. Bollards had been installed on the pavement to stop motorists from driving onto the gardens.

'Over there,' Kovic said, pointing to the ground-floor flat of the house in the centre of the row.

She reached back into the car, took out a folder full of documents and closed the door behind her.

The pavement was cloaked in a layer of black ice. Kovic walked ahead, shuffling along with small, careful steps, arms held out to keep her balance. She stopped at the gate and pointed to the post box. The name *Molly Ahlander* was printed next to the number of the flat they were visiting.

'Is he married?' Blix asked.

Kovic leafed through the documents.

'The mother,' Kovic clarified. 'She's dead. He lives alone.'

Four car tyres were stacked up next to the front door. Two white plastic chairs had been propped against the wall of the house. An old indoor exercise bike was wrapped up in a sheet of tarpaulin.

Blix rang the bell. He wanted to find out what kind of relationship Ahlander and Ruth-Kristine had and what the phone call two days before New Year's Eve had been about. Simple questions he could have asked over the phone. But he wanted to see Ahlander's reaction to them.

No one answered the door. Blix tried again. He could hear the chime of the doorbell ringing through the flat, but he knocked twice more anyway, hard. There was a large window to the left of the door. The curtains were partially drawn. Blix cupped his hands to the glass and peered inside. A kitchen. There was a cup and a used ashtray on the table. A couple of plates stacked up by the sink. On the counter was a box full of what appeared to be old stereo parts.

Behind Blix, Kovic had started rifling through the papers again.

'No employer listed,' she said, as if she had read his mind.

'I'll call him,' Blix decided, taking his phone out. He typed the number in as Kovic read it aloud. Straight to voicemail.

Blix turned around and looked back at the car park.

'Did you bring the printout from the vehicle register?' he asked.

Kovic nodded. 'He drives an old Toyota.' She found the right document and read out the licence-plate number. '2008 model, RAV4,' she added. 'Silver.'

Blix's gaze roamed over the parked cars. Some had clearly been driven recently, others were still coated in snow. He couldn't see any that matched the description.

There were a few garages behind the car park, but they looked as if they belonged to another part of the housing estate.

'Let's see if the neighbours are home,' Kovic suggested.

Blix nodded and walked to the flat on the right as Kovic took the one on the left.

A boy of around ten years old opened the door to Blix.

'Hi,' Blix said. 'Are your parents at home?'

The boy shook his head. Blix introduced himself, but didn't mention that he was from the police.

'I'm actually trying to get hold of your neighbour,' he said, nodding in the direction of Sophus Ahlander's flat. 'Have you seen him today?'

The boy shook his head. A cat appeared from inside the flat and peered out between the boy's legs.

'When was the last time you saw him?' Blix continued.

The boy shrugged. Blix sensed that he wasn't going to get anything out of him and ended the conversation.

Kovic was waiting for him on the pavement.

'Nobody home,' she explained.

Blix rubbed his hands together.

'Well, that was productive,' he stated.

# 21

A fresh layer of condensation had formed on the inside of the car windows. Emma didn't want to start the car and attract any attention. When Blix and Kovic returned, she slid further down into the seat. She wondered whether she should continue following them, but presumed they would just be heading back to HQ. Anyway, she was more curious about who they had been trying to get hold of. After she had watched the Passat drive away, she opened the door and climbed out.

A taxi drove past with someone in the back seat. Emma stopped, took her phone out and pretended to be reading something while the passenger paid and got out. It was a man in his forties. He stepped onto the footpath but walked past the flat that Blix and Kovic had visited.

There was a post box attached to the fence. Molly Ahlander.

Emma took a picture of the name before she lifted the lid and saw that it was stuffed full of various advertisements and junk mail. She looked around, pulled some of them out and among them found a white envelope addressed to a Sophus Ahlander. There was no return address. The date that had been printed across the stamp was unclear, but it looked as if it might have been the 28th of December. The Friday between Christmas and New Year's Eve. Come to think of it, today might have been the first day the post was being delivered again, after the holidays.

She put the letter back. An elderly woman carrying a shopping bag was making her way towards her. She had ice grips attached to her shoes and they were making a crunching sound as they met the ground beneath the ice. It looked as if she were heading to the house that Kovic had tried.

Emma stepped out in front of her.

'Hi, I'm sorry to bother you, but do you know the people who live here?' she asked, nodding over to the flat behind her.

'I used to,' the woman replied.

Emma waited for her to elaborate.

'Molly and I were neighbours for almost twenty-five years,' the woman explained. 'When she passed last summer, her son inherited everything. The car, house, cabin. I met him at the funeral. But I haven't spoken to him since.'

Emma tried to form a picture of Sophus Ahlander. If his late mother had been about the same age as the neighbour, then she envisioned him as a man around the age of fifty.

'Does he live alone?' she asked.

The woman transferred the shopping bag over to her other hand.

'I've never seen anyone else there,' she said.

'What does he do?'

The woman shook her head. 'He doesn't work,' she answered. 'The last thing I remember Molly saying about him was that he worked in a company that sold firewood and Christmas trees.'

'Do you know where he might be?' Emma continued.

The woman moved the shopping bag back into her other hand.

'I haven't seen him for days now,' she said, and started walking off.

'Right. Thank you for the help.'

# 22

'She's been in Larvik,' Kovic said, looking up from her phone.

From the driver's seat Blix threw a look; he wanted to know more.

'In Haugseth's car,' Kovic explained. 'I've just had a response from the Norwegian Public Roads Administration. On Boxing Day, she drove past a toll booth on the E18, on the way to Larvik. She then came back on the same road the day after.'

A car with a trailer overtook them. Blix tightened his grip on the steering wheel. Mapping the movements of a victim was a core part of any investigation. At some point the victim would cross paths with the perpetrator. If you could find that crossing point, you could solve the case.

'What was she doing all the way down in Larvik?' Kovic pondered.

Blix pulled into the outside lane and accelerated.

'We have to go to Kolbotn,' he said. 'I want to talk to Haugseth again. He knows more than he's letting on.'

Blix felt a vibration in his jacket pocket as they reached the exit to the motorway. He pulled his phone out a fraction and glanced at it, his other hand still on the wheel.

He had thought it would be Emma, but it was Iselin. The message began with a 'Hey' and a smiley face, then a question about what time he was planning on getting off work. He didn't read the entire message, resolving to read it properly later.

Haugseth's lorry was running idle in the driveway when they arrived.

'There's the car,' Kovic said, pointing towards an old, black BMW parked in front of the open garage.

Blix parked up. Svein-Erik Haugseth came out of the garage, wiping his hands on an old rag. He greeted them with a nod.

'Any news?' he asked. 'I was thinking about going to the hospital this afternoon.'

'Her parents are travelling over from Spain tomorrow,' Blix replied.

'I've never met them,' Haugseth said. 'Ruth-Kristine didn't have much contact with them.'

Kovic pointed to the car. 'Was that the car she took over Christmas?' she asked.

'Yes.'

'Can we take a look?'

Haugseth nodded, pulling a keychain out of his pocket and pressing the fob to unlock it.

Blix opened the driver's side door. The car was surprisingly tidy.

'How much money did you lend her?' he asked.

'Three thousand kroner. And she never paid me back.'

'Did you talk to her while she was away?'

'I couldn't get hold of her,' Haugseth replied. 'I think she'd turned her phone off.'

'Did you know where she was?'

Haugseth didn't respond, he just shrugged.

Blix bent over and looked under the seat. Nothing there.

'The car has been in Larvik,' he said. 'Did she know anyone there?'

'Not that I know of,' Haugseth answered, rubbing his hands on the filthy cloth.

He hesitated a moment, before adding: 'I thought she might've been in Denmark.'

'You think she took the ferry from Larvik?' Kovic suggested.

Haugseth nodded. 'I cleaned the car out after she'd used it,' he explained. 'It was full of rubbish. Danish drinks cans and take-away boxes. It looked like she'd been living in it.'

'And you didn't talk about it?'

'She didn't want to. She was angry when she got back, and stressed.'

Blix closed the car door. 'What did you do with the stuff she left in the car?' he asked, looking over at the bins by the fence.

'It's all still in there,' Haugseth nodded. 'At the bottom.'

'What could she have been doing in Denmark?' Kovic asked.

Haugseth's answer was rather vague:

'She always got involved in things she shouldn't have been. Had quite the talent for it.'

'What was she involved in this time?'

'I don't know, but when I found out where she'd been, it got me thinking...'

Blix was now starting to piece together what Haugseth was suggesting, and realised they were going to have to pull it out of him.

'What were you thinking?' he asked.

'That she'd been to Denmark to pick something up.' He hesitated again. 'Drugs or something else illegal,' he carried on. 'Which would explain why she was acting as she was. Why she was so stressed and evasive, and why she'd turned off her phone. You know, so she couldn't be traced by the police.'

'Has she done that before?' Kovic asked. 'Smuggled drugs?'

'Not as far as I know, but she suddenly had all this money and refused to say where she'd got it from.'

Blix waited impatiently for him to elaborate.

'It always seemed to happen around Christmas,' Haugseth added. 'Last year she bought me a new TV, and the year before that she gave me a new iPhone. The most expensive one.'

'And she did the same this year too?'

Haugseth shook his head. 'No, this year, I got a jumper and a few bits and bobs. Or, last year, even, seeing as it's already January.'

Kovic walked over to the bin. 'Do you mind if we take what you cleared out of the car?'

She opened the lid without waiting for an answer. Haugseth walked over to her and helped to pull out the other bin bags until he found the right one.

'Here you go,' he said, handing it to her.

# 23

Blix received another text when they climbed back in the car. Iselin again. This time, she had just sent a question mark. He read the previous message. She wanted to meet up, but didn't say why.

He typed out a reply, saying that he would probably be working late but that they could have dinner together. Out, at a restaurant, somewhere. She replied immediately: A thumbs up.

'I'll contact the ferry company, get a copy of their passenger lists,' Kovic said.

Blix nodded and started the ignition.

'She might not have been travelling alone,' Kovic added.

The lorry in front of them ejected a huge cloud of exhaust.

'Shall we try Nina Ballangrud before we drive back?' Kovic asked.

Blix's thoughts were elsewhere.

'Who?' he asked.

'Ruth-Kristine's addict friend,' Kovic explained, yawning as she said it. 'I can't get through on her phone. She lives in Manglerud. It's on the way back.'

Blix put his phone into the space between the seats. 'Let's do that,' he said.

Kovic entered the address into the sat nav.

'Does she live alone?' Blix asked as they drove out onto the E6.

'According to the information we've got,' Kovic nodded.

The map indicated that they would be there in two minutes.

Kovic opened the folder she had been holding in her lap and found the print out of Ruth-Kristine Smeplass's phone log.

'Nina Ballangrud was the last person to call Ruth-Kristine,' she said.

'When was that?'

'At 22:07 on New Year's Eve,' Kovic replied. 'A short conversation. Only ten seconds.'

They pulled up in front of an old block of flats, one of the only ones in the area that had not yet been restored. Advent candles and Christmas decorations were visible in several of the windows.

Kovic got out first. She located the right entrance and found the doorbell with the name Nina Ballangrud.

'Not home,' Kovic concluded after waiting about a minute.

The next doorbell down was labelled Tore Halvorsen. Blix tried that one. Not long after, a man's voice answered.

'Police,' Blix said. 'We need to get inside.'

Without hesitation, the door buzzed as the lock opened from inside; it seemed this wasn't the first time the police had asked to be let in. Kovic pulled the door open.

Nina Ballangrud lived on the third floor. A man stood in the doorway of the flat opposite hers.

'Halvorsen?' Blix asked.

The man nodded.

'We're here to speak to Nina Ballangrud,' Blix explained. 'Have you seen her?'

'It's been a few days,' the man replied.

'So she's not home?'

'I don't know.'

The man stood there in the doorway while Blix knocked on Nina Ballangrud's door. No response.

Kovic pulled out a calling card, wrote a short message and stuck it in the doorframe. The man across the hallway went back into his flat and closed the door.

Back in the car, Kovic searched for the phone number of Nina Ballangrud's parents and called it as they drove back to HQ. Blix listened as she introduced herself and explained why she was calling. Then the tone of her voice changed, as if she had been told something interesting.

Blix's own phone started to ring. He recognised the number but couldn't quite work out where from. He lifted the phone to his ear so as not to interrupt Kovic's conversation.

'It's the fingerprint lab,' a woman's voice said. 'We've examined the image you sent over. I was told that you needed the answer immediately.'

'Have you found anything?'

'A total of six different fingerprints,' the woman stated. 'One of them is yours.'

'Brilliant,' Blix replied with a sigh. 'Have you identified any of the others?'

'Two of them. Several prints from both the left and right hands of Christer Storm Isaksen, and the remaining prints – a right thumb and a right index finger – belong to Ruth-Kristine Smeplass.'

'Ruth-Kristine Smeplass,' Blix repeated. 'You're sure about that?'

'We'll send an official report to verify,' the woman confirmed.

'What about the envelope?' asked Blix. 'Did you find any on that?'

'Two sets of fingerprints,' the woman answered. 'Christer Storm Isaksen's, and an unknown print.'

'Not Ruth-Kristine Smeplass then?'

'No, hers were only on the photo.'

Blix tried to work out what that could mean, but couldn't think straight.

'I'll send the written report within the hour,' the woman concluded.

Blix thanked her and looked over at Kovic who was now sat holding her phone in her lap. He let her go first.

'Nina's mother was planning on calling us,' she said. 'They've not heard from her since New Year's Eve.'

## 24

Although the carpet muffled the sound of the cleaning trolley, Amy Linh still tried to be as quiet as possible as she wheeled it down the hallway. She cast a quick glance down at her list. Rooms 614, 615 and 616 were done. 617 was supposed to check out later, so she carried on walking past.

She knocked on the next door down.

'Housekeeping.'

The words came out like a whisper. She cleared her throat and tried again, a little louder.

'Not today,' a voice answered from inside room 618. 'I don't need anything.'

She asked one more time, just to be sure.

'No thanks', the man repeated.

Amy Linh took hold of the trolley again and carried on pushing it down the hall, back into the silence. She liked the silence. It gave her space to think. Her imagination thrived at work. Sparked by the small insights she gained into other peoples' lives, just by cleaning up after them, or from stealing brief, curious glances at their belongings. A used condom, or the residue of some bodily fluid left on the bedding. A gift bag or box from somewhere expensive, opened but packed away again – the garment still inside. A receipt from a fancy restaurant on the bedside table. Several glasses of wine and a taxi back to the hotel. Some of them didn't even bother to hide the fact that, at some point since she'd last been in to clean, they had snorted a line of cocaine. Amy Linh would make a note of everything she saw or encountered at work, saving it all to write her own stories later on.

A door opened just ahead. A man and woman emerged from the room and began walking in Amy Linh's direction. She moved the trolley closer into the wall and looked at the man, noticing that he didn't seem fully awake yet. He had deep bags under his eyes, and his cheeks were red – as if they had been shaved recently with a razor that had been a little blunt. The woman's hair was wet. As they passed, Amy could hear that her breathing was shallow – as if she were annoyed about something. Neither of them replied when Amy Linh gave them a quiet hello, just carried on as if she wasn't there.

A late night, or maybe an early morning. Perhaps he had snored, or she had. Maybe their few days away at a hotel in Norway's capital had lived up to their expectations, or they could have been in a rush to get back to normality. Children, work, a car they might have to take to the repair shop. Her imagination ran wild.

As for her own story, she had long fought to forget it. After the Americans had left her home country in the 1970s, the peace they had been promised had only resulted in more warfare. And since her father had taken the side of South Vietnam, they had been forced to flee in a raft, along with nearly fifty other refugees. They had all come close to falling overboard more than once. Then they were finally rescued by a Norwegian cargo ship, and were, at long last, given food and drink, and were taken to Singapore. From there, they travelled to the Philippines. They had to stay there for two years, before they could eventually continue on to Norway.

It was in Manila that Amy Linh lost her sister. They had not caught the pneumonia in time. With no money, it had been impossible to get her the medication. Twelve years on earth, that was all. Their escape, and the journey itself, had impacted and shaped her family in ways none of them would talk about. But what they had been through was still visible, etched into their faces. Their story could still be heard in the silent cries of a grief that they never let out. In the arguments that raged between them whenever they found them-selves without clothes or food.

It was for that reason that Amy Linh had made her mind up.

She wasn't going to suppress the story she carried with her any longer. She was going to write it down. She was going to tell everyone about Nha Trang. What the city had been like before the tourists had discovered its bay and pristine beaches. The sounds she would wake up to every morning. The motorbikes. The doorbells. The horns from the boats signalling their way back into the harbour with the catch of the night. And she would write about her sister.

619 didn't take long to clean. The guest was meant to be staying for two more days, so she only had to change the bed linen and the towels, put an extra toilet roll in and clean the bathroom. She also folded some of his clothes for him. In and out in less than ten minutes.

There was a tray with a dirty plate, an empty glass and some cutlery left on the floor outside 620. He had been staying at the hotel since the day before New Year's Eve. Alone. Amy Linh had seen him before. He always stayed in the same room.

She wanted to knock on the door and check to see if everything was okay. If he needed anything. He had kept the *Do Not Disturb* sign on the door for three days in a row. He didn't usually do that. She could hear that the TV was on, but no one was moving around inside.

Her thoughts got carried away again. What if something had happened? What if he was in there, dead, or unconscious?

If the sign were still there tomorrow, Amy Linh said to herself, she would knock and check.

# 25

The blinds in the office windows had been pulled shut and the lights dimmed. Gard Fosse was sat behind his desk. The clock on the wall behind him showed that it was already after five o'clock.

Blix walked in, leaving the door wide open behind him.

'We're going to have to take a closer look at the circumstances around Ruth-Kristine Smeplass,' he announced.

Fosse leant back in his chair and looked up at him.

'What kind of circumstances are we talking about?'

'We have footage of her from the CCTV outside City Hall,' Blix began. 'Acting strangely, going from one bin to the next, before stopping right next to the one with the bomb.'

Fosse loosened his tie. He was the only one in their department who actually wore his uniform every day.

'Her flat has also been broken into sometime over the last twenty-four hours,' Blix continued. 'And her boyfriend suspects that she was involved with some drug-smuggling operation just before New Year's Eve.'

'I don't see how any of that relates to the explosion,' Fosse commented. 'Petty crimes. They always turn up when investigating these larger cases. You know that. They can't be prioritised.'

Blix ignored him and carried on, informing him about the photo Christer Storm Isaksen had received in prison.

'I've just found out that Ruth-Kristine's fingerprints were on it,' he said. 'And her closest friend, Nina Ballangrud, has been reported missing too. No one's heard from her since New Year's Eve. The Missing Persons Unit have got most of their personnel wrapped up in the investigation into the bombing now, so they don't have enough people to help us out with this. The smartest thing to do would be to look into it ourselves.'

'Sounds as if you've looked into it a lot already,' Fosse replied.

Blix considered him. For Fosse, the department was simply a

machine that processed cases, hopefully with the least amount of re-sistance. Its effectiveness was measured only by the number of cases processed and the time it had taken to complete them. He didn't want his staff to do any extra work that might fall into the responsi-bility of the other departments.

'I have a bad feeling about this,' Blix said, aware that argument wouldn't have any impact on Fosse. 'The father of Ruth-Kristine's missing friend works for NRK,' he added, knowing full well that this, at least, was a language Fosse understood. 'I don't want the case to be left on the shelf.'

He avoided telling him that Rolf Ballangrud was actually em-ployed in the kitchen of the broadcasting company's cafeteria.

'Fine,' Fosse said, making a gesture with his hand, as if to wave him out. 'But don't take too much time on this one.'

'I'll ask Wibe and Abelvik to help out,' Blix added, now on his way out of the door. 'They're back from the Christmas break now. Maybe we'll find her before the day is over.'

He closed the door behind him and headed back to the office, where Kovic had already gathered Nicolai Wibe and Tine Abelvik, all of whom were now waiting for him at the conference table. Wibe was a down-to-earth police officer with a background in undercover surveillance. He was an expert when it came to tracking people, both online and on the ground. Blix and Abelvik had worked on patrol together. She was a few years younger than he was but had gained a lot of experience working in various other specialist units.

'As far as we know, this should be a basic missing-persons case, but it may also be connected to the New Year's Eve bombing,' Blix began. 'One of the most severely injured is the closest friend of the woman who is now missing.'

Wibe pulled towards him the photo of Nina Ballangrud that Kovic had printed out.

'I want to look into the possibility that the bomb was not just ran-domly placed, but was targeted at Ruth-Kristine Smeplass,' Blix continued.

He went through the outline of the Patricia case again, noticing the scepticism on the faces of the two new team members.

'What about the bomb in Frogner Park?' Wibe asked. 'The bomb squad reported that it had been made in the same way as the one at City Hall, just not as powerful. Which would suggest that the same person or group was behind the attack, and given the fact that the second one was placed in a rubbish bin as well, that seems plausible. But what you're saying is that the New Year's Eve bomb was an attempted murder? That sounds ... wrong.'

'I understand why you would think so,' Blix said. 'But there are a lot of reasons why we should look into Ruth-Kristine.'

He told them about the break-in at her flat, her trip to Denmark, her bizarre behaviour along the harbour just before the explosion. And finally, the cross they had found on the bin she had ended up standing next to.

Kovic took over. 'One of the last people to have been in contact with Ruth-Kristine was the now-missing Nina Ballangrud,' she explained, showing them the phone log.

Wibe studied the records.

'Have you spoken to the taxi driver?' he asked, pointing to the line that showed Ruth-Kristine's call to the taxi company.

'I called them fifteen minutes ago,' Kovic replied. 'They're looking for the details of that trip and who the driver was, and then they're going to get him to call me back.'

Abelvik took the printout of the phone log.

'Do you have the records from Nina Ballangrud's phone as well?' she asked.

'Not yet.'

'What about the activity on her bank account?'

'We've requested it,' Kovic assured her. 'We have just received the card details for Ruth-Kristine though,' she added. 'She paid for a taxi at 23:27 on New Year's Eve. And that's the last time her card was used.'

'Maybe Ruth-Kristine and Nina were both in the taxi that night?' Abelvik suggested.

'Nina wasn't injured in the explosion,' Kovic said. 'The divers have checked the fjord, and the video feed has been reviewed to account for all the casualties and injured.'

'Maybe she was involved?' Wibe offered. He fished a bag of snus from behind his lower lip and put it back in its container. 'Made sure Ruth-Kristine was there for the explosion?'

'And then disappeared after that, you mean?' Abelvik asked.

Wibe shrugged. Blix held his face in his hands as he thought through it.

'They were both addicts,' Wibe continued. 'Maybe Smeplass owed her money or something?'

'There are easier ways to kill someone than trying to blow them up outside City Hall,' Kovic interrupted. 'Besides, her flat had been completely upended. All because someone was looking for cash? Valuables?'

Wibe didn't answer.

'And where did she go, anyway?' Abelvik asked.

Kovic's phone rang and she walked a short distance away to answer it. Blix started to gather the papers together, indicating that the meeting was over. He gave Wibe and Abelvik the task of tracking down Nina Ballangrud, while he would try to find Sophus Ahlander himself.

'I also want you to go to Ruth-Kristine's flat and do a tactical search this time. See if you can find something that might explain what she had been up to in the few days before the explosion, or what the intruder could have been looking for.'

Kovic came back over as everyone was getting up.

'That was the taxi driver,' she said, holding up the phone. 'The trip was booked under Ruth-Kristine's name. There was only one passenger. A woman. She was picked up at Holmlia and driven into the city centre.'

'He's sure about that?' Blix asked. 'Just one woman?'

Kovic nodded. 'He remembered the trip because he was worried he wouldn't get paid for it.'

'Why?'

'The payment wouldn't go through until the third attempt. According to the driver, the passenger kept typing in the wrong pin number.'

'Maybe she was nervous?' Wibe suggested.

Blix pushed the chair back under the table. He had expected to hear that both women had been in the taxi into the city centre.

'So did Nina Ballangrud stay at Ruth-Kristine's flat then, or...?' Abelvik asked, trailing off.

No one had an answer.

'Right, well,' Blix started. 'We know what happened to Ruth-Kristine. Let's try to find Nina.'

The four investigators went their separate ways. Blix went to grab a cup of coffee before sitting back down behind his computer screen. Kovic had pulled out the bin bag they had taken from Haugseth, and was in the process of looking through the contents left over from Ruth-Kristine's trip to Denmark.

'Anything interesting?' Blix asked.

Kovic shook her head. 'Just rubbish. No receipts or paperwork that could tell us anything about where exactly she had been in Denmark, or what she was doing there.'

Blix turned his attention to the screen. He had already created a new folder titled Sophus Ahlander. It only contained the most basic information thus far. Ahlander was forty-six years old, had no permanent employment, no children or registered cohabitants. Both parents were dead – the father died fifteen years ago, and the mother last summer. Ahlander had inherited the flat and reported the move. He had also inherited a car and a cabin in Undrumsåsen, in Vestfold county. He had sold the car and had bought a Toyota RAV4 instead.

His criminal record included a few drug misdemeanours, three convictions for car theft, a few burglaries and one case of fraud that had been dropped. What Blix was really looking for was anything that might indicate Ahlander's involvement in Patricia's disappearance. He had no concrete hypothesis about it – it was more an intuition. Right before Knut Ivar Skage had been murdered by Patricia's father, he had admitted to his part in the kidnapping. He had suggested that Ruth-Kristine was behind it. Blix had been looking for a person who had been in both of their social circles. Ahlander's name hadn't turned up at the time, but he could be the common denominator. To move forward with the case, he would have to find something solid that showed that Ruth-Kristine Smeplass, Knut Ivar Skage and Sophus Ahlander knew each other ten years ago, at the time Patricia disappeared.

Kovic stuffed the rubbish back into the bin bag and tied it up.

'I'm going to see if there's any food left in the cafeteria,' she said. 'Want anything?'

Blix shook his head and used two fingers to type Ahlander's name and birth details into the intelligence database, which contained all sorts of information that they had gathered, such as statements given by informants, surplus details from other investigations, material from the surveillance of known criminals and general tip-offs that had been sent in. A few results came up regarding a car-theft case, implying that Ahlander had been involved to a much greater extent than had been acknowledged at the trial. His name also popped up in a few other drug cases, but only with a peripheral role.

One entry attracted Blix's attention. It was a tip-off that had come in a little over eight years earlier – a phone call that had been made soon after the broadcast of an episode of *Wanted*, a TV programme about unsolved criminal cases. One feature had been dedicated to the murder of a man in Alna three years before. A pedestrian had been run over and killed, and the driver had sped away. The accident had occurred on a poorly lit stretch of road, late at night. The body hadn't been found until the next morning.

Paint residue on the victim's body and shattered glass found at the scene suggested that the car involved was a burgundy Ford Focus. A witness had seen a similar car travelling at high speed in a nearby street that night. It was missing a headlight and had two people inside.

Neither the car nor the driver had been found.

In the programme, the widow of the murdered man had begged for answers from anyone who knew anything about what had happened. An anonymous tip-off had named Sophus Ahlander as the driver, and had revealed that he had been driving a stolen car around that time.

Blix read the entry again. The phone number of whoever had given the tip-off hadn't been included. Probably a private number. There was no information about whether the caller was male or female either, but the fact that Ahlander had been convicted of car theft several times gave the tip-off some substance.

Blix waited as the computer struggled to load the case files. They showed that the case was still unresolved and had been given the closure code 014: insufficient information regarding the perpetrator.

Blix scrolled through the list of documents and saw that Ahlander had been called in for questioning after the programme had aired. There was a short statement. He had denied the anonymous accusation. And as it had been such a long time since the incident, it was impossible for him to account for where he had been and what he had done that night.

Towards the end of the interview, he was encouraged to offer any reasons why someone would accuse him of the crime. He had no answer for that either, but didn't try to hide the fact that he had previously been found guilty of stealing cars. He also believed that the car he owned at the time was the same model as the one they were looking for, which he thought might have led to the accusation. His car, however, had been blue. He gave them the licence-plate number, and an investigation had followed to try and find the current owner of the car, to ascertain that it was originally blue and hadn't just been repainted.

Blix printed out a transcript of the interview and read it again.

Something about it made him uneasy, but he couldn't quite put his finger on what or why. In an attempt to find out more, he entered the licence-plate number Ahlander had given. It was, as he had said, a blue Ford Focus from 2006. The current owner was a man with an Arabic-sounding name who lived in Lillestrøm.

He typed a few commands in and loaded the list of previous owners. The car had changed ownership a number of times. It had also been registered with an insurance company at one point, indicating that it had been involved in a serious collision.

Sophus Ahlander had owned the car between 2007 and 2009. Blix straightened up when he read the name of the previous owner. Ahlander had bought the car from the Autokvick car repair shop in Kalbakken. That didn't necessarily have to mean anything in itself, but Blix recognised the name: it was Knut Ivar Skage's garage.

This was exactly what he was looking for.

A missing link between the man who had already admitted to being involved in Patricia's kidnapping, and Ruth-Kristine Smeplass. It was only a small connection, but it was enough for him to start an internal inquiry into Sophus Ahlander. He included a note requesting that he be notified immediately once Ahlander had been found.

# 26

The article dedicated to Ruth-Kristine was long, and it had taken Emma more time than usual to write it, what with the sheer amount of facts she had had to find and include.

The piece recounted the story of a woman who had not had an easy life, largely due to her mental-health struggles. Most of it had been covered in the newspapers years ago, so Emma didn't feel guilty for bringing it back to the surface, but she made sure to write it all in a way that would generate sympathy for Patricia's mother.

She also included some lines about what she had gone through herself on New Year's Eve, before she had found Kasper, that is. The panic that had spread across the square after the explosion. The chaos, the smells, the sounds. The cold gusts of wind coming off the fjord. She also recycled some of the details she had included in the article she had originally written about Blix rescuing Ruth-Kristine.

Emma was pleased with her work. It was a good story, as good as unhappy stories could be, anyway. And she had come up with an idea for another article while working on it. A parallel article based on what had happened to Patricia's father. How he had ended up in prison after murdering the man who just might have had the answer to what had happened to his daughter. She just had to get hold of him first.

After sending the article to Anita, Emma sat and let her mind wander. As soon as she stopped doing anything, her thoughts returned to Kasper.

She had packed up his things and put them in the guest room. But it still felt like he was there.

Before he died, she had wondered if she would miss him when he returned to Denmark. If their relationship might have been heading into a sort of indifferent phase. Now that she missed him more than her heart could bear, she wondered if she only felt that way because she would never see him again, or if she might, in fact, have loved him.

Emma closed her eyes for a few seconds and shook her head. She couldn't, and wouldn't, think about that, or him. *Think about work instead*, she told herself. *Do something. Don't sit still.*

She called Blix, who surprised her by answering on the first ring.

'Any news?' she began.

'About what?' Blix asked.

'The bombings.'

'Not as far as I know,' he replied. 'But that's PST's responsibility. You'll need to contact them, or ask Gard Fosse.'

'Wollan can do that,' Emma commented. 'I'm not working on that case anyway, not directly.'

'What are you working on then?'

'I'm looking into Ruth-Kristine Smeplass. Any news about her?'

Blix sighed. 'I spoke to the hospital earlier this afternoon; they said that they'd let me know if there's any change in her condition.'

'Have you found out any more about what she was doing by the harbour that night?'

'No,' Blix answered. 'We're trying to contact the people she had been in touch with in the few days beforehand, but that hasn't resulted in anything so far.'

Sophus Ahlander, Emma thought to herself. She wrote his name in capital letters on the notepad in front of her, but didn't mention anything to Blix.

'I want to talk to her ex,' she said instead. 'Patricia's father.'

'Why?'

Emma told him about the article she had written, and how she wanted to write another about Christer Storm Isaksen.

'Do you know what prison he's in?'

Blix hesitated, as if he were thinking about whether that was information he could share with her.

'Oslo Prison,' he replied after a minute.

Emma picked her pen up again. 'Has it been long since you last spoke to him?'

Again, it took some time before he answered. 'I spoke to him yesterday. Briefed him on what happened to Ruth-Kristine.'

'What did he say?'

'I can't give you that information, Emma.'

Emma chewed on the end of the pen. 'Can you give me a hand getting in to see him?'

'That's not something that I or the police can help you with,' Blix replied. 'You'll have to take it up with Correctional Services.'

His answer irritated her. He sounded reluctant. He must be able to arrange a meeting if he wanted to.

She let it go and changed the subject. 'A name has cropped up,' she began.

'Right?'

'Sophus Ahlander,' she read from her notepad. 'Who's that?'

She heard Blix gasp.

'Where did you get that name from?'

'I can't say,' she replied.

'Come on,' Blix said. 'I've just helped you out. This could be important.'

'How important?' Emma asked. 'Important for the Patricia case?'

'Among other things,' Blix answered. 'He's a person of interest in the case. Where have you found that name?'

Emma searched for an excuse. She couldn't think of anything.

'How interesting?' she asked instead. 'Does he have something to do with the kidnapping?'

'It's too early to say.'

'Was he not looked into at the time?'

'Emma,' Blix said sternly. 'What do you know about Sophus Ahlander?'

'Nothing,' she admitted.

'You said his name had cropped up?'

Emma bit her bottom lip. Blix deserved an answer. An honest answer.

'I followed you,' she said.

'What do you mean?'

'Earlier today, when you didn't have time to talk. I was parked outside HQ and saw you and Kovic leaving. I followed you, to Ahlander's flat.'

'Followed us ... why?'

'On an impulse. It looked like you were doing something important. I just wanted to see what that might be.'

'Emma...' Blix's voice sounded accusatory.

'Sorry,' Emma said hastily. 'I was borrowing the company car—'

Blix interrupted her. 'I'm getting another call,' he said. 'I have to take it.'

'Sure. Talk later.'

Emma put the phone down, stretched, and realised how hungry she was.

# 27

'Hi,' Iselin said. 'It's me. What are we doing about dinner tonight?'

Blix transferred the phone to his other ear. He had completely forgotten.

'I've booked us a table for eight o'clock tonight at Benjamin,' he lied.

'Do you mean *Le* Benjamin?' There was a teasing tone in her voice.

'Yes.'

Le Benjamin was a French bistro at the southern end of the Grünerløkka district. They had eaten there together once before. She had sorted everything that time. He just hoped that they would have a free table on a weekday so soon after the holidays.

'I'll see you in half an hour,' Iselin said, and hung up.

Blix pushed himself away from the desk and pulled on his jacket. As he made his way out, he searched for the number, called the restaurant and asked them to hold a table for two.

His daughter turned up at eight o'clock on the dot, wearing the dark-blue puffer jacket he had bought for her the Christmas before last. She had a bag draped over her shoulder.

She greeted him with a wide smile and a warm hug. Blix held her close for a few extra seconds, before giving her a quick kiss on the cheek and asking her how she was.

The bag slipped off her shoulder. 'I'm doing okay,' she said, heaving it back on again. 'How are you?'

'Yeah all's well with me,' he answered.

'Good to hear,' she smiled. 'Shall we go in? I'm starving.'

Blix opened the door for his daughter and followed her inside, into the aroma of garlic and sautéed mushrooms. Iselin had taken charge and was already asking about their reservation. Blix noticed that several people turned and stared as she walked by, probably recognising her from the reality TV programme she had participated in the previous autumn.

'Can I get you a drink to start?' the waiter asked once they had sat down.

Iselin looked at her father and answered: 'He's probably heading back to work after this,' she said, nodding at Blix. 'But I'll have a glass of red wine.'

'Just water for me, thanks.'

The waiter disappeared. Blix looked at Iselin and smiled. Shook his head.

'What's up?' she asked.

'Nothing, I just can't get used to the fact that you drink wine now,' he replied. 'I swear it was just a few weeks ago that you refused to drink anything other than milk.'

Iselin sent him a smile as if to say *how embarrassing*.

'I'm not twelve anymore, Dad.'

'True, but I'm still your dad.'

She grinned. The waiter returned and they ordered. Mussels *au gratin* in a tomato and onion sauce for Blix, an autumn salad with veal sweetbreads, chicken liver and blackcurrants for Iselin.

Blix put the menu down. They spoke for a while, just small talk, before Blix leaned across the table slightly. Iselin had said that she wanted to talk to him about something.

'You said you were doing okay,' he said. 'Not that everything was okay.'

'Is there a difference?'

Blix straightened his napkin. 'The former could mean that everything might not be okay, but that you're dealing with it,' he explained.

'I forget that you're a policeman,' Iselin commented, taking a sip from her glass.

'What is it?' Blix asked. 'Is something bothering you?'

Iselin sat still for a while, holding the glass in her hand. 'I need somewhere to live,' she said.

Blix raised his eyebrows.

'Mum and I had planned to stay at Jan-Egil's house while he goes to Singapore for work ... but she's decided to go with him now. I can't take care of that massive house by myself. And anyway, I think they might want to rent it out.'

Blix thought of all the hours Iselin had spent in therapy, of everything she had been through after being on *Worthy Winner*. How fragile and scared she had been, how long she had spent like that. He wasn't sure if she had managed to put it behind her yet. And now Merete was going to leave her daughter, all by herself, just like that?

Blix felt a wave of anger crash over him.

'They're not leaving for a few weeks yet anyway, not until after my birthday.'

'That's not that long,' Blix said.

'No.'

She looked as if she were thinking about it. The food arrived.

'Mum hasn't called you, has she?' she asked.

Blix shook his head. He picked up the spoon, but sat there with it in his hand without starting.

'Have you argued?' he asked, looking down at her bag.

Iselin didn't answer immediately.

'I thought about renting a studio flat,' she said at last. 'I've saved up a bit now so should be able to afford it.'

In the wake of the reality show's explosive finale, the TV company had decided that Toralf and Iselin, the two finalists, should share the grand prize of one million kroner, even if that wasn't technically allowed in the rules.

'Or I could come and stay with you?' she added.

'With me?'

'At least until I can find my own place.'

Blix tore off a chunk of bread and dipped it in the bowl, thinking about his tiny flat in Tøyen. Quite the contrast to the house that Merete, Jan-Egil and Iselin had been living in in Holmenkollen for the last three years. Much more of a contrast than he'd care to think about.

'Of course you can,' he said, popping the chunk of bread into his mouth.

Her face lit up. 'You don't have to change anything for me,' she said eagerly. 'I can shop and sort … things for myself. And I won't be home much. I'm sure I'll stay over at Toralf's a lot too, so you won't see too much of me anyway.'

'Stay over…?'

Iselin sent him an exasperated look. 'Are you surprised to find out that I occasionally spend the night with my boyfriend?'

Blix didn't have a chance to respond.

'Even if you refuse to believe it, I'm not Dad's little girl any longer,' she finished.

Blix took a sip from his glass of water.

'I know that,' he said quietly.

'So what's the problem?'

He thought about how he should reply, about how he, himself, had never been particularly good at living with other people.

'Have you already packed?' he asked, glancing down at her bag again.

'A little,' she replied.

He nodded, smiling at her.

'So that's all sorted then?' she asked. 'I can stay with you, at your place? Just for a while, at least?'

Blix raised the spoon to his mouth, hiding his moment of hesitation. He had actually been planning on driving out to Haslum once they finished, to see if Sophus Ahlander were back home, but that could wait until the morning.

'You are always welcome, my darling,' he said with a smile. 'Any time.'

'Thanks, Dad,' she said, returning his smile.

# 28

The way Blix had reacted when she mentioned Sophus Ahlander had convinced Emma that there was something more going on, something related to Ahlander. She tried looking him up, but couldn't find him on social media or in the newspaper text archives. The only result she had actually managed to find was the document that proved he had inherited his mother's house and cabin.

She looked at the notes she had jotted down while on the phone with Blix, the doodle she had drawn of a small cabin with a chimney on the roof. Maybe Sophus Ahlander was at his cabin? The neighbour hadn't seen him for days.

She checked the inheritance document again. Ahlander's cabin was in Undrumsåsen, Vestfold county. The document included an address. Emma highlighted it and copied it into Google. It was located in a particularly isolated area, north of Tønsberg. With a few more clicks, she found that it would only take about an hour to drive over there.

The company car was parked outside. Anita insisted that she was starting a new and healthier chapter of her life, which entailed walking to and from work instead of driving there and back. It might be worth a try, Emma thought. She would get there before it got too late, before nine o'clock at least. On the other hand: if Ahlander wasn't there, she would have wasted a good two hours. And if it turned out that he *was* there, she wasn't even sure what she would ask him. What she did know though, was that the police had been to his door, and that they had left with no answers.

Emma pushed the idea aside, grabbed her iPad and started to read the information she had collected about Christer Storm Isaksen instead. She had called the prison and spoke to one of the officers. He had agreed to pass her request on to Isaksen, but couldn't promise that she would hear back from him.

She scrolled past the parts she had already read. It looked as if he hadn't agreed to any interviews after his sentencing. It certainly couldn't have been the case that no one had asked. If her request to interview him in prison was accepted, it would make for a rare and interesting article. His situation was unique. He had been convicted of murdering the only person who knew something about his daughter's disappearance. If he did agree to meet her, she would have to have something to offer him. Something that would make telling his story worthwhile.

Her thoughts strayed back to Sophus Ahlander and the cabin in Undrumsåsen. Blix had said that Ahlander was a person of interest in the Patricia case. The silence of the flat, the thought of spending the rest of the evening wallowing in it, thinking of Kasper, prompted Emma to grab the car keys.

The display on the sat nav showed that the drive would take one hour and seven minutes. She was six minutes away from her destination when it told her to turn off the main road and onto a gravelled lane that wound its way into a dense forest.

There was less snow in the south than there was in Oslo. Just the occasional mound dotted along the side of the road. After a few hundred metres, the road veered right and up an icy incline. The rear wheels started spinning about halfway up. The car struggled, jolting back and forth. The tyres managed to grip an exposed patch of gravel, gaining traction and pushing her forwards momentarily, only to slide backwards again. The car gave up altogether, forcing her to slam her foot onto the brake pedal to stop it from sliding all the way to the bottom of the slope.

The sat nav indicated that she was only 320 metres from the cabin.

She let the car roll smoothly back into the dark, reversed a short distance and thought about trying again. Deciding not to, she pulled over onto the verge and got out.

It was dark outside. It took a moment for her eyes to adjust. Over to the east, she could hear the distant sound of the traffic on the E18. The stars were scattered across the sky above her.

She tugged a knitted beanie out of her coat pocket, pulled it down over her ears and wrapped her scarf tightly around her neck before setting off on foot. Once or twice she thought she glimpsed the tyre tracks of a car other than her own.

The lane led to a small, brown cabin. There was a car parked out front. Lights were on in a few of the windows. She could smell the smoke billowing out of the chimney.

Emma hesitated. She stood there for a few seconds, before continuing on towards the cabin.

It had been built on top of white foundations. The paint was flaking off the walls in some places, and there were clumps of green moss growing out of the ground near the foot of the cabin. It was right in the middle of a large area of rugged terrain. Boulders were scattered across the landscape and trees surrounded it, shielding the cabin. A cloth rag was hanging from a cord that stretched between two trees. Three empty bottles stood on a homemade wooden table, with four tree stumps placed around it like stools. A dark-grey satellite dish was fastened to the wall.

Emma stopped. On the drive down, she had wondered how she would start the conversation, and she still wasn't sure of what to say, or how to introduce herself. She walked to the foot of the front steps, running through the options in her mind, only to stand there, feeling a sudden, deep discomfort. Ruth-Kristine and Patricia had been her reason for coming here. Patricia could have even been transported to the very place where Emma was standing right now, kept here, hidden away while everyone was looking for her, ten years ago. The man inside the cabin might have played a part in that. The thought had started to turn her discomfort into fear.

She registered a faint sound coming from inside the cabin. She was about to take a step backwards when the front door flew open. It happened so abruptly and with such force that it hit her square in the face. She was knocked over, landing on her back. A man was standing in the doorway, brandishing a fire iron. The light from the solitary bulb above the porch fell over the large, round face and the wild, grey beard.

'Get out of here!' he shouted, raising the rod.

Emma crawled backwards as she heard the sound of the iron slashing through the air. She tried to push herself up, but slipped.

'Leave!' he roared. 'I want nothing more to do with you!'

Emma managed to get to her feet and ran. She could hear the man as he chased after her.

# 29

'I should have tidied up earlier,' Blix apologised. 'But I've had a lot on with work recently.'

Iselin hung her jacket on one of the hooks in the hallway and kicked off her boots.

'Will you catch him?' she asked.

'Who?' Blix replied, picking up a pair of his socks from the floor.

'The bomber,' Iselin said. 'Isn't that what everyone's working on?'

They had made it through dinner without talking about it.

'I'm working on another lead,' Blix replied, clearing some of the junk mail off the cabinet as they passed through the hallway.

'What kind of lead?' Iselin pressed.

'Something to do with one of the people injured in the explosion,' he answered.

'The one you rescued from the water?'

Blix smiled. 'You've read about it?'

Iselin nodded. 'Do you think she has something to do with it? A suicide bomber, or something like that?'

Blix opened the door to the spare room. 'No, not like that,' he answered.

Iselin walked in. The walls were bare, and the room was empty, except for a desk, a cupboard and a bed with a bare mattress.

'There's some bedding in the cupboard,' Blix said, pointing at it.

Iselin took the bag off her shoulder.

'This is great,' she said.

Blix paused on his way back to the living room and turned to look at her. 'You need to let your mum know that you're here,' he said.

'She knows,' Iselin said. 'I sent her a text.'

'Good,' Blix nodded, looking at his watch. It was already eleven o'clock. 'I'll call her tomorrow.'

He walked into the kitchen, loaded the dishwasher and turned it on, then got started on cleaning up the living room.

Iselin disappeared into the bathroom with her toiletry bag. Blix slumped onto the sofa and turned on the TV, only to get back up again to check what was in the fridge. A few eggs, a tube of cheese spread and an unopened jar of raspberry jam. That was it. He had a few bread rolls in the freezer.

He sat back down and flipped through the channels. Iselin finished in the bathroom and joined him in the living room, wearing just her shorts and a baggy T-shirt.

'Do you have a spare key?' she asked, sitting down.

Blix jumped up and went to get the spare key from the cabinet in the hallway.

'What are your plans for tomorrow?' he asked as he handed it to her.

'I was thinking of going to see Toralf.'

'Do you need help picking up more of your things from your mum's house?'

She nodded. 'But I can get Toralf to help me with that.'

'I can help a bit after work tomorrow,' Blix offered.

Iselin smiled. 'Thanks,' she said, standing up. 'I'm going to bed.'

'Goodnight, darling.'

She kissed him on the cheek and left.

Blix sat there for a while, paying no attention to what was happening on the screen, until he got up and went to bed himself.

At quarter to five, Blix was woken by a phone call. He blinked a few times, fumbled about, trying to find his phone on the nightstand, and answered it. The woman on the other end introduced herself as Ada Haugen, the operations manager for the south-eastern police district.

Blix cleared his throat. 'Okay,' he croaked.

'We have a note here that you wanted to be contacted immediately if we came across Sophus Ahlander,' the woman explained.

'That's right,' Blix said, sitting up.

'Sophus Ahlander was arrested following an incident outside Tønsberg at 01:23 this morning,' she continued.

'So you have him in custody?'

'Correct.'

'What was the reason for the arrest?'

'It's a bit complicated,' the operations manager replied. 'A recovery vehicle was called out because a woman, a journalist, had driven off the road near Sophus Ahlander's cabin.'

'A journalist?'

Blix felt an uncomfortable tightening in the pit of his stomach.

'Yes, an Emma Ramm,' the operations manager clarified. 'She works for news.no. Do you know her?'

Blix swallowed hard. 'I know who she is,' he replied. 'How is she?'

'Fine, I think,' she answered. 'She has a few grazes and some minor injuries. We took her to the emergency room. Ahlander chased her with a fire iron, and she sustained the injuries when she slipped. She got to her car and out onto the main road, but ended up skidding on the ice and driving into a ditch. It was the vehicle-recovery company who alerted us, actually. When we found out what had happened, we decided to bring Ahlander in.'

'Good,' Blix commented.

'And when we went to arrest him, we discovered some drugs at the cabin,' she continued. 'So he'll have to answer for both the drugs and the incident. Is there anything you want us to do, seeing as you asked to be notified?'

'I'll drive down to you,' Blix replied, thinking quickly about the meetings he had that day. The first was with Ruth-Kristine's parents at the hospital.

'How long can you hold him for?'

'As long as you need to get here.'

# 30

The door to Anita Grønvold's office was closed. Emma shuffled a little in the hard visitor's chair. Both her hip and arm were sore after her encounter with a ditch in Undrumsåsen the previous night.

'I'm really sorry about what happened to your car,' she said. 'I've filled out the damage report. The workshop said it should be ready in a week.'

Anita dismissed it with a wave.

'He came after me,' Emma continued. 'I thought he was going to follow me in his car as well. I panicked. The road was just sheet ice. Everything went wrong.'

'What were you doing there in the first place?' Anita enquired.

'I went on an impulse,' Emma began. 'I had a feeling that Sophus Ahlander had something to do with the Patricia case.'

'What made you think that?'

Emma raised her hand to touch the plaster above her eye, covering the place where the door had hit her. She told Anita about how she had followed Blix and Kovic, and had then gone to Undrumsåsen to find out who Sophus Ahlander was and what he knew.

'At night, in the dark, alone?'

Emma didn't try and justify what had turned out to be a complete lapse in judgment.

'But I didn't have time to say who I was or what I was there for,' she explained. 'He just charged at me. I think he thought I was someone else.'

Anita stared at her. A long, scrutinising stare.

'Do you think we should cover it?' she asked. 'It's not often that journalists are threatened in such a way.'

Emma shook her head. She wasn't interested in that kind of attention.

'We'll publish your article about Patricia anyway, and the one about Ruth-Kristine being one of the injured in the City Hall explosion,' Anita said. 'So at least we've got our bases covered if it does turn out that Ahlander is involved in some way.'

She put the papers she was holding aside, as if to say that they were finished talking about it.

'Have you slept?' she asked.

'A few hours,' Emma answered. 'I had planned on talking to Patricia's father today.'

'In jail?'

She nodded. 'I've already spoken to the prison. They were fine with it, but I'm waiting for a reply from Isaksen.'

Her phone started to ring before she could finish telling Anita about her plans.

'It's Blix,' she said, frowning. It was rare that he would call her first, and so early in the morning.

'I'm sure he'll have found out what happened by now,' Anita said, gesturing to Emma that she should answer.

Emma stood up, but didn't leave the room.

'Did I wake you?' Blix asked.

'No, no,' Emma replied. 'I'm at work.'

'I heard you had a rough night. How are you?'

'Fine ... or just about,' Emma said, feeling the plaster above her eye again.

'What happened?' Blix pressed. 'What did you talk to him about?'

'I didn't talk to him,' Emma explained. 'I didn't even get that far.'

Emma looked up and met Anita's gaze.

'Do you know if he's been questioned yet?' she asked. 'If he explained why he reacted as he did?'

'No, not yet. I'm going down to Tønsberg sometime this morning.'

Emma paced restlessly over to the other side of the room, turned around and walked back.

'How is he involved in all this?' she asked.

'He's one of the last people Ruth-Kristine Smeplass spoke to,' Blix explained.

'But what does that have to do with the investigation?' Emma asked. 'Why is it so important for you to talk to him?'

'It's just routine questioning,' Blix replied.

Something about his tone made Emma question whether he was telling the truth.

'Maybe it's all related to Patricia,' Emma suggested.

Blix remained quiet for a moment.

'She might be a part of it,' Blix conceded. 'I've got to go now. I just wanted to check in and see how you were doing.'

Emma wanted to continue the conversation, but could tell that Blix's mind was on something else.

'I'll call you this afternoon,' she said. 'After you've spoken with Ahlander. You know, it's really down to me that you have him in custody.'

There were a few seconds of silence, as if Blix were taking a moment to think about what she had said.

'Sure,' he eventually replied. 'But I can't promise that I'll have any more answers for you.'

## 31

'Any news?' Kovic asked.

She sat a fresh cup of coffee on the table in front of him and nodded at his phone, before taking a seat behind her own desk.

Blix shoved the phone back into his pocket and told her how he had been woken that morning by a phone call from the operations centre in Vestfold. How Emma had gone looking for Ahlander at his cabin.

'I'm driving down to Tønsberg after we've met with Ruth-Kristine's parents at the hospital,' he finished. 'Where are Wibe and Abelvik?'

'On their way to Nina Ballangrud's flat. They're meeting a locksmith there. Perhaps they'll end up finding her in there, dead from an overdose or something.'

Blix raised the cup to his mouth. 'Let's hope that it's not *or something*,' he said, turning to his computer screen. They had half an hour before they had to leave for the University Hospital at Ullevål. He wanted to use that time to review everything they had collected during the investigation so far, so he could give Nikolaj and Sonja Smeplass as many details and answers as possible. They were sure to have a lot of questions.

'They've found photos of the perpetrator of the bombing in Frogner Park,' Kovic said.

Blix rolled his chair over to her desk. She was looking at a map of the city centre, markers plotted across it from the various CCTV cameras that had captured footage of him.

'It's the same man we saw by the harbour,' Kovic said, clicking on a blue marker in the Majorstua district.

An image of a man walking along the pavement. He was facing away from the camera. Blix tilted his head. The man was dressed in the same clothing he had been wearing in the surveillance footage they had of him following the explosion on New Year's Eve. He was carrying a shopping bag from *Kiwi* again.

'They've started calling him the *Kiwi* man,' Kovic commented.

'The media?'

Kovic nodded.

'This is on his way to the park.'

She clicked on the red marker from the same camera.

'And this is four minutes after the bomb went off.'

It was the same man, but without the shopping bag. He was walking away, head bowed. It would be impossible to identify him from the recordings. CCTV cameras were often mounted either on a roof or so high up on a wall they couldn't be vandalised, so they were usually angled down at the ground, making it impossible to see people's faces properly.

'Same man, same type of bomb,' Kovic summarised. 'I don't see how you can still think this has something to do with Ruth-Kristine. It has to be a coincidence that she was there at the exact moment the bomb went off.'

'Maybe,' Blix conceded.

'He must come from somewhere around this area,' Kovic continued, pointing at the middle of the screen and drawing a circle.

Blix agreed. The site of the explosion in Frogner Park was about three kilometres northwest of City Hall. The circle Kovic had drawn was between the site of both bombs and was the area in which the CCTV had caught him walking before and after the explosion at the harbour. The footage they had found before and after the explosion in Frogner Park showed that he had walked to and from the exact same area.

Majorstua.

'We should survey everyone who lives in that district,' Kovic said. 'Contact all the hotels and landlords.'

'You can be the one to tell Gard Fosse and PST how to do their jobs,' Blix suggested.

Kovic smiled and suppressed a yawn.

'He might just have parked his car somewhere there, though,' Blix pointed out, pushing himself back round to his own desk.

'We have to leave in ten minutes,' Kovic reminded him.

Blix nodded. He studied the record from Ruth-Kristine's phone log, looking again at how she had repeatedly tried to contact Sophus Ahlander in the days before New Year's Eve.

'She's been to his house,' he said.

This time it was Kovic's turn to roll over to his desk. Blix pointed to the line that showed one of the last times she had tried to get hold of him, on the 30th of December. The call had gone through the phone mast next to Haslum tram station.

'Maybe that's why he went to stay at his cabin in Vestfold?' Kovic suggested, rolling back round again. 'To get away from her.'

Blix loaded the entire document the telecommunications company had sent over and looked more closely at the other data.

'I think we might have missed something,' he said.

'Like what?'

'The data we've got stops at nine o'clock in the morning of the first of January,' Blix began.

'That's when we contacted the phone company,' Kovic nodded. 'The records are saved from up to three months ago.'

'But there's activity on her phone from after midnight,' Blix said.

Kovic scooted over again. He angled the screen towards her.

'We've only been looking at her calls and texts,' he said. 'But her phone was still connected to the internet after the bomb went off. A lot of other activity has been recorded throughout the night. Data traffic, as if someone had been using the internet or were searching for something online.'

'Her phone was never found,' Kovic recalled, squinting at the column detailing which base station had been activated.

'They're all coming from Holmlia, all night,' Blix said.

'Maybe she left it in the flat?' Kovic wondered.

'But who was using it?'

Kovic shrugged. 'I don't know enough about this,' she admitted, standing up. 'We can't tell what kind of activity that is. Maybe your phone automatically downloads updates or something?'

Blix thought about it.

'We have to find that phone,' he said.

'We know it's not in her flat at least,' Kovic commented.

'We'll have to put a trace on it,' Blix concluded. 'Someone might still be using it.'

'I'll sort that,' Kovic said, pulling on the jacket that had been draped over the back of her chair. 'But now we really have to go.'

# 32

The hospital ward Ruth-Kristine was being treated on was full. Blix approached a doctor to get an update on her condition.

'She had to be put into a medically induced coma, and she's now on life support and all her vital functions are under constant observation,' the doctor explained.

'Will she survive?' Kovic asked.

'It's still too early to know for sure,' the doctor replied. 'But even if her condition does stabilise, she will most likely be in a vegetative state after coming out of the coma.'

Blix swore internally. He had hoped that he would be able to talk to her at some point.

The doctor received a message.

'Her parents have just arrived,' he announced. 'I'll talk to them in my office first.'

'Take as long as you need. We'll be in here,' Blix said, pointing towards the waiting room.

Twenty minutes later, the doctor returned with Nikolaj and Sonja Smeplass. Blix approached them with his hand outstretched. Nikolaj Smeplass took it immediately. His palm was clammy. His wife nodded at them. Her cheeks had fresh traces of tears.

Blix started to say something, but was interrupted.

'We want to see her first,' Nikolaj Smeplass said. 'We can talk afterwards.'

The doctor led them down the corridor, pushed open a door and let the parents go in first.

Blix and Kovic entered and stood just inside the room, while Nikolaj and Sonja Smeplass approached the bed cautiously, as if afraid that their movements would inflict further harm.

Ruth-Kristine Smeplass was lying under a duvet, bandaged from head to toe. Her face was almost entirely covered. The beeping from the machines surrounding her filled the room. A nurse had been standing next to the bed, but moved aside when they entered.

Sonja Smeplass's hand shot up to cover her mouth. She started crying again. Nikolaj Smeplass put an arm around her, pulled her close to him. They stood like that for several minutes. Sonja Smeplass sniffled.

'Can I...?' She cleared her throat and turned to the nurse. 'Can I hold her hand?' she asked a little clearer, but still as quiet as a whisper. 'Can I touch it?'

'Yes, but hold the left one,' the nurse answered. 'The right one is ... bandaged.'

The Smeplass couple moved over to the other side. Blix and Kovic watched their slow, careful movements. Gently, Sonja Smeplass lifted the duvet and extracted Ruth-Kristine's hand. It looked like any ordinary hand. The skin was smooth, just a little paler than normal. No wounds.

Sonja Smeplass held it tenderly. Squeezed it lightly. Stroked it. Turned it over, and let it rest in her own hand.

A sound came from somewhere deep in her throat.

'What is it?' her husband asked, as if he had noticed a change in his wife's demeanour.

'I don't know,' she answered. 'It feels strange, in a way. Smaller, thinner.'

She turned to the doctor, as if she had just realised something.

'Have you taken her ring?' she asked.

The doctor glanced at the nurse.

'That's routine procedure,' he explained.

Sonja Smeplass turned to her husband. 'The one from your mother,' she said, angling the pale hand towards him so he could see. 'She wouldn't have taken it off herself. You were happy about that, it meant that she wouldn't sell it.'

Blix felt the indent on his finger, the place where he had worn his wedding ring for years. He started to feel unsettled, an uneasiness in the pit of his stomach. Blix walked over to the bed and looked at the hand of the woman lying there. The pale fingers showed no trace of her having worn any ring.

'Could she have worn it on the other hand?' Kovic asked, noticing the same thing.

Sonja Smeplass glanced over at her daughter's other hand, which was heavily bandaged.

'No,' she replied. 'Definitely the left.'

Blix looked at the doctor and thought about the activity that had been logged on Ruth-Kristine's phone after the explosion.

'Can we ... see any other part of her?' Nikolaj Smeplass asked. 'She had surgery on her left knee when she was fourteen. She was left with a huge scar afterwards.'

The nurse turned to the doctor, who nodded in approval. He walked to the bed and lifted aside the duvet for them.

Most of the leg was bandaged, but the knee was visible.

Sonja Smeplass's hand hovered over her mouth again. Blix saw the same thing they had seen. No scar.

'This is not Ruth-Kristine,' Nikolaj Smeplass said, pointing at the person lying on the bed in front of them. 'This is not our daughter.'

# 33

'Why the hell are you only just figuring this out now?' Gard Fosse bellowed down the phone.

'The identification was based on the fact that Ruth-Kristine's bank card was found in her jacket pocket,' Blix said. 'And all the other circumstances pointed to it being her. No one has seen her since New Year's Eve. The last thing we know for sure that she did, was book a taxi into the city centre.'

'That's not enough information to have gone public with,' Fosse snarled.

Blix wanted to remind his boss that it was actually his decision to inform the media.

'Her parents have only just been able to come and see her,' he said instead. 'They live abroad.'

'Hasn't anyone else been to visit her?' Fosse raged. 'No one could have found this out before now?'

Following routine, Blix had asked the hospital staff to keep a visitor list, but he hadn't had time to look at it yet.

'Her face was wounded in the explosion,' he said. 'It's completely bandaged up.'

'We're going to look like idiots,' the police superintendent snorted. 'Releasing the wrong ID of someone on their deathbed.'

Kovic rolled her eyes. She was stood next to Blix and could hear the whole conversation.

'So who is it, then?' Fosse carried on, just as aggressively. 'Who is she?'

'We believe it might be Nina Ballangrud,' Blix said. 'Her friend.'

'You believe?!'

'We know that she was the last person Ruth-Kristine was in contact with over the phone, and she has been missing since New Year's Eve too. She was most likely the one who took the cab from Homlia and paid with Ruth-Kristine's bank card. There is every reason to believe that—'

'We're not going to *believe* anything,' Fosse interrupted.

'No, of course not,' Blix said. 'We are working on finding out who it is. Both Ruth-Kristine Smeplass and Nina Ballangrud are registered on the fingerprint database. We'll have answers in a few hours.'

Fosse took a deep breath.

'This means that Ruth-Kristine is alive then?' he continued, his voice a little calmer.

'Maybe,' Blix replied. 'Maybe not. She hasn't been heard from since New Year's Eve. It's a mystery in any case, and finding her is our top priority.'

There was a moment of silence on the other end of the line.

'Fine,' Fosse said finally. 'We must deny this publicly. Let me know the second the fingerprint analysis comes back.'

Blix walked into the hallway where Ruth-Kristine's parents were waiting. He didn't know what to say, but he tried to approach the situation as gently as possible.

Nikolaj Smeplass shook his head. 'Making us go through something like that?' he muttered. His voice was trembling. Blix could hear his indignation, but traces of relief too.

Blix apologised. It sounded flat and empty, but he had to say it, to let them know.

'We're happy to know she's alive at least,' Nikolaj Smeplass continued.

Blix glanced at Sonja. She refused to look at him.

'Do you have any idea where she might be?' he asked.

'We haven't had much contact with her in the last couple of years,' Nikolaj said.

'Why not?'

'She didn't want to. Wanted to live her own life, was what she said. We ... tried to call her every now and then, but she shut us out.'

Blix took a notebook out of his jacket. 'And she gave no explanation as to why that was?'

'No, it...' Nikolaj looked over at his wife. 'We don't really know why it turned out that way, but it was after everything that had happened with Patricia. Everything fell apart after that.'

Blix jotted down some notes.

'No friends she would visit?' he continued. 'Who might live elsewhere, outside of the city?'

They shook their heads simultaneously.

'What about her sister?' Blix asked. 'You said the other day that you didn't think they had much to do with each other. But we know Ruth-Kristine called Britt two days before Christmas. Twice, in fact.'

'Is that so?' Nikolaj replied. 'I ... I didn't know anything about that. We ... haven't spoken to Britt in the last few days.'

'You haven't?' Blix looked up from his notebook.

'No, we haven't been able to get hold of her.'

Kovic came over to them. She was putting her phone back into her jacket pocket and nodded briefly at Blix.

'We haven't had any luck getting in touch with her either,' Blix said.

He looked down at the notebook, mostly to have something to do while he thought.

'Where are you staying while you're in Norway?' Kovic asked.

'We had hoped that we could stay with Britt,' Nikolaj replied. 'She inherited the house after we moved to Spain. We're heading over there later on. But we're going to visit Sonja's sister first.'

'If Ruth-Kristine contacts you, or if you manage to get hold of her in any other way, you must let me know immediately,' said Blix. 'Either me or someone else in the police.'

The couple shared a look again.

'We will,' Nikolaj answered, nodding at Blix.

'Great. Thank you. And again, I'm so sorry.'

Ruth-Kristine's parents left the room through the sliding door. Nikolaj let Sonja go first. He placed a gentle hand on her shoulder.

'Well that was uncomfortable,' Kovic said bitterly once it was just her and Blix in the room.

Blix took a deep breath.

'Right,' he said. 'Let's see if we can find the visitor list. It might prove interesting.'

They walked back to reception. A nurse in his late twenties started searching through the papers on the desk. Blix glanced at his watch.

'Do you mind taking care of the fingerprints?' he asked. 'I have to go down to Tønsberg to talk to Ahlander.'

'Ann-Mari Sara is going to work on it,' Kovic nodded. Sara was one of the forensic technicians. 'I've already organised it with her.'

The nurse handed Blix a clipboard with a ballpoint pen attached to it.

'She hasn't had many visitors,' he said.

Blix saw that there were only three names listed – Svein-Erik Haugseth, Mona Grandre and Christina Gjerdrum. The first was her boyfriend. The others had been mentioned somewhere in passing before, two of her friends. Their arrival times showed that they had come together.

'Hm,' he muttered.

'What is it?' Kovic asked.

'Her sister hasn't been to visit.'

He looked at Kovic, and added:

'Isn't that a bit odd?'

# 34

It was much easier organising a visit to see Christer Storm Isaksen than Emma had expected. He wanted to meet with her. The prison officer who had called her back had said that it usually took three to four weeks to book a visit, but that the situation was a bit different for journalists. She was even allowed to visit outside the usual visiting hours. All she had to do was give them her social security number so they could check her criminal record.

She had never been inside a prison before, and was gripped by a sudden feeling of claustrophobia when the door to the visiting room closed behind her, and the gaunt officer left to fetch Isaksen.

The room looked as if it had been recently renovated. The furniture was new, and the walls were bare, as if no one had had the chance to hang anything on them yet.

She walked over to the window and stood there, staring into the courtyard. A few birds were up to something in one of the flower beds. She lay her hand against the glass and felt a rush of uncertainty and nervousness.

The door opened. She turned. Christer Storm Isaksen was escorted in. He looked much older, but she still recognised him from the photos she'd seen in the newspapers.

'Hi,' she said, stretching out her hand. 'Emma Ramm, from news.no. Thank you for agreeing to meet with me.' She could hear her voice shaking.

Isaksen shook her hand and stared at her. She had been face-to-face with a murderer before, but as their eyes met, she felt no fear. Just pity.

He let go. The officer instructed her on how to use the intercom for when the meeting was over. And then they were left alone.

'Shall we sit?' Emma suggested.

Isaksen nodded and took a seat.

'Why are you here?' he asked.

It dawned on Emma that Isaksen probably didn't have access to the internet so wouldn't have read the article she had published about Patricia and Ruth-Kristine. She was prepared for the question, nevertheless.

'I'd like to talk to you about your daughter,' she said. 'And Ruth-Kristine. I don't know whether you've heard that—'

'I know about the explosion,' he interrupted. 'Is that the only reason you've come?'

'I would like to talk to you a bit about ... everything that happened to you,' Emma said. 'It could be related to what's going on now.'

'Have you heard something about Patricia?' Isaksen pressed. 'Something new?'

Emma shook her head. 'Unfortunately not,' she answered. 'But what happened to Ruth-Kristine on New Year's Eve may have triggered some movements in the case. I'd like to talk to you about it.'

Isaksen looked disappointed. Like he had been hoping for something. He opened his mouth and began a new approach:

'You haven't...?' he began, but it seemed as if he changed his mind. 'Who have you spoken to, before coming here?' he asked instead.

'I've spoken to Alexander Blix,' Emma replied.

His eyes flashed. 'What did he say?'

'Blix doesn't say much,' Emma smiled.

'Did you talk about the photo?'

Emma tilted her head. 'What photo?'

Isaksen shook his head. 'Forget it,' he said. 'Who else have you spoken to?'

'Just my boss, Anita Grønvold. She wrote a lot about the investigation, at the time. What happened to your daughter, it consumed her. She was obsessed, and the more I work on this case, the more I get sucked into it too. If I can help in any way, to find out what happened, I'll do it.'

The room was silent. Distant shouts came from somewhere above them. The sound of a metal door slamming shut.

'Someone out there has to know something,' Emma continued,

gesturing towards the window. 'Your story could make them come forward. To get in touch, to help you.'

Isaksen leant back in his chair, took a long, deep breath and slowly released it again.

'Sure,' he said. 'Let's talk.'

# 35

Tønsberg Police Station was located in the town centre. One of the local investigators, who introduced himself as Jan Olimb, met Blix at the entrance.

'Ahlander has admitted to everything,' he said, giving Blix a copy of the case file.

Blix flipped through them.

'What did he have to say?' he replied.

'That he mistook the journalist for someone else.'

'Who?'

'He wouldn't say, other than that he thought she was a woman with some issues who had been bothering him for a while.'

Blix nodded, thinking of Ruth-Kristine.

'On top of that, he admitted to being in possession of and using hash,' Olimb continued. 'So we're all done and ready to release him, but I understand that you wanted to talk to him first?'

'I would like to see the cabin first actually,' Blix answered. 'Do you have the keys?'

'I can find them,' Olimb replied. 'But if we're going to keep him here any longer, you'll have to tell the police prosecutor what you suspect him of.'

Blix met his gaze. 'I'm working on the investigation into the bombings,' he explained, examining the investigator to see his reaction.

'Is Sophus Ahlander involved?' he asked.

'That's what I'm trying to figure out.'

'The journalist said that she had approached him about something connected to an old missing-persons case,' Olimb said. 'But she was reluctant to answer as well.'

'Several cases seem to have become intertwined,' Blix said, looking down at his watch and noticing how little time he had.

The investigator disappeared inside the station and returned with a clear plastic bag holding two sets of keys.

'I'll go with you,' he said, passing the bags to Blix. 'The other keys are for his house in Bærum. You might want to have a look round there too?'

Blix thanked him. He had hoped to look through the cabin alone, but couldn't decline Olimb's offer.

They took Blix's car, with Jan Olimb giving him directions all the way to the cabin. A red sign on the brown cabin wall welcomed them in large, ornate letters.

The keys to the front door were attached to a keyring with a Mercedes pendant. The lock was stiff, as if the cabin hadn't been used that often.

Blix entered first, walking through the small hallway and into a living room that had a white fireplace and a half-full log basket next to it. Empty beer bottles and a plateful of food had been left on the creased, mint-green tablecloth covering the dining table. There was a sofa, two armchairs and a leather foot stool. Old newspapers and magazines were stacked up on the table next to the armchair.

'What are you looking for?' Jan Olimb asked.

Blix didn't answer, and carried on, heading further into the cabin. What he was looking for, was anything that could prove that Patricia had been there. There were two small bedrooms with bunk beds. Blix lifted the mattresses, looked in the cupboards, finding nothing of interest.

A small bathroom with a toilet, walk-in shower and a sink. The cabinet next to the sink contained a few toiletries. A mop and bucket were tucked away in a larger cabinet in the far corner of the room.

The kitchen was small and cramped. It had an old stove, a dark-blue counter and shelves upon shelves of canned food, visible behind the panes of glass.

There was a staircase that led from the kitchen up to the loft. Blix climbed up. There were four beds – with duvets, pillows and mattresses but no covers. The layer of dust on the floor indicated that there hadn't been anyone there for a while.

Blix went back downstairs and into the smallest bedroom. If Patricia had been there, it would most likely have been this room that they kept her in.

He found a strand of hair on the pillow and wondered if he should bag it up and take it with him, but he let it go. Instead, he lifted up the mattress and shifted the panels aside to look underneath.

'What exactly are you looking for?' Jan Olimb asked again.

Blix studied him. The other investigator was quite a few years younger than he was, but seemed experienced and had a jovial manner that radiated confidence.

'I'm wondering if a child has been here,' he answered.

'A child?' Olimb repeated.

Blix put the mattress down again. 'Patricia Storm Isaksen,' he explained.

'Bloody hell,' the other investigator exclaimed. 'I read an article online about that earlier. Her mother was injured in the explosion. They aren't sure whether she'll survive.'

Blix hadn't read the article himself, but he presumed it was Emma's piece that news.no had released.

He chose not to elaborate on how thin the basis for his suspicions of Ahlander was, or the extent to which he believed Ahlander was involved in the bombing.

'Patricia was in a pushchair when she was kidnapped,' he explained instead. 'The blanket she was covered with was white on one side and pink on the other. It had an elephant with big ears and a long trunk on both sides. A pink elephant on the white side, vice versa on the other. The same on the pillow. There was a white, crocheted blanket in there as well, and a toy chain with colourful shapes that had been clipped on to either side of the canopy.'

Jan Olimb pulled out a small torch from a clip on his belt.

'I'll search in the other room,' he said.

'Great. She was wearing white tights, a bodysuit and a Winnie-the-Pooh jumper,' Blix continued, now reading from the report he'd just pulled from his jacket pocket. 'There was a baby-changing bag, a grey one, attached to the pushchair's handle. It contained a bottle, a few dummies, antiseptic cream, sachets of baby porridge, flannels, nappies and some wet wipes,' he concluded. 'Things like that. It was ten years ago, but the cabin doesn't look like it's been used that much.'

They worked in silence. Searched every room, every cupboard and every drawer. Blix was just starting to take all the pots out of the cupboard under the kitchen counter when the local investigator shouted to him from inside the bathroom.

Blix stopped and stood in the doorway. Jan Olimb was sitting back on his heels, kneeling in the middle of the floor.

'Under the cabinet,' he explained, pointing with his torch.

The cabinet was raised on four legs, about ten centimetres from the floor.

'What is it?' Blix asked.

Olimb didn't respond, but made room for him and passed him the torch.

Blix kneeled down. He leant forwards, bowed his head and aimed the light.

Dust and old bits of fluff had gathered in the space underneath, but tucked into the far corner was a pink dummy with a picture of a teddy bear on it.

Blix could feel his heart rate increasing. His mouth was dry, and he was starting to feel dizzy.

'I didn't want to touch it,' Olimb said in a low voice.

'Smart choice,' Blix replied.

He grabbed his phone and took a few photos. He got up, walked back to the doorway and took some more photos of the entire room. He envisioned a child, crying. She had probably spat out her dummy. Imagined how it had landed on the floor and rolled under the cabinet. It could have been there for the last ten years.

Jan Olimb had found a pair of latex gloves and an evidence bag.

'You do it,' he said, passing the equipment to Blix.

Blix pulled the gloves on, lay down on the floor and fished out the dummy.

'Do you think there might be DNA on it?' Olimb asked.

'I don't know,' Blix said, almost whispering. 'But you can bet on your life that I'm going to find out.'

## 36

Christer Storm Isaksen spun the two glasses on the table to face him and filled them with water from a plastic jug.

'What kind of movements do you mean?' he asked, repeating what she had said: 'movements in the case'.

Emma searched for a way to explain the very little she actually knew about it.

'I understand that you believe Ruth-Kristine was involved in the kidnapping,' she began. 'That she had an accomplice, who in turn was helped by Knut Ivar Skage, who looked after Patricia.'

Isaksen took a sip from his glass.

'The police searched for the accomplice,' Emma continued. 'There had to have been a man who Ruth-Kristine knew, and who had no experience dealing with children.'

He gave her a quick nod.

'They couldn't find anyone who matched the profile at the time, but perhaps it would be possible to find him now.'

'How so?' he asked.

'They may have resumed contact,' Emma suggested. 'What happened to Ruth-Kristine on New Year's Eve has now prompted the police to look into her again.'

'The police were here,' Isaksen said. 'Blix. He didn't say anything about that.'

'Have you heard the name Sophus Ahlander before?' Emma asked. 'Was he mentioned at all around the time Patricia disappeared?'

Isaksen shook his head. 'I would have remembered. Who is he?'

'One of the last people Ruth-Kristine spoke to the day before the explosion,' Emma explained. 'He fits the profile. No children. And no siblings with any children either.'

Isaksen sat, holding the glass of water in his lap.

'Interesting,' he said.

'The police have him in custody,' Emma continued.

Isaksen's eyes widened, and Emma had to tell him about what happened to her when she tried to get in touch with Ahlander.

'What is your opinion now, all these years later?' she asked. 'Are you still convinced that Ruth-Kristine had something to do with it?'

It was as if something had awoken within the man. An anger that, although not directed at her, she could feel radiating off him from the other side of the table.

'I said it from the start,' he said. 'She was furious with me when she wasn't granted custody, and for only being allowed to see Patricia under supervision. It was degrading, she said, and I can understand that, of course. But her temper...' He shook his head. 'It scared me, a few times. And even though I don't think it really meant all that much to her to be a mother, it was definitely important to her that I wasn't allowed to be a father.'

'She wanted revenge, you mean?'

'Something like that, yes.'

'But what do you think happened that day?' Emma continued. 'What happened to your daughter?'

Isaksen traced his finger thoughtfully around the rim of the glass.

'I think she sold her,' he said finally. 'It happens. It sounds absurd, but I've read a lot about it. Ruth-Kristine never had money.'

Emma put her glass down, pulled out a pen and notebook.

'But don't those kind of things take a lot to pull off?'

'What do you mean?'

'I mean, to sell a child. I wouldn't even know where to start.'

'Ruth-Kristine was involved with the wrong kind of people,' Isaksen said with a sigh. 'So I have no doubt that she knew someone who knew someone who could get the ball rolling. Human trafficking is big business. It's not that difficult to imagine that it happens in Norway too. Or that Ruth-Kristine got someone to take her out of the country, or ... that something went wrong, and she's buried somewhere.'

'But wasn't Ruth-Kristine involved in the search for your daughter, those first few weeks after her disappearance?'

'Oh yeah,' Isaksen said, with a bitter smile. 'She was. But she was smart, and if she wanted to get away with whatever she had done, she didn't have any other choice. Of course she had to help. Cry on TV, cry in front of the journalists. Sleep as little as possible, so she could look as devastated as possible.'

'You think it was an act.'

'I *know* it was an act.'

'What about the neighbour who was with Ruth-Kristine on the day Patricia was kidnapped?' Emma continued. 'Jette Djurholm. Do you think she was part of the act as well?'

Christer shrugged. 'I don't know much about her,' he said. 'I never met her. But I do know that Ruth-Kristine was good at manipulating people. Djurholm was probably just a pawn to her, like everyone else.'

Emma nodded.

'How did you and Ruth-Kristine meet in the first place?' she asked carefully. 'If you don't mind me asking.'

Isaksen looked as if he were reminiscing.

'I ... was drinking a lot in those days. I don't even remember where I met Ruth-Kristine, but it was at some bar or some party in Oslo. She came home with me. I sent her off in a taxi a few hours later. Didn't think anything more of it, until she turned up at my door just over three months later, telling me she was pregnant.'

'And she was sure that you were the father?'

'Yes,' he said with a smile. 'But I insisted on making sure. She was right, I *was* the father. And it ... changed my life. I didn't want the child to grow up without a father, so ... Ruth-Kristine and I, we tried to make it work. We made an honest attempt, but it didn't take long to realise that we were miles apart on ... too many things. She wasn't completely clean, but I only realised that later on. She was always tired. Depressed. I caught her drinking, for one thing, and smoking. You shouldn't do that when you're pregnant.'

Isaksen raised the glass to his mouth, looking as if he were deep in thought.

'So we were on a collision course from day one,' he said, instead of taking a drink from the glass. 'And it eventually resulted in this sense-less battle about custody and everything else under the sun. I'm not proud of what happened back then, but I just thought it wasn't good for Patricia to have someone like Ruth-Kristine in her life on a daily basis. It could've been disastrous. And,' he added. 'It was.'

Emma wrote down a few brief notes, then tried to lead the conversation to the night Isaksen had become a killer. Once there, she let him tell the story as it came to him.

'I had promised a reward,' he explained. 'The police had advised me not to. They said it would just coax out the liars and impostors, and that it wouldn't contribute anything to the investigation other than delays and distractions. But nothing else had worked, so I promised a hundred thousand kroner to anyone who had any information. It was a small amount, if we're talking about the value of Patricia's life, but it was a balanced amount too, as Blix called it.'

Isaksen drained the glass before continuing.

'When I met Skage, he wanted more. We argued. I'd had an uneasy feeling about the whole situation, and had taken a knife ... So, yeah...' He looked away, around the room. 'You know what happened.'

He cleared his throat before the silence settled between them.

'But he knew something,' he added after a long pause. 'He knew who took her, he just wouldn't say it.'

Emma nodded. She asked a couple more questions and got some extra details about the sequence of events, as well as Isaksen's own reflections on everything that had happened. The story that was beginning to take shape was personal, captivating.

They went on to talk about the trial, the prison sentence itself, his doubt and feelings of helplessness. About the time he had had with his daughter, how he missed her, and the grief.

'When are you out?' she asked to round off the interview.

'August.'

'Have you thought about what you will do?'

There was a moment of silence.

'You mean with work, that kind of thing?'

Emma nodded.

'No, not yet,' he said. 'It depends on what happens.'

'What do you mean?'

'With Patricia,' Isaksen clarified. 'If they find her. If not, I'll have to look for her myself.'

Emma put the pen down. She had got exactly what she had wanted. At the same time, however, she felt as if he were keeping something back.

# 37

Via the screen on the wall, Blix watched as Sophus Ahlander was led into the interview room. His lawyer was already sat in there waiting for him. Ahlander threw his arms out and shook his head. There was no audio transmission, so Blix couldn't hear the exchange between them, but it was clear that the atmosphere in the room was tense.

Blix was just preparing to head in himself when his phone rang. It was Kovic.

'The results for the fingerprint analysis have come back. It is Nina Ballangrud,' she said. '*She* was the one who was injured in the explosion.'

Blix wasn't surprised.

'What about Ruth-Kristine's phone?' he asked. 'Have you started tracking it?'

'Yes. It looks like it's gone completely offline. The last time any data was recorded on it was on the first of January at 09:43. There haven't been any other calls or texts since New Year's Eve.'

'Is it still being traced?' Blix enquired.

'We'll be notified whenever it's used again,' Kovic confirmed.

'Good.'

'What's going on in Vestfold?'

Blix glanced up at the screen. Ahlander had sat down. The lawyer was looking at his watch.

'I'm using one of the interview rooms here,' he said, proceeding to tell her about the dummy they had found during their preliminary search of the cabin.

'One of the officers is on their way to you with it now. I want Ann-Mari Sara to take it when it gets there. She needs to get the lab to put everything else on hold. I have to know if Patricia's DNA is on it.'

There was a knock on the door. Jan Olimb appeared.

'They're ready,' he said with a nod towards the screen.

Blix ended the conversation with Kovic.

'Me too,' he replied, tucking the phone back into his pocket.

He entered the narrow interview room and introduced himself. The lawyer representing Ahlander was Vidar Rødland; he'd travelled down from Oslo.

'My client has already given a full confession,' he said. 'Although it could be deemed as a case of negligence, he has nonetheless pleaded guilty to causing bodily harm by opening the door too forcefully, such that the journalist was hit in the face, and to his subsequent threatening behaviour. He has also pleaded guilty to drug use and possession. I don't know what else you could want. There's nothing in the documents I've been sent that would suggest there are any grounds for keeping him here this long.'

'I have a few unanswered questions,' Blix said.

The lawyer crossed one leg over the other and looked at Ahlander. Ahlander shrugged.

'Let's get this over with,' the lawyer said, nodding at Blix. 'But let me remind you that this Emma Ramm did not at any time or in any way make it known that she was a journalist.'

'No, she didn't get the chance to.'

'She should have called first and organised a meeting, instead of approaching my client in such an inappropriate way.'

'How long have you had the cabin?' Blix said, unperturbed, turning to face Ahlander.

'What do you mean?' he asked. He sounded irritated.

'You inherited it from your mother after she died last summer, right?' Blix continued.

'Yes, that's right. Dad bought it in the eighties.'

Blix leafed through his papers. 'In 1983?'

'Yes,' Ahlander nodded. 'He died fifteen years ago.'

'Have you spent a lot of time there?'

Ahlander shook his head. 'No, there's nothing there,' he replied. 'No ski slopes or anything. There are a couple of lakes for fishing nearby. Dad loved that kind of thing. Being out in nature. Not for me. And Mum's legs got so bad that there wasn't anything she could do there either. Most of the time, it was just Dad up there by himself.'

'So how many times would you say you've been to the cabin since your father died in 2004?' Blix asked.

Ahlander shrugged, the corners of his mouth turning down into a frown. 'I've no idea,' he said. 'Once a year, maybe. Why?'

Blix didn't answer him. This initial conversation was just to ensure that Ahlander couldn't construct a plausible excuse later on as to how the dummy had ended up at the cabin.

'Who has keys to the cabin?' he carried on.

'Me.'

'Just you?'

'Yes. There are two keys. I have both.'

'Has the cabin ever been loaned or rented out to anyone?'

'No?'

'Have you ever taken any friends, acquaintances or anyone else there?'

'I guess so. A few friends.'

'Have there ever been any trespassers? Break-ins, that kind of thing?'

Sophus Ahlander shrugged again, looking like he was unsure of where the conversation was going. 'No...' he answered.

Blix took a few notes, and checked to make sure that the red light was on, that the interview was being recorded.

'Have there ever been any children at the cabin?' he asked.

He watched the man sat on the opposite side of the table, saw how the question triggered a physical reaction in him. He stiffened, eyes darted up to look directly at Blix.

'No,' he replied, swallowing. 'Not that I know of.'

The lawyer glanced over at his client. He looked as if he wanted to interrupt, but didn't.

'Not even when your father was there?' Blix continued.

'I don't know about that. I was just a kid when he bought it.'

Blix checked his papers. 'You were twelve?'

'Yes.'

'Could your father have had any other children with him at the cabin?'

Ahlander thought about it, but shook his head: he couldn't think of anyone.

The lawyer leant forwards. 'What is this about, exactly?' he asked.

His expression was cautious. Blix imagined that he was probably speculating about a case of paedophilia.

'Right then,' he said, ignoring the lawyer's question. He flipped a page of his notebook over, as if to signal a change in topic, then leant over the table slightly.

'Did you think it was Ruth-Kristine looking for you last night?' he asked.

A few beads of sweat had appeared on Ahlander's upper lip. He opened his mouth, but closed it again without answering.

'Who is Ruth-Kristine?' the lawyer asked.

'Ruth-Kristine Smeplass,' Blix said, without taking his eyes off Ahlander. 'How do you know her?'

'She's just a friend,' Ahlander replied without looking up. 'From a long time ago—'

The lawyer cut him off, looking like he'd suddenly realised something. 'Is this to do with the Patricia case?'

'First and foremost, this is to do with Ruth-Kristine Smeplass,' Blix answered. 'She's been missing since New Year's Eve.'

The lawyer snorted. 'What are you talking about?' he asked. 'She was injured in the first explosion. I read about it a few hours ago. That same journalist had written about it. Emma Ramm.'

'You can't believe everything you read,' Blix commented. Then addressed Ahlander again. 'You were one of the last people she spoke to on the phone,' he said. 'Altogether, a total of twenty-one calls were recorded, but you only picked up twice. Once on the twenty-ninth of December, at 17:02. A conversation that lasted for four minutes and thirty-four seconds.'

Ahlander stared down at the floor.

'What did you talk about?' Blix pressed.

The lawyer stood up. 'We're done,' he said.

'And why is that?' Blix asked.

'This interview has taken a direction that involves matters that do not relate to the case my client has been charged with,' the lawyer answered. 'This all sounds like some sort of conspiracy, especially considering the person involved in the first case against Ahlander is the journalist publishing false information about this other case.'

Blix looked over at Ahlander. He wanted to continue questioning him, to ask how he had known Knut Ivar Skage, but knew that he had pushed him as far as he could this time.

'We're going to expand your charges and transfer you to Oslo,' Blix said.

'For what?' the lawyer challenged.

'For the kidnapping and false imprisonment of Patricia Storm Isaksen.'

# 38

Kalle's Choice was packed, even on the first floor, where Emma's usual table was. She still managed to find a free spot, a little further inside the café than where she liked, and once she sat down, took a sip of the latte she had just bought. With the help of her earphones and some music, she managed to shut out the noise of the room around her.

The visit to Oslo Prison and the conversation she had shared with Christer Storm Isaksen had made a lasting impression on her. Isaksen gave off an aura of grief and despair, even all these years later. She had a clear plan in mind as to how she would construct his story, but it would have to wait.

She browsed through the search history on her phone and found the article about Ruth-Kristine and her neighbour, Jette Djurholm. Emma wanted to talk to Jette. Ten years on, she may see things differently. Perhaps she had changed her perspective, about everything that happened back then.

She couldn't find a phone number for her, though, and tried googling the name instead, only to be met with the same news articles she had read earlier. However, a quick search through the Danish yellow pages told her that there was a Jette Djurholm who lived in Horsens.

Emma called the number. She let it ring for a while, before sighing and hanging up.

She saved the number. It was three minutes to three. She could call Blix.

He surprised her by picking up immediately. Emma could hear that he was in a car.

'I've spoken to Patricia's father,' she said, hearing the pride in her voice, in the fact that she had actually managed to pull it off.

'In prison?' Blix asked.

'Yes,' Emma said. 'He told me everything.'

'Everything?' She thought she sensed an uneasiness in his voice, as if he were afraid that Isaksen had said too much, or had mentioned something he shouldn't have.

'You can read about it,' she said, instead of pushing the matter any further. 'What did Ahlander say?'

'He confessed to the bodily harm and threatening behaviour charges,' Blix said. 'You can apply for compensation for what happened.'

'I was thinking more about Ruth-Kristine,' Emma said. 'What did he say about her?'

Other than the sound of the passing traffic in the background, the line was completely silent. As if Blix was working out what to say.

'Are you there?' Emma asked, pushing for an answer.

'There's been a development...' Blix began, only to hesitate again.

'What is it?'

'The woman in the hospital is not Ruth-Kristine Smeplass.'

Emma had been absentmindedly fumbling with the cable attached to her earphones, and now she accidentally pulled one of them out.

'What did you say?' she had to ask, shoving it back into her ear again.

'The injured woman, it's not Ruth-Kristine,' Blix repeated.

'But...' Emma began, not sure where to even start.

'It is true that the woman we rescued from the harbour after the explosion was registered at the hospital as Ruth-Kristine Smeplass,' Blix continued. 'I don't know how you got the name, but it's wrong.'

Emma thought of her sister, who had tracked it down for her.

'But ... we've been talking about Ruth-Kristine this whole time,' Emma protested. 'Gard Fosse confirmed that it was her. I've just written an entire article based on her. Other media outlets have picked it up.'

'We also had reason to believe that it was Ruth-Kristine,' Blix said, adding that Fosse would be sending out a press release later that day.

Emma lay her free hand on her forehead, trying to gather her thoughts. She could try and get ahead of the police, but would need some solid facts to get an article together first, so that the mishap couldn't be traced back to her and news.no.

'Who is it then?' she asked.

Blix paused again.

'Come on,' she pleaded. 'I have to be able to clear this mess up.'

'A friend of Ruth-Kristine's,' he replied. 'Nina Ballangrud.'

'You're sure of that?'

'Yes.'

'But how could this happen?'

'They're saying it was a misunderstanding and then a series of unfortunate circumstances.'

Emma noted that down. She could make it look like it was a mistake the police had made. It *was* their mistake.

'What sort of circumstances?' she asked.

'I can't go into detail,' Blix replied.

'How did you find out about the error?' she continued.

'You've got all the details I can give you,' Blix said. 'More than that, actually.'

Emma thanked him.

'But you didn't hear any of this from me,' Blix added. 'You will have to get confirmation from the lead investigator.'

'Sure,' Emma said. 'But can you tell me where Ruth-Kristine Smeplass is now then?'

'We don't know either,' Blix answered. 'She's been missing since New Year's Eve.'

Emma's eyebrows furrowed. 'What do you mean? Missing how?'

'I have to go,' Blix said. 'You'll need to talk to Fosse.'

He hung up.

Emma felt restless, now that there seemed to be some movement in the case. She wanted Blix to tell her more about Ahlander, to ask him what kind of impression he'd had of Jette Djurholm, those times he had questioned her.

She sat, still wearing her earphones, unsure of who to call first.

Anita Grønvold or Gard Fosse. She called the police superintendent, feigning a relaxed tone.

'I'm meeting with Ruth-Kristine Smeplass's parents in a bit,' she began. 'And I wondered if there were any new developments in the case, anything I should know before I see them?'

It was just on the verge of being a complete and utter lie. She intended to meet the parents, of course, but the way she had phrased it had made it seem as if the meeting were imminent.

There was a grunt on the other end of the line. 'Have they not said anything?' Fosse asked.

'Who? The parents? About what?'

She heard Fosse release a long sigh. 'We are in the process of organising a press briefing in which we will be withdrawing the information about the identity of one of the injured,' he said.

Emma feigned surprise, and then teased out of him the same information Blix had given her a moment earlier. And then she pretended to be annoyed.

'I have already written a comprehensive article based on the information I received from you yesterday,' she said.

'We had the same information as the hospital, and had every reason to believe it was correct,' he added in what seemed like an attempt to divert the blame.

'So you're apologising?' Emma replied.

'Absolutely,' Fosse confirmed.

Emma noted: *The police apologise.*

'Will you be saying that the police made a mistake?'

Fosse didn't take the bait. 'We'll be going through everything and will evaluate what happened,' he said instead. 'And then we'll learn from it.'

Emma thanked him for the conversation, took her earphones out and raised the cup to her lips. The coffee was cold. She put it down, opened up her laptop and hammered out just over a thousand characters, the word 'scandal' taking precedence at the top of the page. She sent the article over to Anita and called her immediately after.

'Read my article,' she said without an explanation. 'I've just sent it over.'

'Jesus Christ,' Anita exclaimed, obviously already making her way through it.

'We should publish it before the press release,' Emma said.

'I'm on it,' Anita answered.

'What are we going to do about the article we published this morning?' Emma asked. 'The one where we named Ruth-Kristine? It's completely out of context now that she's not one of the victims.'

'What do you think?'

Emma bit her bottom lip.

'I think we should retract it,' she replied. 'But then I can write a new article about her mysterious disappearance. That way I can include some of the information from my meeting with Christer Storm Isaksen too.'

'Good plan,' Anita said. 'Maybe you can try and get a new statement from her parents as well.'

# 39

Amy Linh stopped outside 620. No glasses, plates or cutlery had been left outside this time. The *Do Not Disturb* sign was still hanging on the door handle.

She knocked anyway, tentatively. It had been four days since she had last been in there. He could be sick, or something could have happened.

There was no response.

She knocked again, a little harder than before.

'Housekeeping,' she added resolutely, pressing her ear to the door.

No answer. The TV, on the other hand, was still on. Someone was talking. Dramatic music.

Four days in a row. Without wanting to be disturbed.

Amy Linh knocked again, trying one more time.

'Housekeeping!'

Still nothing. She thought about it for a few seconds, before pulling out her key card and unlocking the door.

'Hello?' she said, opening the door. 'Housekeeping.'

She took a hesitant step inside. 620 was one of the nicest rooms on this floor. In the entire hotel, in fact. It was actually a suite. She stood in the hallway. No shoes on the floor, no jacket hanging on the hook. No one was in. There was a briefcase on the floor next to the umbrella stand, but that was it. She wasn't disturbing anyone.

The hallway led into a larger room with a sofa, dining table and desk.

The TV she could hear from the hallway was in the bedroom. She announced her presence again and continued further into the suite. The bathroom door was closed. She decided to check the bedroom first. Amy Linh could feel her heart rate rising; still no one had replied. She had heard stories about housekeepers who had found dead bodies. She hoped for the love of God that wouldn't happen to her. The thought made her feel guilty at first. It would, of course, be terrible for the person who had died, and his loved ones. But still.

She walked forwards tentatively, her shoes making a distinct clacking sound against the dark-brown parquet floor. She peeked into the bedroom. An unmade bed, a duvet that had been cast aside, as if the guest had only just gotten up. One of the pillows was on the floor. The other three pillows were still on the bed, one of them at the foot end. A suitcase was propped up against the wall. One of the wardrobe doors was open.

There was no one there.

She wanted to turn the TV off, but left it as it was. The sound was actually welcome company for the torrent of thoughts charging through her head.

Where was he?

Amy Linh walked back into the living room. The bin next to the desk was filled to the brim. Some of the contents had overflowed onto the floor. There were two bags propped up against it. One of the towels from the bathroom had been left scrunched up on the desk.

She moved closer. Lifted the towel slightly. There was a mortar underneath. The pestle was lying on the surface beside it. Residue of some kind of powder on both. Some of it was on the desk too.

She lifted the mortar to her nose and sniffed, but didn't recognise the smell.

She picked up one of the bags from the floor and peered inside. A reel of wires and a small container with a diesel label on the side. A pair of black rubber gloves were folded up on the desk chair.

She was gripped with the sudden feeling that she shouldn't be there. That she should get out immediately. She turned around, but stopped abruptly.

A sound from the door. The electric buzz of the lock.

It opened.

A man stepped inside and was in the process of taking off his scarf, before he came to a halt, realising she was there.

'Hi,' she said quickly, trying to smile. 'Housekeeping.'

She looked down at the bag still in her hands. Put it down hastily. The man stood in the hallway, his eyes searching the room behind her. Amy Linh lowered her gaze. Stared at his boots instead. Beige leather with bright-blue shoelaces. They were muddy, and had probably soiled the carpet in the corridor.

'Do you need anything?' she asked, realising as she did that her voice was trembling. 'Fresh towels?'

The man shook his head slowly. Amy Linh tried to smile, but couldn't force her face to do it. He just stared at her. Dead eyes. Expressionless.

'In that case,' she said, noticing that her voice was really shaking now. 'I'll carry on.'

She walked past him. Through the hallway. Into the corridor. It was only once she had closed the door behind her, that she realised she needed to breathe.

# 40

The traffic on the motorway came to a standstill as Blix approached Oslo. He turned off at Bygdøylokket and made his way through the back streets. As always during the afternoon rush hour, the screen on his phone lit up continually with notifications warning him of the chaos on the roads.

With the traffic moving so slowly, he pulled out his phone and dialled Iselin's number.

'Hi, Dad,' she answered, picking up straight away. 'Are you at work?'

'Yes,' he said. 'I won't be home for a while yet.'

'That's fine. I enjoy my own company.'

'Did you get any sleep last night?'

'I slept like a rock,' she replied. 'I might go for a walk in a bit. Is it safe to go into the city centre?'

'What do you mean?'

'Just thinking about the rogue bomber.'

Blix took a moment, thinking about how he could answer her.

'There's no reason for you to worry,' he said, hearing just how stupid that sounded. 'That's what he wants.'

*Maybe*, he wanted to add. They were still struggling to work out his motives, or even to decide whether there was more than just one perpetrator.

'Let me know where you're going though,' he said.

'Dad,' Iselin replied, accusingly. 'You never asked me to do that when I was living with Mum.'

Merete, he thought suddenly. He had planned on calling her today, but it had completely slipped his mind.

'It's different when you're living with me,' he answered. 'You're my responsibility now.'

'I'll send you a text when I figure out where I'm going,' she said. 'And I promise I'll be home before the kids' programmes start.'

Her teasing made him smile.

'I've got to get back to work, my darling. See you later.'

'See you.'

As soon as he hung up, he called Kovic and asked her to gather their small investigative team for a meeting.

Upon arrival on the sixth floor of police HQ, he found them waiting for him at the large conference table. He had asked Ann-Mari Sara from forensics to join them too, and she was now sat there with Kovic, Wibe and Abelvik. Blix had also requested that the police prosecutor, Pia Nøkleby, attend. Gard Fosse had not been invited, but he'd taken a seat at the end of the table regardless.

Blix quickly brought them up to speed on what had happened in Vestfold, and why he now believed that it was Sophus Ahlander who had kidnapped Patricia.

'The link to Skage seems solid,' he said, taking a sip from his coffee cup. 'I've found the notifications of sale for a total of six cars that had been exchanged between them in the years leading up to Patricia's kidnapping. These two probably knew each other quite well. Ahlander also confirmed that he used to be friendly with Ruth-Kristine too. The question is, just how long ago was that? We had kept an eye on Ruth-Kristine's social circle at that time, in the hopes of identifying anyone she knew who fit the criteria – who could be a potential suspect. But we never came across Ahlander. We need to do things differently this time. Focus on Ahlander's social circle, and see where Ruth-Kristine fits in.'

The police prosecutor straightened up. 'The Patricia case has officially been reopened,' she began. 'I have started the process of pressing charges against Sophus Ahlander, but we need more information before we can proceed.'

Blix nodded. If they couldn't find any DNA on the dummy, they risked having to let him go.

'So you're saying that dummy has been under a cabinet for the last ten years?' The objection came from Wibe.

'I agree that it sounds far-fetched,' Blix said. 'But I also know how easily things can get lost in a household with young children. It's not all that rare to find things again much later, often in the strangest places. Beneath cabinets you rarely ever clean under, for example. Or at least not in my house, anyway.'

Wibe held up two hands, as if admitting that he wasn't any better at cleaning either.

'We received the dummy just before two o'clock,' Sara reported. 'I've spoken to one of the senior forensic techs. She was optimistic. They may have preliminary results for us sometime tomorrow morning.'

Kovic leant forwards. 'I've submitted a request for a copy of his phone records,' she said.

'Good. We need to find out who he's spoken to recently, besides Ruth-Kristine Smeplass.'

'I'm still waiting on the data from Nina Ballangrud's phone, although that's not exactly relevant anymore,' Kovic continued. 'But we'll probably have that by tomorrow.'

Blix took notes.

'We've searched her flat,' Wibe said. 'We didn't find anything that looked like it could be connected to the case.'

'What about Ruth-Kristine's flat?' Blix asked. 'Have you checked there again too?'

Abelvik nodded. 'Nothing there, either,' she said. 'We've also gone round and interviewed some of her friends, including Mona Grandre and Christina Gjerdrum, the ones who were on the visitor list. They'd been told what had happened by Haugseth, her boyfriend, and had gone to visit her, but they hadn't been allowed in.'

'Did they say anything?' asked Blix. 'Or know anything?'

'Nothing specifically related to the case, but both of them, as well as the others we spoke to, mentioned her mental-health problems and long-term drug addiction. She was generally described as a woman who had never really had her life in order.'

'Did any of them have anything to say about Patricia?'

'Nothing other than the fact she never spoke about her. She resented it when people brought it up.'

Blix's phone started to ring. It was a number he had saved, but without a name. He let it ring out.

'We went to see her boyfriend again,' Wibe continued once Blix's phone had gone silent. 'He insists that he hasn't heard anything from Ruth-Kristine, and he reassured us that he would let us know if he does hear from her.'

Gard Fosse had been sitting quietly at the end of the table.

'Good,' he said, clearing his throat. 'This is certainly interesting, but there is still a lot of dust that needs clearing up from the wake of the bombings. They need more people. There is a limit to how much time you can carry on with this for. We need clarification.'

The police prosecutor agreed. 'We have to make a decision on whether we'll be taking Ahlander into police custody within the next twenty-four hours,' she said. 'When can we expect the next interview?'

'Tomorrow,' Blix replied. 'As soon as I get the results for the dummy. If they find Patricia's DNA on it, it won't be a problem getting him into custody.'

Kovic's phone began to ring as well. She had placed it on the table in front of her. Blix saw the number on the screen. It looked like the same person who had tried calling him.

'See what they want,' he said.

Kovic picked up her phone and walked away from the table. Blix watched her as she listened to the news on the other end of the phone. She nodded, hung up and returned.

'That was the hospital,' she said with a sigh. 'Nina Ballangrud died twenty minutes ago.'

# 41

On most days, Amy Linh would walk all the way from the hotel in Majorstua to her home on Sars gate in Sofienberg, but she decided that, just this once, she would take public transport. She wanted to get home to her cat as soon as possible, to the leftovers of yesterday's noodle soup and a quiet evening under a blanket in the living room. After such a long day at the hotel, she was tired and hungry.

She got on the tram at the stop towards the end of Vibes gate and sat in one of the vacant single seats right at the front, glad that she didn't have to sit so close to a stranger. She could lean her head against the rattling windowpane as the tram clattered and whined its way laboriously through the city centre. She closed her eyes and longed for the peace and quiet of her flat. A cup of tea after dinner. Her laptop perched on her knees, if she could be bothered to do any writing, that is. Or maybe she would just read the book she had been neglecting for the last few days.

The lights of the city camouflaged the dark sky above them. The winter, which felt as if it was only getting longer and longer with each year, had seized Oslo in its icy grasp. The pavements were covered in the grit that had been scattered across the ice. People walked tentatively, holding on to each other. But the cold, slippery surfaces never phased Amy Linh. The dark days, on the other hand, that was a different story.

Just as the winter darkness began to set in, the darkness within welled to the surface. It was rare to find her doing anything after work. She washed and cleaned all day long at the hotel. At home, she couldn't even be bothered to clean up after dinner. The first few weeks after Christmas were always the worst, when the evenings and winter months seemed endless.

Ten minutes later, a voice rang out from the speaker above her, announcing that the next stop would be Oslo Central Station. Amy Linh manoeuvred her way back towards the nearest door. She was not alone in trying to position herself at the exit. As the tram jud-dered to a halt, she steadied herself on the back of one of the chairs. Others were not so vigilant and bumped into her, without offering her so much as an apology.

A face of someone further back in the crowd caught her attention. There was something familiar about it, but she didn't have time to look more closely – a teenager who was so tall he almost brushed his head along the roof of the compartment had pushed in front of her. In the chaos that ensued as the tram came to a complete stop and people began to shove their way out, she lost sight of the man.

She hurried out into the evening and down the stairs leading to the underground. She was only going to Grønland Station, one stop down the line. A cold gust of wind passed through her as she hurried by a homeless person kneeling on a piece of cardboard, hands out-stretched in the form of a bowl. The flame of the small candle beside him flickered in the wind.

While she waited on the platform, it suddenly came to her that the man she had seen on the tram looked like the guest from room 620. She wondered if he would complain to her manager at the hotel, not just because she had let herself into his suite when he had hung up a *Do Not Disturb* sign, but because he had also caught her snoop-ing through his things. That, she knew, could be grounds for dismissal. She definitely shouldn't have done it. But she hadn't been able to stop herself.

She was only on the Metro for about a minute before she got off. The Grønland underground station was huge, and it took her a few minutes to weave her way out into the fresh air. Amy Linh made her way onto Tøyengata, through the powerful scent of incense and spices. She had a strange feeling that someone was following her, but when she turned around, there was no one there.

The Botanical Garden came into view just ahead. The garden had been one of the reasons she had chosen to settle in Sofienberg. When it was enveloped in snow, as it was now, she would spend the day wandering around in there, imagining what it would look like in full bloom, what it would smell like, this green oasis, overflowing with all the plants and flowers the world had to offer, nestled in the centre of Norway's capital. It gave her something to look forward to. Something that made the long evenings of the Norwegian winter a little more bearable.

Taking the path through the garden would shave about five minutes off her walk home, and she was pleased to see that the gate was open. The garden was spacious, wide and hilly, with several paths that zigzagged between the trees and bushes. They were sparsely lit during the winter – the only negative thing about taking this route on a cold, dark evening such as this.

Amy Linh was halfway up the steep incline, the highest point of the garden, when a jogger emerged over the hill, running in the opposite direction. He kept a good pace. She turned and watched with admiration at how easily he kept his balance on the icy surface. As she did so, she noticed a person in a dark coat behind her who had also chosen to walk the same path through the garden. His face was shrouded in darkness. She turned again and sped up. She felt her heart rate increase, noticed how hard she was pushing forwards as her feet met the slippery ground below, saw her breath start to crystallise in the icy air in front of her. She was irritated with herself for having not packed her ice grips when she left home that morning.

It wasn't much further. Just up to the highest point of the hill before she could speed up again. She looked behind her. The man was closer now, she could hear that his breathing was heavy too, an indication that he had been straining to get up the hill as well. She was just approaching the top now, but could hear that he was closer, almost right behind her. The sound of his footsteps. She spun round. In that moment, she realised who it was. She recognised the beige shoes. The laces. The face that was momentarily illuminated by a lamppost nearby.

She stopped, she knew he would eventually catch up with her. She knew that he wanted something.

With a quaking voice, she asked, 'What do you want from me?'

He stopped directly in front of her. 'How many people have you told?'

It was the first time she had heard his voice. It wasn't as deep as she had imagined, but it was colder, hollow.

'Told about what?' she stammered.

'That you were in my room today, that you looked through my things.'

'No one,' she answered hastily, regretting it instantly. 'No. Wait. Several people.'

He didn't say anything, just carried on staring at her, until he looked away, then around them, and seemed to come to the same realisation she had: there was no one else there. The jogger was gone.

Amy Linh swallowed.

'I wish I could trust you,' the man said, taking a step closer. 'But I'm afraid I can't.'

# 42

While Emma had been stood at the counter, buying herself a sandwich and another latte, a breaking-news notification from the Norwegian News Agency popped up on her phone – an update that the New Year's Eve bomb had claimed its fifth life. She rushed back to her table and opened the notification. The police had published the name of the person who had been killed, Nina Ballangrud, hiding in this new update the press release they had planned to publish, and simultaneously rectifying the fact that they had misidentified Ruth-Kristine Smeplass as the injured woman.

It was a tactical move. The latest death would make the headlines, instead of their blunder regarding the woman's identity.

She opened her laptop and went into the news.no website, looking to see how Wollan had reacted. His article was posted one minute ago. He had only had about an hour to gather enough information about the correct victim. He had been sending her details as he found them.

Nina Ballangrud had been a promising member of the Bækkelaget handball team, but a serious injury had ruined her chances of a career. He hadn't included the fact that her use of painkillers had eventually led to her drug addiction. Nor that she had grown up in a house of alcoholics, or that she had been abused by her father. He had, however, given plenty of attention to the opinions of a former police investigator who criticised the current investigation and disapproved of Gard Fosse's handling of the entire situation.

She took a bite of the sandwich. The article with Isaksen's interview would have to be postponed even longer. The rewriting of the article about Patricia's disappearance and now that of Ruth-Kristine was quite a lot more complicated than she had anticipated when she suggested to Anita that she could just edit it. Instead of tying it to the bomb on New Year's Eve, she would have to write it as a missing-persons case, angling it around the fact that she was the victim of the police's misidentification, and that the search for her had therefore begun more than two days late. Still, there was something missing. She needed something personal.

Emma had tried calling both of Ruth-Kristine's parents, but neither was picking up. She could go via Blix to see if he knew where they were, but was reluctant to ask him. She could also try the sister again. There was something strange about the way she had behaved and how reluctant she'd been to talk when Emma had called in on her on New Year's Day. Maybe she saw things differently now.

A young couple sat down at the next table. Emma packed her things and left the coffee where it was, but took the rest of the sandwich with her out to the rental car. As she wasn't used to driving through the city centre, she typed Britt Smeplass's address into the sat nav, and concentrated as she followed the directions, gradually recognising her surroundings. With only slight difficulty, she managed to manoeuvre the car into a tight space on Aschehougs vei, just a stone's throw away from where Britt Smeplass lived.

The curtains were still drawn. None of the lights were on. She made her way to the front door anyway. There was a biting chill in the air, and a wind that made Emma's cheeks tense up almost immediately. The last time she was here, the dog had warned its owner of her presence long before she had even had the chance to ring the doorbell. This time, there was no reaction from the four-legged inquisitor, not even after Emma rang the doorbell. She tried knocking, but couldn't hear any movement inside.

A car drove by. Emma waited a moment before walking over to the post box. There were a few promotion leaflets from the usual furniture chains. Two recently tied bin bags were stuffed into the wheelie bin. Emma stood there for a few seconds, thinking about what to do. She didn't want to leave, so she walked around to the back of the house. Dead leaves from the autumn had frozen into some of the patches of ice around the garden. Traces of paw prints and some piles of old faeces were dotted about here and there. She tread carefully up to the porch and walked right up to the window, cupping her hands around her face to see inside. Emma half expected to see a body on the floor in the dark, naked, lifeless, but she tried to shake those thoughts away. She knocked on the window, to no avail. Britt Smeplass wasn't home.

Emma got back in the car. It was starting to get dark. She was met with the sight of her own face in the rear-view mirror. She looked exhausted. She hadn't slept more than a few hours last night, after the accident and the questioning that had followed at the police station in Tønsberg.

She turned on the ignition. The headlights reflected off someone wearing a high-vis vest. A woman walking her dog. Emma pulled out and drove around them, looking back in the mirror as she passed. It looked like Britt Smeplass's dog. Eddy, wasn't that its name?

Emma drove for about a hundred metres before she decided to turn back. She slowed down and rolled past the woman with the dog again. The dog turned its head towards the car. It had a large white blotch around one eye, just like Eddy, but she didn't recognise the woman. She was small and stocky.

Emma pulled over, jumped out with the engine still running and crossed the street.

'Hi!' she said. 'Excuse me.'

The dog barked.

'Is that Eddy?' Emma asked, pointing at the dog.

'Yes,' the woman replied suspiciously. 'Do you know him?'

'No, but I know the owner.' Emma tried to smile. 'I've just been to Britt's house,' she said, turning her body slightly in the direction of the house. 'But she's not home.'

Emma introduced herself. As did the woman. Trine-Lise Melbye.

'No, Britt's not home,' she said. 'I'm looking after Eddy while she's away. I usually do. I like it. I think he likes it too.'

She smiled down at the eager guy.

'Do you know where Britt is?' Emma asked. 'I need to talk to her about something.'

'Have you tried calling?'

'Yes,' Emma lied.

The woman shook her head. 'I actually don't know where she's gone.'

Emma thought for a moment.

'When did she leave?'

'This morning.'

Eddy started tugging on the lead.

'Do you know if she'll be away for long?'

'Three days, max. But it seemed as if she wasn't entirely sure.'

'You know her well, by the sounds of it,' Emma continued. 'What with you looking after her dog and all?'

'Yes, quite well, I'd say.'

'Do you know if her sister visits much?'

The woman's brows furrowed slightly. 'She was here quite recently.'

'Was she?'

'Yeah, I saw her,' the woman said. 'Very early one morning. Not that I was watching, but I happened to see them from the kitchen window.'

'When was that?'

'I'm not sure. The days all seem to blend into one at the moment.'

'But can you remember if that was before or after New Year's Eve?'

Melbye considered the question. 'After, I think. New Year's Day, maybe? But they definitely stood outside for quite a while, talking on the front stairs before Britt invited her in.'

Emma mulled the information over for a few seconds. Eddy was now straining forwards with all his weight, pulling the lead tight and huffing impatiently.

'We should get a move on,' Trine-Lise Melbye said. 'Hope you manage to get in touch with her soon.'

'Thank you. And thanks for stopping to talk.'

# 43

The investigation was at an impasse. There was little Blix could do to move forwards without finding out the results of the dummy's DNA analysis.

He pulled out his phone and started typing out a text to Iselin to say that it wouldn't be long until he was home. If she was in, he could bring a pizza.

The moment he pressed send, the phone rang. It was Emma. He stood up and walked in the direction of the toilets. Halfway down the corridor, he had a quick glance around him before answering.

'Ruth-Kristine has been to visit her sister recently,' Emma began. 'And now Britt's gone too.'

Blix thought of all the unsuccessful times they had tried to call her. Of the visitor list at the hospital without Britt's name on it. Emma filled him in about how she had met one of the neighbours who was looking after Britt Smeplass's dog while she was away.

Blix turned and walked back towards his workstation. It could be simple, he thought: Britt didn't visit her sister in the hospital because she knew she wasn't there.

'Thank you for letting me know,' he said.

'Any news about Ahlander?'

He was itching to tell her about the dummy.

'Not yet. How are you?'

'Fine,' Emma replied quickly. 'I've been trying to get in touch with Jette Djurholm, Ruth-Kristine's neighbour. Her alibi. Do you think she could be directly involved in the disappearance?'

Blix ran his hand through his hair and surveyed the office.

'I can't discuss details about the case with you,' he said. 'But that was something we looked into, of course.'

'And?'

Blix saw no reason to continue that particular conversation.

'Is it a good idea for you to be working this much, after everything that's happened recently?' he asked instead.

He had expected a moment of hesitation on the other end.

'I might go to Denmark for a few days,' Emma replied. 'Depending on when Kasper's funeral is.'

'That sounds like a good idea.' Blix approved.

'It feels like something I have to do, anyway.'

Blix said that he understood how she felt.

'I'll look into that, by the way – about Britt Smeplass,' he concluded. 'But I've got to go now.'

'Of course,' Emma replied. 'Keep me updated, then. If you can.'

'I'll try.'

As he hung up, he noticed he had received a reply from Iselin:

*Pizza sounds great. I'm not going out after all. Safety first!*

She had ended the text with a smiley face. He sighed, leafed through his papers and found Britt Smeplass's phone number. The call went straight to voicemail. He didn't leave a message, deciding to call Nikolaj Smeplass instead.

'I'm sorry to have to disturb you again,' he began. 'We've been trying to get hold of Britt. Have you spoken to her?'

'Not at all while we've been here,' Nikolaj Smeplass replied. 'We've tried too, but we've not been able to get through. Sonja and I had thought about going over to look for her.'

'Do you have a key?'

'Yes.'

'Can we meet you at her house as soon as possible?' Blix asked. 'We're on our way there now.'

'Why's that?'

Blix dodged the question. 'We need to talk to her,' he replied instead. 'Have a look around the house.'

Smeplass hesitated, before answering. 'Sure. We'll leave now.'

Blix hung up and called Kovic and Abelvik over.

'We need to head over to Grefsen.'

Once in the car, Blix delegated the tasks. He would talk to the parents, while Abelvik would search the house for any clues as to whether Ruth-Kristine had, in fact, been there, and where they'd both disappeared to. Kovic was assigned the job of talking to the dog sitter and the other neighbours.

Nikolaj Smeplass met them outside Britt's place.

'Sonja decided to stay at her sister's,' he explained. 'What is this about?'

Blix looked at him intently. 'We have reason to believe that Ruth-Kristine has been staying here.' He pointed at the house. 'We need to verify that. And we need to find both of them.'

Smeplass looked confused, but he eventually nodded and took out the key, letting them in. While Abelvik started examining the house, Blix sat down in the living room with Smeplass. They slowly worked their way through the usual topics. The relationship between the sisters, his daughters' friends and acquaintances, what kind of contact he and his wife had had with them recently. And they discussed Patricia, and the time that had passed since she had disappeared. Smeplass had nothing new to contribute.

Blix was relieved when Abelvik waved him out into the kitchen.

'It looks as if someone's stayed overnight at some point,' Abelvik said in a low voice. 'The bed in the guestroom has been slept in, and there are two red-wine glasses in the dishwasher.'

'They may have been in there for a while,' Blix commented. 'For all we know.'

Kovic entered the kitchen. 'One of the neighbours saw a taxi outside here this morning,' she said. 'Two people were sat in the back.'

Blix and Abelvik exchanged a look.

'So they might have left together?' Kovic asked.

Blix looked into the living room, where Smeplass seemed to be immersed in something on his phone.

'We have to find that taxi,' he whispered. 'Try and confirm that it was them.'

The others nodded.

'We know for sure that Ruth-Kristine hasn't used her phone since

New Year's Eve, and that's after her name accidentally ended up plastered across all the papers. So, to me, that sounds like a person who's gone into hiding. She may have done so here.' He gestured around them with his hand.

'Britt hasn't been interested in talking to anyone over the last few days either,' he said. 'And she told her neighbour that she would be away for a few days. Let's check all the main transport hubs first.'

'I'll call Wibe,' Abelvik said as she took out her phone and walked to the other side of the room.

'We need to talk to the airlines as well,' Blix continued. 'Have them check their passenger lists. And then we need to start tracking Britt's phone.'

Nikolaj Smeplass came into the kitchen.

'What is going on, exactly?' he asked.

Blix glanced quickly at Kovic, before he turned to Smeplass and said:

'That is a very good question.'

# 44

By the time Emma arrived home, it was already quarter past eight. She sat down to finish writing up her interview with Christer Storm Isaksen, but she had too much going on in her head to settle.

She turned on the loudspeaker that she kept on the windowsill, putting on a playlist of slow and contemplative instrumental music: *Moods From Norway*. She stood there, staring out of the window, before turning to sit in the deep armchair in the corner, pulling her legs under her and tugging a blanket over to lay across her lap. Thoughts of everything that had happened over the last few days flowed freely around her head. Something didn't add up, she thought. Or, she corrected herself, there was a lot that didn't add up. And Patricia's mother seemed to be at the centre of all of it. Emma tried to search for an explanation, for where she could have gone, but didn't land on anything that seemed logical or sensible. Ruth-Kristine could be anywhere.

She leant back, resting her head against the chair. The sound of a violin and piano began to blend into one, before being cut off by a loud ringing. Emma yanked her phone from her trouser pocket. It was an unknown, foreign number. Denmark, she suddenly realised.

'Hi, Emma,' a woman's voice said on the other end. 'It's Asta.'

Emma felt her heart skip a beat. Kasper's mother.

After Kasper had died, she had only spoken to Jakob. She immediately felt the grief overwhelming her again and had to fight to keep her tears from flowing.

'Hi,' she said weakly. She pushed her shoulders back a little and stared over at the window.

'How ... are you doing?' Asta asked.

Her voice was cautious, gentle. Emma didn't know how to answer.

'I've been better,' she said eventually.

She started to pick at the fluff on the blanket that was draped across her lap.

'How about you? ... All of you?'

'Oh, you know,' Asta replied with a heavy sigh. She stayed silent for a while, before continuing. 'It's been ... difficult.'

'I understand.'

A long silence followed.

'I actually just wanted to call and let you know that we'll be coming to Oslo tomorrow. To bring him back. We ... we'd like to see him before he ... travels, and we wondered if ... whether you wanted to come with us?'

'Come with you ... what do you mean?'

'If you wanted to come see him,' Asta said. 'They have finished the autopsy now, and...'

Emma closed her eyes. The last thing she wanted to do was see Kasper.

'I thought he had been sent back already,' was all she could manage to say.

'No, it's taken quite a while,' Asta replied. 'I don't know why.'

Emma searched for what to say next.

'When do you get here?' she asked.

'We're flying out from Billund at ten tomorrow morning. So I guess we'll be in the city a little before noon, maybe. We can call you?'

Emma closed her eyes again. It annoyed her that she couldn't bring herself to say no. Instead, all she could manage was, 'Please do.'

# 45

The lift was packed with investigators, some of whom looked as if they had only just woken up. It trundled up to the sixth floor of Police Headquarters. Blix read through the morning's headlines on his phone. They were now entering the fourth day after the first explosion, and the media was becoming critical. The demands for answers and explanations were gaining momentum.

He stopped at the coffee machine on his way into the open-plan office. Wibe came and fetched him.

'We think we've found Ruth-Kristine and her sister on a recording from Oslo Central Station at 12:54 yesterday afternoon,' he said. 'They were heading to one of the platforms.'

'Which train did they take?' Blix asked, suddenly feeling more awake.

Wibe led Blix to his desk, where an image from one of the CCTV cameras had been left open on the screen. Two women were walking towards platform eighteen. There was a certain resemblance between them, one woman had features similar to Ruth-Kristine, although it had been a few years since Blix had last seen her.

'That train went to Gothenburg,' Wibe explained.

'So they're in Sweden,' Blix said, sipping his coffee.

'Arrived at 16:50,' Wibe added. 'There are only three stops before Gothenburg, all of which are on the Swedish side of the border. I've sent the missing-persons photos over, so the Swedes are assisting, looking through their surveillance footage from Gothenburg Central Station and the other stops.'

'Good,' Blix nodded.

He strongly doubted whether that would be of much help. Britt and Ruth-Kristine would have been in the large Swedish city a long time ago, and from there it was just a short distance by ferry, plane or train to every corner of Europe. In theory, the sisters could be any-where.

Kovic had come in early too.

'Any news?' Blix asked, after reiterating to her how important it was to get hold of the sisters' electronic data.

Kovic sat down. 'The taxi company confirmed that Britt Smeplass booked a trip from Aschehougs vei to Oslo Central Station,' she continued. 'Paid by card.'

'At least that's one thing that correlates,' Blix replied.

'Have you heard back about the dummy analysis yet?' Kovic enquired.

'Not yet,' Blix replied. 'It has to go through the DNA database before I'm told.'

He pulled his phone out of his pocket and lay it on the desk in front of him, to make sure it would be ready for whenever that update came.

Gard Fosse emerged from his office shortly after eight o'clock and made a beeline to their workstations.

'Crime Scene Investigation are currently at the Botanical Garden,' he announced, looking at Blix. 'A death; suspicious circumstances. They're requesting assistance from a homicide investigator.'

Blix groaned. 'Are they sure it's murder?'

'They've said that it's a young woman,' Fosse answered. 'Someone had tried to hide the body.'

'We can't take that on right now,' Blix protested, gesturing around them, as if to highlight everything else they had going on.

'It's your job,' Fosse pointed out. 'I don't have anyone else I can send.'

'But we might be awaiting a breakthrough in a case we've been working on for almost a decade,' he argued, and quickly updated Fosse on the investigation.

'So you're really just waiting for a DNA analysis and phone records to track down the Smeplass sisters?'

'We're not *just* doing that.'

'No, but pretty much all of our resources are tied up in the investigations into the bombings. I've given you free rein to work on other things. But now one of you will have to take the lead at the Botanical Garden.'

Blix sighed heavily. 'Brilliant.'

Fosse returned to his office. Blix looked at his investigators.

'I can take it,' Kovic offered.

Blix mulled it over for a few seconds. Kovic had never been the lead investigator on a homicide case before. But there had to be a first time.

'Sure,' he said. 'Just call if there's anything.'

Kovic threw her jacket on and disappeared. Blix turned to the stack of papers on his desk. He read through the documents from the initial investigation, connecting the dots and drawing up an outline so that he was thoroughly prepared for the interview.

The results arrived at 09:02.

The woman calling was from the DNA database team. Her name was Gitte Kollemyr.

'You requested an urgent analysis of a sample marked B-8 for Case 2019000372 from the South-Eastern Police District?' she said in a formal tone.

'A dummy,' Blix confirmed. 'I'm the one responsible for that case.'

'A DNA sequence has been found on the item,' the woman continued. 'It is identical to a DNA profile from a missing person relating to Case 150293 from 2009, from the Oslo Police District.'

'Patricia Storm Isaksen,' Blix said.

'I understand it's related to that case, yes,' Kollemyr replied.

'Just so we're clear – is it a match?' Blix asked, holding his breath.

'The samples are one hundred percent consistent,' the woman said.

It felt as if his heart had imploded. His theory was correct.

Now they had him.

# 46

Two police cars, an ambulance and an unmarked police car were parked on the pavement outside the southern entrance to the Botanical Garden. Kovic pulled up behind them. The snowflakes were descending horizontally, landing thick and fast, in wet splotches on the windscreen.

She stayed in the car for a moment, collecting her thoughts, before pulling the lapels of her jacket right up to her chin and pushing the door open. A taxi drove by slowly as she made her way round the car.

A uniformed officer was standing at the gate, hands behind his back. He was moving his weight from one foot and to the other, as if trying to warm his legs up. A thin layer of snow had settled on his shoulders.

Kovic pulled her ID card from inside her jacket and held it up for him.

'On the left,' he said, pointing out the correct path for her.

Kovic thanked him with a nod and shoved her hands deep into her pockets. After six months of working in homicide with Blix, and with her previous experience behind her, she felt more than equipped to take on the responsibility of a murder investigation, but she still felt nervous. It was vital that she did everything right. The initial phase was crucial. Everything had to be done as soon as possible.

Both the car belonging to the forensic technician Ann-Mari Sara and the Crime Scene Investigation van were parked at the top of the steep hill. The barrier tape was already up. A flash of light shone out from somewhere behind the nearby trees.

A few onlookers had gathered around. A man with a dog stepped aside as Kovic edged through them and introduced herself to the officer guarding the barrier. He noted her name and arrival time before lifting up the tape for her.

The narrow footpath wound its way through the trees and shrubs. On her way into the bushes, she nodded briefly to two of the paramedics who were on their way back out.

The dead woman lay hidden beneath some branches. Tracks in the snow beside her suggested that someone had attempted to cover her up. Her eyes were open. A few crystals of ice had formed on her eyelashes. Her face was blue and frostbitten. As if she had been lying there for some time.

Ann-Mari Sara was squatting at the woman's feet, her back to Kovic, not realising yet that she had arrived.

The investigator from the Crime Scene Investigation unit walked over to her. She recognised him. Edvald Rognlien. A man in his late forties, sporting a few grey streaks in his dark hair. He wore thick glasses that were spattered with droplets of water. The eyes behind them were always calm. Kovic recognised a sincerity in them.

'So they've sent you,' he noted, sounding neither satisfied nor dissatisfied.

'What have you got?' Kovic asked.

'The alert came in at 07:48 this morning,' Rognlien explained. 'A jogger found her after coming into the forest to relieve himself.'

He mentioned the name of the jogger.

'We've questioned him.'

Ann-Mari Sara straightened up and approached them.

'Looks like she was strangled,' she said. 'There are blue marks on her neck.'

Kovic peered over to see them.

'And then she was dragged in here?' She turned, indicating the path.

'Hard to tell, with the fresh snow,' Abelvik chimed in. 'But she's probably been here since yesterday.'

Kovic looked over at the body again. Nothing to suggest that there had been an attempted rape. Her jacket was still zipped up, her trousers hadn't been unbuttoned.

'What do we know about her?'

'Her name is Amy Linh,' Rognlien replied. 'Having said that, we should probably be a bit careful about coming to conclusions like that so quickly these days.' He sent Kovic a quick smile. 'But she had an ID card in her bag for what I presume is her workplace. There's a picture of her on it. And there's a certain resemblance.'

Rognlien pulled out an evidence bag from the folder he was holding and passed it to Kovic. She studied the image through the plastic.

'Hotel Gyldenløve,' she read aloud. 'That's in Majorstua, I think.'

'On Bogstadveien,' Rognlien confirmed.

Kovic realised that he had already carried out the first few essential tasks.

'Where does she live?' she asked.

'On Sars gate,' Rognlien replied, turning to point in the right direction. 'About five hundred metres that way.'

'Family?'

Rognlien shook his head. 'According to our records, she lives alone.'

Kovic turned to Ann-Mari Sara. 'Does she have any keys on her?'

Sara walked over to her trunk and pulled out a labelled evidence bag with a key chain inside. 'Found in the right jacket pocket,' she said. 'She had a wallet on her too, the cards and cash left inside, the phone untouched too. It's still got some battery left. I'll make sure it's unlocked with her fingerprints, so you can access it.'

Rognlien's phone rang. He checked the number and turned the screen off.

'What do you want us to do now?' he asked.

Kovic was rather taken aback by the direct question. It sounded like a challenge. Rognlien was almost twice as old as she was, and had far more experience.

'I want to map out her movements and circle of friends,' she answered, thinking she was taking a bit too long to reply.

A murder investigation had one of two starting points. She was either a random victim, or Amy Linh was taken out because she was who she was. The latter meant that someone had a specific motive and that the perpetrator was someone she knew.

'We've not found any relatives,' Rognlien said. 'But she may have some family where she's from. Vietnam.'

Kovic nodded and took the bag with the key chain. She would start with her flat.

She stood there a moment longer, staring down at the dead woman. Then she turned and left.

# 47

Emma stood in front of the fridge, staring at the contents, trying to work out if there was anything in there that she actually wanted to eat.

She'd had a restless night, drifting in and out of sleep. Lying there, thinking about Kasper, and his parents, and what it was going to be like to see them again. The images of Kasper at the harbour had resurfaced, but now she had started imagining him on the cold autopsy table too. How the pathologist had sliced into him, plucked the shrapnel out of his body.

She grabbed an apple, pushed the fridge door closed and was met with a reminder that she was supposed to have a session with Gorm Fogner at eleven o'clock. The card with the details of the therapy appointment was stuck to the fridge. She hadn't heard anything from him, other than the text on New Year's Day. He must have found out that Kasper had died. His name had been mentioned in almost every news report since Wednesday.

She took a bite of the apple, sat behind her laptop and pushed aside the half-empty coffee cup she had left there the day before.

The article about Christer Storm Isaksen was still not complete; she was finding it impossible to collect her thoughts and make a proper start. She had spent that morning scrolling through news websites and social media. Fear that the bomber might strike again reigned. The newspapers had several theories, as did the people commenting on the articles. The criticism of the police and PST had become even more intense.

What Emma couldn't quite understand, was how and why Ruth-Kristine was first believed to have been a victim of the explosion, and then reported missing somehow. If the two things weren't connected, it was certainly a bizarre coincidence. The kind of coincidence she didn't believe in.

It was half past eight. Still early, but she could probably get away with calling Jette Djurholm. She found the Danish phone number. Ruth-Kristine's former neighbour didn't pick up this time either.

She spent some time researching where exactly Ruth-Kristine had been living at the time of Patricia's disappearance and discovered that it was the same address she lived at now – in Holmlia. There could be other people who lived there at that time and who still lived there too.

The chairman of the housing association was called Mustafa Jamal Hayd. She considered calling him to see if he might have any information, but decided to just take the rental car and drive over there before her therapy session.

It had started to snow, and the drive took longer than the sat nav estimated. A boy with a school satchel ran past, through a flurry of snow, but other than that, a strange silence enveloped the low-rise block of flats as she arrived. No one to talk to.

She found the chairman's phone number and called him. He picked up.

'You're not the only journalist to have come up here,' he said after Emma introduced herself. 'The police, too. A few times.'

He explained that he lived in one of the terraced houses, but offered to walk over to meet her. He turned up five minutes later.

'Do you know her?' Emma asked with a nod towards the block.

'Not really,' Mustafa replied. 'There have been a few complaints, every now and then. Loud music, being too noisy, but I've never had any problems with her.'

'Were you living here when her daughter disappeared?' Emma enquired.

'I've lived here for sixteen years,' Mustafa said, a touch of pride in his voice, as if it were an achievement in itself. 'I've been chairman for the last eight.'

'You must like it here, then, by the sounds of it?'

'I must say, I really do. And there's quite a lot to keep track of. It's easy to combine with work, luckily.'

'What do you do?'

'I run my own IT company. Server support.'

Emma nodded.

'Do you remember Patricia? Her daughter?'

His expression changed. From warm and welcoming to something more sober. Sad, even. He nodded.

'Such a sweet girl,' he said, although somehow Emma had the impression that he didn't actually remember her. 'Always happy,' he added. 'But she lived with her dad most of the time, so I didn't see her often.'

He shook his head gloomily.

'It was terrible, what happened. It really affected us. For a long time. I would say that it still affects us, actually. Or at least, we often think about what could have happened to her.'

'So do I,' Emma said. 'That's why I'm here.'

'Oh?'

'I'm trying to get in touch with Jette Djurholm, or some of Ruth-Kristine's other neighbours from around that time,' she said. 'Do you remember Jette?'

Mustafa thought about it for a moment.

'The Danish woman? Quite short, blonde hair, a little plump?'

'She's from Denmark, yes,' Emma said. 'But she's not picking up when I call.'

'They were neighbours, that I can remember. Jette and Ruth-Kristine.'

'Can you tell me about them?'

He sent Emma a quizzical look. 'What do you mean?'

'Were they good friends? Did they spend a lot of time together?'

'I can't really say. Jette didn't live here for that long, no more than a few years anyway, maybe not even that. But I did see them outside together quite often, over at the play area between the two buildings with their kids. Remembrance Park, as we call it.'

'So Jette had children as well?'

Mustafa nodded.

'I have five myself,' he said, smiling. 'One of them was the same age as Patricia. They would have been in the same class.'

'Can you remember if Ruth-Kristine used to spend much time with anyone else back then? Other people who lived here, I mean.'

Mustafa seemed to be thinking hard, trying to remember.

'No, it was mostly Jette, I believe.'

Emma started to feel as if she had come out here for nothing.

'As chairman ... you don't happen to have the contact information for Jette or her husband, do you?'

Mustafa considered it.

'It's been a while ... I don't think they left anything behind. I can have a look through my documents though. I might find something.'

Emma thanked him and tried to think of anything else she could get out of him.

'What were the police doing here?' she asked.

'Someone had broken into her flat,' Mustafa answered. 'It's been a long time since anything like that happened here.'

Emma raised her eyebrows. 'When was that?'

'New Year's Day. I showed them in when they arrived.'

'Do you know if they found whoever did it?'

Mustafa shook his head again. 'No idea.'

Emma checked her watch. She would have to leave if she were going to get to her appointment on time.

'Thank you for all the help.'

Mustafa smiled.

'Anytime.'

# 48

Blix printed out the results of the DNA analysis and made his way to the interview room where Sophus Ahlander and his lawyer, Vidar Rødland, were waiting. Copies of all of the documents from the Patricia case were stacked up on the table between them.

Both stayed in their seats when Blix entered the room. Ahlander looked like a completely different person. All the colour had drained from his face.

'Have you been able to get some sleep?' Blix asked. 'Any breakfast?'

Blix forced himself to speak as gently and politely as he could. The lawyer answered for his client:

'Yes, he's been treated well enough. But I don't think he's eaten much.'

Blix stared at Ahlander for a few seconds, before turning on the room's recording function and going through all the formalities.

'Let's start by talking about Knut Ivar Skage,' Blix said. 'How do you know him?'

Ahlander stared at him, surprised by the question.

'Old acquaintance,' he said quickly.

'Ah, so him too,' Blix said.

'What do you mean?'

'Ruth-Kristine Smeplass was also an old acquaintance of yours.'

Ahlander didn't respond.

'Was that a question?' he eventually asked.

'Knut Ivar Skage admitted to Patricia's father that he had been involved in the kidnapping,' Blix continued, unperturbed. 'He had been asked to help take care of the child, after the fact.'

Neither Ahlander nor his lawyer responded.

'Skage owned a car repair shop,' Blix carried on. 'You have been convicted of, among other things, car theft. I think that you were delivering stolen cars to him. That you dismantled the cars, and he would use the parts.'

'Knut Ivar Skage is dead,' the lawyer reminded him.

Blix looked down at his papers as if he hadn't heard and ticked off the first bullet point. He wasn't looking for confirmation about the car thefts. It was just something he had to get through first, to draw a clear picture for Ahlander as to how the police were approaching the case.

'I think that, towards the end of his life, Skage tried to clean up some of the mess he had made,' Blix continued, pushing a newspaper clipping across the table. 'Three weeks before he was murdered, *Wanted* aired on TV3, reporting on a story about an unsolved murder, a hit-and-run. A tip-off came in that named you as the driver of a stolen Ford Focus.'

'That accusation was dropped, I checked out,' Ahlander commented, pushing the newspaper clipping that referred to the case back across the table.

Blix left the newspaper clipping where it was and made sure to speak clearly as he continued:

'I think that the car ended up in Skage's garage, and that it was Skage who, three years later, tipped off the police. He was attempting to clear his conscience, just as he was when he contacted Patricia's father. He had nothing to lose by telling him what had happened. Skage was terminally ill, he didn't have long to live. He wanted to give the little girl's father the answers he was looking for, and he wanted to try and secure the reward too – which he was probably planning on giving to his own children before he died.'

Rødland made an arrogant hand gesture, clearly indicating that whatever Blix believed, it was of no interest to him.

'You trusted Skage,' Blix continued without taking his eyes off the interviewee on the other side of the table. 'He'd kept quiet, even though he knew you had hit someone with your car, had left them for dead. So when you called him for help, to take care of Patricia, you knew he was a man that you could count on.'

'I hope you have evidence to support these allegations,' Rødland said.

Blix pushed the newspaper clipping back to Ahlander's side of the table.

'There were two people in the car that killed that man,' he said. 'Witnesses tell us that there was a woman in the passenger seat.'

Ahlander ran his tongue nervously over his lips. Blix leant back in his chair. The picture he wanted to present had started to take shape.

'The descriptions fit Ruth-Kristine Smeplass,' he finished. 'She had something on you. She knew what you had done, so when she contacted you to ask for help kidnapping her own daughter, it was almost impossible for you to refuse.'

'Has Smeplass given a statement about this?' Rødland interjected.

Blix ignored the question and pulled a set of documents out, including the report that outlined the results of the DNA analysis taken from the dummy.

'I have a few documents here,' he said, pushing them over to the defence lawyer.

Rødland picked them up. 'I would like to go through these before we continue,' he said.

'There's not much there,' Blix replied. 'Just an evidence report showing the discovery of a pink dummy with a teddy bear on it during a preliminary search of your client's cabin in Undrumsåsen yesterday. There is also a copy of the request I submitted to the laboratory for an analysis. The results came in a little over half an hour ago. They're in there too.'

Blix fixed his gaze on Ahlander. The man's eyes had widened, his pupils had expanded, as if the lights had suddenly been turned off.

Rødland repositioned his glasses. 'Am I right in understanding that a DNA profile has been found and that there is a consistent profile in the DNA database?'

'Correct,' Blix nodded.

'It doesn't say who, it's just a reference to a case number.'

Blix leant forwards and pointed to the thick stack of documents on the table. 'Case 150293 from 2009,' he said. 'Patricia Storm

Isaksen.'

Ahlander lowered his head into his hands. Sat like that for quite some time. Blix waited for one of them to say something.

'I think I need to have a few words with my client,' Rødland said flatly. 'Alone.'

'By all means,' Blix said.

He reached forwards and stopped the recording. Glanced up at the camera and had to force himself not to grin. A surge of emotions erupted inside him. The kind of emotions that only occurred when you were on the verge of a major breakthrough. And with that breakthrough being on a case that had plagued him for nearly ten years, the adrenaline was particularly exhilarating.

Blix left the room and waited on the other side of the door.

It only took a couple of minutes before Rødland came to get him, with the words: 'My client would like to make a full, unreserved confession.'

Blix glanced at his watch. It was barely ten o'clock. It had gone much faster than he had anticipated.

'About what?' he asked.

Rødland sighed heavily.

'The kidnapping of Patricia Storm Isaksen.'

# 49

He pushed himself up from his knees, but couldn't bring himself to look down at the toilet bowl. Swallowed, but wished he hadn't. The taste of bile, of old, previously digested food, made him groan and grasp hold of the sink. He didn't bother waiting to see if the water was cold or not, just bent down until his lips met the tap. He opened his mouth and drank a few gulps, swallowing them down, just to have any other taste in his mouth. He turned the water off and straightened up. Came face-to-face with a man in the mirror who he almost didn't recognise, whiter than a ghost.

Was he really going to go through with this?

He thought about Ruth-Kristine. The plans. Carmen's daily routine, the route she would always take home from the Tangenten Nursery. The park. The bushes. Everything that could go wrong. The money he would get. The bills he had to pay. The aftermath.

When she had come over the night before, it had been exactly like he had dreamt it would be. They had shared a bottle of wine. They had sex on the sofa while the TV played in the background. She made the first move. She was so grateful and happy that he would do this for her.

'Everything's going to be great,' she had said. 'Our lives are going to be so good.'

She had repeated the instructions again before leaving. Serious, at that point.

'Remember, you can't tell anyone I've been here today. No one can know. Christer's going to think I did it, and the police will think so, too. They'll investigate me anyway. Thoroughly.'

He had nodded.

'And you can't, under any circumstances, call me. The police will be keeping an eye on who I've been in contact with over the last few weeks. You know I'll come to you as soon as I can, but it could take a few days. I have to do the kind of things I would have done if it had actually happened.'

'It is actually happening.'

'Whatever. You know what I mean. Go out, look for her, that kind of thing.' She had looked him deep in the eyes. 'I need to know that you can do this, Sophus. That you'll go through with it, that you won't freak out.'

He blinked a few times as he stared at his own reflection. He felt as if he were going to throw up again.

The fresh air did him some good. He felt his skin, warm one moment, cold the next. He climbed into the van and turned on the ignition. He leant over the wheel for a few moments, before hoisting himself up, telling himself it would all be fine.

He left the car in a side street near the park and walked, legs trembling, in the direction of the nursery. Yanked his hood down firmly over his head and made sure not to make eye contact with anyone he passed. He had made this trip several times over the last few days, so he knew how long it would take. Upon arriving outside the nursery, he realised he had taken two and a half minutes less than the day before, and that he was way too early, so he sat on a bench a few hundred metres away, only to jump up again a few seconds later. He had run out of cigarettes. He ran into the nearest corner shop and rushed back, anxious that he might be too late.

And he was.

Her pushchair was gone.

'Fuck,' he swore to himself. He began to run, as fast as he could, and there, a few hundred metres away, on the path in front of him, was her dark Spanish hair. He recognised her quick pace. Sophus glanced around as he slowed down, paying no attention to the weather, nor to the fact that his breathing was now fast and heavy. Again, he could feel his stomach churning. He tried to suppress it. The taste of cigarettes and bile. He hadn't managed to eat anything that day, and he really needed the toilet as well.

As he edged closer, he noticed that she was wearing earphones. Good, she wouldn't hear him coming. There were people everywhere, on the path, on the road, standing around talking to each other, pram to pram. A large, heavyset woman came running towards them at a slovenly pace. Sophus could barely feel the ground beneath his feet. But his heart, he could feel that, in his throat, neck, stomach. In his legs.

They were approaching the trees he had checked out beforehand. Carmen was only twenty metres ahead of him now. Bloody people! He sped up again. Came a little closer, just ten metres behind her. He matched his speed with hers. Looked around. There were still a few people nearby, but they weren't looking at him, weren't looking in his direction. They were heading up a small hill. Five metres behind her. Four.

People?

He had no idea. Didn't think, only heard Ruth-Kristine's urgent voice in his head. *I need to know that you can do this, Sophus. That you'll go through with it, that you won't freak out.*

# 50

'Sounds as if you were lucky,' Blix said, looking at Ahlander.

Sophus snorted. Luck only scraped the surface. He had hit Carmen as hard as he could – she hadn't seen the attack coming. Then he had pushed her into the bushes, tucking her legs in so that they wouldn't stick out, taken the pushchair and carried on walking with it. To the van.

'And then you drove her to the cabin.'

Blix's voice made him jump. Ahlander nodded.

'I need you to answer,' Blix said. 'For the recording.'

'Yes,' he said, clearing his throat.

'Did you have a car seat for her?'

'Car seat? No, I ... just put her in the van. In the pushchair, like she was when I took her. She was asleep, so I didn't think about it. And I was stressed as fuck as well, just wanted to get away, fast as I could.'

'You didn't secure the pushchair with anything?'

'I don't know ... don't remember. But I must've done. Put the brake on anyway. I think.'

He noticed the policeman's expression. It was the same on the lawyer's face. Contempt. Pity too, maybe. It didn't surprise him. He hated himself as well. Hated what he had done. But he had tried to find a way to live with it. To forget. And now, at long last, he was re-lieved that he could finally tell someone what he had done. He had held it in for so long.

'So you got to the cabin. What happened after that?'

Ahlander took a deep breath. 'Not that much, really. I took her inside. She'd woken up by then.'

'How did she react when she saw you?'

'She cried,' he said. 'At the top of her lungs. I ... didn't know what to do. I'd never looked after a child before.'

'Ruth-Kristine hadn't thought about that part then, when she gave you the assignment?'

Ahlander threw his arms up. 'There were obviously not that many people she knew who would go through with it.'

'So you suddenly had a child to look after, a crying child, and you didn't know how long it would be until she would come back? That was the deal? You would stay at the cabin, with Patricia, for an unknown number of days? And Ruth-Kristine would come ... whenever she could?'

'That was the deal, yes.'

'Did she ever mention what her plan would be, for Patricia?'

'No.'

'And Patricia continued to cry?'

'Yes, she ... I mean, I'm not stupid, I knew I had to try and comfort her, give her food and change her nappies and everything, but ... nothing worked, she just cried and cried. It drove me up the wall.'

'And that's when you called Knut Ivar Skage?'

'Not that early,' Ahlander said. 'I tried, for two or three days. She slept and such, stopped crying then, but as soon as she woke up, she'd start again. And that's when I lost it. And Ruth-Kristine just never turned up.'

He could hear the anger in his own voice. Still.

'I ran out of nappies,' he continued. 'And food, for her and me. And I couldn't just go to the shops, could I? Couldn't take her with me, with everyone looking for her. And I couldn't just leave her there, on her own.'

'How did you get him on board?'

'Hm?'

'How did you convince Skage to help out? Just called him up, like: "Hi, I've kidnapped a young child, I need help taking care of her?"'

'No, I...'

Ahlander thought back.

# 51

He paced back and forth in the cabin. Stared at the phone, then at the child, who was toddling about, making incomprehensible, high-pitched noises.

She was hungry.

That must be it. And he had food, *that* wasn't the issue. But there was nothing that she would eat, other than the yoghurt, and he had run clean out. He had tried *lapskaus* – that chunky kind of stew, the one that comes in a can. Tried sweetcorn when that didn't work, but she had just spat them out again. The bananas had gone down well, but he had none left. She had teeth, it was just that she wasn't particularly interested in using them.

The worst, though, were the nappies.

And the clothes.

He hadn't managed to work out the nappies, and she had already leaked through both the nappies and the clothes that he had bought beforehand, several times. He had tried washing them, and had rinsed her off in the shower, but when she'd been stumbling around the cabin afterwards, nappy sagging halfway down her thighs, she did it again. And then the shit had ended up all over the floor as well.

*Whatever you do, do not contact anyone.*

The very last thing Ruth-Kristine had said to him before she had left that night. That no matter how bad things got, no matter how long he had to wait, he must not call anyone. But that was before the delirium had begun to creep in. Before the sound of constant screaming had made him hold his hand over her mouth a few times, just for a second of silence. When he removed it, she would scream even harder, even louder. And now she was starving, poor thing. That must be what was bothering her.

Ahlander glanced at his phone. He needed help. He couldn't go on like this.

Knut Ivar, he thought.

Knut Ivar could be trusted. He hadn't said anything when he and Ruth-Kristine had turned up at his garage in a car with streaks of blood across the dented bumper, as well as a broken headlight. Ahlander was certainly no actor, so he knew that the lie he had fed Knut Ivar, about some unfortunate deer, wasn't convincing. But it hadn't mattered. Knut Ivar had kept his mouth shut.

Ahlander walked into one of the other rooms and dialled his number.

'Howdy!' his friend shouted down the phone, feigning a Texan accent. Ahlander couldn't bring himself to say anything at first. One utterance about the little girl and he would be going beyond the point of no return.

'Can ... I trust you completely?' he finally said.

'Trust me?' Knut Ivar started to laugh. 'Of course you can trust me, Sophus.'

'I mean it, Knut Ivar.' Ahlander could hear the desperation in his own voice. 'I need help, and I don't think I have anyone else I can ask.'

A momentary lull down the line.

'What is it?' Knut Ivar asked. 'What's happened?'

'I ... can't tell you over the phone. But before I say anything else, I need to be sure that you won't tell anyone that I've called you, not a single word to anyone. Can you promise me that? No one!'

'Yeah, yeah, of course,' Knut Ivar assured him.

Ahlander heard as Knut Ivar walked from one room into another, presumably the office at the back of the garage, and listened as he closed the door behind him.

'What's going on?'

Ahlander took another deep breath before continuing.

'I need you to come to the cabin. You know where it is, right?'

'I know the area,' Knut Ivar said. 'But I'm sure I can find it if you give me the address.'

'I need you to drive over, straight away. I don't care what excuse you give your wife, just make sure you can leave for a while without anyone getting suspicious. Especially ... now.'

'What do you mean?'

'I'll explain everything when you come. How soon can you get here?'

Knut Ivar seemed to take a moment to consider it.

'Give me a couple of hours, I can probably come straight from work.'

'I also need you to get a couple of things for me on your way over.'

He was waiting for Knut Ivar outside when he drove up to the cabin, three and a half hours later, a bag full of bananas and yoghurts in hand. Ahlander held his hands up, palms open, and walked towards him.

Knut Ivar approached him, suspiciously.

'I'm sorry for calling you,' Ahlander said, almost in tears. 'There's no one else I can trust.'

'You said that, and I said that you can trust me.'

'Whatever happens?'

Knut Ivar studied him for a few seconds before turning to look at the cabin. The sound of the crying child had reached them outside.

'What the hell have you gotten yourself involved in, Sophus?'

He could feel his eyes welling up. Afraid of what was going to happen in the next few hours, in the next few days, what Knut Ivar would say ... or do.

'You can still turn around,' he said in a trembling voice, 'and then you'll never know what I've done.'

'Come on,' Knut Ivar replied. 'I'm here, aren't I? I've told the wife that I'd be away for a few days anyway. I can't go home now.'

Ahlander sighed. There was really no going back.

'You'll regret saying that when you...' He sighed. 'Just ... come in.'

# 52

'How did Knut Ivar react when he saw Patricia in the cabin?'

'He...'

Ahlander stopped, thought back.

'He was in shock, naturally. At first. But Knut Ivar had been involved in a lot of shady things in his time, so he knew that he was basically an accomplice the second he'd entered the cabin. So, after yelling at me for a few minutes, he got on with it.'

'He ... got on with it?'

'Yes, taking care of her, that kind of thing. Bathed her, sorted her nappy out, put it on properly. He found some sort of cream thing in one of the bags from the pushchair. She was sore, obviously. Poor thing. He knows what to do, with kids. And he made me go to the shop to buy some dummies for her.'

He nodded at the picture on the table between them.

'I soon realised that it would be a good idea to buy several of them. She kept losing them everywhere, all the time. Dummies,' he said, a small smile appearing on his face, 'must be the world's best invention. Stopped the screaming anyway.'

Neither Blix nor the lawyer smiled back. Ahlander waited a few moments before carrying on:

'Didn't take him much time to get some food in her, and for her to get used to him too, comfortable. He played with her. Messed about and made funny faces. Got her to smile. It ... was nice to see.'

'But Knut Ivar couldn't stay for long?'

'No, and I didn't want Ruth-Kristine to see him there either.'

'So he left. Eventually. A few days later?'

'Yes. He showed me how to do everything. With her, I mean. I got the hang of it in the end. And kids adapt to change quite quickly.'

'And then Ruth-Kristine finally came?'

'Yes. Probably about a week or so later.'

'How did she know where the cabin was?'

'She'd been before. We would drive up every once in a while, whenever I had found myself a nice car.'

Blix looked down at the notebook on his lap, before carrying on:

'What we, and by that I mean all of Norway, want to know is what happened after that.'

Ahlander stared at the floor. He grabbed the glass of water in front of him and drained it. Let out a deep sigh.

'It was like she was a completely different person that day.'

'In what way?'

'Didn't give me a kiss, or hug or whatever when she got there. Nothing. Just parked outside and marched towards me with these brisk, determined steps. Screamed at me: "Where is she?" Aggressively as well, as if I'd done something wrong? Didn't say hello or thanks or anything either. I asked her why she'd taken so long. "Have you not seen the newspapers?" was all she said. "Have you not watched the news?"'

Ahlander imitated her, putting on a waspish voice.

'Then she went into the cabin, walked into the back room and snatched the girl off the floor, as if she were picking up a jumper she had left behind. Didn't hug her, didn't talk to her. Just said: "You can go now."'

'She said that to you?' Blix asked. 'That *you* could go?'

'Yeah, I hadn't understood what she meant either, or what was going on, so I ... asked.'

'What did she say?'

'That it wasn't any of my damn business. And that she didn't have much time.'

Blix lowered the pen to the notepad, but didn't write anything.

'Then she asked for the keys to my cabin.'

'Why did she want the keys?'

'She wouldn't say at first. She answered eventually, sneered at me: "Do you want me to leave the door unlocked when I go?"' Again, imitating her sharp tone.

'So you gave her the keys?'

Ahlander sat in silence for a few moments. Then he nodded.

'You just drove away? Alone?'

'Yes. At that point I was just happy to leave, get out of there.'

'Did you never find out what happened to Patricia?'

Ahlander shook his head, answering 'no' as he did.

'You didn't find out afterwards, either?'

He recalled the drive home. Of how he had thought about Ruth-Kristine and everything she had promised him. How loving she had been that first time, how hostile the next.

When the coverage of the case began to calm down, she'd turned up at his doorstep with the money – less than the amount she'd originally promised.

'We can't be together,' she had said. 'Not right now, anyway. It ... just won't work.'

He had accepted it, at that time. He had understood. And as the weeks and months came and went, it was just as well. He had gotten away with what he'd done. What had happened to the girl remained a mystery to the police and the media, to Christer Storm Isaksen and everyone else.

But Ahlander thought he knew.

'What do you mean?' Blix asked. 'What do you think you know?'

Ahlander took a deep breath. 'A few days before I ... kidnapped the girl, Ruth-Kristine had asked if...'

He stopped himself.

'She asked you what?' Blix pressed.

Ahlander locked eyes with him before he answered:

'She asked if I kept a shovel at the cabin.'

# 53

A bouquet of festive flowers stood wilting on the table of the therapist's office. A small, folded card had been fastened to it with a strand of gold thread. A thank-you gift from another patient, perhaps.

When Emma had accepted the offer of therapy sessions, she had envisioned herself lying on a couch, the therapist sat nearby, writing notes and analysing her very soul.

That was not the case with Gorm Fogner. He had a regular office, with a small seating area, just a few sofas and chairs. Nothing weird or intimidating about it. It was like going to an informal doctor's appointment, without the doctor urgently rushing through everything because they had more patients waiting outside.

At her first appointment, she had been given some forms to fill out and a sheet with a set of standardised questions to answer. It had felt strange, categorising her feelings. On the other hand, it was easier to do that than try and explain in her own words what she was finding so painful and difficult.

It was pure luck that she had ended up with Gorm Fogner. He was one of several therapists the police had recommended, and he could see her right away. He was in his early forties. Meaning that he was old enough to have gained some experience, but not so old that he was set in his ways, or was tired of meeting with patients.

She soon realised that talking to Fogner was almost like doing a spring clean of her mind. It helped her to sort through her thoughts in a faster, more thorough and more gentle way than she would have done alone. She was always the one to choose the topic and lead the conversation, basing her decisions on what she thought would be most important to explore. Gorm Fogner listened, reflected on what she said, proffered ideas, contributed suggestions and helped put things into perspective. They weren't all that different from the conversations she would sometimes have with her sister, except for the fact that the therapy sessions were solely about her, so there was no two-way communication that required effort on her part. That was why she liked it. There was no Irene to burden with her issues, so she didn't have to worry about what her sister would think and feel, she could just concentrate on herself and what she was struggling with. It felt good to put her own experiences into words, with someone she had no contact with otherwise in her everyday life.

'I don't know how it must feel, but I do understand that you are hurting,' Fogner said as she sat down.

Emma was aware that this was probably something he said to all his patients, but it still did the job, made her relax her shoulders.

'Would you like to go through what happened?' he added.

She hadn't felt as if she had wanted to before, but she realised then that she did need to talk through the events of New Year's Eve, one more time.

New details emerged. A used-up sparkler sticking out of the snow, a scarf floating on the surface of the water as Blix plunged into it, a champagne cork on the ground next to Kasper.

It was easy to repeat the facts, but it was harder to verbalise the grief, the heartache. To describe the fatigue that had taken over her body, the mental turmoil, the lack of motivation and how difficult it was to do anything. It felt like a tsunami of excruciating emotions, and the one thing that made everything so much harder was the over-whelming guilt.

'I feel like it's my fault Kasper died,' she said.

'Why do you think that?' Fogner asked.

'He wouldn't have been there when the bomb went off if it hadn't been for me,' Emma explained. 'I left the party. He came looking for me.'

'Why do you think he came after you?'

The question made Emma reach for the tissue box. Kasper had come after her because he cared about her. Because he wanted to be with her.

The realisation of what she had actually meant to Kasper didn't help lessen her feelings of guilt; knowing that she wasn't thinking

about him the entire time just weighed even more heavily on her conscience. It had only been four days, barely even that, but she was
already busy with other things that felt important to her. Patricia's
disappearance from 2009. The mother's disappearance ten years later.

She tried to describe this feeling – that she was neglecting Kasper
because she was keeping her mind occupied with other things.

'A lot of people expect someone who is grieving to behave in a
certain way, as if they know how that person should heal, but there
is no single solution for how one deals with grief,' Fogner assured her,
smiling as he did so.

'I was laughing about something Anita said yesterday about my
driving skills,' Emma continued, explaining how she had driven the
company car into a ditch. 'It was like I'd forgotten.'

Gorm Fogner moved his head from side to side. 'I have also experienced loss and mourning,' he said, bringing up something personal
for the first time. 'I know what it's like to feel such intense sorrow,
even though I can't describe what the grief you are going through must
feel like. What I do know is that you will smile and laugh long before
you feel any happiness. But it will come. The happiness will return.'

Emma wanted to ask who he had lost, but decided against it.

'I'm just so tired,' she said instead.

Fogner studied her.

'Are you having trouble sleeping?' he asked.

'Yes,' Emma admitted.

'Dealing with grief uses up a lot of energy,' Fogner said. 'I can fill
out a sick note for you.'

Emma shook her head. Taking time off work was not an option.

'You can get medication to help you sleep,' Fogner suggested.
'Grief is not only mentally draining, it can make you physically ill
too. It's vital that you get some rest.'

Emma thought about how hard the nights had been, and how
good it would feel to wake up rested.

Fogner stood up, pulled a set of keys out of his pocket and unlocked a drawer behind his desk.

'You can get the first few tablets from me,' he offered. 'Then I'll write a prescription for you, and you can use it if you feel like it.'

Emma nodded. Gorm Fogner sat at the desk and filled out all the necessary forms.

'You don't have to wait until tonight,' he said, handing her a strip of four tablets. 'You should try and sleep once you get home.'

Emma took them. She didn't know whether it was the conversation with the therapist that had been exhausting, or whether it was the accumulated lack of sleep that was catching up with her, but she wasn't going to say no to the advice. She wanted to go home and lie down.

# 54

'I need to get the search dogs out to the area as soon as possible. Immediately. Today.'

Blix took a few steps towards Gard Fosse's desk.

'The last time you were in here, you said you thought that Patricia may still be alive,' Fosse reminded him. 'Isaksen had received a school photo of her at the prison, with Ruth-Kristine's fingerprints on it.'

'I don't know who the girl in that photo is,' Blix replied. 'But we've just discovered where Patricia was kept after she was kidnapped, and that Ruth-Kristine had been there with a shovel.'

Fosse said nothing.

'More snow has been forecast for tomorrow,' Blix added. 'For Vestfold too. I don't think they've had any snow there today.'

The police superintendent shook his watch out from the sleeve of his uniform and returned Blix's gaze with his own sceptical one. 'It takes over an hour to drive down to Undrumsåsen,' he began. 'And it'll take a while to rally the dog patrol.'

'I know. That's why I've paused the interview. To get the ball rolling.'

Fosse looked as if he were contemplating the idea.

'It starts to get dark down there by about four o'clock, if that—'

'The dogs can work in the dark,' Blix interrupted. 'And it isn't exactly the world's largest forest. If Patricia's buried in there somewhere, I can't leave her in there any longer than I absolutely have to.'

Again, it took a few seconds for Fosse to answer.

'I'll see what I can do.'

'Great. Thank you.'

When Blix returned to the interview room, some of the colour seemed to have returned to Sophus Ahlander's face.

Blix got him to go through his story one more time. Asked him to elaborate.

'When she kept calling you before New Year's Eve, what did she want?' he asked.

'It was hard to understand what she was after,' Ahlander replied. 'But she needed help again. She was probably hopped up on pills or some other shit, but she was saying that I had helped her with Patricia that time, and she needed me to help her again now. There was no one else she could go to, she said.'

'What did she need help with?'

Ahlander paused.

'She was scared of a guy.'

'Scared?'

'Yes, I don't know why, or who it was – I didn't ask. I tried to hang up after that. But she just continued to screech at me. She was pretty incoherent.'

'Describe the screeching ... even if it was difficult to work out what she was saying,' Blix requested.

Ahlander sighed.

'The only thing I managed to figure out was that she was going to meet someone or other and needed help from someone else who she could trust. I'd done enough for that woman already. I told her that, but she didn't let up.' He rolled his eyes.

Blix checked his notes before continuing.

'When was she planning on meeting whoever it was?'

'New Year's Eve, I think. Which made it all the more unbelievable.'

'Did you get the impression that the meeting had something to do with Patricia, seeing as she had used her as an excuse to try and rope you in?'

Ahlander hesitated before he answered:

'I didn't really think about it that way at the time,' he began. 'But now you mention it ... maybe, yeah. But I couldn't possibly say it was definitely to do with Patricia.' He shook his head. 'I'd tried to forget about everything that happened back then, but she wouldn't stop calling. Turned up at my house a few times too, calling as she stood outside. I pretended I wasn't home. In the end, I went to the cabin, for some peace. And then some woman turned up at my door one night, who, from a distance anyway, looked like Ruth-Kristine, so I thought, for fuck's sake, that's enough now.'

He sighed heavily.

'I hope she wasn't too shook up afterwards, that journalist.'

Blix's mind momentarily diverted to Emma.

'Did Ruth-Kristine say anything about what was planned after this meeting she had to go to?'

'No. And I didn't ask either.'

Blix glanced down at his notebook.

'Where do you think Ruth-Kristine is now?' he asked.

Ahlander shrugged.

'I have absolutely no idea.'

# 55

Emma stood with the small, white sleeping pill resting in the palm of her hand as she let the water run, waiting for it to turn cold. She was reluctant to swallow it, but felt drained all the same. She was tired, but not in a way that meant she was sleepy. That said, she wouldn't get anything done until she had managed to get a few hours' sleep, she told herself.

She filled the glass, placed the pill on her tongue and washed it down.

A second later, the phone rang. Emma took a deep breath before answering.

'Hi, it's Asta.'

Asta. Kasper's mother.

'Our plane landed a little over an hour ago,' she said, 'and we didn't have any luggage to pick up. We'll be in Oslo slightly earlier than planned. Where are you?'

Emma wasn't sure how to answer. She looked around. Her eyes rested on the computer, the loose notes on the kitchen table.

'I'm at work,' she said.

'We're meeting with the police first, one of the family liaison officers,' Asta continued. 'He'll be telling us how he can help with the case and everything, and then we'll go to the University Hospital afterwards, where ... Kasper is.'

That was as much as she could bring herself to say.

'I can't join you, unfortunately. It ... I can't, I don't have time.'

It was silent on the other end.

'You have to work ... now?'

The sound of sirens erupted somewhere in the distance. Emma walked to the window, looked out.

'Yes. I'm sorry,' she said. 'I can't leave, not right now.'

She was about to say that Kasper would have understood, but chose not to. Even though she didn't explicitly say it, Emma could hear that Asta Bjerringbo was disappointed, sad.

'Maybe I can find some time a little later?' Emma offered.

'We had hoped that you might want to come back with us, to Denmark,' Asta said. 'With Kasper. His coffin will travel back on the plane tonight too. The Norwegian police have organised everything. I asked them to book a seat for you as well. His brother, and the rest of the family, would like to meet you.'

'I understand,' Emma said. 'This is ... all a bit sudden. I'll see what I can do.'

Asta thanked her and hung up.

Emma took a deep breath and tried to shake off her guilt. She checked the box of sleeping pills to see if there was any information about how long they worked for, but there wasn't. She could check online, but couldn't be bothered. Instead, she walked into the bedroom, took off her wig, undressed and crawled under the duvet.

# 56

Tine Abelvik stood waiting outside Amy Linh's flat on Sars gate. Kovic used the keys they had found at the crime scene to let them into the building. They stamped the snow off their boots and allowed the door to close slowly behind them. The smell that met them was something like a mixture of wet dog and oriental spices. There was a pram partially blocking the staircase. Eight post boxes were fastened to the wall in two perfectly straight rows. Bright red, as if brand new. Kovic found Amy Linh's name and, with her phone, took a few photos of the names of the other residents.

'We should talk to all of them,' she said. 'See if anyone knows anything.'

Abelvik nodded.

It wasn't the first time Kovic had been inside the home of a person who had recently died. As a single woman, she was not unfamiliar with the silence that could fill an empty flat, but there was something about a home to which the owner would never return. A different kind of emptiness. It was charged, more powerful. It was in the walls and the ceiling, almost as if they knew that someone was gone, as if they were grieving for them.

Amy Linh's flat was small and cramped, with parquet laminate flooring and walls painted white. A red-and-blue raincoat hung on a hook closest to the entrance, next to a black umbrella with a broken rib poking out. Hats, mittens and scarves had been scrunched up and tucked away in a basket on the floor. Lined up beside the basket were a pair of wellies, ankle boots, one of which had a hole in the toe, and some trainers that looked like they might have been white once.

A tame yet inquisitive *meow* was followed by the pitter-patter of paws against the laminate flooring and the appearance of a black cat from out of the kitchen. It stopped in the doorway, as if it were scrutinising the visitors. Kovic bent down and tried to lure it over, but the cat just stared at her warily, before it turned and walked back into the kitchen.

Kovic straightened up. 'Let's see what we can find,' she said.

Abelvik started in the hallway, making her way towards the bedroom, while Kovic took the kitchen. There was a receipt stuck to the fridge, one of those vouchers from the plastic-bottle recycling machines that you could claim some money back with. She mustn't have had the chance to cash it in. Magnetic letter tiles – some had been organised into a few well-chosen words, the rest scattered randomly across the fridge. A handwritten recipe. A credit note from a clothing shop. Tickets to see an Icelandic artist in concert in a few months' time. A photo of an older Asian woman sat on a staircase outside a dilapidated house; she didn't seem particularly happy to be photographed.

The kitchen reminded Kovic of her own. A half-loaded dishwasher, a used saucepan left to soak in the sink. A strip of tablets, ibuprofen, had been left on the counter. A bowl of clementines. A book with what she presumed were Vietnamese recipes. Perched on the windowsill were several pot plants and a rustic candlestick with the candle almost burned down to the wick. A tall jar with kitchen utensils stood below.

What Kovic was looking for was something that could tell her what Amy Linh had been up to over the last few days, and who she had spent that time with. Everything was of interest. A receipt from a restaurant, a cinema ticket, a note with a phone number.

Kovic's gaze travelled across the room, up and down, side to side, slowly, as she had learned during her training, but not too slowly either, as Blix had instilled in her. She had to let her first impression form by itself, to trust it. Even though Amy Linh's flat wasn't exactly a crime scene, the principle was the same. Let her instincts lead her, at first. And then proceed methodologically.

The cat had settled next to an empty food bowl under the table. Kovic glanced around for something she could give it, but couldn't see anything obvious. She looked up and noticed a calendar fastened to the wall. Amy Linh's plans for the month had been written across it in various colours. An appointment with the chiropractor, 9th of January. ELENA had turned twenty-eight at the beginning of the month – a drawing of a blue balloon accompanied that entry. Amy Linh was supposed to start yoga classes next Tuesday. She was also meant to attend a writing course for beginners on a Monday later in the month. And every Sunday, written throughout the entire calendar, was a note to remind her to call her mother.

Kovic moved on into the living room, where she met Abelvik.

'No trace of any visitors,' she said. 'Doesn't even own a single sex toy.'

Kovic let her eyes wander while Abelvik spoke.

'Only one toothbrush in the bathroom. She was healthy too, from what it seems. No medicines in the cabinet, other than the usual. Plasters, paracetamol.'

There were even more plants on the floor in the living room. A TV stood on top of a small, white stand. A large amateur painting hung on the wall behind it. The painting depicted a small boat, full of people, in the midst of a violent storm. Amy Linh had several bookshelves too, mostly holding foreign literature.

On one of the small coffee tables, next to the armchair, was a used cup and a notebook with a pen attached to it. Kovic sat down, imagining that she were Amy Linh. She picked up the notebook and browsed through it, realising immediately that it had been well-used. It was full of journal entries, written in neat handwriting.

Kovic flipped to the final page, dated the day before Amy Linh had been murdered. The entry consisted of a few notes.

*Why alone at the hotel? For days, behind a locked door?*
*– secret lover(s)*
*– hiding from someone*
*– taking some time off*
*– has done something bad*

There were several other entries made up of questions about, and descriptions of, various guests from the hotel. The kind of life she imagined they had, details of the clothes they had packed, the things they had bought, the receipts from places they had visited. Considering the way Amy Linh wrote about the guests, there was little to suggest that she had actually interviewed any of them. In some instances, she described them right down to the moles on their faces, and even the size of shoe she thought they might wear. She had included no names.

Kovic showed Abelvik the last entry.

'She was going to start a writing course,' Kovic added. 'These look like writing exercises.'

Abelvik had a brief flick through the notebook.

'It's good she had a cat,' she commented. 'There wasn't much else going on in her life.'

Kovic looked around. There was a laptop on the floor, next to a stack of books. She picked it up.

'Can you take this and the notebook back to HQ?' she said as she stood up. 'Maybe they'll provide us with something to go on.'

'What's the next step?'

'The hotel she worked at,' Kovic answered. 'If her life was as lonely as it looks, her colleagues were probably the people who knew her best.'

# 57

The questioning of Sophus Ahlander had taken almost five hours. It had been an exhausting exercise in concentration. A headache had begun to pulse behind Blix's right eye. He was going to have to try and find a few painkillers, and something to eat.

The door to Gard Fosse's office was closed. Blix knocked and popped his head in, without waiting for an answer. The room was empty.

He needed to confirm whether the search dogs were on their way to Undrumsåsen. Then he would have to get down there himself. It was eerily quiet in the spacious, open-plan office. Neither Wibe nor Abelvik were there. One junior investigator was busy on the phone, another appeared to be engrossed in something on their computer screen. Other than those two, the place was completely empty.

Blix grabbed a spotted apple that someone had left on a plate, took a bite out of it and headed back to his desk. He picked up the phone to call Oslo Prison, and asked to speak to Christer Storm Isaksen.

'What is it?' Isaksen asked the second the line was connected. 'Has something happened?'

The line crackled. Blix pressed the phone closer to his ear.

'Yes,' he said. 'It ... There is something. And I didn't want you to find out about it on the news. We ... have arrested someone. He's been charged for kidnapping Patricia.'

Silence.

'Are you there?' Blix asked eventually.

'Who?' Isaksen enquired.

Blix hesitated. He knew the question would come, but had decided to withhold the details for now.

'One of Ruth-Kristine's old acquaintances,' he replied.

'So I *was* right,' he said, thoughtfully. 'She was in on it.'

'There is certainly a lot of evidence to point to that,' Blix said. 'But there are a lot of questions we still need to find answers for.'

'Where is she?' Isaksen interrupted. 'Did he say what he did to her?'

'He took her and looked after her for a few days until Ruth-Kristine took over. He doesn't know what happened after that. Ruth-Kristine might be the only person who does know.'

'And where is she?'

'We're looking for her. She's missing.'

He could hear Isaksen's ragged breathing on the other end of the line.

'Her fingerprints were on the photo,' Blix continued. 'Along with prints belonging to several other people.'

'Did she deliver it then?'

'We don't know,' Blix admitted. 'We don't know anything other than the fact that her fingerprints were on the photo.'

Silence again. The sound of Isaksen's shallow breathing.

'You have to talk to Jette Djurholm,' he said suddenly. 'She was Ruth-Kristine's alibi the day Patricia disappeared. Now you *know* that Ruth-Kristine was involved in the kidnapping. Maybe Djurholm was involved too.'

Blix understood where he was coming from. There were recordings of Ruth-Kristine and Jette Djurholm together that day, from one of the CCTV cameras at the shopping centre, captured at the same time Patricia had been kidnapped. That had obviously been a part of Ruth-Kristine's plan, but it didn't necessarily mean that Djurholm knew anything.

'We'll talk to her,' Blix assured him.

'She has to know something,' Isaksen persisted. 'She might know where Patricia is.'

Blix could hear in Isaksen's voice just how much the news had affected him.

'I shouldn't have told you over the phone,' Blix said. 'I should have let you know face-to-face, but I haven't—'

'What's his name?' Isaksen interrupted.

'Hm?'

'The man you arrested. Who is it?'

'We have to wait to—'

'Is it Sophus Ahlander?'

Blix was taken aback.

'How—?'

'Just answer the question – is it him?'

'Do you know him?'

'No. Is it him?'

Blix couldn't help but tell him the truth.

'It's him, he's the person we've arrested,' he confirmed. 'But there is still a lot we don't know. How do you know about Sophus Ahlander?'

He was quiet for a moment.

'A journalist was here,' Isaksen answered. 'She mentioned him.'

Emma, Blix thought. The information had come full circle.

'Right,' he said. 'I have to hang up now. I just wanted to let you know.'

'Find her,' Isaksen begged him. 'Just find Patricia. She's alive, I am *sure* of it.'

# 58

Despite the old-fashioned name, Hotel Gyldenløve was a modern hotel with a colourful interior.

Kovic joined the queue for the reception desk, behind a German couple checking in. When it was her turn, she discreetly revealed her ID card to the receptionist and asked to speak to the hotel manager.

The man behind the desk nodded, lifted the receiver and pushed one of the keys. It only took a few seconds before he said in a hushed voice, 'The police are here, they want to speak with you.'

Kovic could just about hear the man's voice on the other end of the phone. She could tell that he was surprised, but couldn't hear what he said. The receptionist answered yes twice, before hanging up.

'He's on the third floor with the caretaker at the moment, but he will be down soon.'

It took all of one minute, before a tall, broad-shouldered man stepped out of the lift. His name tag only displayed his surname – Rønning – but he introduced himself by his first name: 'Theodor,' he said with a friendly handshake. 'But everyone calls me Teddy.'

'Is there somewhere we could talk in private?' Kovic asked.

'We can use my office,' he said, pointing to a small room to the side of the reception.

Kovic followed him in and closed the door. All that separated them from the guests in the lobby was a glass wall with one frosted strip at chest-height running along the length of it.

'Can I get you anything?' Rønning asked before he sat down.

'No, thank you,' Kovic replied, taking a seat on the other side of the desk. 'I'm here about a suspicious death.'

Rønning tilted his head.

'One of your employees was found dead early this morning,' Kovic continued. 'Amy Linh.'

Rønning's jaw dropped.

'Amy,' he said. 'How...?'

'She was probably killed yesterday afternoon or evening,' Kovic continued. 'We need to know where she was and what she was doing before then.'

Rønning looked stunned.

'I spoke to her yesterday,' he spluttered. 'She was at work.'

'Do you know what time she went home?'

'Her shift ended at four o'clock, but I don't know if that's when she left. We don't have a clock-in, clock-out system here.'

'What has her behaviour been like recently?'

Rønning paused.

'I'm not quite sure I understand the question?'

'Could something have happened to her here that may have led to her death?'

Rønning thought about it.

'I have a hard time imagining that would be the case,' he concluded. 'But I'm not the one she had the most contact with.'

'Who should I talk to?'

'Housekeeping.'

'Is there somewhere I could interview them?'

'I'm sure we have an available meeting room,' Rønning said.

Kovic stood up. 'Great,' she said.

The hotel manager found a room for her at the end of a corridor, next to the toilets. Kovic met the employees, one after the other. There were eight of them at work that day. None of them knew Amy Linh particularly well. They had no contact with her outside of work, and they were usually so busy on the job that they never really had time for small talk. They didn't know if she had a partner, didn't know the names of any of her friends or acquaintances. All in all, they painted a picture of a woman who mainly kept to herself, who was unassuming, reserved and introverted. An innocent woman, Kovic thought as she left the hotel.

# 59

The names of towns and villages along the Oslo Fjord whistled past the car. Sande, Holmestrand, Horten. Blix was sat in the back seat, resting his head against the window. They only had about three hours of daylight left. A little longer, maybe. He pulled his phone out and dialled Merete's number.

'Are you sure you have time to talk now?' she asked. 'With everything going on?'

'I wouldn't have called if I didn't. Where are you?'

'At home. Doing a bit of packing.'

'For ... Singapore?'

'Yes, you know ... we'll be there for quite a while. A completely different country with a completely different culture. You've got to plan a little differently.'

Blix had no idea what she was talking about.

'It was probably a bit of a surprise, finding out that I was going too?'

'It certainly came as a surprise to your daughter, anyway.'

'Not really, but that's probably how she made it sound.'

Blix didn't have an answer for that.

'So what's going on then? Why have you decided that it's okay to leave Iselin now, while she's in the state she's in?' It came out a little harsher than he had intended.

Merete sighed and was silent for a moment, before she began:

'Firstly: Your daughter is tough, so she's coping pretty well, given the circumstances. Secondly: I have been her mother and then some for twenty years and nine months. I'm the one who's been there for her while you studied and worked and dealt with ... your stuff.'

'I have—'

'Wait, I am not done. I have never, as long as I have known you or your daughter, done anything that has been *just* for me. The longest trip I've ever been on was to Budapest, and that was only for three days for work. And yes, you and I went to Copenhagen a few times, but now, for the first time, I – *I* – have the opportunity to go on an adventure too. Experience something. Be something other than someone's mother or cheerleader. This is a chance for me to see some of the world for myself. And Iselin has Toralf, and you, and some friends who can take care of her, so she's not alone. She just won't be depending on *me* for once.'

Blix struggled to find anything to say.

'I just thought it was odd that she was living with you one day, and had suddenly moved out the next,' he answered finally.

'I thought so too,' Merete said. 'But she's still got a bit of teenager in her. She's miffed that I didn't invite her to come with us, so she probably wanted to demonstrate that by being a bit dramatic. And I can understand it, but I've said that she can come to visit, and that I would like to chip in and help her pay for the tickets and such, even though she probably has more money than I do at the moment.'

Blix nodded. 'What are you planning on doing over there?'

'I don't know yet. Travel around. Think about what I want to do with the rest of my life. Take a course or two. Start painting or become a yoga instructor – no clue, really. Jan-Egil will have to work a lot, so I'll have quite a lot of free time.'

'When do you leave?'

'In eleven days.'

Blix didn't know what to add to that, other than: 'Have a good trip. I'll take care of Iselin.'

'Thank you.' She sounded happy. 'Say hi to her, from me. Tell her to come over for dinner with us before we leave. Maybe you would both like to come? Next Sunday works?'

Blix thought about it.

'Thank you for the invitation,' he said. 'But I don't think that would be a good idea.'

'Why not?'

He couldn't tell her the truth, that he still found it harrowing to see her with another man. Merete had always been careful and avoided being too affectionate while Blix was there, but he had noticed them anyway, a shared look, or a gentle hand on the other one's arm. It had always jolted him, like a stab in the heart.

'I'll tell Iselin to call you, so you can organise something. I have to get back to work.'

He hung up and sighed heavily. Looked out of the window and avoided meeting the gaze of the driver in the rear-view mirror.

The young police officer sitting in the passenger seat received an update. He read it, typed out a quick response and turned round to inform Blix.

'The cadaver dogs are ready.'

'The search dogs,' Blix corrected him. 'That's good.'

He had used the specially trained sniffer dogs before, but not for a case as old as this one. The search had been under way for about half an hour when Blix and the other officer arrived. There were three dogs in all. The dog handlers were equipped with searchlights, although it looked as if they had enough natural light for the time being. Several floodlights had been set up as well, all connected to the electricity supply at the cabin.

'Have any of them detected anything yet?' Blix enquired.

'Nothing so far,' the head of the dog section replied, showing Blix a map of the search area, divided into segments.

Blix was pleased that he had the forethought to put some extra layers on. He walked around by himself mostly, but he was connected to the search teams by radio, and was never far enough away that he couldn't still see them. The occasional clamour of barking dogs would pierce through the silence, obscuring the sound of his feet as they trampled the forest floor. The twigs that snapped beneath him, the moss that sighed under his weight.

He scanned the ground for areas where it might be possible to dig at least half a metre into the ground. But that looked like it could be almost anywhere. The sense of unease grew with every step he took. Ruth-Kristine might have been in here, somewhere. Patricia might be buried somewhere close by.

Had she been murdered by her own mother?

Blix knew all too well that desperate people could carry out grotesque, inhumane deeds. There were plenty of examples of parents who had killed their own children without having any well-thought out reasons for doing so. And Ruth-Kristine was a peculiar woman. Suicidal one moment, furious the next, and after Patricia had disappeared, she, too, had disappeared into a spiral of drugs, cigarettes and alcohol.

He had just started to deliberate whether he should get back into the car, when the radio crackled:

'Possible discovery,' the voice reported.

Blix responded immediately. 'Where?'

Blix made his way over as the voice started to give him directions.

'Under a massive, felled tree. Looks as if it came down a long time ago,' the voice added.

The man on the other end guiding him, it wasn't long before Blix saw the crowd of people and dogs ahead. The light from one of the torches penetrated the incipient darkness that had started to settle between the tree trunks.

Blix was met by a uniformed officer, holding a dog back on a tight lead.

'It picked up the scent immediately,' he said, pointing to the upturned tree.

A gaping hole had been exposed where the roots were ripped out of the ground. Blix took a few steps closer and let his own torch wander across the mouth of the opening, which was about two metres long and a metre wide.

He bent down and felt the forest floor. It was hard, cold, but not impossible to dig into. A feeling coursed through his entire body. She was here.

Blix turned around and asked for a shovel. In the light provided by the surrounding torches, he swept away the top layer of moss and heather. Then he pressed down with the tip of the shovel, not too hard. He felt his way into the ground, carefully, starting about halfway into the centre of the opening. With every shovel full of soil that he cast aside, he grew warmer, angrier, and more and more anxious about the sight he was about to be met with.

The hole widened. Something was starting to peek through the surface. The corner of a black plastic sheet.

Blix let go of the shovel, knelt down and started using his hands.

A black plastic bag. It had a gash in it from where the shovel had broken through. A light piece of cloth was poking out.

Someone took a photo.

'Help me, please,' Blix requested.

One of the officers knelt beside him. Together they eased the plastic bag out of the ground and laid it down gently beside the hole. Blix prised it open to reveal the twisted bundle inside. It was tangled up in a weather-beaten bedsheet, as if the cloth had been used as a shroud. Beneath the thin fabric, Blix could feel what he knew to be the knuckles of a small child's hand.

# 60

The train to the airport drifted silently through the Romeriks Tunnel. The utter darkness had a mesmerising effect on Emma. It was as if she had forgotten how to blink. The pitch-black inside the tunnel blurred everything within. The walls streamed past. The occasional light would come into view, but even with the rhythmic precision of the train, her eyes never really registered them. The yellow glow only sent her deeper into the trance.

Emma had made her mind up the moment she got up that morning. She would follow Kasper home.

She had thought that the sleeping pill would make her groggy, but she felt well rested. She had called and talked to Irene, realising then that the only thing she really could do was return to Denmark with Kasper's parents. Not only because she felt that she owed them that respect, but because she knew that her conscience would plague her if she didn't. Although, on the other hand, she now felt like she had failed Anita, and her job. She had slept through most of the day, and hadn't sent in anything new. And now she was leaving. She hung on to the excuse that it was the weekend, all the while aware that neither Anita nor Henrik Wollan would be taking any time off, not now that people were so desperate for information.

The train lurched momentarily, jerking Emma out of her daze. Her eyes settled on her own reflection in the window, and she was repelled by the paleness of her face. As if there were no life left in it.

The air pressure in the carriage adjusted as the train left the tunnel. The lights of Lillestrøm Station temporarily replaced the darkness before the half-light of the evening returned, obscuring everything other than the contours of the fields and the trees on the other side of town.

Emma was dreading the time she would be spending with Kasper's family in Århus. Surrounded by their grief and pain, all while they tried to be good hosts. She didn't like spending that much time in other people's company, or at least, she didn't tend to stay the night in other people's homes. Her discomfort grew as she approached the airport. She thought that Kasper's family might not actually want her to visit. She was a stranger. She and Kasper hadn't been together that long. They probably knew that she wasn't particularly keen to go with them either. It was like volunteering to perform in a play, a tragedy, where everyone had to take a role they would rather not have.

She pushed the thought out of her mind, and instead, ended up thinking of Blix. He had promised to keep her updated on any developments following the interview with Sophus Ahlander, but she hadn't heard anything.

The train pulled into Oslo Gardermoen Airport, only nineteen minutes after leaving Oslo Central Station.

Emma had been to Copenhagen several times. It was a comfortable journey. This time, she would be on a smaller plane, heading down to Billund, somewhere in central Denmark.

Picking up the suitcase that she had hastily packed earlier that day, she towed Kasper's suitcase behind her, struggled through the ticket barrier on the platform and joined the queue trailing up the escalators towards check-in. Through the flurry of people, she spotted a large man with a grey-and-white beard waving at her from under one of the notice boards.

Jakob Bjerringbo let go of the luggage trolley he had been holding and approached Emma with a warm, welcoming smile. Emma set her suitcases aside and accepted his embrace.

'It's so great that you're coming back with us,' he said in his deep, baritone voice, letting go of her and holding her at arm's length, looking at her properly. Then he noticed the suitcase at Emma's feet. His ordinarily jovial, open and friendly face dropped.

'Is that...?' He pointed to the black suitcase to Emma's right.

'Yes, it's Kasper's.'

Jakob stood there, staring at it as if he had x-ray vision, as if he could see an entire life unfolding behind the hard plastic.

'Let me take that for you,' he said at last, forcing himself to smile again. Emma thanked him.

They walked over to Asta, who had deep bags under her eyes and looked like she had very recently been crying. She, too, opened her arms and pulled Emma in close, although in a much briefer, cooler hug.

'How long will you be staying?' Jakob asked. 'We've planned a memorial service for Sunday. The funeral won't be until later next week.'

'It depends,' Emma answered hesitantly.

'On work,' Asta said. It sounded like an accusation.

'Yes,' Emma replied. 'That too.'

Jakob looked over at his wife, before reassuring Emma: 'We understand.'

He picked her suitcase up and added: 'Let's get you checked in.'

They walked over to the SAS desks. Everything that had been left unsaid now lingered in the air around them, so much so that Emma felt the urge to ask how everything had gone at the hospital earlier that day, but she couldn't bring herself to do it.

She wondered how Kasper's coffin would be loaded onto the plane, and whether there was anything they would have to do when they landed, but she didn't ask about that either. A funeral home would most likely take care of the logistics.

They made their way through security, and were meandering through the duty-free shops, towards Gate E6, when Emma received a text. The message was from a number she had contacted recently. It took her a few seconds to realise that it belonged to Mustafa, the manager of the housing association where Ruth-Kristine lived.

*Hello. Found the name. Jette Djurholm's husband is called Jens-Christian Kvist. They didn't leave a forwarding address for their post, but I did find an old mobile number. Think it's Norwegian. Maybe he still uses it?*

Mustafa had included the eight-digit number. Emma replied and thanked him for his help, before saving Kvist's name and number into her phone. She wondered if she should try to contact him then and there, but figured it could wait until tomorrow. Tonight was for Kasper. And his family.

# 61

The forensics team from the local police station had taken over the site, which was nestled in behind the trees. They had carefully unwound the sheet, revealing the small bones within, and the remains of body tissue that had not yet decomposed. A clump of hair had gathered beneath the skull.

Blix could not remember the last time he had felt so empty. To stand above this scene, an incomplete childhood, to take it all in, filled him with a grief so intense that, at first, he could neither say nor do anything. He had just stood there, staring down at the small child who someone had decided would not be allowed to carry on living. Who had lay there, under just a few centimetres of soil, for so many years.

A part of him had been relieved that the investigation that had haunted him for so long was finally over. Until those emotions had transformed into rage.

When Blix finally got back home, it was already half past eleven. He went straight into the bathroom and scrubbed his hands clean. Not just to remove all the dirt that was lodged under his fingernails, but to cleanse himself of the feeling of inadequacy. He knew they had done everything they possibly could at the time, ten years ago, but he couldn't escape the fact that Patricia had still been alive for several days after she was kidnapped. If they had only managed to do even more during those first few hours, those first few days, she could have survived. It was something he was going to have to learn to live with.

'Dad?' Iselin called from the living room.

Blix had completely forgotten that she was living with him. When he reached the living room, she looked up, meeting him with a brief smile. The TV was on behind her, a programme about how various families survived in Alaska. Blix had no idea when his daughter had become interested in that kind of thing.

'Hi, darling,' he said, realising for the first time just how sombre he sounded.

'How's it going?' his daughter asked from the sofa.

'Oh, it's...' Blix replied heavily. 'It...'

He took his phone from his pocket and left it on the kitchen table, next to where the newspapers and letters from the last week had started to pile up. Blix wasn't even sure what day of the week it was.

He pulled his jacket off and started tidying up. Iselin was still watching him.

'So it's that bad,' she said.

Blix made no attempt to hide how he was feeling. He didn't see the point in keeping it to himself either, so he sat down and told Iselin what had happened.

'Poor little thing,' she said when he was done. 'What did her father say?'

'I haven't told him yet.'

'Why not?'

'We have to be absolutely certain first.'

'Oh, yes, of course.'

On the screen, one of the programme's participants was having some trouble with a snowmobile – they had managed to get trapped in an icy river.

'And how are things with you, darling?'

Iselin glanced at him quickly, before looking down and staring at something on the floor.

'I tried calling you,' she said. 'Earlier.'

He felt a wave of guilt for having not answered.

'I'm sorry,' he said. 'I was busy.'

'I get it.'

'Was it something important?'

'Not anymore,' she smiled, shaking her head.

Blix smiled back. 'I have to leave for Denmark tomorrow,' he said.

'What for?'

'I just need to question someone who has moved there. We're

looking at the case in a whole new light now, and she may have information she didn't quite grasp the gravity of at the time.'

'Can I go with you?'

Blix smiled and shook his head. 'It won't be a fun trip, darling,' he said. 'And I'll be home before dinner.'

She nodded, but he could tell that she was disappointed.

'Are you hungry? Want me to get you anything?'

'No, but thanks.'

Blix had stood up and was on his way to the fridge when Iselin spoke up:

'I've been wondering if I should apply for police college.'

Blix stopped and turned back to face her.

'I've been thinking about it for a while,' she continued. 'I think it looks … interesting.'

*Interesting*, Blix thought. After the day he had just had.

'I think the work would suit me.'

Blix didn't know what to say. The years he had spent in the police force had shaped him, made him who he was today. They had destroyed his marriage, had even stolen a few years from his relationship with Iselin. And Gard Fosse, his best friend from police college, was now a person Blix could no longer spend time with without feeling uncomfortable.

He thought about all he had seen, all he had experienced. Everything he was going to have to face, come to terms with, in the years to come. With Iselin in training as well, and then out in active service, he would always be worrying about how she was dealing with the dangers she would inevitably be exposed to, the fates she would eventually meet. His entire body was urging him to steer her away from the track she was heading towards, but he couldn't bring himself to do it, not when he could see the sparkle in her eye, the expectation that grew in the charged seconds that ticked by as she awaited his answer.

# 62

Emma woke up early, in what had once been Kasper's childhood bed. It wasn't even half past seven yet. It was still dark outside.

She grabbed her phone and checked to see if anything had happened back in Norway overnight. The latest headline on news.no was about a murder in the Botanical Garden. Wollan had taken that case. Emma skimmed through the first few paragraphs and concluded that the police had little to go on.

She had slept with her wig on – something she never did at home. She got up and went to the bathroom, took it off to shower, then got ready. It was half past eight by the time she re-emerged from the bathroom. She felt a pang of hunger, but most of all, she felt the discomfort of being in someone else's home. As if she was an intruder and shouldn't be there.

Emma followed the aroma of coffee into the kitchen, where Jakob was bent over, peering into the fridge. His pyjama bottoms had slid a little too far down. Emma looked away quickly.

'Oh, good morning,' Jakob said, once he realised she was there. He straightened up, yanking his pyjama bottoms back into position again as he did so. The unnatural pose had caused his face to turn bright pink.

'Did you sleep well?'

'I did,' Emma lied. 'How about you?'

'Oh, you know. It's not been particularly easy to get much sleep these last few days.'

He paused, before continuing.

'But I slept a little. Coffee?'

'Yes please.'

He shot over to one of the cupboards just above the machine, took out a cup and filled it with coffee.

'Just say if you want any milk or sugar.'

'Black coffee is fine.'

He handed it to her and poured his own. They stood there, both aware of the awkward silence between them.

'Are you always the first one up in the mornings?' Emma asked.

Jakob considered the question. 'Yes ... I like to get an early start. To make breakfast for our guests, when we have any. To be in here, enjoying the smell of the coffee. Maybe start to get a little hungry, as I wait.'

He smiled.

Emma was starting to like Jakob more and more. Maybe because there had been so much of him in Kasper. Their smiles were almost identical. That great sense of humour. Kasper liked to be up early too, playing the host when she had been to visit him in Copenhagen.

'You must excuse my wife,' Jakob said. 'She's not handling this very well.'

'There is nothing to apologise for,' Emma insisted.

'She looks at all this like ... like it's an attack on *her*, personally. What has *she* done to deserve this? This grief, this punishment?'

Jakob stopped himself, busied himself with one of the drawers.

'Sorry,' he said, collecting some cutlery. 'I didn't mean to...'

Emma smiled and shook her head slightly, trying to show that there was no need for him to apologise.

'Is there anything I can do?' she asked, in an attempt to change the subject.

Jakob smiled again and shook his head. 'No, no, you have a seat, I'll get some food sorted.'

Emma did as she was told. An immediate restlessness came over her. The desire to get out. Leave. Be alone. She wished she had brought her bike with her.

Jakob had found a loaf of bread, some butter and a pack of deli meats. He had just begun making a batch of scrambled eggs, when Emma asked if he had a car she could borrow. He turned up the heat on the stove before answering:

'A car? Yes, I ... certainly do,' he said.

'I just fancy having a bit of a look round.'

Emma wasn't sure why she had lied, but Jakob nodded as if he understood, answering:

'Sure, of course.'

He disappeared into the long hallway and returned a moment later, a bunch of keys in his hand, from which he removed a large, thick key. It had a dark-blue Ford logo on it.

'Drive as much as you want,' he said hospitably. 'There should be a full tank in there.'

'Thank you.'

'More coffee?'

Emma declined, content to eat a slice of dark rye bread with some liver pâté, before she headed out, glad that the rest of the house had not yet woken up.

# 63

The first flight to Copenhagen left from Oslo Gardermoen Airport at 06:05. Seeing as there were no morning flights that flew direct to Billund, Blix got on the earliest flight to Denmark that he could. He was picked up from Kastrup Airport by Lone Cramer, from the National Police of Denmark. Blix didn't know anyone else in the Danish police who would show up at such short notice. They had met last autumn through the investigation into the countdown murders, and he had found her to be both a diligent investigator and a friendly person.

'Did you get *any* sleep last night?' she asked with a chuckle.

Blix smiled back and shrugged. 'Two hours, tops.'

Cramer guided them through security and led him out to a marked police car parked right outside the main entrance.

'What have you found out about Jette Djurholm?' Blix asked as he got in.

Cramer took a folder from off the top of the dashboard and handed it to him.

'She's had a few speeding tickets,' she said, pulling out and heading immediately onto the motorway. 'That's all. Married, one child. She works part-time in a nursery. Leads a pretty normal life, basically.'

Blix flipped through the papers.

'You could call her and organise a meeting first?' Cramer continued. 'Make sure she's home.'

'I don't want her to know I'm coming. That way she won't have time to prepare before I get there.'

'You think she's hiding something?'

Blix mulled it over.

'Not necessarily, but I've already questioned her three times, and every single time, she gave the exact same information, right down to the same words, the same expressions. Identical, every time. It was kind of impressive, in a way.'

'You mean, like she'd memorised what to say?'

'Maybe. And she always seemed a little restless.'

Back then, he had written this off as a fear of authority. Some people got quite anxious when they had to explain themselves to the police, and this often manifested itself in nervous behaviour, erratic movements. It wasn't uncommon for people to practice what they should say in police interviews either, to avoid misunderstandings. But now that Ruth-Kristine's role in the kidnapping seemed undeniable, Blix needed to look Jette Djurholm in the eye when he asked her the same questions, one last time.

They crossed the bridge from Amager over to the larger island of Sjælland, and continued heading further south.

'How far is it to Horsens?' Blix asked.

'It usually takes about three hours,' Cramer replied, pressing her foot down on the accelerator. 'But with a bit of luck we should get there in about two and a half.'

Blix took his phone out and scrolled through the Norwegian news websites. Nothing new.

Kovic had called him a couple of times the previous evening, with a few practical questions regarding the homicide at the Botanical Garden. She had nothing to go on and had no more leads to guide the investigation. There were no witnesses, no solid evidence at the crime scene, no conflicts in the victim's closest relationships. It felt like he had left her in the lurch, with such a difficult task.

Emma had contacted him the evening before too. A text to say that she was also on her way to Denmark. Which meant she was already here. She hadn't elaborated on why she was coming or what she was doing. Blix was afraid that if he answered her, he would be at a loss for words if she asked about Ahlander. They needed radio silence surrounding the investigation for the time being, until all the pieces were in place.

He sat back and stared at the road ahead.

'Recline the chair a bit and get some sleep,' Cramer offered.

'Sleep? At this speed?' Blix said. 'Like that's even possible.'

Cramer smiled and tilted her head back against the headrest.

They had driven over the Storebælt Bridge and were approaching Fyn when Blix's phone rang. It was Ann-Mari Sara.

'Hi,' Blix said, picking up immediately. 'What's going on?'

'That's a damn good question,' Sara replied.

'Oh?'

She sighed heavily into the receiver, and started: 'You know those knuckles you dug up in Undrumsåsen yesterday?'

'Yes?'

'You were right to say that the bones belonged to a small child, about a year and a half old.'

Again, there was a moment of silence, before she continued:

'But it's not Patricia.'

# 64

Kovic looked up and was met with her own reflection in the mirror above the sink. Her face was pale, eyes bloodshot. She rubbed the sleep out of one of them. She seemed so much older than she actually was.

The voices coming from some of the other investigators reached her from the hallway, but no one came into the bathroom. She was glad of it. She needed a few minutes to gather her thoughts.

The investigation into the murder of Amy Linh was in its second day, and they still had no solid direction to go in. Kovic hoped that the autopsy and the forensic examinations of the body might give her something, but that didn't stop her from thinking that someone else should be leading the investigation. Someone with more experience.

The door opened behind her. A cleaner came in. Kovic turned on the tap and washed her hands. Dried them, and walked out. At least Amy Linh had no relatives she had to meet, to give updates on their progress, Kovic thought to herself as she walked to her desk.

Her phone rang the moment she took a seat.

'This is Teddy,' the man said on the other end. 'Theodor Rønning, from Hotel Gyldenløve.'

Kovic grabbed a pen.

'There's someone here who you might want to talk to,' Rønning went on.

'Who?'

'Elena Vilensky,' Rønning answered. 'She was off work yesterday, but she's here today. She worked a lot of shifts with Amy. Said that Amy had been upset when she left work on Thursday.'

'What about?'

'Something about a guest who had been behaving strangely,' he replied. 'You can talk to her if you want?'

Kovic had already stood up. 'I'm on my way,' she said.

It wasn't even nine o'clock yet, Kovic thought as she strode over to the lift. They were meant to be going over the case at eleven. Maybe she would have something to give them by then.

The traffic was light at that time of the morning. It took her less than fifteen minutes to get to Majorstua. She swung into a vacant parking place in one of the side streets.

Elena Vilensky was a slender woman in her mid-twenties.

Kovic introduced herself and sat down in one of the empty chairs beside Rønning.

'Tell me about the guest,' Kovic requested. 'What exactly happened?'

Elena blew her nose on a small pocket tissue first.

'He frightened her.'

'Who?'

Elena took a moment to compose herself. A tram rattled by on the street outside. Sirens started wailing in the distance.

'Amy worked on the sixth floor,' she began. 'I'm on the fifth. That's where the linen room is, and where the trolleys are kept. I was cleaning one of the rooms. She was done for the day, and she passed on her way back with the trolley. I called out to her, but she kept going, as if she hadn't heard me. So I went after her. I could tell that something had happened. She had this distant look in her eye. It took quite a while before I could convince her to tell me what was going on.'

She sniffed again, clasped the tissue in her hand a little tighter.

'There was a room she couldn't get in to clean. The guy staying there never took down the *Do Not Disturb* sign, so in the end she went in anyway.'

Kovic remembered what she had read in Amy Linh's journal, the prompts she had written, her speculations about why someone would want to isolate themselves for days on end.

'Go on...'

Elena glanced at her boss and back at Kovic.

'He came back while she was in there,' she explained, hesitating again.

'What happened then?'

'I don't know...' Elena answered. 'She didn't say anything else. From what I did get out of her, I gathered that it had been unpleasant. That he had scared her.'

'Do you know which room he was staying in?'

Elena shook her head.

'But it was on the sixth floor.'

Behind his desk, Rønning had lifted himself slightly out of his chair and was looking over the top of their heads, out into the lobby. Kovic turned. Through the frosted glass, she could see the flashing blue lights of numerous police cars out on the street. She got up, crossed the room and was at the door in just a few steps. Within seconds, the lobby was full of uniformed officers.

The receptionist accompanied one of them to the hotel manager's office. Kovic recognised him. It was Claes Stenberg, head of the police tactical unit. In one swift determined motion, he shoved the door open, found Theodor Rønning and announced:

'We're evacuating everyone from this building, now.'

# 65

The Danish roads were wide and smooth. The landscape consisted of windmills and farms, as far as the eye could see. Herds of cows grazed among the bright-green fields, even though it was still early January. It was a light but cloudy day. Powerful gusts of wind nudged the car occasionally. Emma held both hands on the steering wheel.

After thirty kilometres or so, she pulled over onto the roadside, picked up her phone and typed 'Jette Djurholm' into the Danish yellow pages website. Ruth-Kristine's alibi and closest friend lived in Horsens, about fifteen minutes away, on a street called Engtoften.

Emma drove out onto the road and concentrated as she diligently followed the directions on the sat nav, soon reaching a residential area. The road she followed was wide, with cycle paths on each side. The hedges surrounding the houses and gardens were immaculate.

Emma turned off onto a side road to the right. Engtoften turned out to be a dead end, but she drove all the way to the end, parking next to a yellow skip, making sure not to block the little footpath that passed through a hedge and led onto another street behind.

The smell of wet grass hit her as she climbed out of the car. She looked at the time and realised it was far too early for an unannounced visit, at least for a Saturday. The drive from Århus had only taken three quarters of an hour, and Jette Djurholm and her family were probably asleep.

Emma decided to have a look round first. Jette Djurholm lived in a large, white, brick house. There was a blue trampoline in the garden. And a greenhouse at the back. There were no cars parked in the driveway, but Emma noticed smoke rising from the chimney. Maybe they were already up.

Emma strode past the post box, which had *Djurholm/Kvist* printed on it, and over to the front door. She rang the doorbell. There was a sign beside it that read: *Caroline, Jette and Jens-Christian live here.* She couldn't hear any movement inside.

Emma pressed the bell again. There was a flicker of movement behind the curtain in the small window next to the door, but she didn't catch sight of who had been peeking through. Only now did Emma realise that the door had a peephole. It felt as if someone were staring at her from the other side.

The door opened an inch. The face of the woman who peered out was sallow, weary. She had unruly, shoulder-length hair and a large, dark mole on her left cheek. She was wearing a brown cardigan over a white sweater. Black jeans. Barefoot.

'Can I help you?'

'Jette Djurholm?'

'Yes?' she answered hesitantly.

The hallway behind her was narrow. There was another door, but it was shut, preventing Emma from seeing any more of the house.

'Hi,' Emma said, smiling. 'I'm sorry to disturb you on the weekend, and so early. My name is Emma Ramm and I work for news.no, an online newspaper in Norway. I've tried calling you a few times?'

There was no sign that Djurholm recognised Emma's name.

'I've been trying to get in touch about a case I'm working on,' Emma continued. 'Patricia's kidnapping, the daughter of your former neighbour in Oslo, in Holmlia. I don't know if you've been following what's been going in Norway over the last few days, but...'

Something about the expression on Djurholm's face made Emma stop mid-sentence. The woman in front of her looked as if she was about to cry.

'I'm trying to locate Ruth-Kristine Smeplass,' Emma continued, cautiously. 'Patricia's mother.'

Djurholm closed her eyes for a few seconds, before they shot open again as she spun round, as if she was checking to see whether someone was standing behind her. Her lips moved.

'Hm?' Emma pointed to her ear. 'Sorry, I didn't hear what you said.'

'Help me,' Djurholm whispered. 'Hurry, you have to tell the pol—'

In the next second, the door behind Djurholm was thrown open.

A dark-haired woman stormed towards them, in one quick, aggressive motion – as if trying to chase Emma away. Instead of pushing Emma out and closing the door, she stopped in her tracks and stared at her. Emma returned the woman's inquisitive gaze. It took a few moments before she realised who she was looking at. Those eyes. That angry, harassed look she had seen so many times in various newspaper articles over the last few days – as if she was permanently mad at the world.

'You,' she hissed, pointing to Emma. 'Get inside!'

Emma looked down. The woman had a gun in her hand.

## 66

Authoritative commands blared through the lobby as heavily armed police officers began to occupy the hotel.

Kovic introduced herself to the head of the tactical unit. She explained what she was doing at the hotel and asked him to do the same.

Claes Stenberg showed her a grainy print-out of an image captured from a CCTV camera, and pointed out to the street, towards one of the businesses on the other side.

'The video analysis has tracked him to here,' he said.

Kovic recognised the man, the one dressed head-to-toe in dark clothing. The bomber.

Stenberg showed the image to the hotel manager.

'Have you seen this man?' he asked. 'Have there been any guests recently who have been dressed like this?'

Rønning shook his head.

'I can't say for sure...'

Stenberg showed the image to the housekeeper who had worked with Amy Linh.

'Have you seen him?'

Elena Vilensky shook her head.

'Do you have him under surveillance?' Kovic asked. 'Do you know if he's currently in the hotel?'

'They're going through the rest of the footage as we speak,' Stenberg replied. 'But they haven't seen him leave. Both the tram and the bus occasionally stop right outside the entrance however, which blocks our view, so it's impossible to be a hundred percent certain. There may be explosives in the building, though.'

The hotel manager had been standing, bewildered, as he listened.

'Is there anything I can do?' he asked.

'We need a master key,' Stenberg answered and turned back to Kovic. 'We have people at every exit and on every floor,' he explained.

'We're evacuating everyone, all the guests and staff, and we'll be going through every room.'

'Start on the sixth floor,' Kovic said, filling him in on what Elena and the hotel manager had told her.

In the lobby, chaos ensued. The guests who had only just arrived were protesting against the fact they were being sent back out, while others were demanding to be allowed back up to their rooms to collect their bags and other items before leaving. The protests and objections were futile. As they were all ushered out, the names of the staff and guests were registered, and they were shown a photo of the bomber. A dog handler from the bomb squad was waiting outside with a springer spaniel, letting it sniff everyone as they passed.

Stenberg was handed a document with a record of all the guests who had stayed at the hotel over the past twenty-four hours, and commanded four armed officers to accompany him upstairs. Kovic followed them towards the stairwell and the sixth floor.

The corridor was empty. None of the rooms looked like they had a *Do Not Disturb* sign hanging on the door.

The specially trained officers began in room 601. Stenberg knocked, leaving it ten seconds before unlocking the door with the master key. Two men entered the room, their weapons held up in front of them.

Kovic hung back, but could see that the room was empty.

'Bring the explosives detection dog up,' Stenberg said into the police radio. 'Sixth floor.'

They left the door open and moved on to the next room. Also unoccupied.

A man in a blue shirt opened the door to room 603. He took a step back when he saw the police officers. Stenberg ordered him out into the corridor. The man did as he was told. He gave his name and other personal details as two of the officers searched his room. One came out with a red puffer jacket, as if to demonstrate that this was not the man they were looking for.

'We have detected a potential threat in the building,' Stenberg explained. 'The hotel is being evacuated. Take only the things that you absolutely need and leave.'

The guest asked no questions. He put on his shoes, grabbed his jacket and a satchel, and moved towards the stairs.

There were no guests in the next room, although it was clearly being used.

The sniffer dog arrived and was taken in to search room 601. Stenberg and his team worked their way through the corridor.

'Someone must have noticed or said something about a guest who's been here for at least five days,' Kovic said. 'Who's been staying since before New Year's Eve too. There can't be many of them.'

'There's nothing mentioned here,' Stenberg said, waving the guest list.

The empty rooms were searched through swiftly, by both the team and the dog.

They now reached the large suites at the end of the corridor. Stenberg stood outside room 620 and checked the guest list.

'The guest has checked out, but it hasn't been cleaned,' he said, knocking anyway. He waited a moment, used the master key and opened the door. Kovic peered in as the men entered the room. The curtains were drawn, and the room was shrouded in half-darkness. The bed was in disarray and one of the cushions from the sofa lay on the floor.

'Clear,' one of the two officers reported.

They left the room and moved on to the next one. Kovic stayed where she was. It was obvious that someone had been staying in that room for an extended period of time, and that it hadn't been cleaned every day. Empty takeaway boxes were scattered across the desk, along with about eight to ten empty bottles that had once contained some sort of soft drink. Two tied-up plastic bags had been left on the floor next to the overflowing rubbish bin. One of them had the *Kiwi* supermarket logo.

Kovic walked into the room. It smelled like stale food. She pulled the curtains aside to let some light in and stepped in a sticky patch on the floor. There was something else beside it. Kovic bent down and picked it up. A piece of wire, about a centimetre long.

She walked back out to the corridor and called to Stenberg.

'Who was staying in this room?' she asked.

Stenberg checked his list.

'Jens-Christian Kvist,' he read. 'Why?'

'I think he might be the man we're looking for,' Kovic answered.

She checked the spelling and logged on to the internal police system to access the national population register.

'No results,' she said. 'Could be a fake name.'

Stenberg called out to the dog handler and pointed to the open door of room 620.

The springer spaniel was let in, working its way around, searching as eagerly as it had done in the first room. Swerving around the room, nose down to the floor, sniffing up chair legs and along the edge of the bed.

And then it lay down flat in front of the two rubbish bags.

'Detection,' the dog handler reported.

'What does that mean?' Kovic asked. 'Is there a bomb?'

'There have been explosives in there at some point in any case,' the dog handler answered.

Stenberg beckoned to them, indicating that they had to leave the room.

'We're locking it down and calling the rest of the bomb squad in,' he said.

Kovic took a few steps back down the corridor, and felt something click, as if all the pieces were falling into place.

Amy Linh had come too close to the bomber.

# 67

'Ruth-Kristine,' Emma stammered. 'What are you doing here? ... Why...?'

Ruth-Kristine made a beckoning gesture with the pistol before she turned to Jette Djurholm.

'You *had* to try it? You had to try to warn her?'

Djurholm did not answer.

'Go in,' Ruth-Kristine told her brusquely, dragging Jette by the arm and shoving her back into the house. 'You too. Get in,' she continued, nodding back to Emma, who looked around quickly in the hope that someone outside had noticed what was going on. But there were no neighbours to be seen.

Emma stepped into the warm hallway.

'Give me your phone.'

Emma cursed inwardly, but obeyed.

Ruth-Kristine held the door to the living room open for her, staring Emma down as she did so. The years had clearly taken a toll. Deep wrinkles burrowed into her forehead. She didn't have any eyebrows left, but it looked as if she had drawn some on. She had a slight overbite. The skin on her cheeks was ravaged by sores. The marks of a difficult life, Emma thought.

Ruth-Kristine scratched at her face feverishly and asked, 'What are you doing here?'

'I...'

Emma wanted to answer, but couldn't find the words. Ruth-Kristine pushed her into the room too. Her sister, Britt Smeplass, was sitting inside.

'Who knows you're here?' Ruth-Kristine asked.

'No one,' Emma said. 'No, actually, one person. Alexander Blix, the investigator. I sent him a text before I left.'

'I don't believe you,' Ruth-Kristine retorted aggressively.

'Give me my phone, I can show you.'

Ruth-Kristine looked as if she were considering it, but ended up stuffing the phone into her trouser pocket.

'What's going on here, then?' Emma asked, trying to gain control of her trembling voice.

Britt Smeplass refused to meet Emma's eye. Djurholm walked over to the sofa and sat down, keeping her distance from Ruth-Kristine's sister.

'Why are you here?' Ruth-Kristine repeated, making a motion with her head towards the sofa, a sign that Emma should sit down too.

'I've been looking for you,' Emma said. 'To try and find out what happened to your daughter. The police in Norway have arrested Sophus Ahlander, and they're looking for...'

Ruth-Kristine paced back and forth across the room – over to the kitchen door, turning on her heel and walking back. Deep in thought.

'Sit down,' she commanded again.

Emma did as she was told. Her feet brushed against a grey cat resting under the table. It didn't seem too bothered.

'You're only making things harder for us,' Britt said.

Emma turned to face her. Britt had wild, wiry hair that reached her shoulders. Her lips were dry and flaky. A gold necklace lay on top of her grey cotton jumper. She leant forwards jerkily, only to sit back just as suddenly.

'How could you have possibly thought this would end well?' Britt carried on, looking at her sister.

'It won't,' Ruth-Kristine said. 'It was never meant to end well either.'

Emma had no idea what the sisters were talking about.

'Why did you bring her into this too?' Britt asked, nodding to Emma. 'She hasn't done anything.'

'Jette tried to warn her,' Ruth-Kristine said, her eyes boring into the Danish woman. 'And anyway, she's come all the way here, from Norway, on a Saturday, and she turns up at this house, this early in the morning, asking about Patricia, asking about me. I'm not taking any chances. Not now.'

She took a step closer to the coffee table in the middle of the room. Staring intently at Jette Djurholm.

'Have you heard anything yet?'

Djurholm glanced quickly at her phone in the centre of the table. Shook her head.

'Send another. Say it's urgent.'

Djurholm pulled the phone towards her and unlocked the screen with her thumb. Under Ruth-Kristine's supervision, she typed out a brief message before putting the phone back down on the table between them.

It only took a few seconds before it vibrated. Djurholm leant forwards and looked at the display, before sagging back into the sofa.

'Two minutes,' she said, looking up at Ruth-Kristine, who nodded and lifted her shoulders up to her ears, as if to draw as much air into her lungs as possible.

She began walking restlessly back and forth across the room again. Emma tried to work out what they were waiting for, what was about to happen. She asked, but none of the other women answered. The atmosphere in the room was electric – a charged silence that engulfed them.

A few sounds reached them from outside. A bicycle being propped up against the front wall of the house. Light steps making their way over the path. A hand on the door handle. Someone entering. A door, closing behind them. Emma looked at Ruth-Kristine, whose face had drained of colour. It looked like she was struggling to breathe.

'Hello?'

The voice came from the hallway.

The voice of a young girl.

# 68

'What are you saying?'

Blix moved the phone from one hand to the other, sitting up straight as he did so.

'It is not Patricia,' Ann-Mari Sara repeated.

'But...'

'I don't know *who* it is yet, but we're working as fast as we can to identify the child.'

'But, is it...?'

'It's a girl.'

'Have you checked the missing-persons database?'

'First thing I did,' she said, a little disgruntled. 'We have no other children from around that time who match our findings.'

'So ... is the girl the same age? Or rather, has she been there for the same amount of time that Patricia has been missing?'

'It's difficult to determine that accurately,' Ann-Mari Sara said. 'But she has been there for a long time, we know that.'

Blix scratched his head.

'We're checking with the neighbouring countries, too,' Sara continued. 'To see whether they have any missing girls who could be a match. We should hear back in the next few hours.'

Blix nodded to himself as his thoughts raced off in several directions. He thanked her for the update, hung up and told Lone Cramer the news.

She sent a quick look his way. 'How is that possible?' she asked. 'Could someone have made a mistake, somewhere? Maybe there's something wrong with the DNA analysis?'

Blix shook his head. He had no explanation to give her, and was simply relieved that he hadn't said anything about the find to Christer Storm Isaksen. But his mind wandered to the photo Isaksen had received. His conviction that it was Patricia.

Maybe he was right.

They drove past a sign that informed them it was twenty-seven kilometres to Horsens. His phone rang again. Kovic this time.

'How's it going?' he asked.

'PST's video analysis team have tracked down the bomber,' she explained. 'He's been staying at Hotel Gyldenløve in Majorstua, where Amy Linh worked. The murder victim from the Botanical Garden. The explosives detection dog sensed traces of explosives in his room.'

'Who is it?' Blix asked.

'His name is Jens-Christian Kvist,' Kovic said. 'We initially thought it could have been a fake name, but he doesn't live in Norway, he lives in—'

'What did you say his name was?' Blix exclaimed, seizing the papers he had been given by Lone Cramer.

Kovic repeated the name.

Blix stared blankly at the document in his hands for a few moments, before blinking a few times and eventually replying.

'I've questioned him before. In the Patricia case, a long time ago. He's married to Jette Djurholm.'

'We've circulated him as wanted,' Kovic continued.

'So we don't know where he is?'

'All we know is that his car crossed the Øresund Bridge a few hours ago. He's on his way home to Denmark.'

## 69

'What's so urgent then? Why...?'

The girl entered the living room and stopped in the doorway. She had a touch of eye shadow on and some light-pink lipstick, with just a trace of glitter. She was wearing ripped black jeans and a hoodie with *FILA* written across the front.

She cast a quick, uncertain glance at Jette, who stood up as if to embrace her but then seemed to change her mind and sank down onto the sofa again.

'Caroline, these are...' Jette hesitated. 'A few friends of mine,' she finished, her eyes on Ruth-Kristine, whose forehead was drenched in sweat.

Ruth-Kristine took a sudden, short breath. A small gasp, accompanied by the realisation that she still had a gun in her hand. She looked around, searching for a suitable place to put it down, but it was too late – the girl had seen the gun, and her eyes widened.

'Sorry,' Ruth-Kristine said. 'It's not ... I didn't mean to...'

She couldn't find the words to finish her sentences.

'I'm not dangerous. I won't hurt you.'

Caroline looked from one woman to another. Ruth-Kristine's words had done nothing to reduce the shock etched into her face.

'Mum, what's happening?'

Jette didn't answer, just closed her eyes. Emma thought that it looked as if she was going to snap at any moment. Ruth-Kristine took a step closer to Caroline, holding the gun behind her back and tucking it into the waistband of her trousers. She stared at the girl, wide-eyed. She walked around her, behind her, taking her in. Ruth-Kristine raised a hand to her, gently, as if to touch her, but withdrew it. Caroline watched her.

'Where's Dad?' she asked, now turning to look at her mother on the sofa. 'Is he not back yet?'

Jette shook her head. 'I don't know when he'll be back, my love.'

'Don't say that,' Ruth-Kristine cut in sharply. 'Do not call her your love.'

The muscles of her face tightened and she squeezed her eyes shut, as if Jette's words had caused her physical pain. Britt got up from the sofa and approached Caroline, a strained smile on her face, holding her open palms up in front of her.

'Nothing's going to happen,' she said. 'We ... just want to talk to you. Right?'

She looked at her sister, but Ruth-Kristine didn't say anything. She only had eyes for Caroline. Emma tried to read Ruth-Kristine's expression. She looked as if she were about to start crying.

'Who are you?' Caroline asked. 'Are you from Norway?'

'Yes, we are,' Britt answered with a warm smile. 'We arrived last night.'

'You stayed here, overnight?'

Ruth-Kristine blinked a few times, like she had suddenly come to. She reached the sofa in two brisk steps.

'Did you not think to tell her?' she snarled, talking through clenched teeth.

Jette didn't look up. She sat, nervously rubbing her hands together.

'Tell me what?' Caroline asked.

Jette still didn't say anything. She had started to tremble. Tears erupted from both eyes simultaneously.

'We were waiting for you,' Ruth-Kristine said finally, turning to face Caroline. 'That's why we're here.'

'Me?'

Ruth-Kristine nodded. 'God,' she uttered, breathing in a sudden hiccup. 'You're...'

She covered her mouth with her hand. Caroline took her phone out, a move that made Ruth-Kristine tense up.

'Sorry,' she said, her tone sharp. 'But I'll need to take that.'

She pointed to Caroline's phone.

'Why?'

'Because...' Ruth-Kristine looked away as she searched for the right words. 'Because I need you to sit down and pay attention to everything I say,' she said eventually. 'This is a story you need to hear. A story about your parents.'

Caroline's eyes darted to her mother, before settling back on Ruth-Kristine again.

'And about you.'

# 70

The scream made Ruth-Kristine sit bolt upright and mute the TV. There were a few moments of complete silence before another shriek cut through the wall between her and the neighbouring flat.

Jette.

Ruth-Kristine stood up, feeling a cold shiver run down her spine. She rushed out into the hall without bothering to put her shoes on and knocked on her neighbour's door. No answer. She tried the bell, unsure if it even worked, before hammering her fist against the door. Behind it, she heard a thump, like something had hit the wall or floor, and then the sound of someone wailing.

She turned the door handle – it was unlocked.

She stepped inside. Shouted: 'Hello?' Cleared her throat. 'Jette? Is everything alright?'

No answer. Shit, she must have really hurt herself, Ruth-Kristine thought as she edged her way further into the flat. No signs of Jette or Jens-Christian.

'Hello?'

Nothing. She followed the sound, a groan that seemed to be coming from the bathroom. She knocked twice, lightly, just with the edge of her knuckles, before pushing the door open.

There she was. Jette, on the floor, her back against the wall. Caroline in her lap. Naked, wet.

Jette was rocking back and forth. Ruth-Kristine wasn't sure if her neighbour had even registered the fact that she was there. She just cried, shaking her head. Her hair was wet, her clothes soaked through. The bathtub was full. There was a yellow rubber duck on the floor, several towels. Jette adjusted her position slightly. There was blood on the wall behind her head.

'What's happened?' Ruth-Kristine asked.

Jette tried to say something, opened her mouth once or twice, but couldn't, overcome with a fresh wave of tears and despair.

Ruth-Kristine walked into the room. Stooped down and touched her friend's knee. Tried to get her to look her in the eye.

'I was just...' Jette was clutching the child. 'I only went into the kitchen for two minutes,' she hiccupped. 'I was just going to get my phone, to take some photos, and then it started ringing ... it was Jens-Christian. He had so much to say. His new job ... he was so happy...'

The muscles on Jette's arms had completely tensed up. Ruth-Kristine was scared that her neighbour was about to squeeze her daughter to death, until she realised that the damage had already been done.

'What am I going to say when he ... when he...?'

Again, Jette was overwhelmed with grief. Emma lay her hand on the child. The baby's soft skin was cold, wet.

'Did she drown?' Ruth-Kristine asked calmly.

Jette couldn't answer.

'Have you tried to revive her?'

Jette nodded.

'Did you call for help?'

She shook her head. 'Don't,' she begged. 'Don't call the police.'

'What should we do then?'

'You have to help me.'

'How can I help?'

'By ... by...'

Jette slammed her head against the wall, again and again.

'What should I do?' she sobbed.

'There's not much we can...'

Ruth-Kristine stopped herself.

'When will Jens-Christian be home?'

'I don't know,' Jette said, hesitating. 'He ... he's going to ... we can't have more children.'

She raised her head to look at Ruth-Kristine. Her bloodshot eyes boring into hers, pleadingly.

'You have to help me. Please, you have to do something.'

Ruth-Kristine didn't know what to say.

'I'll be here when Jens-Christian comes home,' she said at last.

'He's going to leave me, he's going to hate me for the rest of his life, he's going to...'

'...understand that it was an accident,' Ruth-Kristine finished.

Jette shook her head. 'They'll lock me up,' she cried.

'No,' Ruth-Kristine said. 'That won't happen.'

'It will!' Jette protested. 'And I'd deserve it, too. Deserve to...'

She threw her head back against the wall again, hard. Ruth Kristine tried to think.

There was nothing to do.

Or, maybe.

No, she told herself. That wouldn't work. *You can't.*

But the thought had taken hold. There was one possibility. Christer, the bastard, had practically taken away her right to be with her own child, had taken away any chance she had of a future with her. It was his fault that Patricia no longer recognised her.

She needed a cigarette.

She needed something stronger.

Jesus, there was a dead child in front of her – she had to think fast. And Jens-Christian would be home soon.

Ruth-Kristine stood up, ran a hand through her hair. She saw her reflection in the bathroom mirror as Jette continued to cry. Ruth-Kristine leant forwards, turned on the tap and rinsed her hands under the icy water. She pressed them to her face, felt how hot her cheeks were. She looked up, met her own gaze, moved down to her slightly crooked mouth. The moles, the liver spots, the tired, worn-out skin. The straggly hair. She thought of Patricia, of Christer, how she could give him exactly what he deserved, make him feel the pain she felt, all while plotting a better future for herself.

Ruth-Kristine turned to Jette, tried to talk, but the words got stuck in her throat.

She tried again, and at last, managed to say:

'We can swap.'

## 71

It began to dawn on Emma what had happened. The journalist in her wanted to interrupt Ruth-Kristine, ask for answers, but she kept quiet, instead focussing on trying to find a way to get them all out without anyone getting hurt.

She looked at Caroline, who was still standing in front of Ruth-Kristine and occasionally glancing over at Jette, who couldn't bring herself to do anything other than stare at the floor and rub her hands. Lift one of them to her face every so often to wipe away a tear.

Ruth-Kristine's eyes were fixed on Caroline as she spoke.

'I wasn't very well at that time,' she said. 'There were a lot of reasons for that.'

She had a distant look in her eye, as if the memories were coming back to her.

'I was frustrated. Angry. And there was one man I was angrier at than any other, because...' She stopped herself abruptly. Her voice had become harsh, like she was reliving it.

'Please,' Jette pleaded. 'She doesn't need to know all this.'

'It's too late for that now,' Ruth-Kristine barked.

'But what good do you think it will do? Now? You're going to ruin her life!' Jette raised her head.

'She deserves to know her story, where she is really from,' Ruth-Kristine said.

'And what do you hope to achieve with that?' Jette continued.

'Justice,' Ruth-Kristine said. 'Vengeance.'

'Vengeance?' The question came from Britt this time. 'You said you wanted to make up for what you've done. That's why you came to me for help. To finally put an end to all this and sort your life out.'

'That was before they tried to murder me,' Ruth-Kristine spat, frowning at her sister. 'They killed my best friend. They killed Nina.'

'So you lied to me?' Britt had stood up. 'To convince me to come here with you. Or did you just need my money?'

Ruth-Kristine didn't answer.

Caroline looked between them, a confused expression on her face. 'I don't understand...' she said.

Ruth-Kristine tried to smile at her. 'No, and that's understandable. But you will. Soon. I promise.'

Caroline looked like she was concentrating, thinking it through.

'But ... there was a child who died then?'

Jette hiccupped. Ruth-Kristine waited a moment before nodding.

'It was a mistake. An accident. She drowned.'

'But...' Caroline still looked as if she didn't understand.

'Can you not just sit down, please?' Ruth-Kristine asked, as gently as she could.

'I don't want to sit,' Caroline replied.

'Well, it's stressing me out, you standing there.'

'Yeah, that's a shame for you then,' she said defiantly.

'Sit down,' Ruth-Kristine said, more firmly this time. Eventually adding: 'Please?'

Caroline rolled her eyes and pulled a chair through from the kitchen. Picked her phone from the table, but put it back down, having checked the screen quickly.

She sat down near Jette. Emma noticed that there was a stiffness to the girl's body language now that wasn't there before. Not as if she were scared though, just resilient.

'The people who you have come to know as your parents,' Ruth-Kristine said, turning to Caroline again, 'are not particularly good people.'

'Oh, coming from *you*,' Jette exclaimed. Her eyes were overflowing with tears.

'I was just trying to help your family,' Ruth-Kristine argued back. 'Help *you*.'

'But at what cost?'

Ruth-Kristine snorted. 'So you're saying it shouldn't have cost you anything? You mean that saving you from prison, the fact that I saved your family, maybe even your marriage – none of that has any value?'

'Of course it does, and we agreed on a price in advance. And we – *we* – stuck to our half of the deal.' It seemed as if Jette had completely forgotten that Caroline was there. Her eyes flashed.

'What are you two talking about?' Caroline asked again. She looked anxious now, scared.

Ruth-Kristine took a deep breath.

'We are talking about a deal I made with your parents,' she replied. 'Almost ten years ago.'

# 72

Ruth-Kristine looked at the tiny bundle of a child, the few tufts of hair on her head. Lying in Jette's lap as she was, it was almost like she was just sleeping.

A cold determination came over her. It was not a child. It was an object.

'We need to decide what to do, and fast,' Ruth-Kristine said, crouching in front of Jette. 'We have a lot to get done, in a short amount of time.'

'It's not going to work,' Jette wept.

'This is the only way,' Ruth-Kristine said.

'What is Jens-Christian going to say?'

'He's going to go along with it,' Ruth-Kristine assured her. 'He'll do it for you. For both of you.'

Jette pulled herself up a little.

'What are you going to do with her?' she sniffed, gazing down at the girl in her lap.

'I'll make things nice for her,' Ruth-Kristine replied. 'Don't think about it.'

Jette lifted her chin so she was looking right at her.

'And you would do this for me?'

Ruth-Kristine answered without skipping a beat.

'I'm sure we can agree on a price,' she said.

Jette gawked at her for a few more seconds before nodding and lowering her head.

'Can you find a bedsheet?'

Jette remained still for a long time, before giving the baby to Ruth-Kristine.

Ruth-Kristine looked down at the dead, naked child. The dead, naked thing, she reminded herself. The thing couldn't have weighed more than ten kilos.

Jette returned. A white sheet in hand.

'Lay it out flat for me,' Ruth-Kristine said. 'On the floor.'

With slow, apathetic movements, Jette did as she was told. Ruth-Kristine bent down and placed the object in the centre of the rectangle. She could hear Jette gasping behind her, before it turned into hyperventilating.

'Maybe it would be best if you go and wait in the living room,' Ruth-Kristine said.

Jette started to sob again; it took a long time before she was able to calm herself down.

'I just want to be with her for as long as possible,' she stuttered and hiccupped between rapid inhaling and exhaling.

'I understand,' Ruth-Kristine said in a resolute voice. 'But we need to get a move on.'

Jette wiped her tears away and sniffed loudly a few times. She looked at her child one last time, before her eyes filled with tears again. She turned and left the bathroom.

Ruth-Kristine folded the fabric over and around, making sure there were no gaps anywhere. It only took a minute, and she was done.

The front door opened. The sound of keys clanking against a bowl or hook on the wall.

'Jette?' Jens-Christians' voice travelled through the hallway. His voice was low, as if he were afraid to wake his sleeping daughter.

Ruth-Kristine was alone in the bathroom with the dead child. She could hear the sound of him slipping his shoes off, hanging up his coat. The sound of Jette gasping, before she started hyperventilating again, weeping loudly.

The sound of Jette trying to speak. Of Jette trying to explain. It came out completely jumbled, none of it making sense. Completely impossible to follow what she was trying to tell him.

'What the hell are you saying?' He was anxious now. She could hear it in his voice.

Some words occasionally broke through Jette's crying. Words like 'dead' and 'drowned'. 'Phone'. 'Bathroom'. 'Ruth-Kristine'. 'Bedsheet'.

Followed by heavy steps surging across the floor. The door in front of her was torn open.

Jens-Christian Kvist stared at her.

At the bundle in her arms.

His eyes widened. Mouth opened in surprise.

He looked at the sheet, the outline of a skull so clear beneath the cloth. The rest of the little body. The legs. The feet.

'It was an accident,' Ruth-Kristine said. 'If you hadn't called her when you did, and if you hadn't insisted that she always has to answer whenever you call, then this wouldn't have happened.'

Distribute the guilt, make sure Jette doesn't take all the blame. Ruth-Kristine knew that they would eventually talk about this moment again, how this happened, in the years to come. It would be dredged up in arguments, and the guilt would destroy them. They would try to blame each other. Or maybe they wouldn't say anything at all. Maybe they would just try to forget the entire affair.

Jens-Christian moved closer, folded back one of the corners of the sheet, revealing his daughter's face. He inhaled, a sharp, painful gasp, before the convulsions took over and the crying began.

Ruth-Kristine waited.

'Has she told you about my proposal?'

She knew that Jette hadn't managed to get that far, but she wanted to take his mind off the situation and onto the solution, and as soon as possible. Away from the despair. But she wasn't sure if he had even heard her. He just stood there, shaking.

Ruth-Kristine had never liked Jens-Christian.

On the occasions he had come home while she was visiting Jette, he'd never greeted her, never smiled at her. Just had that look on his face, the disappointment that Jette was friends with people like *her*. Ruth-Kristine knew it. She had encouraged Jette more than once to stand up for herself, not to be so submissive and obedient, but Jens-Christian had some kind of power over her. Sometimes one look was all it took, and Jette would know what he wanted her to do. Even now, as he stood there in front of her, his upper body sagging forwards, trembling, hunched over as if someone had punched him, Ruth-Kristine found it impossible to muster up any compassion for him.

A solution.

Progression.

They didn't have much time. *She* didn't have much time.

'I know of a way out of this,' Ruth-Kristine said. 'But for this to work, you have to do exactly what I say.'

## 73

'As I said, I had my own child at that time. A gorgeous baby girl, but I was never allowed to see her. I...'

Ruth-Kristine stopped herself and looked down at her feet.

'And I thought they were going to restrict my visits even more, that they were going to take her away from me altogether, so I...'

She paused again, before carrying on:

'Jens-Christian wouldn't hear of it, to begin with. It was out of the question, he said. Never in all his life would he even think of doing that. "Are you completely insane?"' Ruth-Kristine imitated him. 'He couldn't see yet, how we were going to make it work. But he understood that there was nothing we could do to bring his daughter back. By swapping, as I suggested, they could carry on with their lives, in a way. They could go back home, to Denmark, with a child around the same age, who didn't look all that different. And children change so much in such a short amount of time anyway – they grow, get taller, their teeth come in, their faces change, even their hair changes colour...'

She threw her arms up.

'If you tell a story with enough confidence and conviction, there's almost nothing you can't persuade people to believe. But convincing your parents to go through with this, that was the one, the only thing, we needed to be absolutely sure of. The second, the most important thing, was...'

She stopped.

'...that we got hold of my daughter in such a way that the kidnapping couldn't be traced back to any of us. I couldn't just pick her up from nursery. I had to...'

Ruth-Kristine looked away.

'I got someone to help,' she continued. 'A guy, who...' She hesitated. 'And then I got help from...' She pointed to Jette.

Emma thought it looked like Caroline had stopped trying to follow the story.

'Jette came shopping with me that day, when Patricia was ... collected. And we hammed it up for the media afterwards when we helped to look for her.'

Jette shook her head. Mumbled something about having been in shock, about not being able to think rationally.

'And although Christer, my ex, was certain that I had something to do with it, we were basically in the clear,' Ruth-Kristine continued. '*We* weren't the ones who had kidnapped my daughter. And the police had come and questioned us too, but we played our roles well. We were good. Convincing.'

She took a breath.

'I told Jette that she had to move back to Denmark with my daughter the second things calmed down. Jens-Christian would stay on in Norway, so it wouldn't look too suspicious. Everything was working out fine, or so I thought, anyway.'

Ruth-Kristine looked at Jette.

'You two needed some time apart. To have some space to grieve, individually. Gain a little perspective.'

Jette didn't reply.

'But what happened to the dead child?' Emma couldn't help herself.

Ruth-Kristine turned towards her, a vexed expression spreading across her face, as if she had completely forgotten that Emma was in the room.

'I buried her.'

'Where?'

'Somewhere nice.'

Emma wished she could take some notes or record everything that was being said, but something told her she was going to remember it all word-for-word. The question was whether she would get the opportunity to tell anyone else.

'So...' Caroline halted. She had an unfathomable look on her face. 'So *I'm* ... My name isn't Caroline?'

Ruth-Kristine shook her head. 'Your name is Patricia. And I'm your real mother. Me.'

Emma tried to compare the face of the girl in front of her with the photo of Patricia she had seen so many times in various news articles. There was a certain likeness. But it was also proof that Ruth-Kristine was right. A child's face could change a lot in a short amount of time.

Caroline – Patricia – blinked rapidly, looking around at them all, one by one. She stared at the woman she had thought was her mother for the past ten years, but Jette would not return her gaze. She continued to look at the floor.

'So ... who's my real dad?'

'The guy I told you about,' Ruth-Kristine said. 'Christer, my ex. I ... He doesn't know about any of this, and things kind of took a turn for him after everything happened. He...' Ruth-Kristine stopped herself.

Patricia was pulling at a loose thread on her jeans, twisting it around and around and around. A tear trickled down her left cheek. She let it fall.

'You mentioned a deal,' she said. 'A deal you made with my parents?'

Ruth-Kristine sucked a deep breath in through her nose and let it out through her mouth, slowly.

'Yes, and that's why we are here.'

# 74

Ruth-Kristine was drenched in sweat. She was cold. But it was the anger that was making her clench her teeth together.

When she was finally able to drive off the ferry, three and quarter hours after it had departed from Larvik, the cars in the queue in front of her would not get out of the way fast enough. She had to get to Horsens. To Engtoften 9. The address that, over the last few days, had become the target of her rage.

It was late by the time she arrived, but a light was still on in one of the windows. Ruth-Kristine parked outside and turned off the engine. For the first time, the thought suddenly struck her that Patricia might be in there right now, that she might even be the one to open the door. How would she react? How would *she*, her real mother, react?

*Idiot*, Ruth-Kristine said to herself. *Patricia has no idea. You're just a stranger to her, like anyone else.* Besides, she would probably be in bed by now.

There was a car parked outside. A Volkswagen, one of the fancy models, so they definitely had enough money. *That* couldn't be the problem.

She rang the doorbell.

Think, if Patricia were to open the door, she repeated to herself. Christ. But it was Jette who stood in the doorway, whose eyes opened wide, who at first could not utter a single word. Neither could Ruth-Kristine, for the first few seconds. Until she asked:

'Where is that useless excuse of a husband of yours?'

Jette still couldn't bring herself to say anything.

'He should have called me three days ago,' Ruth-Kristine carried on. 'And he should have met me in Oslo too, as he usually does. Where is he?'

The words came out as if she was firing them from a machine gun. She could hear it herself. A moment later, Jens-Christian appeared in the doorway behind Jette.

'Ruth Kristine?' he asked in amazement. 'What are you doing here?'

She snorted. Right, like he had no idea what was going on.

'When *you* don't get in touch, *I* have to.'

'Get in touch?' he asked, moving around Jette. She shifted, made some room for him. 'We agreed that we wouldn't have any more contact with each other after last year. That was the deal. Ten years.'

An uneasiness swept over Ruth-Kristine. Ten years. That might have been said. But back then, at that time, ten years had felt so far away, so far into the future. Anyway, she couldn't remember agreeing to that.

Jens-Christian looked around, checking that none of their neighbours were watching, before carrying on: 'We agreed that we would pay you a set sum every year. For ten years,' he repeated in a lower voice. 'The final payment was last year. When we last met, we agreed that we'd settled our debt to you. Don't you remember?'

Ruth-Kristine thought back. She really didn't remember.

'We met at the lake, at Sognsvann.'

A hazy memory drifted back to her. They had always carried out the handover like a top-secret operation, something Jens-Christian had picked up in the military. The Sognsvann lake had been one of their usual meeting places. She remembered it, but not that it would be the last time. But maybe he was right?

'The time before last, we said that the final amount would be a little higher than usual, seeing as we hadn't considered regular inflation or anything.'

Ruth-Kristine felt even more uncertain. She remembered buying Svein-Erik a particularly expensive Christmas present last year. Shouldn't have done that. It was money she could have spent on other things. And now she was broke.

'Well,' she said. 'That no longer applies.'

'What?'

'I gave you my daughter, and I should be paid for that. Where is she? Is she here? Patri—'

Jens-Christian took a rapid step towards her and clasped his hand hard over her mouth. The move took her by surprise. It was useless to put up a fight. She already knew how strong his grasp was.

'Get a grip of yourself,' he said firmly. 'I'm not letting go until you've calmed down. Do you hear me?'

She struggled a little before finally giving up. It was getting hard to breathe.

'Bloody hell,' Jens-Christian said as he released her. 'You've lost it.'

Ruth-Kristine caught her breath again and tried to compose herself.

'Look at you, withdrawal symptoms and all,' Jens-Christian spat.

Jette was stood beside him, a worried expression plastered across her face. She looked around, checking for neighbours this time. Ruth-Kristine couldn't care less.

'I want to see her,' she said.

'That's not happening. And that was part of the deal too.'

'I want to see her,' Ruth-Kristine repeated. 'I want to see that she's okay. See that she's alive.'

'Of course she's fine,' Jette said. 'And of course she's alive.'

'You've lost a child once before,' Ruth-Kristine said. 'You could do it again. You took my daughter from me.'

She was crying now, overwhelmed by an emotion that startled her. She had thought about her daughter occasionally over the years, but never with such longing as she did at that moment. Christer was right. The psychologists were right. She was not fit to be a mother. But now, now she knew that she wanted to be. That she should be. That she should have been this entire time. She was sure she would have managed it. Gone to rehab. She could have stopped drinking. Got a job.

'You have to leave now,' Jens-Christian said. 'Before Caroline wakes up.'

*Caroline.*

'That's not her name.'

'Yes,' Jens-Christian said sternly. 'It is.'

'And what will you do if I refuse to leave? Call the police? That would be an interesting conversation: Hi, Jens-Christian Kvist here. Our child drowned ten years ago, so we stole another one and came back to Denmark, but now the child's mother is here, asking for more money. Oof.'

Spit flew out of her mouth as she spoke.

'I want to see her,' Ruth-Kristine repeated once more. 'And then I want more money. I'm not leaving until I've got both.'

That seemed to stop them.

Jette looked at her husband, who looked as if he were deep in thought.

'You can't see her when you're like this.'

Ruth-Kristine was about to protest, but he had a point. If she were allowed to see or meet Patricia again, she couldn't behave like such a strung-out wreck.

'We can do this one last time,' Jens-Christian said with a deep sigh. 'I can come to Oslo, like always. With money. But only if we agree that it's definitely the very last time. We can't have you coming to our home like this. I can't live in fear of that. I don't want Caro— ... I don't want her to open the door one day, and there you are.'

Ruth-Kristine thought it through. She had come to Denmark with no other plan than to return with her money. For a few moments, while Jens-Christian explained the details of the old deal, she had thought she would have to go home without a single penny. But now she saw an opportunity to make a tidy sum in another way. In a few days.

'But I still want to see her,' she said.

Jens-Christian sighed and shook his head, but he didn't object this time, something Ruth-Kristine interpreted as a sign that he was giving in.

'Fine,' he said at last. 'We're planning on spending the New Year's weekend in Oslo anyway, all three of us. Caroline complains every year that we don't do anything special for New Year's Eve. We can spend the day together, in Oslo.'

He looked at Jette, who nodded.

'But I can't risk you making a scene, so if you want to meet her, then it has to be somewhere public, and you have to be sober. All that ... shit you've got in your body, get rid of it. Do you understand what I'm saying? Those are the conditions. Take it or leave it.'

Ruth-Kristine considered it. It was odd, how things could change so quickly. In the space of one evening, having had no desire to see Patricia whatsoever, to now, feeling as if it were the most important thing in her life.

'I can do that,' she said eventually.

'Good. Then let's meet in the square between the harbour and Oslo City Hall at midnight, for the fireworks. I'll contact you in the usual way closer to the time, to organise a meeting place.'

# 75

Ruth-Kristine stared at Caroline. Patricia.

'I'm guessing no one told you about a trip to Oslo for New Year's?'

Patricia glanced at Jette quickly, before shaking her head.

'Dad had to work,' she said.

Ruth-Kristine nodded slowly. 'I suppose he did. In a way. Have you been following the news, over the last few days?'

Patricia shook her head again.

'So you haven't heard about the explosions in Oslo?'

'Oh, that. Of course I have.'

'Right, so you know that five people died that night, at the harbour?'

Patricia shrugged.

'One of them was my best friend,' Ruth-Kristine said.

Patricia still didn't seem to be that affected by what Ruth-Kristine was telling her.

'And one of them was my boyfriend,' Emma said, clearing her throat.

Ruth-Kristine turned sharply to face her.

'His name was Kasper,' she continued, attempting to gain a bit of sympathy, to open the dialogue between them. 'His parents live in Århus. That's where I've driven from this morning. They're probably wondering why I haven't come back yet.'

Ruth-Kristine didn't say anything.

Britt got up from the couch and walked towards the kitchen.

'Where are *you* going?' Ruth-Kristine challenged, failing to hide the suspicion in her voice.

'The toilet,' Britt answered. 'I've heard this story before, so...'

She edged past the coffee table and towards the door. Emma watched Britt cross the room and disappear into the hallway, closing the door behind her.

'I've been wondering about something.' Emma turned her head

back to Ruth-Kristine. 'Why was Nina Ballangrud, your friend, waiting in the square that night in the first place, instead of you?'

'I couldn't go,' Ruth-Kristine answered. 'I had ... I was having a rough time with the withdrawal symptoms over Christmas. I tried,' she insisted. 'I tried so hard to get clean. But the day before New Year's Eve, I caved.'

She looked down at her feet.

'I knew that if Jens-Christian saw me while I was still on something or with withdrawal symptoms as severe as those were, I wouldn't get my money, and I wouldn't get to see Patricia. So I asked Nina to go instead. Just to show up, to get the money. And then come back.'

Ruth-Kristine stopped for a moment, before continuing.

'I told her she would get a cut. She was even more hard up than I was, so I loaned her my bank card. I had enough money on it to get her into town, maybe back again.'

'But how did you think that would work?' Emma couldn't help herself. 'Jens-Christian would see that it wasn't you. Did you think he would just give Nina the money like that, no questions asked?'

Ruth-Kristine paused before answering:

'I told Nina everything. Everything I've just said. So that meant there were several people who knew the truth about Patricia and Caroline. We thought that Nina could explain that to him. How dangerous things could get. Meet him by the rubbish bin and force him to give her the money.'

There was a brief moment in which Ruth-Kristine looked as if she were ashamed of what she had done.

'But what about Patricia?' Emma pointed to her. 'Was Nina meant to just tell *her* everything as well?'

'That was the last resort,' Ruth-Kristine explained. 'If Jens-Christian wouldn't hand it over. Nina would threaten to tell Patricia. When we were going through the plan initially, we didn't really expect Nina to be able to get that much across over the sound of all the fireworks, but Nina wasn't scared to do it if she had to.'

Ruth-Kristine sighed heavily.

'But, of course, Jens-Christian didn't have Patricia with him, did he?' she continued. 'So she never had to. No, instead, he had devised a plan to get rid of me.'

'So, after New Year's Eve, you realised you had survived an attempted murder?'

Ruth-Kristine nodded. 'I realised that there was a man here in Denmark who wasn't interested in wasting any more of his money on the past. A man who wanted to get rid of his biggest problem, once and for all.'

## 76

Lone Cramer had activated the blue lights and notified her colleagues in the Horsens police department. She had also called headquarters in Copenhagen and asked to be sent any information they had on Jens-Christian Kvist.

Blix told her all he could remember. Kvist had a background in the military, and he had led several international mine-clearing operations. When Patricia disappeared, he had been given a civilian job as a researcher and chemical engineer for a firearms manufacturer.

'So he knows how to make a bomb?' Cramer asked.

'It's not out of the realms of possibility,' Blix replied.

Blix thought back to the lock on Ruth-Kristine's front door, how it had been melted away. Of the traces of explosives found in Kvist's hotel room in Oslo. But he still couldn't work out what role Jette Djurholm's husband could possibly have in the kidnapping.

'We focussed on his wife at the time,' he told Lone Cramer. 'She and Ruth-Kristine were close friends. The possibility that her husband could have been involved wasn't something we considered.'

'But in what way could he be involved?' Lone Cramer asked. 'What connection is there between his role in this and in Patricia's disappearance? What's he doing setting off bombs in Oslo?'

'The bomb was meant for Ruth-Kristine,' Blix replied.

'But there were two bombs,' Lone Cramer reminded him.

Blix searched for a reasonable explanation. One bomb was far more powerful than the other. The second was far weaker than the first. Maybe he made the second bomb first, but wasn't sure if it would be powerful enough.

He offered the theory to Lone Cramer.

'He must have miscalculated the force for that first one,' he concluded. 'It probably wasn't meant to kill anyone other than Ruth-Kristine Smeplass.'

'What was the point of the other bomb then?' Cramer wondered.

Blix turned in his seat to face her. 'To mislead us,' he suggested. 'Make us believe that the first bomb had nothing to do with Ruth-Kristine.'

'Make you think it was an act of terrorism.'

Blix nodded. 'And he succeeded. So much so that pretty much all of our resources have been tied up in investigating the possibility that it was a terror attack.'

The phone in his lap started ringing. He didn't recognise the number, but answered anyway.

'Stefan Molt calling.'

Blix took a second to place the name. Molt was an investigator in Kripos' specialist investigation department for sexual offences. Now wasn't the best time, but Blix let him talk.

'I've looked at the picture you sent us,' Molt continued. 'It's an official school photo, but you know that already. These kinds of pictures are often taken at the start of the school year, but I would estimate that the girl is around eight years old. Her braces indicate that she's a few years into school already. Otherwise she would be too young for orthodontics. Some schools take new class photos every year. The name of the photographer is usually included somewhere on the photo, but not on this one.'

Lone Cramer's phone was wired up to the console. It vibrated. She picked it up, steering with one hand.

'The girl is from one of the Nordic countries,' the specialist investigator added. 'Probably Denmark.'

'Denmark?' Blix repeated. 'What makes you say that?'

'There's a light switch on the wall, on the right-hand side of the photo,' Molt explained. 'A round one with a type of rotary switch not used in Norway. They were common in Danish buildings in the seventies.'

Blix felt something click as all the pieces started to fit together. In the seat next to him, Lone Cramer was snapping her fingers, trying to get his attention.

'I'll send you a report through shortly,' Molt concluded.

Blix thanked him, hung up and turned to Cramer, who was still on the phone.

'Right,' she said. 'But keep a low profile. We don't want anyone in there to panic.'

She waited for a minute before nodding.

'Great. Thanks.' She hung up.

'What is it?' Blix asked. 'What's going on?'

'The emergency services just received a phone call from a residence in Horsens,' Cramer said, pressing her foot harder on the accelerator. 'Britt Smeplass, a Norwegian. Recognise the name?'

'Yes,' Blix answered eagerly.

'She's just called from a toilet in the house belonging to Jens-Christian Kvist and Jette Djurholm.'

'She's what?'

'And she made the call with a phone registered under their daughter's name, Caroline Djurholm. Smeplass asked us to get there as fast as possible. Ruth-Kristine Smeplass is holding the family hostage, and she has a gun.'

'Is Jens-Christian there too?'

'No, but there is a Norwegian journalist.'

'Hang on, what? A Norwegian journalist?'

'Smeplass couldn't remember the name, and she couldn't stay on the line any longer, said she had to get back to the others.'

Emma, Blix thought. It couldn't be anyone else.

'We've instructed Smeplass to keep the call going. So we've got a hostage situation that could easily escalate. Britt Smeplass said her sister is out for revenge. I don't know what for.'

An image of a scenario began to take shape, but he still didn't have enough details to make sense of it all.

'Right then,' he said. 'We need to intercept Kvist before he gets home.'

Cramer looked sideways at him and said:

'I think we might be too late.'

# 77

Emma was fascinated by the pieces of the puzzle that were slowly connecting in front of her. But she still had so many questions. One of which was why hadn't Jens-Christian Kvist left Oslo after he had detonated the first bomb?

She asked Ruth-Kristine, who stopped to think about it.

'After driving all the way down here, I asked to use their toilet before I went back home. I took one of the photos on the wall. Stole it. I hadn't seen my daughter since she was a baby, and all of a sudden, there she was.'

She looked away.

'I also took it because I needed something to use as blackmail. I wanted to make sure that Jens-Christian actually came, and that he brought my money and my daughter. When he called me a few days before New Year's Eve, he hadn't even realised that the photo was gone.'

She shook her head.

'He was furious, unsurprisingly. Demanded I brought it with me when we met.'

'What did you say to that?' Emma asked.

'That there was no way in hell that was happening,' Ruth-Kristine said.

It was starting to dawn on Emma why Ruth-Kristine's flat had been broken into on New Year's Day. Jens-Christian had been hunting down that photograph – the only thing that could connect him, and them, to the past.

'It was a stupid thing to say,' Ruth-Kristine carried on. 'It just wound Jens-Christian up even more. I'm not actually sure if he'd had thought about doing what he had tried to do to me *before* I had taken it, but that's why I called Sophus. I needed someone I could trust, someone who could be with me in case ... someone who could...'

She didn't finish the sentence.

'I should never have asked Nina to...' She shook her head.

The living room was deathly silent. Britt came back in and walked back to her seat on the sofa.

'So, where is the photo now?' Emma asked.

'I'm not sure. I had it earlier. I think I left it at Britt's house.'

'I sent it to Christer,' Britt said.

Ruth-Kristine glared at her sister. 'You did *what*?'

'I wasn't sure how honest you were being when you told me you wanted to make up for all you had done. I took it to give it to the police. But I changed my mind. Instead, I put it in the prison post box, with Christer's name on the envelope.'

Ruth-Kristine stood there, gaping at her.

'But ... he'll show the police!' she roared at last. 'Then they'll know that Patricia is alive!'

Britt shrugged. 'You've hidden the truth from that man for ten years,' she said. 'You, all of you, have been deceiving us – everyone. He deserves to know that his daughter is alive. Why do you think I came with you, paid for your trip? To help you commit yet another crime?' She shook her head. 'It's time you sort this out. The three of you.'

'So you didn't know your sister had a gun with her then?' Emma asked.

Britt shook her head. 'I had no idea she was planning on taking everyone hostage either. I trusted her. Thought that for once she'd actually decided to do the right thing, but...' She gestured as if it were obvious.

Ruth-Kristine looked lost for words.

'What happens now?' Patricia asked. 'What is it you want, exactly? Why are you here?'

Ruth-Kristine continued to stare into space for a while, before she lifted her chin, looked at Patricia and pulled the gun out of her waistband, holding it firmly against the side of her thigh.

Patricia gasped. Jette stiffened.

In the same moment, they heard the slamming of a car door on the drive. Ruth-Kristine turned her head at the sound.

'I'm here to wait for your father,' she said. 'And I think that might be him now.'

# 78

Ruth-Kristine raised a finger to her lips, over-exaggerating the motion, making sure that everyone in the living room had seen it. She tightened her grip on the gun. Her knuckles whitened.

Patricia slid off the chair and next to Jette on the sofa. Jette looked desperately like she wanted to hold a protective arm around her, but daren't. Britt Smeplass leant forwards and rested her elbows on her knees, unable to keep her legs still.

Emma tried to control her breathing.

'Is he not coming in?' Britt asked.

'He might be in the garage,' Jette said quietly.

Outside the entrance, they could hear the sound of footsteps, some fumbling at the door. A key in the lock. A handle creaking, the door opening. Other than that, it was silent. No 'hi, I'm home', no question to see if anyone was there. Ruth-Kristine aimed the gun at the hallway door as it started to open slowly.

Jens-Christian Kvist stepped inside.

Emma studied him. A man of average height, with only a few traces of hair left on his head, sporting a light beard. He stood there, leaning forwards slightly, his hands buried deep in his jacket pockets, but not exactly surprised about the situation he now found himself in. He made eye contact with Emma and held it for a few seconds, most likely wondering who she was and what she was doing there. But he didn't say anything.

Emma felt a rage burning deep within her. This was the man who had murdered Kasper, who had taken the lives of several others in Oslo. She fought the urge to charge at him, attack him.

'I thought I told you to leave,' he said calmly, looking at Jette. 'Take Caroline and go to your mother's.'

'I was going to,' Jette said with a bowed head. 'But I didn't get the chance.'

Jens-Christian Kvist took a few steps towards her.

'She is wanted by the police in Norway,' he said, pointing at Ruth-Kristine. 'Missing. It wasn't that difficult to work out that she would turn up here, was it?'

He jerked his head towards their daughter. 'That she would come here. For her.'

'Yes, but...'

'Yes, but what? I told you to get out of here!'

'They arrived almost immediately after you called.' She nodded to Britt and Ruth-Kristine.

'And Caroline had already left for Malene's. For a sleepover.'

Kvist snorted and shook his head. Ruth-Kristine looked unsure of what to say, how to proceed.

'And now you're going to kill me, is that it?' Kvist asked, gesturing wildly with his left hand. 'Going to get your revenge?'

His right hand remained inside his jacket pocket. He had something in there, Emma realised, shuffling away slightly. A weapon, perhaps. It wouldn't be impossible. He could have picked something up in the garage before he came in.

Ruth-Kristine didn't seem to have noticed.

'You killed my best friend,' she sneered. 'You tried to kill me.'

Kvist glanced quickly at Patricia, who was staring off into the distance. Paralysed. Scared.

'Have you...?' Kvist indicated her.

'I've told her everything, yes.'

He waited for a moment.

'So what's your next step, once you've killed me? Go on the run for the rest of your life?' He shook his head. 'You won't even make it out of the country. And then you'll end up in prison too, just like the guy you got to kidnap your daughter. Have you even given that a thought? He's been arrested now, by the way. I'm assuming it's him, anyway.'

'None of that matters,' Ruth-Kristine said. 'My life is already over. It's probably only a matter of time before Christer...'

She stopped and shook her head.

'My life has been a living hell for as long as I can remember. I've often thought about ending it, just for some peace and quiet.'

'Ruth-Kristine...'

'It's true,' Ruth-Kristine said, turning to face her sister. 'I have been so close, so many times.'

'Why not take all this to the grave with you then?' Kvist asked arrogantly. 'So the rest of us can carry on, live our lives, happily, together. As a family.'

He looked over at Emma momentarily, who understood that there was no place for her or Britt in such a scenario.

Jette made an almost inaudible sound. 'Happy,' she scoffed. 'You think we're happy? After all that happened since we lost Caroline?'

'Since *you* lost Caroline,' Kvist said.

Jette shook her head, as if they had had this discussion too many times before.

'And now you've murdered...' She stopped herself, remembering that Patricia was beside her. 'You think we could just carry on like normal after ... after...' Jette couldn't bring herself to say it.

'What should I have done then? Keep paying up every year? Paying and paying and paying? We would never be free of her. This was the only way, and you know it. You knew what I was going to Oslo to do.'

'No,' Jette said firmly. 'I did not know that. We never spoke about it.'

'Yes we did,' he argued.

'I don't remember that.'

Emma wasn't sure who to believe, but that didn't matter right now. They were at an impasse, and everything depended on what Ruth-Kristine was planning to do with that gun. What Kvist was plotting.

Emma tried to make her own plan. Time was running out. She could try to creep closer to the front door, but then she would have to pass Kvist.

But there was no other way out.

'Do you think you're the only one with a weapon?' Kvist asked, looking at Ruth-Kristine.

The remark made her take a swift step back and glance quickly at her sister, but she kept the gun pointed at him.

'Do you think you're the only one who came prepared?'

Ever so slowly, Kvist removed his hand from his jacket pocket and presented them with the object he had been holding on to the entire time. A hand grenade.

# 79

Lone Cramer held her foot firmly on the accelerator, blue lights on, but no siren. The other drivers moved obediently onto the hard shoulder.

Blix called Kovic and updated her on the hostage situation.

'Jens-Christian and Jette have a daughter the same age as Patricia,' he said. 'I think the remains we found in Undrumsåsen may belong to her. It's all starting to come together.'

'The girl in the photo...' Kovic began, but stopped that line of thought. 'This is insane.'

'Emma Ramm is in there too,' Blix continued. 'She's one of the hostages.'

'How has she managed that?'

'No idea,' Blix answered. 'I thought she was in Denmark for Kasper, with his family.'

'How are the Danes responding?' Kovic asked.

'We're about three to four minutes away,' Blix explained. 'They've got police stationed there already, assessing the situation as it unfolds. I'll call you as soon as I know more,' he finished.

A few minutes later, Lone Cramer pulled up behind one of the many police cars parked along the road leading to Engtoften 9. Blix waited at the car as she took the lead. She spent the first few minutes receiving updates. More and more uniformed police officers appeared at the scene around them. All armed. Two ambulances had parked as close to the property as was deemed safe. Blix feared how this might end. With that many hostages, there was a lot that could go wrong.

Cramer joined Blix at the car again.

'That's Kvist's car,' she said, pointing to a dirty SUV in front of the garage.

'We've tried calling him, but he's not answering,' she continued. 'Britt Smeplass stayed on the call when she returned to the living room. We can hear what's going on in there, but it's a bad line. Sounds like she's got the phone in a pocket.'

'The curtains are drawn too,' Blix commented.

'Yes, we're completely blind, but we have some sound to go off at least.'

She pointed to a large panel van that had *Incident Commander* printed across the side, indicating where the current one-way communication was being monitored.

'You've tried calling the other phones in the house as well?'

'Yes. Neither Jette Djurholm nor Emma Ramm are answering.'

Blix cursed inwardly. He wanted to go in, involuntarily took a few steps closer to the house, but stopped, ran his hand through his hair, and remained where he was.

'Let's get in,' Cramer said, nodding at the van.

## 80

Kvist held the grenade out in front of him. He had inserted his finger into the ring attached to the safety pin. Emma didn't know much about explosives, but she did know that a little jerk was all it would take for that pin to come loose. If he dropped the grenade, they would have no more than three, maybe four seconds to find cover. In a living room like this, there wasn't much to hide behind. One of the sofas, the coffee table, the armchair. The table seemed solid. Solid enough to take the edge off the explosion.

'Dad,' Patricia said, her voice trembling. 'What are you doing?'

Kvist didn't answer her, just stared at Ruth-Kristine.

'Go ahead, shoot,' he told her. 'Get your revenge. But you'll take everyone else down with you. Including Caroline.'

'Her name is not Caroline.'

He snorted. 'You gave up the right to be her mother years ago,' Kvist spat. 'What *you* have suddenly decided now, means nothing.'

Ruth-Kristine looked somewhat disconcerted. Caught off guard.

Thoughts raced through Emma's head. She could see no way to resolve the situation, but she stood up anyway. Ruth-Kristine and Jens-Christian Kvist both glared at her. Emma locked her eyes on his and shut everything else out, even as she felt the fury raging inside of her. The fear coursed through her body, making her legs numb and her breathing irregular.

Still, she spoke: 'Haven't you two caused enough damage?' Her voice quaked. She crossed the floor to stand between them.

Ruth-Kristine's gun was aimed right at her. Kvist still had the grenade in his hand, as if he were readying himself to yank the pin out at any moment. His eyes were dark and expressionless.

'Who the fuck are you?' he asked, looking at her disdainfully. 'And what are you doing in my house?'

'My name is Emma Ramm,' she said. She took a step towards him, an intense sense of defiance overwhelming her. 'I had a boyfriend called Kasper Bjerringbo,' she continued. 'Do you know where he was on New Year's Eve? He was just a few feet away from that bin you planted the bomb in.'

Emma's story didn't seem to have bothered him in the slightest.

'So you're here for revenge too?'

The thought had made a muscle in his cheek spasm, the corner of his mouth curved upwards into a faint smile.

'We can solve this, Jens-Christian,' Jette Djurholm interrupted. Her voice was quiet, resigned. 'Let's just try to end this in a civilised manner. Accept our punishment...'

'Shut up,' Kvist shot back, without looking at her. 'Continue, Emma Ramm,' he said, now with a wry smile. 'What's your plan? Are you going to attack me? Try and take this?' He shook the hand the grenade was in ever so slightly.

'Think about it,' Emma pleaded, unable to stop her voice from shaking. 'You are already responsible for the loss of so many lives. No one else has to die.'

She turned to Patricia. Stretched a hand towards her, encouraging her to stand up. Patricia hesitated, looked at Jette for a second. Jette shook her head and placed a determined hand on her daughter's arm. Patricia took a moment, as if she were thinking it through, before she tore herself free.

'What are you doing?' Kvist asked.

Patricia got up and watched Ruth-Kristine as she walked past. Grabbed Emma's outstretched hand and stood beside her.

'This girl has been your daughter for almost ten years,' Emma said. 'Look at her.'

It took a while, but Kvist shifted his eyes from Emma to Patricia.

'Have you not loved her as your own daughter? Don't you love her?'

Kvist didn't answer, just lowered his gaze. He mumbled something, but Emma didn't catch it. In the corner of her eye, she could see Britt fumbling with something in her trouser pocket. Saw as she moved her hand to rest on her thigh.

'What did you say?' Emma asked, trying to get through to Kvist.

'I said no.'

He pushed his chin forwards and resumed eye contact. 'It was never the same. She could never be Caroline. Not really. She was just a constant reminder of what I had lost.'

Kvist only looked at Emma as he spoke. Emma could feel Patricia's grip around her hand tighten, could feel the girl's whole body begin to shake beside her.

Kvist turned to his wife. 'You're absolutely right. For once. This family is a joke. To think, all the hours I've wasted trying to convince myself that everything was fine, that we were doing the right thing back then.'

He turned to Ruth-Kristine.

'Did you think we would just carry on with our lives like nothing happened? You thought we would just forget?'

'It must have been hard...' Emma started.

'It's been hell!'

'But this...' Emma gestured to the hand grenade, '...this doesn't solve anything.'

Kvist paused.

'The pain would be over,' he said. 'We wouldn't have to feel anything, anymore.'

'You're probably right, but it's not up to you to decide that for the rest of us,' Emma argued. 'We're all in pain too ... Christ. But I want to be the one to decide how to deal with that, myself.'

She looked around the room, as if to see if she had any support. Her eyes landed at Britt, whose hand slid from her thigh to the sofa. Kvist noticed the movement too.

'What have you got there?' he asked abruptly, removing his finger from the ring and back onto the pin.

He crossed the room in a few short steps, leering over Britt, who was pushing herself deeper into the cushions of the sofa. She had a phone in her hand, the display turned on. She yelled into it:

'He's got a grenade!'

Kvist forced the phone out of her hand. He studied the screen in disbelief. Even at a distance, Emma recognised the three numbers – 112. The police. The call had been connected for over fifteen minutes.

Kvist glared unblinking at Britt, who seemed to be anticipating his fury. Emma looked at the grenade. This was her chance. Now, while Kvist was distracted with the phone, with Britt.

But she was too slow.

Kvist hung up and approached the window.

## 81

A heavy silence settled inside the incident commander's van.

'Call her back,' ordered the tall man next to Lone Cramer.

The man sat at the control panel carried out a few procedures, initiating a new phone call. The rhythmic ringing filled the cramped space in the back of the van. They stood there, waiting for someone to pick up.

No one did.

Blix looked up at one of the many monitors displaying live images of each side of the house. He noticed a curtain flutter. The brief glimpse of a face peeking out.

'Kvist,' Blix said, snapping his fingers and pointing. The others had noticed it too.

'He's seen us. He'll try and barricade himself in.'

The call ended. The silence returned.

'Try again,' the incident commander said. 'He will have to answer sooner or later.'

'But we can't provoke him either,' Blix commented. The incident commander and several of the other people in the van turned to him.

'It's important that he thinks *he's* the one in control here,' Blix added. 'So he doesn't do anything reckless.'

'We have done this before,' the commander pointed out.

Blix held up his hands. 'Sorry,' he said. 'But...'

He searched for the right way to explain.

'Most of the evidence suggests that he is responsible for a number of murders in Oslo, so I would say that it's quite likely that he thinks he has nothing to lose. And the fact that we're here now too, will probably exacerbate it.'

The incident commander considered Blix for a few seconds before turning to face his colleagues.

'What else do we know about him?'

'He used to be in the military,' one of them started. 'Most likely

suffered severe trauma during the time he served carrying out international mine-clearing operations. We're building a psychological
profile of him as we speak.'

The incident commander gestured towards the house.

'We don't have time to wait for a profile,' he started. 'I want everything we've got on him. Now!'

'He's forty-two years old,' Lone Cramer said. 'Has a brother in
prison for a charge related to violent crime. He's the son of a plumber.
Mother died when he was sixteen. Suicide.'

'He has regular appointments with a therapist,' contributed the
officer who had been working on the psychological profile. 'For the
last eight or nine years. We don't have access to the therapist's case
files or notes, but I would imagine that he was referred because of his
time in the military. It can't have been an easy job, mine removal in
Afghanistan. It must have taken a toll on his nerves, that kind of
high-pressure operation.'

'Or it could have something to do with the fact that he may have
lost his daughter ten years ago.' It was Blix who contributed this time.
'And that he's had to live with the fact that he kidnapped a child, and
as a result, has had to put on this façade for the outside world, all this
time,' he continued.

The incident commander turned to face him directly now.
'Explain.'

Blix spent the next minute telling him what he had uncovered in
Norway the day before, and how the discovery of the body might be
connected to the current event.

'Right,' the incident commander said finally. 'Keep calling that
number. We have to get him to talk. And then we get the snipers in
position.'

It rang four times. Five. On the sixth ring, it stopped. Someone
picked up. The audio recording system started automatically.

'Hello,' the man said as he leant towards the microphone. 'My
name is John-Mikael Rasmussen. Is this Jens-Christian Kvist I'm
talking to?'

No answer, just fumbling, crackling, at the other end.

'Don't come any closer.' His voice was cold. Void of emotion.

'We won't,' Rasmussen rushed to answer. 'Not if you don't want us to.'

Kvist didn't answer, but he didn't hang up either. Blix kept his eye on the incident commander. Observed as he took over, tried to establish a dialogue.

'How many people are in there with you?'

'It's too late now anyway.'

'What do you mean?'

Kvist didn't answer, just repeated, 'Don't come any closer.'

He hung up.

# 82

Kvist chucked the phone aside, pulled the ring on the grenade and tossed the pin away from him, so that it sailed along the floor and collided with the fire guard.

'Right then, how are you going to do this?'

The question was directed at Ruth-Kristine. Emma stared at the grenade in his hand. His fingers were pressed down on the trigger mechanism. She felt paralysed.

Ruth-Kristine looked as if she were figuring out what to do next. Britt pulled one of the cushions from the sofa and held it up in front of her. Jette was desperately trying to pull Patricia back to her, urgently trying to hold on to her, protect her, but Patricia stayed where she was, next to Emma.

'How am I going to do this?' Ruth-Kristine repeated his question, looking Kvist in the eye. There was a calmness in her voice. A determination.

'As fast as I can,' she said, aiming the gun at him. A tear ran down her cheek.

She pulled the trigger.

The bullet hit Kvist in the centre of his chest. The impact made him stumble backwards, knocking over the lamp behind him. Patricia threw a hand over her mouth and stifled a scream. The scruffy grey cat shot out from under the table and into the kitchen. Kvist covered the wound with one hand as blood flowed between his fingers. He looked down at the grenade, like he was making sure that he still had control of it.

He sank to his knees.

Jette approached him. Britt stood up. Everyone was watching him. The distant, glassy look in his eye. His breath, growing faster and faster. The life draining out of him with every second. His grip around the grenade, getting weaker.

Emma wanted to run at him, to try and wrestle the grenade out of his hand, but she felt a steadfast hand holding her back. Ruth-Kristine braced herself. As she did, the grenade slipped out of Kvist's hand and thumped against the parquet flooring, slowly rolling away.

Emma wrenched Patricia down to the ground and flipped the coffee table onto its side. She pressed her to the floor and was about to follow suit. They only had a matter of seconds. Tenths of a second. Before she, too, ducked behind the table, she caught a glimpse of Ruth-Kristine, throwing herself onto the grenade. Emma let out an involuntary shout, before she threw herself down and waited for the explosion.

# 83

The force from the explosion shattered the windows. The ground shook. Fragments of glass burst out of the frames. The pressure wave reached Blix and Cramer outside. They crouched down, crossing their arms in front of their faces, protecting themselves from the debris flying through the air.

Blix's first thought was for Emma. Emma and Patricia. God, there was no way they could have survived.

He tore towards the house. The walls were still standing. The windows were gone. He heard the shouting begin around him, he saw the officers advancing with their weapons, raised in front of them.

Blix shouted into the house: 'Emma!'

No answer. He held on to one of the empty window frames and heaved himself up and into a bedroom. The Danish police were yelling commands to each other somewhere behind him. Blix carried on, further into the house. Parts of the ceiling had come down. Furniture and most of the Djurholm's belongings had been flung to the ground. Dust was still swirling through the air, like a dense fog.

Blix rubbed his eyes. Could smell something on fire. Something charred. But there was another smell, too. Like metal, or blood. He shoved a chair aside and shouted again, preparing himself for the worst.

One of the walls was on fire. Orange-and-blue flames surged upwards, quickly filling the room with smoke. Blix continued through the house, suddenly noticing a small movement. It was a foot, shifting under several layers of wood and torn plasterboard.

He could hear something now too. Breathing, moaning, from one or more people. Groans, someone who was hurt.

The sound of police officers making their way into the room from the other side, through a broken patio door on the opposite side of the house. Someone shouted for a fire extinguisher.

There was a crater in the floor. An opening through which Blix could see down into the basement.

He walked around it, stepping over a severed leg, other human remains. A sound behind him made him spin round. Behind an overturned coffee table was a child. She had sat up, her face was coated with soot and ash. Some of it had been washed away by fresh tears that were running down her cheeks.

Blix had no doubt of who it was. He recognised her from the photo that Christer Storm Isaksen had received.

He lifted her up and carried her towards the patio. Stepped over a few cushions – some completely torn apart, some intact. The feathers were still cascading to the ground around them.

A paramedic approached them. Blix passed the girl over and returned to the living room.

The fire was now tearing through the wall. He could feel the heat. The wind channelling in from outside had only galvanised it. A police officer was in the process of emptying a fire extinguisher over the flames, putting out the worst of them.

Blix coughed, bent down to move aside the remnants of a chair, lifted away what was left of the rug. A twisted metal bar that had once been a lamp. The TV had tipped over. The doors of the china cabinet were destroyed, the contents pulverised.

'We've got another one, they're alive,' one of paramedics yelled.

Blix turned, needing to see for himself if it was Emma, but saw instantly that it was Britt Smeplass. She moaned as she was helped to her feet. She spluttered a few times. Several people were in the process of pulling the garden hose into the house. Hot steam filled the room.

Blix had to get out, get some fresh air. He staggered out into the garden and felt a strange combination of grief and victory. And despair. Grief, from the fact that yet more lives had been lost. Victory, in knowing that the case was finally over. Despair, as he thought of Emma.

He pictured her. Her light hair. The sparkle in her eyes, that perceptive gaze. Her sharp tongue. The tough mask. She had experienced her fair share of evil throughout her life. Yet, despite that, she had grown up to become a person whom Blix appreciated immensely.

'Are you okay?' Lone Cramer asked behind him.

Blix turned round to meet his Danish colleague.

'I don't know,' he replied.

And then he saw her.

Two paramedics were supporting Emma as she climbed out of the ruins of the house. She was bleeding from a gash on her forehead, and she had a few other minor wounds to her face. Her hair was a sooty mess. She was limping, but stopped and looked up. She locked eyes with him, a confused expression on her face, as if she had never seen him before. Then she squinted against the daylight and sent him a faint, sad smile.

# EPILOGUE

*Five months later*

It had been a long time since Christer Storm Isaksen had bothered to shave. When he tapped the razor against the porcelain sink for the last time and looked up to meet his reflection in the mirror, his face showed the slightest trace of a smile. He just about recognised himself.

He rinsed his face. He had nicked the skin on his neck slightly so that a few, small red spots had appeared, but it didn't matter.

The clothes he had prepared the night before were draped neatly across his chair. He had ironed the white shirt and set a new crease into the dark-blue trousers that he hadn't worn for several years.

He was happy. Excited. Nervous too, he had to admit. What if she didn't like him? What if she was anxious herself, about meeting yet another murderer? What if she was completely devastated after all that Ruth-Kristine had put her through earlier that year, after all she had found out?

Christer knew that he was going to have trouble holding back the tears, even if the girl sat in front of him wasn't really someone he knew, and even if the child-welfare representative was there too. But it *would* be Patricia. *His* Patricia, regardless of whether she had been living under a different identity for well over ten years. But she would, fundamentally, be the same. At least that was what he told himself.

Ruth-Kristine had actually sacrificed herself for her. Threw herself onto the grenade and made sure that Jens-Christian Kvist couldn't take everyone else with him.

Christer looked at the clock on the wall. Twenty-three minutes left until she arrived. He pulled on his shirt, socks and trousers. Took a deep breath and thought of Patricia, of what her life would be like in the years ahead. He would be out in four months. He was her biological father, but she had lived in Denmark for her entire life. That's where all her friends were. Her handball team. She'd had another mother for all those years too, who was now in prison, just like he was. Christer had no idea whether Patricia would keep in contact with Jette Djurholm, or how that would pan out, but either way, it was all about what Patricia wanted.

Her visit today had only been organised because Patricia had requested it herself. Christer wondered what she would ask him. Why had he become a killer? No, she probably knew that, if she had been allowed to read about the case. Would she ask if he remembered any of the sixteen months he had spent as a single parent, when it had just been the two of them, him and her?

It was a time he had thought he remembered everything about. Those first few days after her birth, the first weeks, all the clothes that she grew out of far too quickly, her first words, her new teeth, her first steps, but the details had become increasingly fuzzy. These days he wasn't sure if she had started walking when she was thirteen or fourteen months old. When did she call him 'Dad' for the first time?

Maybe that's what she would call him today?

His own thoughts made him shake his head. Don't expect too much. She must still be traumatised, and that would likely be the case for several more years, perhaps for the rest of her life. But he hoped that they would slowly be able to find a way to live together. Nothing would make him happier.

He paced back and forth inside the little cell. Glanced up at the clock. Checked to see how he looked. Tied his shoelaces, pulled up his socks, straightened his shirt. Then glanced at the clock again. Seventeen minutes. It was seventeen minutes the last time he checked too.

He wished he had something to give her. A gift, something she wanted, something she could appreciate and hold on to between now and when he would be allowed out. But he had nothing.

Eighteen minutes turned into ten. Then five. He checked

himself over in the mirror one last time. The red marks had calmed down a bit. Good. He lifted his shoulders high and breathed as much air into his lungs as he possibly could.

Right.

Now, he was ready to meet his daughter again.

# ACKNOWLEDGEMENTS

Thomas: So Jørn.

Jørn: Yes, Thomas?

Thomas: It's us again.

Jørn: So I've been told.

Thomas: So it is written, in fact.

Jørn: Hm?

Thomas: We have written another book.

Jørn: Oh yes. Yes we have.

(beat)

(beat)

Jørn: Which one is this again?

Thomas: *Smoke Screen*.

Jørn: Ah, yes. The one with the little girl.

Thomas: Yes. We have to give our thanks.

Jørn: We do.

(beat)

(sigh)

(beat)

Thomas: How's your dog?

Jørn: Theodor is fine, thanks for asking.

Thomas: Was he instrumental in you finding your wits and your words this time around as well?

Jørn: No.

Thomas: Really?

Jørn: Yes. Truth be told, he never really was.

Thomas: Oh.

(beat)

Jørn: You should know me by now, Thomas. I make up stuff for a living.

Thomas: Right. That's what you do.

(beat)

(beat)

Jørn: He's still a very nice dog.

Thomas: Are you sure?

Jørn: Yes. I'm telling the truth now.

Thomas: Glad we got *that* cleared up.

(beat)

(beat)

Jørn: So, how did we end up writing this book, then?

Thomas: I don't remember.

Jørn: Me neither.

(beat)

(sigh)

(beat)

(sigh)

(sigh)

Thomas: Maybe if you took your dog for a walk—

Jørn: I remember now.

Thomas: Good. Tell me.

Jørn: You wrote one word.

Thomas: Yes?

Jørn: Then I wrote one word.

Thomas: Yes.

(beat)

Jørn: I'm kidding.

Thomas: I hope so.

Jørn: I really don't remember.

Thomas: Me neither.

(beat)

(sigh)

Thomas: You know, we're supposed to be quite smart people.

Jørn: I know.

Thomas: Quite brilliant minds, coming up with plots and stuff.

Jørn: I know.

Thomas: And here we are, heads empty.

Jørn: I know.

Thomas: People will wonder how on earth we even manage to write one book, let alone fifty, like you have.

Jørn: Fifty-seven.

Thomas: You're kidding me.

Jørn: I don't think I am.

Thomas: You don't *think* ... never mind.

(beat)

(sigh)

Jørn: Can't we just say the same thing as last time?

Thomas: We kept on talking about your dog the last time.

Jørn: Yes, but ... the others. The others we mentioned.

Thomas: You mean, like, our families and stuff?

Jørn: Yes!

Thomas: They deserve to be mentioned again, for sure.

Jørn: So let's do that, then.

Thomas: Yes.

(beat)

(sigh)

Jørn: I would like to thank my family.

Thomas: I think we've covered that, Jørn.

Jørn: No, but I mean: my wife, Beate. My kids, Sondre and Marte. They deserve to be mentioned, because ... you know.

Thomas: I'm sure they'll be happy to read that.

Jørn: What about you?

(beat)

(beat)

Jørn: Thomas?

Thomas: Oh. Yes. Sorry. I'm going to be somewhat original here.

Jørn: Oh. How so?

Thomas: I'm going to thank my parents.

Jørn: Is that original?

Thomas: Maybe it isn't. I don't know. But they put me here on this earth. And for that I'm eternally grateful.

Jørn: That is sweet.

Thomas: Well, yes. It's also true. I owe them everything. Plus, my kids are teenagers now.

Jørn: What do you mean?

Thomas: What I mean is that *they* should be thanking *me*, not the other way around. They didn't help me write this book. In fact...

Jørn: But they're sweet, right?

(beat)

(beat)

Jørn: Thomas?

Thomas: Oh. Yes. Sorry. Yes they are. Of course they are. I love them to bits.

Jørn: Good. Theodor and ... Henny, right?

Thomas: Yes.

Jørn: Same as my dog.

Thomas: I know, Jørn.

(beat)

(sigh)

Jørn: You know there are medications you can take for your dog allergy?

Thomas: I know, Jørn.

Jørn: Just saying.

(beat)

(sigh)

Jørn: Our publisher!

Thomas: Yes, Jørn?

Jørn: We need to thank her.

Thomas: Yes we do. Karen Sullivan.

Jørn: She's wonderful, isn't she?

Thomas: She really is.

Jørn: A true writer's advocate. And a brilliant editor.

Thomas: All of the above. For sure.

Jørn: And she has some great people around her.

Thomas: Indeed she does. West Camel, for instance.

Jørn: West is the best.

Thomas: I'm sure he's never heard *that* one before.

Jørn: But he takes care of our book.

Thomas: He does. And we get to blame him afterwards for all the mistakes he didn't find or correct.

(beat)

Jørn: There are mistakes in our book?

Thomas: Of course not. 😑

Jørn: So...

Thomas: I'm kidding, Jørn. West really *is* the best.

(beat)

(sigh)

(a dog is barking)

Thomas: We should thank Cole as well.

Jørn: Cole?

Thomas: Cole Sullivan, Karen's son.

Jørn: Ah yes. The one we're getting all the emails from?

Thomas: The very one. He's doing a heck of a job marketing our books.

Jørn: He is.

(beat)

(sigh)

Jørn: We have to thank Megan, too.

Thomas: Megan?

Jørn: Megan Turney, our translator.

Thomas: Ah yes. Thank you, Megan. You did a marvellous job. You were quick and efficient about it, too.

(beat)

(sigh)

Thomas: Oh, I know one more we need to thank.

Jørn: You have a hamster I don't know about?

Thomas: No, I'm allergic to them, too.

Jørn: So who, then?

Thomas: It's not really *one*, it's ... (clears throat) a lot of people.

Jørn: Hm?

Thomas: The readers, Jørn.

Jørn: Oh. Yes.

Thomas: Quite a few of them read and loved the first one we did together.

Jørn: Yes.

Thomas: Even without the help of your dog.

Jørn: Imagine that.

(beat)

(sigh)

Jørn: So we're done, then?

Thomas: I think so.

(beat)

(beat)

Jørn: How old are your kids again?

Thomas: I don't even want to know.

(beat)

(sigh)

Jørn: I'm going to take my dog for a walk.

Thomas: I'm not even sure you have a dog now.

Jørn: I do, Thomas. Theodor is his name.

Thomas: So you keep telling me.

(beat)

(sigh)

Thomas: We're going to have some fun, writing our next books together.

Jørn: We are.

Thomas: Enjoy the walk. Bring your notebook.